IF ANGELS FALL

IF ANGELS FALL

Rick Mofina

Pinnacle Books
Kensington Publishing Corp.
http://www.pinnaclebooks.com

PINNACLE BOOKS are published by

Kensington Publishing Corp.
850 Third Avenue
New York, NY 10022

First Printing: February, 2000
10 9 8 7 6 5 4 3 2 1

Printed in the United States of America

This book is for Barbara, Laura, and Michael

ACKNOWLEDGMENTS

The realization of a first novel is never a solitary achievement. I wish to thank my family, my literary agent, Mildred Marmur, and her associate Jane Lebowitz, the legendary Inspector Ed Erdelatz (retired) of the San Francisco Police Department's Homicide Detail, Ann LaFarge and the crew at Kensington, Carsten Stroud, Margaret Dyment, the nuns of St Michael's Academy and Holy Rosary School, Ken McGoogan, Paul Reid, Wendy Dudley, Mary Gilchrist, Peter Way, Dorothy Proctor, Sharon Sellitto, Holly Desimone, Bill Thompson, Peter Bloch, Mary Aikins, the SFPD, the San Francisco FBI, the Royal Canadian Mounted Police, Calgary Police Service, and numerous friends in law enforcement throughout North America who offered their support and a glimpse into their hearts.

I also want to thank all of my friends and colleagues in the news craft. I know you have been there and I know you know.

1

Danny saw the girl again.

As the subway train eased out of the Coliseum station, he looked up, captivated by her frozen smile, her vacant stare, and the fact that she never spoke.

Never.

She was dead.

Her throat had been cut and her body stuffed into a plastic garbage bag hidden in Golden Gate Park.

She was two years old and her name was Tanita Marie Donner. Two eleven-year-old girls from Lincoln Junior High found her during a science class field trip.

"She looked like a little naked doll," Natalie Jackson, one of the girls, told a San Francisco TV station.

That was a year ago. The nightmares were now less frequent for the schoolgirls. For most San Franciscans, Tanita's murder was fading from memory although her face still stared from bus shelters, store windows, and bumper stickers, an image as familiar to the Bay Area as the Golden Gate or the Transamerica pyramid. For a time, it embodied San Francisco's anguish. A blurred, grainy blow-up of a color snapshot, Tanita timidly showing her tiny milk-white teeth as Mommy coaxed a smile. Two pink butterfly barrettes held back her brown hair. She was wearing a cotton dress with lace trim, and crushing her white teddy bear to her chest. Her dark eyes shining like falling stars.

REWARD screamed in bold, black letters above her head. Below were details of when and where Tanita was last seen alive. Twenty-five thousand dollars was offered for information leading to an arrest in her murder. No takers.

Tanita Marie Donner's killer was still out there.

As the train worked its way through the transbay tunnel of the Bay Area Rapid Transit system, three-year-old Daniel Raphael Becker remained transfixed by a poster of Tanita Marie Donner.

"Who's that, Dad?" he asked his father.

"Don't point, Danny. She's just a little girl. Now please sit still. We'll be home soon."

Nathan Becker settled back in his seat, opened the business section of Saturday's *San Francisco Star,* hoping to finish a story he began at home that morning before he and Danny left for the game. Nathan was a systems engineer who commuted by CalTrain to Mountain View. The article was about his firm which was on the brink of a revolutionary breakthrough. The game was a yawner, the A's were embarrassing the Yankees. Danny was bored, so they left the Coliseum after the fifth. Just as well, because now they had to go all the way to Daly City to pick up some artist's brushes for his wife, Maggie. Nathan had promised. It was a long ride, and he wished he hadn't let Danny talk him into taking BART. He got his fill of trains during the week. They'd cab it home from the shop.

* * *

The day started like a typical summer Saturday for Nathan and Danny, with one of their weekend-buddy excursions.

"Want to go to Oakland and see the A's game today, Dan?" Nathan was making scrambled eggs while Maggie slept upstairs.

"Can we do the wave, Dad?"

"You betcha."

Danny laughed.

Nathan buffed his son's hair and watched him eat. Danny's eyes radiated innocence. Blood of my blood. Miracle baby. How he loved him. But his promotion to department head meant longer hours and rationing time with Danny to weekends, leaving him to survive the week with glimpses of his son asleep, glimpses stolen after tiptoeing into his room at the end of another pressure-cooker day.

Jordan Park was a sedate neighborhood sheltered with stands of feather-duster palms, a community of Victorian houses with billiard-table-green lawns. An oasis for young professionals that was not quite as pretentious as Pacific Heights. Today Nathan got to prove how unpretentious he was. Danny wanted to take BART to Oakland.

"Let's take the Beemer, Dan. We'll put the top down?"

"I want to ride the train like you do, Dad. BART goes right under the bay."

"I know it goes right under the bay." Nathan sighed. "Okay."

Before they went, Nathan left a note on the fridge and, reluctantly, his BMW in the garage. He and Danny walked to California, hopped a bus, then a cable car to Embarcadero Station, where an escalator delivered them at a funeral pace into the subway system winding throughout the Bay Area.

* * *

After she heard them leave, Maggie Becker rose from bed, showered, put on her robe, then made a pot of Earl Grey Tea. She curled up on the sofa in the living room with the Arts section of the newspaper, savoring an empty house. Later, she dressed in faded jeans and a Forty-Niners sweater, then climbed upstairs to her studio. It was a large, bright room with hardwood floors, and a bank of floor-to-ceiling windows overlooking their backyard rose garden and the treetops, framing her view of a small park where trumpeter swans glided in a manmade pond.

This was Maggie's sanctuary.

It was here she had mourned the miscarriage of her first child, lost after she fell from a step ladder while wallpapering the nursery. Her uterus was damaged, the doctors said. The chances of her carrying a baby to term were now three in ten. They suggested adoption. A few months later, Nathan started leaving her brochures from agencies. Maggie threw them into the trash. She refused to let a cruel, freak accident rob her of motherhood. Nathan understood. So it was here, while watching the swans, Maggie's prayers were answered. It was here, when she became pregnant with Danny, she sat with her hands pressed to her stomach, begging God to let her keep this baby.

God had heard her.

Their healthy baby boy was delivered by cesarian section. They named him Daniel after Nathan's father, and Raphael for the Italian painter, whose work Maggie adored. Danny was her hope, her light, her angel. His birth reaffirmed the love between her and Nathan and resurrected the artistic dreams she had buried with the loss of their first baby. Here, in this refurbished attic, Maggie produced a succession of inspired water colors, which sold regularly at a gallery down the peninsula.

Maggie pulled off the tarpaulin covering a landscape in progress, collected her brushes, and inhaled the fragrance of paints and freshly cut grass wafting into her studio.

Her life was perfect now.

The train came to the next stop. The automatic doors opened. Dank air rushed into the car as Danny watched the people leaving jostle with those getting on. Then a short warning chime echoed. "Doors closing," Danny said. He had picked up the routine. Three seconds later, the doors closed. The train jolted forward, gathering speed, pulling them deeper into the tunnel system.

"How many more stops, Dad?"

"Uh-huh," Nathan said, eyes locked onto his newspaper, oblivious to the new passengers crowding the car. He had slipped comfortably into his commuter habit of losing himself in his newspaper.

Danny looked at his dad reading. He was bored, so he stared at his own hand and counted his fingers. Remembering the hotdog he had at the game, he licked his lips and wished for another one. He yawned. He looked up across the car at Tanita Marie Donner's face, slid off of his seat, and stood next to it, facing the poster.

"I'm just going right here, Dad."

"All right," the newspaper said.

The train wavered. Danny steadied himself, noticing a tiny, silver chain dangling from the ear of a teenager down the aisle. It glinted rhythmically with the train's rocking motion, like a hypnotist's watch, bidding Danny closer. He stepped carefully around the outstretched, tanned legs of a boy studying a motorcycle magazine, head bobbing to music leaking from the headset of his CD player. Suddenly a skateboard shot at Danny. He tensed before it was stopped by a scuffed Reebok worn by a girl in an oversize sweatshirt. Danny moved on, paying no

attention to the other passengers until he stood before the teenager wearing the chain. His face was ravaged by acne. His jet-
black mohawk hair was greased into six-inch spikes frozen in
coiffured explosion. He wore black boots, torn black pants, a
black T-shirt with a death's head that was partially hidden by
his silver-studded black leather jacket.

Danny pointed at the chain. "What's that?"

The teenager ceased chewing his bubble gum, left his mouth
open, and giggled as if he'd just been tickled. His girlfriend
giggled, too. Although her hair was fuchsia and her chains
smaller, her appearance mirrored her boyfriend's right down
to the gum chewing. They were holding hands. The teen leaned
toward Danny, turned his ear to him, and shook the chain.

"This is my lucky charm." He grinned. "You should get
one."

The girl playfully grabbed her boyfriend's groin, pouting
and asking Danny: "And what's this?"

It was called a *PEE-nus*. Danny knew because his mother
answered the same question for him one night when he was in
the tub. He'd forgotten the word, but he clearly recalled the
function.

"Do you have to pee?" Danny asked, triggering the couple's
laughter as they stood to leave.

The train was slowing, Danny was bumped from behind,
nearly knocked off his feet. He was trapped in a forest of legs.
The automated public address barked the station's name. Danny
tried to return to his dad, but was blocked by a skateboard,
shopping bags, a briefcase, a knapsack. People crushed together,
inching him closer to the doors. He panicked, clenched his tiny
hands into fists, and pounded on arms and legs, but couldn't
break free. The train stopped. The doors whooshed open. Danny
was pushed out of the car with the crowd, crying out for his
father as he tripped, falling hard onto the cold, grimy, concrete
platform. People swirled about him, drowning him. A ghetto
blaster throbbed with a menacing beat. No one could hear

Danny crying. Frantic, he struggled to get to his feet. A cigarette butt stuck to his hand. He pinballed from one grownup to the next. Disoriented, his only thought was to get back on the train. He heard the warning chime.

Get back on the train! Get back on the train! Get back!

Danny felt a pair of large, strong hands lift him.

Nathan heard the chime, lowered the newspaper, and turned to Danny beside him. Gone. Damn that little— He threw the paper down, threading his way from one end of the car to the next looking between seats for Danny. What the hell—? He can't be gone.

He can't be gone!

The driver's whistle bleated again. Nathan's pulse quickened. He ran to the end of the car again, pushing people from his path, searching underneath every seat.

"Hey, asshole!"

"Christ, pal—"

"M-my son, Danny . . . I'm looking for my little boy, he's . . ."

The doors closed and the train jerked forward.

"No! Wait!" Nathan yelled for the train to halt.

The train gained momentum.

Where is my son?

Bile rushed up the back of his throat. Gooseflesh rose on his skin. Through the window, on the platform, he saw Danny in the arms of a stranger disappearing into the crowd.

Nathan knocked an old woman out of his way and lunged for the train's emergency brake.

"No! Please! No, No!"

Tanita Marie Donner stared down at Danny's father.

2

A skeleton crew was on duty in the newsroom of *The San Francisco Star* when Danny Becker was kidnapped.

Tom Reed, a crime writer, was finishing a short hit on a seventy-two-year-old rummy stabbed with a nail file by a fifty-two-year-old whore. Some dive in the Tenderloin. The whore was watching the A's game on the tube above the bar. The rummy wanted her to work her break. She was feeling bitchy, and wanted to finish her beer and her nails. His fingers went where they shouldn't have and he bled to death at her table. Nobody noticed for half an inning. Turns out the guy had helped build the Golden Gate. He was the seventieth homicide of the year. Reed summed up his life in two tight graphs, then punched a command on his computer terminal, sending the story to Al Booth, the assistant metro editor working in the bullpen.

Reed downed the remainder of his tepid coffee. Three hours into his shift. Could he stick it out today? Hungover. Again. Rubbing his temples, surveying the crap pinned to the half-wall of his cubicle: Police numbers, a yellowing article on his winning his second national award four years ago for investigative reporting, a photograph of his wife, Ann, and Zach, their nine-year-old son who wants to be a reporter. Like my dad.

Here was his life, or the illusion of it. Reed's sources rarely talked to him these days. His award-winning work was forgotten. It was coming up on six months since Ann took Zach and moved to her mother's. His life was disintegrating, and like an animal gnawing at a wound that refused to heal, he returned to the clipping file and the story that initiated his disgrace. The case of Tanita Marie Donner.

Reed had led the *Star's* coverage of her abduction and murder, right up until the suicide, the lawsuit, and his suspension. It was nearly a year since he last wrote about Donner and the man he believed had killed her. The case was unsolved and the paper, stinging from the scandal and embarrassment, was now content with superficial coverage of it. But Reed couldn't leave it alone, exposing himself to headlines he had virtually memorized:

POLICE SEARCH FOR ABDUCTED BABY . . . SCHOOL GIRLS FIND TANITA: MURDERED . . . FEW LEADS IN MYSTERY SLAYING . . .

Then he came to the grainy news pictures of Franklin Wallace. The beginning of the fuckup, and it all came back to him. Hard.

He had rushed to Wallace's home and rung the doorbell. He was chasing San Francisco's biggest story. He had found Tanita's killer.

The door was opened by a pudgy little man with a candle-white face, thinning blond hair, a wispy mustache. Mid-thirties. Five-six.

"Franklin Wallace?" Reed said.

Rick Mofina

"Yes?" his voice had a southern lilt.

Damn, the tip was true, Reed thought.

"Mr. Wallace, I am Tom Reed. I am a reporter with the *Star*—"

"Reporter?" Wallace's expression darkened subtly.

"Did you know Tanita Donner? She lived a few blocks away."

Wallace's lips did not move. He was measuring Reed, remaining silent, frozen. Reed repeated the question.

"Yes, I knew Tanita."

"I understand she attended your Sunday school day care?"

"Once or twice. She was not a regular. What is this about?"

"Mr. Wallace, may I come in? I have some questions, important questions, I would like to ask you."

Reed caught it. A twitch in Wallace's eyelid, an unconscious reaction so slight he almost missed it.

"What questions?"

"May I come inside?"

"What questions? What is this about?"

Wallace's hand tightened his grip on the door frame. Reed was losing him; this might be his only chance. "Mr. Wallace, do you have a record for child molestation in Virginia?"

"What? A record?"

"I have it confirmed, sir."

Wallace swallowed, licking his lips. "You have it confirmed?"

"Yes, just now. I would like to talk to you about some other information I have. It is very serious."

"Why? No. Please. That was long ago. Please, I have a family, a job. You must not print anything. Please, I don't know what you're driving at coming here with this."

"I've been told your fingerprints have been found on items linked to Tanita's murder."

"What? I can't believe that!"

What little color Wallace had melted from his face. He was

wan, his eyes, revealing the truth. He was guilty. Guilty of something. Reed knew it. He was standing inches from a child-killer.

Wasn't he?

At that moment, Wallace's daughter appeared, clinging to her father's leg, a tiny Leave my-daddy-alone scowl aimed at Reed. Red jam was smeared on her chin, reminding Reed of blood.

"I had nothing to do with what you're suggesting."

Wallace slammed the door.

Reed cleared his throat and went to the next clipping:

SUNDAY SCHOOL TEACHER COMMITS SUICIDE . . . "HE WAS INNOCENT": WIDOW . . . REPORTER BLAMED FOR TEACH-ER'S DEATH . . . WIDOW SUES S.F. STAR . . . TANITA'S KILLER "IS OUT THERE": POLICE . . .

Reed removed his glasses, burying his face in his hands.

The day after she buried her husband, Rona Wallace held a press conference. It was on the same doorstep where Reed had questioned Franklin Wallace moments before he locked himself in his daughter's bedroom and fired both barrels of a shotgun into his mouth.

"My husband was a decent man, and a loving father," Rona Wallace read from a prepared statement. "He took successful counseling for his problems, which occurred more than a decade ago when he was clinically depressed over the death of his mother. The San Francisco Police and the FBI have told me today, to my face, that my husband was initially checked and quietly cleared as a possible suspect in the death of Tanita Marie Donner. He knew and loved that little girl." She sniffed.

"I attribute his tragic death to the allegations raised in the abhorrent and false reporting of *The San Francisco Star* and have begun civil action. Thank you."

Rona Wallace took no questions. When she finished, she asked if Tom Reed was present. "Right here." Reed raised his hand.

Cameras followed her as she walked to him, her reddened eyes finding his. Without warning, she slapped his face. "You know what you are and you know what you did," she said, then walked away.

Reed was stunned.

Reporters pelted him with questions. He was speechless. The TV gang loved seeing him get his comeuppance. The networks picked it up. Public criticism from police made him a pariah The incident ignited editorials and columns across the country about press ethics. Reed couldn't sleep without drinking—he doubted everything in his life. He argued with Ann, screamed at Zach, and was once on the brink of hitting him, squeezing his arm until he yelped in sheer terror.

"Wake up, Reed. I brought your medicine."

A steaming cup of coffee was set before him, the aroma mingling with the scent of Obsession. "Anything shaking, Tommy?" Molly Wilson settled in at her cubicle, next to his, her bracelets clinking.

"A drunk knifed by a whore." He sipped the coffee. "Thanks."

Wilson was hired four years ago from a small Texas daily. She had a master's degree in English literature. A relentless digger, she was a strong writer. Her brunette hair was cut like Cleopatra's, she had perfect teeth, and always smelled good.

"Why are you here, Wilson? It's your day off."

She switched on her terminal, flipped open a notebook, and

began typing. "Got to finish a feature for Lana. She moved up my deadline."

Reed grunted.

"Thanks for asking, Tom. It's about men who kill, and the women who love them. Hey, you're being naughty. Can't leave that Donner story alone."

Reed said nothing.

"Why do you keep doing this to yourself, Tom?"

"Do what?"

"Forget the story. The police fried you because they screwed up and needed a scapegoat. Benson suspended you because he needed a scapegoat too. It was only a week. Everybody knows he put the entire thing on your shoulders. It was a year ago. Forget it and move on."

"I can't."

The muted clatter of the *Star's* police scanners flared, then faded. Reed and Wilson glanced across the newsroom at the summer intern monitoring transmissions.

"Tom, it wasn't your fault."

"I pushed hard for it."

"Yes, but if that dipshit in homicide had explained how Wallace's prints were on the evidence, like you begged him, you would have backed off. You wanted more time on the Sunday School teacher stuff, but Benson was horny for the story. They pushed hard, too. We will never know the truth, Tom."

Wilson's eyes were sympathetic. She resumed typing. Reed went back to the clippings.

"Why have you got the Donner file, anyway?"

"Anniversary's coming up. I'm going to pitch a feature."

Wilson rolled her eyes. "You really are nuts. This rag is not going to let you do that. They'll pass it to a G.A., or some dink in Lifestyles. Besides, isn't Tanita's mother in hiding?"

"I have an idea, but—"

The scanners grew louder.

They turned to the small office tucked away in the far corner of the newsroom. The "torture chamber." A glass-walled room with twenty-four scanners monitoring hundreds of emergency frequencies in the Bay Area. The incessant noise inspired the room's name. Experienced listeners kept the volume low, but when a major incident broke, the sound increased.

"Something's happening," Wilson said.

Simon Green, a summer intern, was monitoring the radios. His face was taut when he stood, jotted a note, then yelled at Al: "Child abduction off BART! Balboa Park! They're stopping the trains!"

Booth grimaced at the newsroom. No one on, except Reed. "Are you clear?"

Reed nodded.

"Take it, Wilson, stick around, you might get overtime."

Across the newsroom, the weekend photo editor radioed a photographer roaming the city to rush to the Balboa Park BART station.

Reed slipped on his jacket, grabbed one of the *Star's* cell phones. "I've got number three, call me with updates, Molly."

"This is eerie. Balboa Park."

Tanita Marie Donner was abducted from the Section 8 housing complex where her teenage welfare mother lived. In Balboa Park.

3

Sydowski and his father had good seats at the Coliseum. Thirty rows up from first. But the game lacked zeal. Entering the eighth, with the A's up by seven over the Yankees, was not exciting baseball.

Sydowski was stiff and hungry.

"Hey, old man," he said in Polish. "I'm going to get something to eat. You want anything?"

"Sure, sure. Popcorn," his father said.

Sydowski patted his father's knee and headed for the concession stand. Sydowski had not wanted to come to the game. He accepted tickets because his boss insisted. Sydowski's old man loved seeing the A's at the Coliseum, but would never ask to be taken because he figured the job kept his son busy.

Standing in line, Sydowski reminisced about the old days. Whenever Boston played the A's, he would drive across the Bay Bridge to Oakland to pay homage to Carl Michael Yastrzemski, a three-time American league batting champion. Yaz took his third title by posting .301, in an era when pitchers destroyed batting averages.

That was perseverance.

That was 1968. The year Oakland got the A's and the San Francisco Police Department got Wladyslaw Sydowski.

Had it been that long ago?

"You know you can take your pension any time, Walt," his boss, Lieutenant Leo Gonzales, often reminded him.

Sydowski couldn't. Not yet. What would he do?

His wife, Basha, had died of Parkinson's six years ago. The girls were grown, had their own children, and had moved away. He had John, his eighty-seven-year-old father, to look after. His old man was something. A Polish potato farmer and barber, he had kept his family alive in a work camp during the war by cutting hair for Nazi officers. Sydowski's old man taught him how to listen, how to read people. Now John lived happily alone at Sea Breeze Villas in Pacifica, tending a vegetable garden, following the A's. He refused to move in with Sydowski, who lived by himself in the Parkside house where he and his wife had raised their daughters and where he now raised champion canaries.

"Sir? That's four dollars?"

Sydowski smiled, showing two gold-crowned teeth as he dug out some cash. The teenage girl smiled back. At six-foot-three, with a solid two-hundred-pound frame, dark complexion, and wavy salt-and-pepper hair, Sydowski was a handsome man.

He knew the hotdog would take a toll on his chronic heartburn, but what the hell? He smothered it with mustard, relish, and onions as the old question surfaced. What would he do if he retired? He was a cop. A homicide inspector. It was his life. To some, he was one of the SFPD's best; to others he was "the arrogant Polack cocksucker." While he was traditionally assigned to break in new detectives, he maintained the detail's highest clearance rate. Senior clicks told rookies Inspector Sydowski knew killers because he was one.

It was near the end of the war. Sydowski was what? Eight or nine? His family was working on a farm in southeastern Germany when he came upon a drunken Nazi soldier raping his twelve-year-old sister behind a barn. Sydowski grabbed the soldier's Luger and held it to the sweating man's temple, forcing him to kneel and beg for his life. Then he pulled the trigger, scattering master race brain matter against the pigsty.

That was another life. Sydowski had erased the memory of it, or thought he had. Somehow the rage he felt then, rage he thought he would never again experience, had returned when he was given the case of a two-year-old girl. The worst part of the job was always the murders of babies. Looking down at their tiny bodies, knowing they never had a chance, that this world had failed them, and it was his job to avenge their deaths. Remembering how he would go home brokenhearted, kiss Basha and the girls, and tell them it was another routine day.

Over the years he had managed to remain detached from his cases, enough so that he could do the job. Although he won most, he accepted losing some. He had no choice. He couldn't solve them all. But the abduction and murder of Tanita Donner was different. It was a year ago. He was the primary and he couldn't close it. At one stage, he felt he was close. Now he had nothing. The thing refused to be solved and it ate him up. Leo had suggested he let fresh eyes go over it, that he concentrate on other files for a time. That didn't last. He had given a piece of his soul to the Donner case. How could he forget about that baby for one goddamned second?

It was raining when he arrived in Golden Gate Park with a rookie and looked into the bag. He remembered the familiar foul smell, the flies and maggots, how she was so white, the gash across her tiny neck, and how *her eyes, those beautiful little eyes, were open and staring at him. Into him. Feeling something break inside, making him ache at that very moment*

to hold her to his chest, in front of all the cops, reporters, and
rubberneckers, all standing there.

Sydowski had crossed the emotional line with Tanita's file.
At the morgue, seeing her doll-size corpse, then taking Tanita's
teenage welfare mother and grandfather from their Balboa
apartment to identify her. How he caught the mother after
she collapsed upon seeing her baby, hearing a groan from the
grandfather, who covered his face with his hands. He was dying
of cancer and had already lost his legs. Remembering how his
wheelchair was held together by coat hangers, how the mother
let her crumpled snapshot of Tanita fall to the floor and started
screaming, and how Sydowski looked to the ceiling.

He knew he would never give up on this one, never let it
go. He had touched Tanita's coffin at her funeral, vowing to
find her killer.

"Here you go, Pop." Sydowski handed a bag of popcorn to
his old man, then took a couple of bites from his dog and tried
getting back into the game. But he'd lost his concentration.

At the outset, the department had put half the detail on
Donner. It was a green light. The FBI assigned a couple of
humps to inflict its jurisdiction. The senior agent was Merle
Rust, a soft-spoken, twenty-year fed with a three-inch scar on
his chin from a bullet that had grazed him during a shootout
with The Order near Seattle in 1984. Rust was as fond of
chewing tobacco as he was of his young partner, Special Agent
Lonnie Ditmire, a by-the-book grad straight from the academy
cookie cutter. He had an all-American smile and believed all
municipal police were bush.

Despite the inevitable friction, everybody worked overtime.
It was always that way with child murders. They hauled in
suspects, Quantico kicked out a profile. They flashed information on the big screen at Candlestick Park and offered a reward.
As weeks, then months, passed, two network TV crime shows

featured the case. The commission turned up the heat for an arrest. Posters sprouted in the Bay Area. But they had squat, until months into the file when something broke.

A beat cop, searching for tossed drugs in the playground in Dolores Park, found Tanita's diaper and the weather-worn Polaroids of two men holding her. The items were hidden in a bag among some shrubs. True to the profile: Two people were involved in the child's abduction and murder. One of the pictured men was Franklin Wallace, a Sunday school teacher who lived near Tanita's housing project. Latents on the diaper matched his. They ran them and discovered Wallace had been convicted ten years ago of molesting a little girl in Virginia. Nothing was known about the second suspect, a tattooed man who was masked in the snapshots.

They kept the break secret, returned the items to the shrubs, and were about to surveil the site with the FBI when Sydowski got a call from Tom Reed at the *Star,* a reporter he knew and respected. Reed was on to the break in the case and wanted confirmation for a story. Sydowski cursed to himself over what he suspected was a dangerous leak, jeopardizing the investigation.

"What do you know, Reed?"

"Franklin Wallace is your boy. His prints are on her diaper and you've got a picture of him with her. He's a Sunday school teacher in the projects with priors. A diddler from Virginia. Is that right?"

Reed was on the money. Sydowski had to be careful.

"Where did you get this?"

"A call out of the blue this morning."

"Who?"

"Get serious, Walt, you know I'd never reveal a source."

Sydowski said nothing.

Reed thought it over quickly, and lowering his voice, said, "If I helped you with information on the tip, do I get a jump on the story, Walt?"

"No deals."

Reed sighed. Sydowski heard a pen tapping, heard Reed thinking.

"I don't know who called. It was a man. Lasted a few seconds. Has to be somebody sick of the commission's shrieking, a cop likely."

"You tape it?"

"No, it was too quick. So, am I on the right track, Walt?"

"No comment. And I wouldn't write a word just yet."

"Come on."

"We never had this conversation."

There was something triumphant in Reed's silence.

"I'll take that as confirmation."

"Take it any way you like, I never spoke to you."

The leak detonated a shitstorm at the D.A.'s office and at Golden Gate Avenue. Reed had called the D.A.'s office, seeking official confirmation for his tip. He got nothing.

Wallace had not yet been formally questioned. Reed was forcing their hand. Rust, Ditmire, and Rich Long, an assistant district attorney, descended on the Hall of Justice and debated the merits of picking up Wallace without yet having built a case against him or his mystery partner. Sydowski wanted Wallace grabbed right away. The agents wanted Wallace under surveillance so he could lead them to his partner. And could they stop Reed's story? More importantly, Ditmire interjected directly to Sydowski, how many other reporters knew?

Offended at the implication that he was the leak, Sydowski stood to confront his accuser, his chair scraping across the floor.

"Take it easy, Walt," Rust said.

At that moment, they received word that Wallace was dead. Shot himself in the head after Reed showed up on his doorstep, asking about Tanita Marie Donner and his record in Virginia. Wallace left a note proclaiming his innocence. Nothing in his house linked him to Tanita's murder.

Long snapped his pencil in two, closed his briefcase, and left with Rust and Ditmire in tow, cursing Sydowski.

The next day, Reed's story identifying Wallace as the chief suspect in Tanita Marie Donner's murder, ran on the front page of the *Star*. Thankfully, Reed didn't know about the second suspect. The John Doe with the tattoos. The D.A. and the feds decided the case might be salvaged if they downplayed Reed's article by saying Wallace was never a suspect, that he was checked because he knew the victim and because of his old record. It was routine and he was cleared long ago, they said. *The San Francisco Star* was writing fiction, again. Sydowski loathed this tenuous approach, but it was all they had.

But it didn't matter. The investigation crumbled. Then it got worse. Wallace's widow sued the paper, then slapped Reed's face in front of all the cameras during a news conference. Reed was demoted, or some shit like that. Sydowski grilled him half a dozen times about details of the call, then they lost touch.

Eventually, the number of bodies on the case dwindled. Sydowski saw less of Rust and Ditmire. Everyone knew it was Sydowski's file. They left him alone. After Wallace's suicide, he had painstakingly rebuilt pieces of the case. No one envied him. But they understood.

After his darkest days, he would go home and sit in his aviary, listen to his birds and think. What was he doing wrong? He came to the hall at all hours, worked at the computer, reread files, and went out on interviews. Nothing clicked.

That had been his year since Tanita Marie Donner's murder, a year in which he rarely took a day off. But he had today. And sitting with his old man at the Coliseum watching the A's and Yankees felt good. For a few hours, he tried to give his mind a rest. As he chewed on the last of his hotdog, he considered going back for another.

Beep! Beep! Beep! Beep!

He switched off his pager, went to a phone and called the duty crew at the hall.

"Homicide, Jackson."

"It's Sydowski."

"Walt, we got a boy abducted just now by a male stranger."

"Got a body?"

"Nope."

"No body. That's General Works. Why call me?"

"It's an order. Comes from the brass. Leo wants you in on this with General and the feebees, right from the get-go. The kid was grabbed from his father on BART at Balboa."

Balboa.

"It's looking bad, Walt."

Sydowski felt his heartburn flare. "Balboa?"

"They're setting up at Ingleside Station on John Young."

"Okay, I'm coming from the Coliseum."

Sydowski hung up and found a uniformed Oakland police officer. He showed him his badge, asked him warmly to make sure his old man got a cab to Pacifica, then gave him several crumpled bills for the fare.

"Consider it done," the cop said.

Sydowski returned to his old man.

"I got to go to work, Pop." He pointed to the officer. "That guy will get a cab home for you."

His father turned to him, nodded, and adjusted his ballcap.

"Sure, you go to work. You do a good job."

Driving across the Bay Bridge to San Francisco, grateful to beat the ballgame traffic, Sydowski was struck by one thought. He wondered if Reed ever got around to figuring that the short, anonymous call he got nearly a year ago had come from Tanita Marie Donner's killer.

4

Tom Reed drove south from downtown in a staff car, a Ford Tempo, bearing *The San Francisco Star's* red, white, and blue banner and the logo: WE'VE GOT SAN FRANCISCO'S STORY.

Talk about cruel irony. He wanted to do an anniversary piece on Tanita Marie Donner's abduction and murder. To set the record straight. To redeem himself. Now this happens. In Balboa.

His knuckles whitened on the steering wheel. Passing a lumbering motor home from Utah on 101, he couldn't shake the Donner story and a million other questions. If today's case was real, would the paper leave him on it? Could he handle it again? Sure. He had nothing left to lose. He had already sacrificed his family to the Donner story.

"We've lost each other, Tom," Ann had said the last time they were out, weeks after Wallace's suicide. It was at a place in Sausalito, with a view of San Francisco's skyline and a harpist plucking a requiem to their marriage. Ann was right. Something between them had died, a fact he refused to admit. He fingered a spoon and met her eyes, shining in the candlelight like they did on their wedding day.

"Tell me, Ann. Tell me how you've lost me."

"Your drinking's out of hand. I've asked you to stop. You don't see what it's doing to us, to Zach, to you."

He rapped the spoon sharply on the table.

"Ann, I've been professionally humiliated, I've been suspended, dumped into a toilet of political crap, and this is the understanding you show me."

"Lower your voice!" she whispered.

He downed his wine and refilled his glass.

"Tom, why can't you realize that you are not infallible?"

"I was not wrong."

"Something went wrong! I don't want to talk about it."

"You brought it up, dear." He gulped more wine.

"You have no idea what Zach and I went through after seeing you on network TV slapped by the widow of that poor teacher."

"That *poor teacher* killed Tanita Marie Donner, Ann!"

"You don't know that. The police said he was not—"

"Fuck the police! Wallace was a twisted child-killer."

"Stop it! Just stop it!" Ann's hushed voice was breaking. A few tense moments passed. She touched the corners of her eyes with her napkin. "We need some time apart," she said. "I'm taking Zach and we're going to stay with my mother in Berkeley."

It was like a sledgehammer blow to his stomach.

"I don't know if I can live with you anymore," she whispered. "If I love you anymore." She covered her mouth with her hand.

They skipped dessert and went home. A few days later, he helped Ann lift suitcases to their van, watching in silence as his wife and son drove away. He went into the house and drank himself unconscious.

Reed found the scene near Ocean at San Jose. Nearby, a tangle of police cars blocked the entrance to the Balboa BART station, lights flashing, radios crackling.

A working-class neighborhood, Balboa was favored with a degree of gentrification at its fringes: a smattering of eclectic boutiques, yuppified houses and apartment blocks. A cop directed traffic around the area. People craned their necks at the yellow crime-scene tape; others watched from windows and balconies.

"Tom!"

Paul Wong, a *Star* photographer, trotted after him, two Nikons dangling from his neck, a camera bag over his shoulder.

"Just pulled in behind you," Wong said. "Isn't this the same place where they found that little girl, Marie something?"

"Tanita Marie Donner."

"Yeah." Wong suddenly remembered everything.

As they headed toward the police tape, they clipped on their press cards. Reed called the paper on his cell phone. Wong banged off a few frames.

"*Star,* Molly Wilson." Police radios were clamoring.

"It's Reed. Got anything for us?"

"Speak up, I'm in the radio room."

"What have you got?"

"A genuine stranger abduction. The kid somehow wanders off the train. Dad gets a one-second glimpse of his boy with a strange man on the platform just as the train is pulling out. He hits the emergency brake bar, kicks out an emergency window and runs after them. But they vanished. Happened that fast. They're pulling out all the stops, bringing in K-9, going door-to-door in a grid for a twenty-block radius. Simon's on his way with another photographer."

"Get a name on the kid and his dad?"

"Father is Nathan Becker, son is Danny. Unlisted. Library's going through driving and property records. Becker is still around, being questioned somewhere. They haven't taken him to Ingleside Station yet. Mom is home alone. They've sent people to tell her and set up for a possible ransom call. No address over the air, but I gather it's near the University of San Francisco, Jordan Park maybe."

"FBI?"

"On their way. Tom, do you think it's connected to Donner?"

"Wallace is dead, Molly."

"Copycat, maybe?"

"Who knows? Call you later."

Reed and Wong shouldered their way to the tape, where a cop lifted it, directing them to a police van in the distance where reporters were clustered around an officer. On the way there, Reed nudged Wong. Across the street, a pony-tailed woman in her thirties, wearing jeans and a sweatshirt, stepped out of Roman's Tub & Shower Boutique. An ID card was clipped to her waist, and she was instructing an officer, pointing somewhere, as they hurried away together.

"Let's go in there," Reed said.

"What for?"

"A hunch."

Bells jingled as they entered. Roman's smelled of jasmine and had an exquisite Florentine storefront displaying overpriced towels. A slim, tanned man with bleached hair was sitting at a small table in one corner of the store with a distraught-looking man. The thin man rose instantly, approaching Reed and Wong.

"I'm sorry, we are closed," he said, arms shooing them away.

"Door's open and there's no sign," Reed said. He noticed

a woman at the rear of the store on a telephone. She was dressed in shorts and a T-shirt, with a laminated ID clipped to her waist. Reed moved quickly, approaching the distraught man at the table. His widened eyes were horror-stricken, his short brown hair messed. He had a long, bloody scrape on one cheek. His clothes were streaked with black greasy smudges. He was staring at nothing.

"Please, you'll have to leave," the thin man said.

"We're here to speak to Mr. Nathan Becker."

Bewildered, the distraught man said, "I am Nathan Becker."

The woman on the phone materialized, and pegging Reed and Wong for press, inserted herself between them and Becker. According to her tag, Kim Potter was a volunteer with a victims' crisis group. "Leave now. This man isn't giving any press interviews."

Wong looked at Reed. They didn't move. Reed looked around Potter.

"Is this true, Mr. Becker? Does this woman speak for you?"

Becker was silent.

"Please leave now!" Potter raised her voice.

"Mr. Becker, we're with *The San Francisco Star*. Do you wish to tell us what happened? I can't imagine what you're going through, but I will respect your answer."

Nathan Becker rubbed his hand over his face, tears streaming down his cheeks. "We have to find him! We have to find Danny. Maggie will be destroyed. He's all we have."

"Yes. What happened?" Reed stepped closer.

"Go get Inspector Turgeon," Potter ordered the clerk. She glared at Reed, angrily punching numbers into the store phone, shouting into it about "a press problem."

Reed would have to hurry.

Trapped alone in his nightmare, Becker began.

"They won't let me search. It was a man, I saw him for less than a second. Bearded, white, about six feet, medium build, sandy hair, wearing a cap. I stopped the train, I ran, it was too late, it happened so fast. I had only looked away for a few seconds. He wandered to one end of the car and . . . and . . . damn it! Why wasn't I watching him?''

Reed took notes, softly asking questions. Becker was clutching a wallet-size snapshot of himself with Danny on his shoulders, laughing as Danny's mom looked up adoringly. The radiant, white, upper-middle-class, professional family. Police were going to duplicate the photo. Wong took shots of it, and of Becker holding it.

''Why would somebody want to take Danny, Mr. Becker?'' Reed asked.

Becker didn't know. His face disappeared into his hands. Wong's camera clicked and the store's entrance bells pealed.

''That's enough!''

It was the ponytailed woman who'd left earlier. Flanked by two uniformed officers, she faced Reed.

''This interview is over,'' she said. The uniforms pulled Reed and Wong aside and she copied their names into her leather-bound notebook. She had hard brown eyes. ''Tom Reed,'' she said. ''Why am I not surprised? Pull this stunt again and you'll be charged.''

''Ever hear of the constitution?'' Reed shot back, glimpsing her waist and ID. He couldn't get her name without being rude.

Ignoring Reed, she stepped back to the front.

''Sorry about this, Mr. Becker,'' she said.

The bells rang and Sydowski filled the doorway, then walked to the store's rear. ''Well, well, well, if this isn't a curse.'' He looked at Reed. ''Everything in order . . . Inspector Turgeon, is it?''

''Turgeon, correct. Yes, all in order.''

''You should have taken Mr. Becker here to Ingleside Station.''

"Mikelson in General wanted him near the scene for now."

"Yeah. I've just spoken with Gord. We'll be moving Mr. Becker shortly. Now, if no one objects, I'll take care of Mr. Reed." Sydowski clamped Reed's arm firmly, escorting him out the rear of the shop. The two patrolmen followed with Wong.

Alone in the back alley, Sydowski backed Reed against a wall and winced. His heartburn, the price he paid for eating that dog, was irritating him. He jabbed his finger into Reed's chest.

"Just what the hell are you doing?"

"My job."

"How'd you find Becker?"

"Instinct. How are you anyway?"

"Delirious. See you're still getting paid to kill trees?"

"Sure, I've been promoted. I'm now the patron saint of reporters who trusted their police sources."

"Thomas, Thomas, ask me if I give two shits," Sydowski said. "Listen *voychik,* you fucked yourself so beautifully you would've made a million as a freak act. I told you to sit on the stuff you had. Didn't I? I was doing you a favor, remember that."

"Still raising little birdies, Walt?"

"They hit the high notes when I line their cages with your work."

An unmarked car inched its way up the alley. Sydowski raised his hand, stopping it at the rear of the store.

"We're taking Becker home now. The wife collapsed at the news."

"What have you got?"

"Beats me."

"C'mon."

"A kidnapping."

"Why did they call you to this? You're Homicide."

He blinked several times. "What do you think, Tom?"

"Do you think it is a copycat?"

Sydowski looked away, and swallowed. His Adam's apple bounced and his face saddened. "Who knows?" he said, his chest burning from the hotdog, the onions. The unknowns. "I have to go."

5

Dropping his last fare of the day at City College, Willie Hampton sighed at the wheel of his cab and began humming a tune from *South Pacific*. Old Willie couldn't restrain his bliss. In three hours, he would strap his vacation-starved butt into the seat of an Oahu-bound 747 and leave the driving to the hacks who don't look back. Take me to Pearl and step on it, Willie chuckled. Gonna get me a lei.

Seaman Hampton of the U.S.S. *California* would pay his respects in person to the boys of the *Arizona*. He would pin on his Distinguished Service Medal and let them know he never forgot. No, sir. Then for three weeks, he would ride at anchor. Willie switched off his radio and was headed for the shop when he spotted a fare near Balboa Park at San Jose and Paulding. A curbside.

No dice, pal.

Willie looked again. The guy had a kid, a little girl draped over his shoulder. Maybe she was sick or something. What the hell? But only if it was on his way. Maybe keep it off the books.

Willie pulled over.

"I'm outta service, but where you going?"

"Logan and Good."

That's Wintergreen. The man didn't look like a rez of that war zone. He had dark glasses, was stone faced. The kid was sleeping, long blond hair. Balloon still tied to her hand. Must've come from the park. Okay, it was on his way.

"Hop in." Willie reached back, popped a rear door. The man placed the kid down to sleep, her head in his lap. "Too much fun for your princess today?" Willie said to his rearview mirror.

"Yes."

Half a dozen blocks later, two SFPD black-and-whites, with lights wig-wagging, screamers yelping, roared by Willie in the opposite direction. He stifled his usual comment on San Francisco's criminal vermin. His fare had dropped his head onto the rear dash.

Aww, let 'em sleep.

Edward Keller was not sleeping. He was praying. Thanking God for His radiant protection in helping him secure the Angel. All of his devotion, watching, planning—the chloroform, the wig, balloon—it had all worked. Gloriously.

Keller floated with his thoughts back, months back, even though time was meaningless to him. His mind was floating . . . floating . . . to . . . *a watery death.*

He repeated it to himself as if it were an incantation.

It was April. *April, death's chosen month.*

Standing at the edge of the pier, gazing upon the Pacific. All that he was, all that he had been, looked back from the still water.

Eyes that haunt my dreams.

Prolonged severe grief reaction, the doctor had called it.

Keller remembered the doctor staring at him, twisting a rubber band. "Accept that you cannot change reality, Edward. And understand that at this institute, those self-admitted take a lower priority. Move on with your life. Find solace where you can."

Keller had found it.

In his visions.

And out there among the fog-shrouded Farallon Islands, where his life ended, and where he would resurrect it. His heart now knew his destiny. It had been revealed to him.

Sanctus, sanctus, sanctus. Dominus Deus sabaoth.

Filling the tanks of the boat, Reimer studied him standing there at the dock's edge, clutching the big paper-wrapped package.

Edward.

That was the guy's name. Reimer couldn't recall his last name. The guy looked—what? Late forties, early fifties? Slim? No. Gaunt, really. About six foot. Could use a haircut and lose that shaggy beard. If Reimer had to be honest, old Ed there looked bad. Seemed to get worse every year. A shame. One of the smartest people Reimer had met. Talked about religion, philosophy, business—when he talked. Sounded like some sort of professor.

But he wasn't.

Reimer knew what he was. Yes, sir. It was a damn shame about him, something the old-timers at Half Moon Bay, those that knew, rarely talked about. Not to Ed's face anyway. What good does talk do? What's done is done. Reimer only wished to hell the guy wouldn't come to him every time he wanted to go out there.

"How you making out with that twenty-eight-footer I put you on to?" Reimer tried not to sound obvious. "She was in pretty good shape when you bought her. Lapstrake with twin Mercs, wasn't it?"

Keller nodded.

"Where you got her docked?"

He didn't answer.

Reimer shrugged, replaced the fuel nozzle on the Shell pump. The *clank-clank* echoed in the morning stillness. The odor of gas wafted from the gas tanks' openings as he wiped the caps with a rag.

"All set," Reimer said.

Keller stepped into the boat, clutching his package. Reimer untied the lines, climbed behind the wheel, adjusted his grease-stained ballcap, scratched his stubble, and surveyed the Pacific. Fine morning. Fog was light. Season would begin soon.

"The usual place?" Reimer said.

Keller nodded and placed two one-hundred-dollar bills in Reimer's hand. It wasn't necessary, Reimer had told him. But why argue? What good would that do? He turned the ignition key. The motor rumbled and he eased the throttle forward, leaving a white foamy wake to lap against the dock.

San Francisco's skyline stretched across the starboard side, the spires of the Golden Gate jutting majestically through a blanket of fog as they made their way to the Farallons. Reimer was born in San Francisco. His father had earned a living running a charter to the gulf from Half Moon for whale and bird-watchers long before it was fashionable. Reimer loved the region, the Pacific's moods and hues, the taste of salt air. He glanced at Keller, his eyes fixed to the horizon. Looking for ghosts. No point in talking to him. Why couldn't he just say no to the man? Reimer shrugged and gave her a touch more throttle, enjoying the wind in his face.

Reimer's boat was a beauty. His mistress. A Searay Seville. A twenty-one-footer. She had a cuddy cabin, a rebuilt V-6 170 horsepower Mercruise. Glided like a dream as they moved into the California current and cut across the coastal shipping lanes.

It was upwelling season and he kept a lookout for blooms of plankton. He could just make the shape of the Farallons twenty-odd miles away, slicing through the hazy mist like shark fins.

That's where it happened. Out there.

Think of other things, Reimer told himself, like the work on his three other charter boats waiting back at the marina. Just think of other things. He watched a trio of Dall's porpoises leaping along port side. He took mental stock of the galley—he knew he'd be hungry by the time they arrived. They might make good time, the lack of wind made for a smooth surface over the navy's submarine playground, which swept southeast of the islands. Reimer knew the region, her history, her mysteries, and her secrets. He looked at Keller again. Ed there was a tragic story. Look at him. Sitting stonelike, clutching that package and staring at nothing. Somebody ought to tell him they are never coming back. Let go, friend, let go. How many years has it been? Let go.

Keller would never let go.

Staring at the churning wake, the white foam against the jade waters, he *heard them. He saw them.*

Pierce. His eldest. Nine years old. Hair lifting in the wind. Squinting at the horizon, scanning the islands. Pierce. Quiet. Resolute. Like Keller. The motor grumbling. Pierce gripping his seat with one hand. The other around his sister, Alisha Keller. Like her mother. Brilliant, beautiful, unyielding. Alisha. Six. Hugging Joshua. The baby. Three years old. The wooden boat. An old speedboat. The last rental. Hammering over the choppy water. Going to spend the day alone looking for whales. Just him and the kids. Joan demanded it. "They have everything but a father." He was furious. He'd juggled meetings. This would likely cost him contracts.

They started late in the afternoon. Had to stop for burgers before they would get in the boat. Couldn't wait until they got to the islands to eat the lunch Joan had packed. Wouldn't wear the life jackets. "Babies wear them," Pierce said. Josh crying when Keller put it on him. To hell with it. Let's get this over with.

Wouldn't go out too far today, sir, squalls comin', the kid at the marina telling him—a pimple-faced grease monkey giving advice to him, Edward Keller, a self made millionaire. Keller ignoring him, ramming the throttle down. Keller didn't understand the buoys. Where is north? Damn. Couldn't read the chart. Hell with it, you could practically see the Farallones. One hundred fifty goddamn dollars. The boat was slow. He hated to waste money.

Spotting a few gray whales on the way temporarily impressed them.

We want to go back.

The hell we will. He would circle the islands, and they would eat their picnic lunch. He would complete his fatherly duty.

The skies darkening. Thunder. It came up so fast.

Lightning and rain. The children huddled. Their wet shiny faces. Time to head back. Maybe they should wait it out on the islands. They were at least a mile off the southern-most island. It seemed close. Hard to say. Some boats far off. Thunder. Rain. Head for the islands. The boat rising. Dipping. A rollercoaster. Something scraping under them, a fantastic thud. A rock?

Then he saw the huge tail and his heart nearly burst from fear.

A whale! Right under them! Cracked the hull!

The children screamed. Water came through his shoes, ice cold. Alisha screaming. Water rushing in! Josh crying.

"Pierce! Alisha! Life jackets! Get them on! Hurry!"

Water crashing over the side now. Cold. The boat yawing. The water rising fast over his ankles. Alisha screaming. The jackets. Can't get them on! Kill the motor. Standing to help Josh. A wave smashing over the gunwale. Something hard hitting his face. Airborne. He was flying. Wet. Freezing. Black. Nothing. Silence.

He was in the water!

Spitting out water. The boat was on its side. The children were in the water. Pierce. Hanging on to the hull. Josh's head bobbing near the stern. Alisha was near the bow.

The life jackets were rolling away. It was so dark.

"Pierce! Get Josh, he's near you!"

Alisha treading water. Joan enrolled them in swimming classes, didn't she? Think! He didn't know if his own children could swim.

They have everything but a father.

Alisha's hand breaking the surface. Grabbing her hair as she went under. Alisha coughing. Crying. "Pierce!" Pierce had Josh. "Good boy, son!" All of them were together. Okay. Think. Keller gasping. Holding Josh to his chest. Alisha and Pierce next to him. Their breath tight, their teeth chattering. His too.

Hypothermia. Shock. Josh silent, nearly out cold. He shook him. Alisha moaned. Stomachache. The burgers and shakes!

The boat gurgling. It's going down. Stay with the boat. But it's sinking! What if there's an undertow? Spotting a light. Thank God. It's something. A buoy? He could make it. He hadn't eaten. He could make it. He had to.

"Listen! We're going to that light! It's not far! Do what Daddy says. We'll be okay! Kick your shoes off! Joshua!" His eyes were closed. Lips blue. "Joshua! Wake up, goddamn it!" Keller shook him again. He woke. Turning his back to Joshua. "Put your arms around Daddy's neck! Now, Joshua!" Cold, tiny arms slipping limply around his neck. "Tighter, Josh, tighter!" Joshua's hold tightened slightly. "Alisha, take my shoulder and hang on!" Trembling hands clutching his shoulder. Alisha whimpering.

"Pierce, grab hold! Hurry!" Pushing off. "Hang on to Daddy. Let Daddy be the boat. Kick your feet slowly. Easy.

Talk to me. We're going to make it. Nice easy strokes." The
water rolling terribly. Breaststrokes. Adrenaline pumping. Doing
fine. Confident. Going to make it.

"That's it. Kick your feet. Keep warm. Think warm. Kick
slowly. Easy. Help Daddy."

Alisha! Her grip loosening, she was drifting away. Carefully
grabbing her arm. "Alisha! Stay awake! Hang on to Daddy!"
Easy strokes. Alisha's crying softer.

*Suddenly his neck is cold. Joshua slipping down his back
and under. Turning, reaching deep, nothing. Alisha, Joshua,
shaken off. "Joshua!" Diving deep, arms flailing, seeing nothing, lungs aching, waves rolling. "Pierce! Alisha!" Nothing.
"Joshua!" shouting, "Someone help me! Oh God, please help
me." Waves tossing him, screaming, "Why don't they help
me? My children are drowning." The darkness. Oh God, please.
The thunder, the waves, white crest, black water now . . .*

. . . jade against the churning wake of Reimer's boat. Silence
after Reimer killed the engine. "We're here."

Keller nodded, but didn't move.

The wake lapping against the boat. The gulls were crying.
Reimer let Keller be, draped a hand over the wheel and looked
off at the horizon. He rubbed his neck, scratched his stubble,
glanced at his watch, started biting his thumbnail. Maybe he'd
get a sandwich.

The boat swayed gently as Keller stood. Carefully, he
unwrapped the package, dropping the paper into the boat. He
studied the wreath. Entwined with white roses, it was beautiful.
He held it before him for a moment, then lifted his head to
hear the boat's wake reaching a cove along the rocky shoreline.
Tranquil here today, like a church after a funeral. Keller placed
the wreath tenderly on the surface. It drifted away.

Reimer saw a great seabird, startled by the boat's wake,

spread its wings and lift off from the cove to fly low directly above them.

Keller heard a flutter of wings. Angel's wings.

He saw something reflected in the water, passing over the wreath.

Here is where his life ended and where he would resurrect it. His heart now knew. It had been revealed to him.

Your children are waiting, Edward.

"Here you go, Logan and Good." Willie Hampton turned to Keller, stopping alongside the curb. "That's twelve-fifty."

Keller gave him a twenty and collected the sleeping child.

"Hope your daughter feels better." Willie fished for change.

"My what?"

"Your daughter. Hope she feels better." Willie held out change.

"Yes. Keep it."

Keller hoisted the child on his shoulder and walked off.

Willie Hampton pulled the door shut, then left Logan for Donevers Street, went four or five blocks before he realized it was a dead end. Damn. He cut over another block west near Wintergreen Heights, the large project. As he doubled back, he spotted his fare with the child just as they entered a sorry-lookin' little house. Don't know your story, friend, but it must be a sad one. Willie Hampton shook his head and returned to humming his favorite tune from *South Pacific.* In a few hours, he would be on a jet to Hawaii.

6

Tiny ponies in hearts galloped across Danny's cotton pajamas, smelling of shampoo. Maggie touched them to her cheek and wept.

Night had come. If she didn't get Danny into bed and read him a story now, he would become cranky. Maggie tried to rise, but couldn't move.

She must be dreaming. She had to be dreaming.

Sitting in her darkened studio, looking at the park, the swans in the pond, the water shimmering in the light of turn-of-the-century street lamps. The distant din of the strangers downstairs. Maggie's painting was nearly finished. She'd been working on it that morning when Nathan called, his voice small, breaking. She'd never heard him like this before. Was he drunk?

"Maggie? Maggie. Something bad has happened."

"Nathan, what is it?"

"The police, the FBI, are going to be there soon."

"Police? FBI? Nathan! What's happened? Is Danny hurt?"

She heard a muffled, coughing sound.

"Nathan!"

"He's gone, Maggie. . . ."

"Nathan, where is Danny!" Her hand shook. Danny was dead.

"A man took him—"

"No! Nathan, no!"

"I chased him. I stopped the train and ran. But I couldn't catch him. The police are looking everywhere—I swear I'll bring him back, I'll bring him . . . I'll be right there, Maggie. I'll be right there."

She sank to the floor, cradling the receiver to her breast. Anyone behind her would have thought she was holding a baby.

This was how Maggie's dream started.

Then the doorbell rang.

It was Gene Carr, the doctor from down the street. Nathan golfed with him at Harding Park. Gene was with men in suits. Police. Saying their names, showing identification. Please sit down, Mrs. Becker.

What is it?

Gene holding her hand.

This is a dream. She knows what they are going to tell her. Danny is dead.

Do you understand, Mrs. Becker?

No.

Your child was abducted by a stranger.

Shaking her head, wiping her eyes.

No.

They were mistaken. This didn't happen to nice families.

No.

Nathan would never allow it. Danny was a special child.

Everyone exchanging glances. Solemn faces. It was no mistake.

It was a mistake. It was.

Punching somebody, shoving the words back down his throat. How dare you tell me this? Get out of my house. Get out now.

Gene and the police holding her.

No, you lying bastards! Where is my baby? You bring me
my baby!

Maggie waking on the living room couch. Someone holding
her hand. Nathan. Eyes red. Gene standing over them. Gene's
wife, Sharon, nearby, hugging herself. Sharon was a distant
relative of the President. She loved raspberry tea. Gene asking
Maggie to take the two pills he gave her, holding Danny's
Goofy glass from Disneyland. She took the pills. One of the
FBI agents, the older one with the scarred chin, watching from
one end of the sofa. The younger one was on a phone. Police
officers moving her grandmother's Louis the XVIth chair, setting up a table right where they stand the Christmas tree. Danny
loved—*loves*—Christmas. A technician quickly installing telephones, a tape recorder, wires everywhere. Gene telling her the
pills would relax her. Where would she be more comfortable?

Nathan suggested the studio. Gene and a policewoman in
jeans helped her upstairs, where she sat staring at the park.

The FBI agents talked to her several times. Did she know
Angela Donner? Franklin Wallace? No. Then the San Francisco
detectives. Others came later. Linda Turgeon, the policewoman
in jeans, sat with her, silently drinking coffee.

"It's after Danny's bedtime," Maggie said.

Turgeon smiled, nodded. She was pretty.

Maggie watched the swans burrowing their heads under their
wings. Funny how dreams could be so real. Strange. But now
it was time to wake up. Time to put Danny to bed.

Someone entered—that big inspector again, the one in the
tattered sports jacket who smelled of Old Spice. He had soft gray
eyes and seemed understanding. He put his hand on Maggie's
shoulder. Maybe now she would wake.

"How are you doing, Maggie?" Sydowski asked.

She said nothing.

"It's important we talk some more. Are you up to talking to me, to helping us?" He sat beside her.

Maggie nodded.

She liked Sydowski's reassuring presence.

"We're doing everything we can to bring Danny home. Anything you can remember that now you consider odd will help, okay?"

"Uh-huh." Her chin crumpled. "This is real, Inspector. Somebody took my baby. I'm not dreaming, am I?"

"No. You're not dreaming."

She buried her face in Danny's pajamas. Her body shook as she wept. Turgeon held her. Sydowski waited. He offered to come back in a little while, but Maggie wanted to go on. They had to find Danny.

He opened his notebook.

"Does Danny have any serious medical problems, allergies, does he take any special medication?"

Maggie shook her head. "When he gets frightened, usually at night, he'll wet the bed. We're seeing a specialist about it."

"What kind of boy is Danny? Describe his personality."

"A good little boy. Friendly. He likes helping with chores."

"How does he get along with other people? Other children?"

"He likes to play with other children, likes to share his things." Maggie nodded with each point. "Gregarious, inquisitive, and he spills his food all the time. You know how children can be."

"I do. Would Danny talk to strangers?"

"We've taught him never to talk to strangers, but he's curious. We're both curious. So, I guess he would, but we'd stop him."

"Does he know his full name, his address, phone number, area code, does he know how to call home?"

"He's only three."

Sydowski saw Maggie's painting of the swans.

"That's quite good. How long have you been painting?"

"Oh"—Maggie touched her nose—"as long as I can remember."

"It's beautiful."

"Thank you."

"Sell many pieces?"

"About three dozen a year."

"I'd like to have the names of each person who's bought one of your works over the last three years as soon as possible. Do you have a favorite artist supply store that you shop at?"

"Yes."

"Do you take Danny with you?"

"Sometimes."

"What are the names of the stores?"

"The Rainbow Gallery and Mueller's Arts and Crafts."

Sydowski wrote it down. "Do you take Danny to any groups, clubs, classes, or local organizations?"

"I'm a member of the Community Association. I go to meetings once a week and usually take Danny with me to the community hall. There's a playroom there and he plays with the other children while one of the parents supervises. We all know each other."

"Have you noticed any strangers hanging around your house in the last little while? Anybody asking for directions?"

"No."

"Have you received any strange calls, maybe somebody getting the wrong number quite a few times?"

"No more than the usual."

"Do you employ anyone, housekeeper, gardener . . . ?"

"A neighborhood boy, Randy Anderson, does landscaping for us."

"Who baby-sits for you?"

"Vicky Harris and Melanie Lyle. They're teenage daughters of friends. We seldom go out. Usually it's the three of us at home."

"Have you ever spanked Danny?"

"We've given him a tap on his bum—" The tears started again. "When he was bad."

"Ever spank him in public?"

"About six months ago. We were grocery shopping and he smashed a bottle of ketchup on purpose. I spanked him right there." Her voice trailed off. "But he's a good boy, really. He was just tired that day and I was impatient."

"Have you and Nathan had any marital problems, have you been seeing a marriage counselor, a clergyman?"

Maggie looked at him.

"No."

"Have you or Nathan ever had an extramarital affair?"

"No."

"I have to ask." He made a note.

"Are you or Nathan under psychiatric care? Have you ever been?"

"No."

"Anyone in your husband's circles you think would do this?"

"No."

"Has your husband ever used or dealt drugs?"

"Absolutely not."

"Does he gamble?"

"No."

"How are you set financially?"

"Comfortable, I guess."

"No heavy debts, large loans?"

"No."

"Do you know Angela Donner or Franklin Wallace?"

"Only from the news last year."

"Would you object to a polygraph test?"

"A lie-detector! My son's missing and you think I'd lie to you!"

"It's routine, but it will help. I am being straight with you."

Maggie covered her mouth with her hands and nodded.

"Good. It really is routine," Sydowski continued. "Can you think of anyone in yours, or your husband's past who might hold a grudge, might have a strong dislike for either of you?"

"No, I can't."

"Is there anyone in your families, or circle of friends or acquaintances, who desperately want children, but can't have any?"

"Just us. Before we had Danny." Tears rolled down Maggie's face.

Sydowski put his big hand on hers.

"Maggie, what we're going to ask you is very important. As soon as you can, we need you to write out a daily schedule, with a detailed hour-by-hour breakdown of the entire family's routine for the last month. What you do, where you go, everything, with all the detail you can provide. Places, names, everything. Inspector Turgeon can help you. It's crucial. Can you do it?"

"I will do anything you ask of us, Inspector."

"Don't answer your phone without us knowing."

Maggie nodded.

"You were very helpful. We'll talk again later."

"Is my son dead, Inspector?" Her voice became ragged. "I know what happened last year with that little girl at Golden Gate Park. I know you and Linda are homicide police, so you tell me right now if you think my boy is dead. You tell me."

Sydowski stood, remembering Golden Gate. The rain. Tanita Marie Donner's body in the garbage bag. Her killer may have just claimed another victim, Maggie Becker's boy. What could he tell her?

"We don't know if Danny's dead. We have no evidence to suggest it. All we know right now is that a stranger took him. Maybe he just wants him for a little while and will let him go. That happens."

Maggie's eyes searched his for a trace of deception until she was satisfied there was none.

"Please. You have to bring him back. He's all I have."

"We'll do everything in our power to bring Danny home. You have my word on that."

Sydowski patted her hand, then returned downstairs.

7

"We've got to stop meeting like this, Walter." FBI Special Agent Merle Rust implanted a chew of Skoal between his right cheek and gum. "How's your old man keeping these days? Down in San Mateo, isn't he?"

"Pacifica. Got a garden, he's fine. And you, Merle?"

"Thought I'd hang it up this year, but the job has a way of interfering with your life sometimes, doesn't it?"

"I wouldn't know." Sydowski sipped his coffee. "I have no life."

They were in the Beckers' kitchen with Ditmire, Turgeon, Mikelson, and Ray Tilly from General Works, who had the lead on the case.

"Let me introduce my new partner," Sydowski said. "Inspector Linda Turgeon. Joined Homicide today from Vice."

"Turgeon. Turgeon?" Rust was remembering. "You Don's girl?"

Turgeon nodded, helping herself and Ditmire to coffee.

SFPD Officer Don Turgeon was working Chinatown twenty

years ago when he was shot and killed shielding a tourist in the cross fire of a gang war. Linda, his only child, was ten years old at the time.

She decided at his funeral to become a police officer.

"I knew Don. He was a good cop," Rust said.

"From Vice," Ditmire said. "Then you don't know the Donner file?"

"I haven't read it yet, I just—"

Sydowski moved toe-to-toe with Ditmire. "What do you know about anything, Special Agent Ditmire, three years out of Club Fed?"

Ditmire stood his ground with Sydowski.

"I know the press is outside, probably chanting your name."

Sydowski inventoried Ditmire top to bottom. "Picking up where you left off, huh, *voychick?*"

"Fuck him, Walter," Rust said. "Lonnie, don't irritate the inspector. I told you he killed a man for doing that."

Killed a man. Turgeon looked at Sydowski. Mikelson and Tilly chuckled. Rust sent a stream of brown tobacco juice down the garbage disposal. "Now that we can feel the love here, let's get humpin'."

Mikelson had arranged through Pacific Bell to run a tap on the Beckers' phone to immediately give them the address of any in-coming calls. Mikelson's crew would also record all conversations. A phone tap was also set up at Nathan Becker's Nor-Tec office in Mountain View where an FBI agent waited to answer any calls. And Angela Donner, Tanita Marie's mother, allowed police to put a tap on her phone in Balboa, in case she received any suspicious calls.

The security cameras on the BART system did not keep tapes, so detectives were interviewing BART station workers and BART Police from every stop from the Coliseum to Balboa. They had dozens of witness statements from passengers to go through. The FBI was running down everybody at Nor-Tec, along with family friends, acquaintances, checking histories, criminal records. They had searched the house and yard three times using canine units. Alerts with Danny's picture went to Bay Area airports, bus and train terminals, cab companies, and police departments. U.S. Postal inspectors monitored the Beckers' mail and boxes in key areas. Bay Area courier services were alerted. Garbage pickup in Balboa and Jordan Park was halted. Summaries of abductions around the Bay and across America over the last year were ordered.

After several separate interviews with Maggie and Nathan, they were convinced Danny had been taken by a stranger.

"Do you think Donner and Becker are linked?" Turgeon asked.

"It's too soon to think anything," Sydowski said.

"If nothing comes tonight," Tilly said, "the Beckers will make a plea for Danny in a news conference tomorrow. The mayor's office is considering a reward. So is Nathan's company. We'll give the TV people some recent home-video footage of Danny. It may kick something out for us."

The sketch artist arrived. Mikelson and Sydowski took him to the den where Nathan was waiting. Sydowski sat at the edge of Nathan's oak desk, next to a small, gold-framed picture of Danny on his mother's lap. Both were laughing. Sydowski set it aside gently, then checked his watch. For more than an hour, Nathan Becker struggled for the sketch artist, trying to describe the face of the man who kidnapped his son. So far, it had been fruitless. Nathan was growing angry.

"Try to relax, Mr. Becker," Mikelson said.

So many faces. They flowed together. Nathan remembered few details other than the beard. The BART people hadn't seen the man as clearly as Nathan had. The kidnapper likely knew about BART's security cameras and avoided them, Sydowski reasoned. He suspected that he was a stalker who had waited for his golden opportunity. But why Danny Becker? From Nathan Becker's account, everyone concluded that his glimpse of his son's kidnapping had lasted half a second. It was a needle in a haystack. Nathan's frustration and anguish increased.

The phone in the study rang.

"Okay, Mr. Becker, let's go."

They rushed to the living room. Additional phone lines had been installed. Two were new numbers, two were extensions. Pacific Bell would have the caller's address in seconds. The phone rang again.

"Nob Hill!" Someone shouted the address of the call.

Tape recorders were rolling, an SFPD hostage negotiator put on a headset to listen in. He had a clipboard and pen, ready to jot instructions to Nathan. The room was silent. Nathan looked at the negotiator. He nodded, and Nathan answered on the third ring.

"Hello . . ." He swallowed. "Oh, Hello, Mr. Brooker." Nathan shook his head.

Sydowski went to the bank of telephones, slipped on a headset and listened to the call. An officer, already listening in, had scribbled the caller's name on a pad: Elroy Brooker, Nor-Tec's CEO.

"I just heard what happened, Nathan. Two FBI agents just left my home. I'm so sorry. How are you and Maggie holding up?"

"We're praying." Nathan sniffed.

"Be strong, Nathan. Never give up hope."

"Did the agents tell you anything?"

"They asked a lot of questions about you and the project. If you were a gambler, or ran up debts you couldn't repay, if you were capable of selling information about the project."

"Yeah?" His voice wavered between anger and disbelief.

"I told them to go to hell and find your boy. You're one of our top people. Outstanding in every way."

Nathan had regarded Brooker as a bumbling, spineless relic.

"Listen, Nathan, I won't tie up your line. I'm going to call the board now. I think we can pull thirty, maybe fifty thousand

from our corporate donations account. It'll be at your disposal,
a reward, ransom, whatever it takes to see your son is returned
safely. As you know, Ruth and I have nine grandchildren. Our
prayers are for Danny, Maggie, and you.''

"Thank you, Mr. Brooker." Nathan hung up. The recorders
stopped. He put his face in his hands.

"Mr. Becker, we should work on the composite," Mikelson
said.

Nathan moved his jaw to speak, looking into his empty hands.

"It's my fault. It's all my fault. I should have been watching
him. I should've been watching him. He's our little boy. He's
the same age as that murdered little girl. What if . . . what if . . .
Oh please, I have to go and find my son."

Nathan bolted for the door. Ditmire grabbed him. Sydowski
helped, and they held Nathan until he finally broke down and
wept.

During the night, an oppressive silence fell on the Becker
home. Sydowski picked up a Giants' ball cap he spotted peeking
from under the sofa. Child-size. Danny's cap? He noticed the
fine strands of blond hair caught in the weave. In Victorian
Europe, parents would cut and cherish locks of hair from their
dead children before burying them.

One of the police phones rang. Ditmire grabbed it, and said,
"One second," then passed it to Sydowski.

"Give me the score, Walt." It was Lieutenant Leo Gonzales.
Sydowski told him everything, while peering through the living
room curtains at the half a dozen police cars, the unmarked
surveillance van, and the news cruisers out front.

"What about Donner, Walt? We got a serial here?"

"It's just too soon, Leo."

"Probably. Can the father ID the bad guy?"

"Don't know. We're working on a composite."

"We got people canvassing all night in Balboa and Jordan

Park. We'll get vice and robbery to help,'' Gonzales said. ''We'll shake down the registry and see what falls out. We're also checking prisons and mental hospitals for escapees, walk-aways, recent discharges, and complaints. Halfway houses.'' Gonzales promised a grid of the park and neighborhood at dawn and bodies to hit the bars, porn, and peep clubs. ''The mayor called the chief. We need this one, Walt.''

''You're talking in obvious terms, Leo.''

''Sorry about your new partner. That was supposed to be official at the hall on Monday.''

''Well, shit happens, Leo.''

''I love you too, dear. Keep in touch.''

Later, Ditmire was in the study with Nathan and the sketch artist. Turgeon was with Maggie upstairs. Rust was reviewing reports. Sydowski borrowed his cellular phone. The press outside could not monitor its scrambled frequencies. He wanted a moment alone and went to the kitchen. He noticed its black-and-white-tile floor, skylights, lace curtained windows. French doors led to the patio and backyard. The table looked like maple. On the refrigerator door, at eye level, was a newspaper clipping with tips on quake readiness. What about kidnappings? Below it, tiny Donald Duck and Mickey Mouse magnets held up a colorful finger painting with a ''D'' scrawled at the bottom. There was a Smurf's calendar next to it. Danny's doctor's appointment was next Friday at two.

Sydowski called his old man's unit at Sea Breeze in Pacifica.

''Hahllow.''

''Hey, Dad. You got home okay?'' Sydowski said in Polish.

''Oh sure, no problems. Sixty dollars for the cab. Do you believe that? I remember when you could buy a house for that.''

''So, who won the game?''

''A's, ten to eight.''

''It got interesting after I left?''

Rick Mofina

"You going to be working all night on this? I saw it on the TV. It's pretty bad. It breaks my heart."

"The ones with kids always break my heart, Dad."

"Why do people do this? What does it prove? It's crazy. Crazy. Better to shoot the sonofabitch!"

"Listen, I'm going to be working hard time on this one, but I'll come down to see you when I can."

"Sure, sure."

"What are you going to do tomorrow?"

"I got to cut hair for John. Remember Big John?"

"The retired bus driver."

"Yeah. I'm going to give him a haircut."

"Good. Well, I got to get back to work, Dad."

"Sure. You better catch the sonofabitch. Shoot him."

"I'm doing my best, Dad. Good night."

Sydowski was tired. He poured coffee and took a bite of a pastrami on rye, delivered by a deli. Turgeon entered.

"So, you killed a man, did you? Who handled the file, Ditmire?" She sat down next to him. "Going to tell me about it?"

"Maybe."

She smiled, took some coffee, brushing back the hair that had curtained over one eye. She was pretty. Reminded him of his daughters. His heart swirled with warm, then sad thoughts.

"I'm sorry, I never knew your dad."

"It was a long time ago, too. Look"—Turgeon shifted topics—"I'd like to go to the hall tonight and read the Donner file."

"Forget Lonnie. I'll bring you to speed. It'll be a long night."

"Fine, but while we're speaking of Ditmire, I appreciate your help, Inspector, but you don't have to protect me."

A scolding. He bit into his sandwich.

Dad, please. You're suffocating me with your loving concern. His oldest daughter would chide him whenever he offered misgivings on her dates. Sydowski understood.

"And," Turgeon said, "for the record, I asked to be teamed with you. Insisted, actually."

"Let's hope you won't regret it. Getting what you want can sometimes be terrible." Sydowski finished his sandwich and coffee. "I need some air. Tell the Hoover boys I'll be outside with this." He left with the cellular phone.

Strolling through the backyard to the park helped Sydowski think. The cool night air invigorated him. At the edge of the pond, he watched the swans sleeping with their heads tucked under their wings.

It could be the same guy who murdered Tanita Marie Donner. Catch this guy and you could clear both. That was the department's thinking. Results were expected fast before it got out of hand.

Sydowski picked up two round pebbles, and shook them like dice. It was just a little too pat. Could've been planned to appear like the first one. Could be coincidence. He looked up at the darkened windows of Maggie Becker's studio.

Sydowski threw the pebbles into the pond, startling the swans.

8

"I visited my baby's grave this morning." Angela Donner felt the eyes of her weekly bereavement group upon her. It was always hard when her turn came.

Don't be ashamed, embarrassed or afraid. We're here together. That was the group's philosophy. Still, it was difficult to face them. Angela was painfully self-conscious. She was an overweight, twenty-one-year-old, living on welfare with her father, who had lost both his legs below the knee to cancer. She couldn't help being uneasy when it was her time to talk. She apologized with a smile.

"Poppa went with me. We brought fresh flowers. We always do."

Angela fingered the pink ribbon, bowed around the folded, grease-stained, take-out bag she held on her lap, like a prayer book.

"Today, when we got to Tanita Marie's spot—it's pretty there in the shade of a big weeping willow—I started pushing Poppa's chair, he points and says, 'Look, Angie. There's something on her stone.' And I could see it. The wind blew this bag up against it. Poppa wanted to complain to the groundsman. But I said no.'' Angela caressed the bag, then squeezed it.

"I took the bag and folded it. I took the ribbon from the flowers from our last visit and tied it nice around the bag and saved it. Because of all the hundreds of stones in the children's cemetery, this bag came to my baby's grave. It came for a reason. Just like of all the babies in this city, mine was murdered.''

The room's fluorescent lights hummed. Angela stared at the bag in her plump hands. The group listened.

"But what's the reason? Why was my baby murdered? I was a good mother. I loved her. Why did someone take her? How could somebody be so bad? Poppa says somebody who would kill a baby must be dead inside already. But why can't the police find my baby's killer? He's still out there. He could kill another baby.'' Her voice grew small. "I know it's been a year, but sometimes, at night, I can still hear her crying for me.'' Angela held the bag to her face and wept softly.

Lois Jensen left her chair, knelt before Angela, and put her arms around her. "Go ahead and let it out, sweetheart. It's all right.''

Lois knew the hurt. Two years ago, her thirteen-year-old son Allan was shot in the head while riding his bike through the park near their home. Lois was the one who found him. She knew the hurt.

Dr. Kate Martin made a note on her clipboard. Her group was progressing. Manifestations of empathy, comfort, and compassion were now common. Not long ago, Lois, who was married to a lawyer in Marin County, would refuse to open up as each of the others articulated their grief. Now, through Angela, Lois was healing. Death, the great equalizer, had taken a child from each woman. Now, like shipwrecked survivors, they were holding fast to each other, enduring.

Dr. Kate Martin had endured. Barely.

While writing, she tugged at her blazer's cuffs, hiding the scars across her wrists. She watched Angela cherishing her take-out bag. For Kate, it was leaves, saved from each visit to her parents' grave.

Kate was eight when her mother and father were late returning home from a movie. Waiting and playing cards with their neighbor, Mrs. Cook. A police car arrived at the house. The old woman put an age-spotted hand to her mouth. Kate stood in her robe, barefoot, alone in the hall. Mrs. Cook talked in hushed tones with the young officer at the door, holding his hat in his hand. Something was wrong. Kate backed away. Something was wrong. Mrs. Cook hurried to her, crushing her against her bosom, with a smell of moth balls, telling her there had been a horrible, awful car accident.

"You are all alone now, child."

Kate was sent to live with her mother's sister Ellen, her husband, Miles, and their three sons on their pig farm in Oregon.

She hated it.

They were strangers who treated her as the dark child who had brought the pall of human death into their home. She was given her own room and everyone avoided her. Her only happiness came once a year when, only for her sake they reminded her, they'd stop work and pile into the family wagon to drive to California to visit the cemetery where her parents were.

Uncle Miles loathed it. "It costs too damn much money and serves no purpose, Ellen," he complained during their final trip together.

Throughout the drive the older boys taunted Kate.

"You never smile. Why don't stay in San Francisco. You piss us off." Quentin, the oldest, was fifteen and loved killing pigs.

"Yeah. Why don't you go and live in the stupid graveyard, you like it there so much? Huh?" Lewis, Quentin's sidekick, was thirteen.

Aunt Ellen told the boys to stop. At the cemetery, after Kate visited her parents' headstone and gathered leaves, they started back to the car. The boys fell behind Kate and started up again.

"We're going to leave you here." Quentin grinned. His eye spotted the dark earth of a freshly dug grave nearby. He nodded to his brothers. In an instant they picked her up. Quentin held her ankles, his brothers had her arms. "No. Quentin, please!" Her leaves floated to the ground. The boys carried her to the open grave.

They dropped her into the grave and looked down on her from its mouth, laughing and showering her with dirt. "Welcome home, Kate." She lay on the cool earth, watching them. Dead silent. Aunt Ellen screamed and screamed as Uncle Miles lifted her out.

"You are all alone now, child."

Uncle Miles had laughed it off. A joke, Kate, only a joke. She was ten. Aunt Ellen studied the horizon. When they got back, Kate took her aunt's sewing shears into the bathroom and sliced them across her wrists. She ached for her mother and father, wanted to be with them. She closed her eyes and lay in the tub, remembering the cold grave.

Quentin, who liked watching her through the bathroom key-hole, found her. Just in time. Aunt Ellen knew Kate had to be rescued. So for the next four years, Dr. Brendan Blake had helped Kate climb out of hell. And at fourteen, she decided to become a beacon to those bereaved of light. There was enough money in her parents' estate for her to attend Berkeley.

Now at thirty-five, Kate Martin was a tenured professor at San Francisco Metropolitan University's Department of Psychiatry, where she was the focus of a small academic sensation. It was rumored that her research into the impact on parents bereaved of their children through unnatural death could lead to a university bereavement studies center.

For nearly a year, fifteen volunteers, all parents of children who had been killed, met on campus every other Saturday to discuss their private torment. The corporeal and psychological toll of each child's death was also measured in journals the parents kept.

Kate looked fondly at Angela Donner. The study was born with the murder of her two-year-old daughter, Tanita Marie. Police had told Kate about a non-profit support group that was working with Angela Donner. Kate offered counseling, to help her cope with Tanita's murder. Then she became convinced more in-depth empirical studies were needed on the impact of children who had died unnaturally.

She submitted a proposal for a research project, but the university's bureaucracy moved at a glacial pace. Despite cutbacks, she knew funding existed. She lobbied the research committee. Eventually the committee members threw up their hands and found her some money a fraction of what she'd requested—but enough for one year. Through the police, victims' groups, personal ads, and notices posted around the campus, she found volunteer subjects for the project.

Now, with less than eight weeks remaining, when the study was beginning to bear fruit, the plug was going to be pulled. Kate was concerned. Patterns were emerging. She'd observed three, possibly four, distinct cycles, and in one case, an extremely unusual phenomenon that exceeded guilt. She was on the verge of understanding it and needed another year. But she would not get another cent from the university. Despite accolades from some colleagues, her request for more funding was denied and her work deemed redundant.

"Previous studies have clearly shown us the cycles you claim to have found, Katie." Dr. Joel Levine, the dean of psychiatry, advised her to wrap up her research, as he cleaned his glasses with his tie. "You can't perpetuate this artificial healing process for your group. It's not fair to them. Some in the department believe you're using your subjects as a cornerstone for a bereavement center. Write your paper, or a book, then move on. Go out on a date. You know, you're far more attractive than you allow yourself to be."

Kate's face reddened with fury, the same way it did at the faculty Christmas party, when the eminent Dr. Levine, married father of four children, groped her breasts and suggested they slip away to "fuck like rabid mink" in the back seat of her Volvo.

"Go to hell," she hissed before slamming his office door, startling an undergraduate in the hall who dropped his books.

As today's session ended, Kate steepled her fingers under her chin and informed the group that she had written to *The San Francisco Star* about the project with the hope that a sensitive article would give them positive exposure, and perhaps inspire the additional funding they needed to continue. She had violated university policy, but she didn't give a damn. It was a matter of survival.

That night, alone in her Russian Hill apartment, taking in her view of the Golden Gate, Kate agonized over her decision. Had she done the right thing? Or was she reacting to Levine's insult? She sipped a glass of white wine and continued reading files. She worried about each member. Most were healing, but she feared for those who might not recover. Ending the study now would mean irreparable damage. Anniversaries and birthdays were approaching—the most difficult times. It was coming up on one year since Angela's daughter was stolen and killed. She was going to have a rough time. Then there was Edward Keller, her most unusual case.

She opened his file. An anniversary was coming up for him. She flipped through her notes, handwritten on yellow legal pads, biting her lip. So many deaths in one incident. He was the most withdrawn group member. The others were referrals from police or victims' groups. Keller was a walkin. He came to her office after seeing a newspaper ad. A somber man with a whispering voice, he embodied pain.

His three children had drowned together in a boating accident. He nearly drowned trying to save them. He believed their deaths were his fault. So did his wife, who left him six months later. His grief went beyond guilt and remorse. Kate worried about him. Privately, she advised him to get independent therapy. He was consumed with their deaths, even though they had died so many years ago. It might as well have been yesterday. His was an abnormal case of sustained grief reaction. He relived the tragedy over and over, condemning himself, begging for another chance. She came to one page that reminded her vividly of the night he stunned the group. She had written his words verbatim: "On certain nights, an energy flows through me, it's hard to describe, it's extremely powerful, but I sometimes believe I can bring them back, that it really is possible." Flagging the note with an asterisk, she'd jotted "Delusional" next to it. She flipped back to the beginning of Keller's file and checked the anniversary date of his children's deaths. It was coming up. How was he going to survive?

Kate yawned, set her work aside, and switched on the late night TV news. The top story was the kidnapping of Danny Raphael Becker. Next came footage of a helicopter hovering over the area, police officers searching the neighborhood, some with dogs, Inspector Somebody saying that the police have no leads, frightened parents vowing to keep their children indoors. A picture of Danny Becker was shown for several seconds, and later a picture of Tanita, the reporter saying police cannot rule out the possibility of a link between today's case and Tanita's murder, which remained unsolved. Kate feared for Angela. There was also some background about the controversy over the Sunday school teacher who proclaimed his innocence, then committed suicide after he was named as a suspect in Tanita's murder. There was file footage of the man's widow slapping the reporter who wrote the articles for *The San Fran-*

cisco Star. Kate groaned. She had forgotten about the scandal over Tanita's case. What was she thinking? Why didn't she write the *Chronicle* or *Examiner?* What had she gotten herself into?

As the news droned, she thought of Danny's parents, Angela Donner, and the people in her group. She switched off the TV, stared out at San Francisco's skyline. More victims. Always more victims. Suffer the little children to come unto me, the malevolent deity.

She smelled mothballs and fresh, cold earth.

You are all alone now, child.

I can bring them back.

9

Tom Reed was ninety minutes away from deadline when he returned to the *Star's* newsroom.

Bruce Duggan, the weekend night editor, leaned back in his chair, entwining his fingers behind his head. His glasses rested atop his forehead, which had encroached upon his hairline. His black eyes peered from a wrinkled face that had settled into a permanent frown after twenty-five years in news. "Anybody else get the father, Reed?"

"No. It's our exclusive. Cops sealed the house. The family is holding a press conference tomorrow."

Duggan thought. "Put the father up high. The art is strong. It's going A-1. Wilson filed a sider on Donner and some background for you. I'll ship it to you. Work in the Donner murder. Is there a link?"

"Nothing official yet."

Duggan replaced his glasses and resumed working at his computer. "I'll need it fast to make first edition."

At his desk Reed entered his personal code and his terminal

came to life, requesting a story. He typed "KIDNAPPED." A black, blinking cursor appeared, ticking off seconds on a blank screen.

Several floors below in the paper's basement, a crew of pressmen readied the *Star's* Metroliner presses. Less than an hour after they started rolling, sixty circulation trucks would rumble from the loading docks into the night, delivering a pound of information to three hundred thousand homes in the Greater Bay Area.

Reed's story would be on the front page, above the fold.

The third paragraph of the story described police combing the area, that an expanded full-scale search for Danny and his abductor was to resume Sunday at sunrise. Reed studied his notes for the strongest quotes from Nathan Becker, flagging the exclusivity of the interview:

"It happened so fast. I had only taken my eyes from him for a few seconds," Nathan Becker, 35, told The San Francisco Star *minutes after he stopped his southbound BART train to chase the man who kidnapped his son. . . .*

Reed brought in Sydowski, identifying him as the primary detective in the Donner case, who was now helping on Danny Becker's abduction, and disclosing that Sydowski had refused to link the two cases.

Reed glanced at his watch, typed a few commands, and captured the background written by Wilson. It began:

Last year two-year-old Tanita Marie Donner's body was stuffed into a garbage bag hidden under a tire deep in a secluded wooded area of Golden Gate Park. Her killer remains free.

"Excuse me?"

Tad Chalmers, an eighteen-year-old copy runner, stood before Reed, tapping a pen on his palm. "I've got this woman on hold who really wants to talk to you. Asked for you specifically."

"Take her name and number."

"She won't leave her name, says it's about the Donner murder."

The Donner murder? Probably a crank. He'd received dozens of nut calls last year when the story broke. Today's news of the Becker kidnapping was exciting the crazies: He should talk to her, just in case. That's how he had gotten the Wallace tip.

"Okay, put her through."

Tad disappeared across the newsroom. Then Reed's line rang.

"Reed."

"You wrote about the girl murdered last year, Tanita Donner?"

"Look, I'm on deadline. Please give me your name and number and I'll call you right back."

"I don't want my name in the paper."

"Listen ma'am—"

"What I have to tell you, I have to say now, while I'm up to it."

"I won't talk to you unless you tell me who you are. You know how people accuse us of making things up."

She gave it some thought: "Florence."

"Got a last name, Florence?"

"Just Florence." She sounded grandmotherly, early sixties, working class, probably watched soaps and game shows all day.

"Why are you calling, Florence?"

"You know about that little boy who was kidnapped today, how they're saying it's just like that little baby girl who got murdered last year, but they don't know who did it?"

"Go ahead."

"I know who killed her."

Sure you do, dear. "What's the killer's name?"

"I don't know his real name."

"Look, I'm really—how do you know this guy's the killer?"

"I heard him confess. He said he did it and no one knows."

"Really? Did you tell the police?"

"I called them. They said they need more specific information from me. But they never came around. Never talked to me. So when that little boy got kidnapped today, I decided to call you."

She continued. "I love crime stories. I read all the papers. Yours are the best, except for that mistake you made about the Sunday school teacher being the killer."

"The Sunday school teacher didn't kill Tanita Donner?"

"Well, not by the way the real killer talks. I wanted you to know what I heard, but don't put my name in the paper. He scares me."

"Do you think the killer also kidnapped Danny Becker?"

"What do you think? You're a smart fella."

"How did you come to hear Tanita Donner's killer confess?"

A moment passed and Florence did not answer.

"Are you clairvoyant, Florence?"

"A psychic? Why no, I'm a Roman Catholic. I sing in the choir at Our Lady Queen of Tearful Sorrows."

"That's lovely, Florence. Listen, I'm really sorry but unless you can be more specific—"

"I heard him tell God that he did it."

Under R, religious nut: bingo!

Suddenly Duggan loomed over him.

"Fifteen minutes." Duggan tapped his watch.

Again, he asked for her full name and number. She refused.

"I've got to go, Florence." Just a lonely old woman. Reed hung up, finished the story, read it, then sent it to Duggan through the computer system.

In the washroom, Reed bent over a sink, and ran the cold water. His tip on Wallace had come the same way, but the guy who called offered something concrete he could check: Wallace's conviction in Virginia. Reed confirmed it and Sydowski confirmed Wallace was the suspect. Didn't he? That Wallace tip had to have come from a cop, the voice sounded like an old source, yet Reed couldn't put a name or face to it. This Florence person was a nut. "I heard him tell God." Sure. But if Wallace killed Donner, why was the file still open? Did the killer call Reed to set up Wallace? That was Sydowski's thinking, but Reed couldn't accept it. For it meant the real killer was still out there. And now, with another child abduction, and in Balboa, it meant another child may be murdered and that he may have truly contributed to the death of an innocent man.

He splashed his face until he washed the fear from his mind.

The few strands of gray invading the temples of his short brown hair were multiplying. He was thirty three. Thirty three and he had nothing. Nothing that mattered. Nothing but his job, self-doubt, and an increasing affection for Jack Daniel's Tennessee Sipping Whiskey. When Ann left, she opened the door to a dark truth, showing him exactly what he was. On the way back to his desk, Reed saw Molly Wilson reading the memos posted on the newsroom bulletin board.

"Hey, Tomster, finish the story?"

"Why haven't you gone home yet?"

"Didn't feel like it. Feel like a beer?"

"I'm tired. It's been a long day. Can I take a rain check?"

Molly stepped closer. He could smell her perfume. "I've given you a handful already, Tommy. When are you going to put them to use?"

He liked her perfect-teeth smile, her ice-blue eyes inviting him to a place he was tempted to enter.

"See this?" A perfect fingernail tapped a memo. "Could be exciting, don't you think?" Molly said before leaving.

It was a managing editor's notice calling for applications for the paper's new South American bureau in São Paulo. Reed

took five seconds to ingest the idea of applying and the conse-
quences of success before returning to his desk for his jacket.

"Any problems?" he asked Duggan on his way out.

"Good piece. Just in time for first."

"I'll cover the Becker press conference tomorrow?"

"No, you're working the night shift in here tomorrow night."

"But I'm the lead reporter on this one."

"Benson called in the order. You're off the story."

Myron Benson, the editor of the paper's largest editorial
department, controlled fifty reporters. Invoking Benson's name
gave any instructions immediate currency. Duggan stared at
Reed. No elaboration was needed. The fuckup last year, and
that Benson had nearly fired him and kept him on indefinite
probation were known facts.

"Fine, fine. I get it."

Duggan gave him an opened white business envelope addressed to the paper. It bore Metro University's seal and came
from a Dr. K. E. Martin of the psych department. Reed's name
had been scrawled on it.

"What's this?"

"Benson wants you to do a feature on this bereavement
group." Duggan nodded at the envelope. "He wants you to
tie it in with the anniversary of the Donner murder and the
Becker kidnapping."

Reed was wounded. Again. He swallowed it.

"Sure. I'll get right on it."

Crumbs and crap, that's what they were feeding him. Reed
tucked the envelope into his jacket and headed for the parking
lot.

10

The distant horn of a tug echoed from the Bay as Tom Reed walked across the *Star* parking lot. Cool Pacific breezes carried the stench of diesel and exhaust from the freeway overhead. The green '77 Comet he had bought after Ann left waited like a lonely, faithful mutt.

Reed never lost his awe for San Francisco—the lights of Coit Tower, the financial district, the pyramid, the hills, the bridges, the Bay.

He ran a red light entering Sea Park, a community of uphill mansions whose views rivaled Russian Hill and Pacific Heights. It bordered a small park dotted by stone tables topped with permanent chessboards. Old European men brought their own worn pieces here to play friendly games and reminisce. Beyond the houses were rows of condos. A sedate community. Gleaming Jaguars, BMWs and Mercedes lined the streets. Precision clipped shrubs and hedges hid the *pong* of tennis balls, the splash of a private pool, and the occasional whispered investment tip.

Reed parked near the three-story Edwardian house where he lived with five other men. The owner, Lila Onescu, was a Rumanian grand dame with gypsy blood who lived in a condo two blocks away. After Ann left with Zach, Reed couldn't bear living alone in their house. A buddy told him of Lila Onescu's place, a jewel in Sea Park, well-kept, quiet. A hundred bucks a week for a room on the second floor where he would share a bathroom and kitchen with two other tenants. This was his home.

Reed creaked up the staircase, welcomed by the typed note taped to his door: "Where is rent? L. Onescu." He was two weeks behind. He would give her a check tomorrow he promised, fumbling for his key.

His room had three bay windows overlooking the Marina District and the Pacific. A dorm-style single bed with rumpled sheets was against one wall. A mirrored dresser stood against another near an ornamental fireplace. A small desk sat opposite the bed, and a tattered, comfortable sofa chair was in the middle of the room, which had hardwood floors and faded green flower-patterned wallpaper. Reed's framed degree, his two awards, a *Star* front page, and silver-framed pictures of Ann and Zach, were leaning on the fireplace mantel, hastily placed in the hope they would be collected at a moment's notice. A stack of newspapers tottered a few feet from the floor next to the dresser. It had started growing the day he moved in—three weeks after Ann moved out of their bungalow in Sunset. When she left, their house had become a mausoleum for their marriage. He had to leave, or be entombed. They agreed to rent their house.

Reed went down the hall to the kitchen for ice. In his room, he poured some Jack Daniel's, stripped off his clothes, casting them onto the pig-sized heap in the corner, slipped into jogging shorts. He opened the bay windows and watched the twinkling lights of the Golden Gate.

All he had ever wanted in this world was to be a reporter. The dream of a kid from Big Sky Country. His dad used to bring him a newspaper six days a week, *The Great Falls Trib-une*. He'd spread it open on the living room floor and read the news to his mother. When he was eleven, he started his first *Trib* route. Trudging through the snow, shivering in the rain, or sweating under the prairie sun with that canvas bag, nearly black with newsprint, slung over his shoulder like a harness. Dad had knotted the strap so the bag hung just so, like an extension of himself. He would read the paper as he delivered it, dreaming of seeing his stories in print. He had forty customers and every day, by the time he emptied his bag, he'd have read the day's entire edition.

Life's daily dramas enthralled him. He became a news addict and an expert on current affairs. In high school, he graduated from newspaper boy to cub reporter, writing stories for the school paper. He was accepted into J School at the University of Missouri, where he met Ann, a business major with big brown eyes and a smile that knocked him out. She was from Berkeley and wanted children and her own shop to sell the children's clothes she would design and make herself. That was a secret, she told him.

He wanted a family, too, but he wanted to establish his career first and maybe write books. The last part was his secret. If you talked about writing books, you'd never do it.

They were married after graduation. A few weeks later, he got a job with AP in San Francisco. Ann was happy to move back to the Bay Area, where she would be near her mother. And Reed was determined to prove himself in San Francisco.

He hustled for AP, breaking a story about the Russian mafia. He was short-listed for a Pulitzer, but lost out. *The San Fran-cisco Star* then offered him a job as crime reporter at twice his salary.

Ann got an administrative post at one of San Francisco's hospitals. At night, she worked on her business plan and cloth-ing designs. He traveled constantly, worked long hours and was rarely home. The years passed. Starting a family seemed impossible.

Then boom. Ann was pregnant. He was stunned. Unprepared.

She had forgotten her pills when they vacationed in Las Vegas. He hinted that she'd done it purposely. Not true, she said. They didn't want to argue. In the following months, they retreated, withdrew into themselves. Ann welcomed the coming of a baby, Reed braced for it.

When he witnessed the birth of their son, he felt a degree of love he never knew existed. But soon, he grappled with his own mortality. It frightened him, overwhelmed him with the realization that he had little time left in his life for accomplishments. He was a father. He feared he would fail fatherhood. He compensated the only way he knew: by striving through his job to leave Zach a legacy as a man who had made his mark. Someone Zach could be proud of. Consequently, the *Star* became his mistress and family. It seemed Ann and Zach became people he appreciated only when needed. They shared the groceries and the furniture. On the surface, he was like any other young husband and father. In truth, he only gave of himself when it was convenient. It was cute how Zach imitated him and wanted to be a reporter, just like daddy. It was reassuring how Ann understood that he never had time for them. But something was crumbling, little by little, day by day. Reed was blind to what had happened, oblivious to Ann's achievement of single-handedly getting her small shop off the ground while raising Zach alone. He had become a stranger forcing them to survive without him.

His fuckup last year on Tanita Marie Donner's murder brought it all to the surface. He had deceived himself about priorities. What he invested every day in the pursuit of vainglory could be had by anyone for fifty cents. But the price exacted from his family and himself was incalculable. Now he was alone in his room with everything he had thought valuable: his

awards, his job, himself, and a pile of newspapers threatening
to spill across the floor.

How could he have been so stupid?

What had he done to Ann? To Zach? He was so sorry. He
had to call them. Had to tell them. Right now. He heard the
chink of glass as he rose to go to the phone and nearly fell
down. It was three-thirty in the morning. He was drunk. Forget
it. Staggering to the bed, he noticed the Metro University envelope sticking from his jacket pocket. Scanning the letter about
Dr. Martin's bereavement research, he scoffed and tossed it.
Then he saw another envelope in his jacket, from the photo
department. The borrowed snapshot of Danny Raphael Becker.
Someone had slipped it in his pocket with a note suggesting
he return it to the Beckers in person. He looked at it for a long
time. Well, this was one story he wouldn't be fucking up.
Tenderly, he propped up Danny's picture on the mantel next
to the little framed photograph of his son, Zach.

11

The phone jangled. Half asleep, Reed grabbed it.

"You up, Reed?"

"No."

Silence. Reed squeezed the receiver. "Who the hell is this?"

The caller sighed. "You sober, Reed?"

Myron Benson's voice rattled him out of drowsiness. Since the fuckup, the metro editor no longer acknowledged Reed in the newsroom. Why was he calling? Bored tormenting him with probation? Did he reach a decision on Reed's fate? Reed hadn't seen today's paper. Did he screw up? Was that it? Was Benson going to fire him now?

"What do you want?"

"Read your story today. Good job getting the father."

Reed waited for the "but."

"I want you to cover the Becker press conference today."

Reed sat up. "Duggan told me last night you pulled me off the story."

"Changed my mind. For now, you will be involved in our coverage. I want to see where this abduction thing is going."

"Well, I have a few theories."

"Shove 'em up your ass. I want solid reporting. Understand?"

"I understand." That you're a fucking prick.

"I also want a feature on Dr. Martin's bereavement research at the university. I read her letter. Tie it in with the Becker case."

"Right."

"And Reed, any incompetence will be noted."

Like pulling the wings off of flies. You loving this, Benson?

Quit moping and do something about it, he decided after shaving and dressing. He had under an hour before the press conference. No time for breakfast. He snatched two bananas to eat on the way. Remembering to grab the snapshot of Danny Becker from the mantel brought him face-to-face with Ann, Zach, and his own guilt.

Quit moping. Do something.

He checked his watch. There was time.

He punched the number. It had been weeks since they had talked. What if she'd called a lawyer? How would he begin? I love you and Zach more than anything and I want us back together. He now realized he may have been wrong and was ready to admit it.

It rang twice.

"Hello?" Ann's mother said.

"Hello, Doris."

"Oh, hello, Tom." No malice. Doris was not an interfering mother-in-law. She was always pleasant to him.

"I see you've been busy." Doris was a faithful *Star* reader.

"Yes." Not knowing what to say, he said, "I hope you're well."

"I'm fine, Tom. And you?"

"Me?" He saw the empty Jack Daniel's bottle. "I'm okay."

"It's so terribly sad, don't you think?"

Was she was referring to the kidnapping, or her daughter's marriage to him? She continued. "That little boy, Danny Becker. His mother and father must be sick with worry."

"I'm sure they are."

The extension clicked.

"Tom . . . ?"

Ann's voice was balm to him. For he accepted that he could have been wrong and wanted to tell her. She and Zach were his life. He knew he could not live without them and he wanted to tell her. But he didn't.

All he managed was, "Hi, Ann."

"Hi. How are you?"

"Well, I've been better. How are you two doing?"

"We're fine."

"Do you guys need anything?"

"Nothing."

"How's the car running?"

"The transmission feels funny."

"It was starting to slip just before you . . ." He stopped himself before saying: just before you left me. "Take it to Otto's. The warranty's still good."

"Okay."

"Want me to make the appointment?"

"I'll do it."

A few awkward seconds passed.

"I read your story today about this horrible kidnapping. If anything ever happened to Zach . . ."

"They're going hard on the investigation. I'm headed to a press conference. Ann, I want to see you, to talk about things."

"It's Zach, isn't it?"

Zach? He was puzzled. "Why do you say that?"

"I thought he might have called you. He's been having nightmares." Her voice became a whisper. "He misses you."

"He misses me?"

Reed seethed with conflicting emotions. What did you expect, Ann? You paint me as some sort of evil leper because I enjoy my job. You yank him out of the only home he's known, take him away from his friends, his neighborhood. He's probably scared to death because of this kidnapping shit. He's got to get up at five-thirty every morning now to be driven across the goddamned bay to school. He's had to miss soccer, which he lives for. You throw his little world into a goddamn blender. He doesn't just miss me. He misses what you took him away from: his home.

Hold everything.

He was wrong. Only a fool would blame Ann. Blame yourself, Reed.

"I miss both of you," he said.

"Then why haven't you come to see him?"

"When you moved to Berkeley I took it to mean that you didn't want to see me. I swear that's what I thought you wanted. I had to fight the urge to see you. I used to park down the street from your mother's house, hoping to catch a glimpse of you."

"You did?"

"I don't know what the rules are, Ann."

"Zach came home from school one day, asking about you and when we were going to stop being mad and all move back home."

"He cuts through the crap, doesn't he?"

They both chuckled faintly, leaving Zach's question alone.

"Ann, I want to get together. I have some things I want to say."

"Well, Zach's been wanting to visit you at the paper. Why don't we drop by and have lunch some time this week?"

"It's a date. Do you think he wants to talk to me for a bit?"

"Sure, just a minute."

Ann put the receiver down. A few seconds later Tom heard the pounding of Zach's sneakers approaching the phone.

"Dad?"

Reed felt something catch in his throat. "You being good, Zach?"

"Yup."

"Are you being nice to Grandma?"

"Yup." Then he whispered, "I even remember to leave the toilet seat down after I go to the bathroom."

"Wonderful."

"Dad, are we going to move back home?"

"We're working on it. We're working on it, okay?"

"Dad, you want us all to move back home, right?"

"Yes, I do."

"Me, too. Mom does, too. I heard her telling Grandma."

"That's good. I'm glad. Anything you want to talk about?"

"That little boy that got kidnapped yesterday, I saw his picture in your paper. Is that boy dead?"

"Nobody knows. The police are working real hard on the case."

"But the police are going to catch the kidnapper, right? They're going to catch him before he takes some more kids, right, Dad?"

Reed ran his hand over his face. "Zach, your mother and I love you, more than you can ever know. Do you hear me, son?"

"I guess." His voice was weak.

"And it's all right to be a little nervous and extra careful to always not talk to strangers. But Zach, don't let things go crazy in your head over it. Don't confuse it with what's happening with us. Okay? Mom and I are working on moving back together."

"But when, Dad? I want to go home. . . ." Zach's voice broke into a gut-wrenching plea that nearly winded Reed.

"I don't know when, son."

Zach was crying softly.

"Zach, it's all right to be sad. I'm sad, too. But you have to be strong and patient for Mom and me. Can you do it?"

"Uh-huh, I'll try."

"We'll do everything we can. Now, I promise I will talk to you again real soon." Reed looked at his watch. "Tell Mom I will call her. Now I have to go, son."

Reed hung up and hurried to his Comet.

12

Danny Becker woke up afraid and hungry. This strange place smelled bad, like animal cages at the zoo. His mouth tasted funny. "Dad!" Danny waited. Nothing. "Mommy! Where are you?"

Danny listened. Still nothing.

Something was wrong. He had his shoes on. Mommy never let him sleep in bed with his shoes on. His breathing quickened. He was so scared, sitting here on this smelly old mattress. The room was lit by a naked, dim bulb casting long shadows on the concrete walls. One tiny window had bars on the inside. Newspapers covered the glass. Danny noticed a cup of milk, plate of cookies, and a sandwich on the floor.

He cried as he ate. The sandwich was peanut butter and jam. Not nice like Mommy makes. The jam was dripping off the sides. The cookies were cream cookies, the fat ones. He remembered being on the subway with Daddy when he got bumped out the door and fell. He was lifted up from behind by hands that were strong like Daddy's. But they weren't Daddy's. They held him funny. At first Danny thought it was a game because they were going somewhere fast. But when the person carrying him stumbled, he said a bad word. Danny tried to scream, but a stinky wet cloth smothered his face.

Danny had to pee. He replaced a half-eaten cookie on the plate, stood up, and looked around. He had to find the bathroom. He went to the door, reached up, gripped the knob, and turned.

It opened.

The hallway was dark. A shaft of light from a TV illuminated a stairway, and distinct, rhythmic *squeak-creak* sounds came from above.

Sniffling, Danny tiptoed up the stairs. He heard a bark. A little blond dog waited for him at the top of the stairs.

It was brighter on the next floor and the bathroom was near the stairs. Danny entered and left the door open so it would be known he was doing the right thing. The dog waited for him at the door. He was friendly and licked Danny's hand.

The TV and the *squeak-creak* grew louder as Danny entered the living room.

". . . here's the pitch; it's a slider inside. Strike!"

Fifty thousand fans at Dodger Stadium roared. Danny froze and took in the room. It was barren. Torn rags and soiled sheets and towels covered the windows. No Mommy. No Daddy.

The walls were filthy. A large table, cluttered with a big computer, papers and maps was pushed to a corner.

Squeak-creak. Squeak-creak.

". . . the Giants are looking good here in Los Angeles . . ."

Baseball. The TV was on a tall stand in the middle of the room.

Squeak-creak. Squeak-creak.

A strange man faced the set, rocking back and forth in a rocking chair. His back was turned to Danny.

"I want my mommy and daddy," Danny said.

The stranger ignored him.

". . . but so far they're giving L.A. a drubbing today . . ."

Squeak-creak. Squeak-creak.

Strewn on the floor beside the man were newspapers. Seeing something familiar, Danny inched closer.

Squeak-creak. Squeak-creak.

Danny saw his own picture in one paper. He saw Daddy's picture, too—he looked worried and sad. Danny shuddered.

Who was that man in the rocking chair? He took half a step backward.

"Home field isn't helping the Dodgers, Frank. . . . Excuse me, Billy. We're going to the network's San Francisco affiliate for an update on the kidnapping of Danny Becker."

Danny's mouth dropped when he heard his name. His eyes were riveted to the set. What was happening?

A man on the TV said, "Good afternoon, I'm Peter McDermid with an EyeWitness News special update." Danny blinked, staring at himself on TV.

Squeak-creak. Squeak-creak.

"Three-year-old Danny Raphael Becker was kidnapped . . ."

What is kidnapped?

". . . from his father yesterday while they were riding home on San Francisco's Bay Area Rapid Transit System subway from a baseball game at Oakland's Alameda County Coliseum. It's believed a man abducted the boy from the Balboa Park BART Station. Danny is still missing. Police say his family has received no ransom calls and that they have no suspects, no useful description of Danny's abductor. Today they are intensifying their investigation. One hundred additional police and one thousand volunteers are helping in the search for Danny. He is the only child of Nathan and Magdalene Becker."

Squeak-creak. Squeak-creak.

The picture of a little girl appeared beside Danny's. He knew her. It was the girl he saw on the subway. The one who never smiled.

"A disturbing aspect in Danny's case is that it happened nearly one year later, and in almost exactly the same area, where two-year-old Tanita Marie Donner was taken from her home. She was murdered three days later in Golden Gate Park.''

Murdered? Is that when you are dead? Is that murdered? *Squeak-creak. Squeak-creak.*

''An unprecedented investigation involving the FBI and San Francisco police has yet to find Tanita's killer. Police refuse to say if Tanita Donner's murder and Danny Becker's abduction are linked. But EyeWitness News has learned the FBI's Behavioral Science Unit, expert in profiling serial criminals, is again assisting.

''There has been an outpouring of support for the Beckers. We go now to a news conference called by Nathan and Magdalene Becker. EyeWitness News reporter Jeannie Duffy is there. Jeannie, give us a sense of the impact the Becker abduction has had.''

Jeannie Duffy stood before a row of TV cameras. Beyond them, a table with a small mountain of microphones and portable tape recorders rose before two empty chairs.

''Peter, the people I've talked to are horrified. The abduction of Danny Becker is every parent's nightmare. They say this kind of thing isn't supposed to happen in their neighborhood. It's something that happens in the movies, but not here. They're taking precautions. Neighborhood watch parties are being formed, children are not allowed anywhere alone, and strangers are regarded with suspicion. A blanket of fear has fallen over San Francisco.

''I talked to a relative of the Beckers' and he told me Danny's parents will offer a substantial reward for Danny's safe return. And the family just released to reporters a home video of Danny at his cousin's birthday party taken two weeks ago. Here's a bit of that now. Danny's the smaller boy wearing a red shirt.''

Danny's cousins, Paul and Sarah appeared on TV with him. Paul kicked a soccer ball to Danny. Sarah was skipping.

The man in the chair stopped rocking, and turned his head slowly to Danny, allowing him to see only half of his face.

Danny took another step backward and searched the room for a door. He wanted to leave. *Now*. The man resumed rocking. *Squeak-creak. Squeak-creak.*

On TV, a man and a woman seated themselves before the microphones. Transfixed, Danny clasped his hands together, blurting, "Mom, my mommy!"

Squeak-creak.

The press conference room was electric with emotion under the lights. Silent, except for the soft flashes of still cameras and the *whir-click* of their rapid-fire motor drives. Nathan and Maggie held hands, sat with their heads bowed, struggling to begin. Maggie brushed her eye. No makeup. Nathan was unshaven. They had not slept.

"I'm sorry," Nathan said. "This is difficult."

They faced some one hundred reporters, photographers, and camera crews. Relatives, friends, and police officials lined one wall.

Squeak-creak. Squeak-creak.

"Take your time," somebody said.

Nathan nodded. The cameras flashed and whirred.

"Danny is all we have," Maggie began. "To the person who has our son, we say please bring Danny back, please let him go, that's all we ask. We beg you. Please." Tears streamed down her face, making it shine. The cameras flashed, reporters made notes.

Squeak-creak. Squeak-creak.

Nathan looked toward his family and friends. "We want to say to the person who has Danny, our only child, please don't harm him. We know you must be hurting to have taken Danny. Our son, Danny. You must be suffering, too, suffering tremendously. We are now suffering together and only you can make things better. We beg you, Danny is just a little boy, please let Danny go. Please."

Nathan brushed his eyes. "We are willing—" He stopped. "With the help of our friends, we are willing to pay thirty-five thousand dollars for information that brings Danny home safely. If the person who has Danny finds it in his heart to return Danny to us, you will receive every consideration. Please bring Danny back safely. Please.''

Several reporters started with questions. Nathan stayed them. "That's all we can say. Thank you.''

"Mr. Becker, a few short questions?'' implored one reporter.

Squeak-creak. Squeak-creak.

"I'm sorry. Please, it's all we can say now. Thank you.''

"Waiiiittt!'' Danny's arms shot toward his mother and father. "Come and get me please. I'll be good. I promise. Mommy. Daddy.''

They left.

The chair stopped and so did Danny's breathing.

The man stood, switched the set off. Danny scrambled to his feet and hurried to the kitchen, afraid to look behind him. He heard the paws of the dog, following him. He could see a door in the kitchen. He reached up and grasped the handle. It wouldn't move. He kept trying. "Home.'' He pulled mightily, kicked the door for not cooperating. The dog yelped. What if he asked the man nicely?

"Home. Please.''

Nothing happened.

Danny looked over his shoulder—the man was across the room, leaning over the big table with all the papers.

"Home. Please!'' Danny sobbed.

The man raised his head, as if hearing Danny for the first time. He turned and faced him, smiling. He looked friendly. Danny noticed a silver cross hanging from his neck. The man squatted, held out his arms, inviting Danny to come to him.

Danny didn't dare move. Something was funny about the man's eyes. They were big and wide the way Daddy made his eyes go when he was Zombie Man. The man stepped closer.

"No! You leave me alone. Stop!'' Danny shouted.

He ran for the basement stairs. The dog scampered after him.

Too small to run down them, Danny sat and bounced along each stair on his bottom as quickly as he could, racing to the room where he woke, slamming the door behind him, hurrying to a corner. Nowhere to hide.

The door's handle turned. The man entered and smiled. Danny pushed himself against the corner. "Leave me alone! Go away!"

The man drew nearer, his black shadow looming against the wall. Towering over Danny, gazing down upon him from a few feet away.

Danny wanted to push himself through the wall, balling his hands into fists, clutching them together against his chest, terrified something bad was going to happen.

"Go away! Go away!"

The man dropped to his knees, stretched out his arms.

"Oh Raphael! Holy Rescuer, Holy Guardian! Years I have suffered. Years I have atoned. Years I have waited and now you have come! You have come!"

Edward Keller was enraptured, arms outstretched, palms to heaven.

"Oh Raphael! The prophet's words are true. 'Through me you enter where the lost are sent.' Raphael. The resurrection has begun!"

Keller bowed before Danny.

Danny cried harder than he ever had in his life.

13

An hour after Danny Becker's mother and father pleaded for his safe return, San Francisco's top detectives gathered in Room 400 at the Hall of Justice on Bryant. Over the years the room had sucked up the sweat, the fury, and the very souls of investigators avenging the dead whose lives had been taken by evil, perpetually manifesting itself in every wicked force imaginable from crack cocaine to the Zebra, from the Dai Hen Jai to the Zodiac.

Enlarged photos of Danny and Tanita gazed from the corkboard Inspector Gord Mikelson had wheeled into place. Beneath their faces a city map was pierced with tiny flag pins. Pink for locations in the Donner case, blue for Becker. Each had a related file. Notebooks were opened. Reports and witness statements were circulated.

"Right off, we've got one unidentified suspect and little else on Becker. No calls, letters, demands. No body," Mikelson said.

"Not yet," someone muttered, alluding to statistics that show that if an abducted child was not found alive within forty-eight hours, the child was likely dead.

"We will have none of that shit here. Understand? Or tomorrow you are working a fucking koban giving directions to a hayseed from Boise." Lieutenant Leo Gonzales, head of the Homicide Detail, unwrapped an imported cigar and squinted at the talent in the room. Among them were Sydowski, Turgeon, and FBI Special Agents Rust and Ditmire. Gonzales made eye contact with everyone, including Captain Miles Beck, Deputy Chief of Investigations, Bill Kennedy, and Nick Roselli, chief of inspectors. Many in the room were unfamiliar with the Donner case. Adhering to the city's no-smoking rule, Gonzales did not light his cigar, though he yearned to. "Although we've got no body, we are concerned with the obvious similarities to Donner, Walt's file. Now listen up." Gonzales nodded to Mikelson. "Go, Gord."

"We have nothing unusual in the twenty-four hours before Danny Becker's abduction. We canvassed their route. A couple of people believe they saw a man follow Nathan and Danny onto the bus. Their descriptions are vague, but generally fit with Nathan's. But we really don't have anything strong in that department."

"What about a composite?" Inspector Art Tippet said.

"The father got a glimpse of the bad guy at Balboa, but his description is unclear. We've got the police artist and Beth at Computer Enhancing working something up."

"The game, anything there?" Tippet asked.

"Working on it with guys across the bay," Sydowski said.

"We've got, hold it"—Mikelson checked his notes—"at last count, one hundred sixty phone tips to sort through, about the same number of E-mailed tips. We expect it all to go up because of the news conference. We've got dozens of re-interviews and we have to go over the family's background again."

"Let's hear it, Gord." Gonzales wanted Mikelson to offer what his gut told him. "Give it up."

"The Beckers stuck to their routine in the twenty-four hours before the kidnapping. The impulse on Nathan Becker's part was to take Danny to the game on public transit and not drive his BMW on the weekend, which he loves doing. That was an impulse. Only someone who was stalking them would know. I think our guy is a stalker."

"That's what you think?" Gonzales said

"I believe our guy knows the Beckers inside out. Probably studied them for weeks, months even."

Gonzales wanted checks for any strange vehicles near the Becker home and a run through parking citations for the area.

"Okay, Walt"—Tippet turned to Sydowski—"is the guy who took Becker our missing link in the Donner file?"

"Wait. For the benefit of everyone coming to this fresh, walk us through Donner, Walt," Deputy Chief Kennedy said. "I want to measure Becker against Donner from square one."

Sydowski knew the case history by rote. "Angela Donner is a single, young welfare mother. She puts her daughter, Tanita Marie, down for a nap in the playpen of the fenced rear patio of their ground-floor suite in Balboa almost one year ago. When Angela goes to answer the phone, someone grabs Tanita, unseen. No witnesses, no physical evidence at the scene. No ransom call, no letters. No demands. Nothing. Three days later, two girls on a science trip find her about eleven a.m. in Golden Gate, in a garbage bag, under a tire."

"Time of death and location, Walt?" Inspector Bruce Paley asked.

"Coroner puts it at eight hours before she was found. She was killed the night before about three in the morning."

"At the park?" Paley asked.

"No. Her stage of rigor indicates she was not killed there. She was held somewhere for three days, then killed and dumped."

"What about the baby's father?"

"Checked out clean. Her throat was cut with a small, tooth-edged knife. Some details of her death are hold-back," Sydowski said. "We had nothing, no weapon, no witnesses. Nothing, except suspicions about Franklin Wallace. We lit up the 'hood, ran everybody in a twelve-block radius of the girl's home. Wallace came up, among others. He was a short-order cook, married, and had a four-year-old daughter. He lived near Tanita, read Bible stories to her and other kids at his Sunday school day care. He also had a ten-year-old conviction in Virginia for molesting a five-year-old girl. He made our suspect list, along with others in the area. We questioned Wallace superficially through a routine canvass. We never went hard at him. He was alibied and we had nothing at the time, which was days after the case broke.

"Quantico's profile leaned strongly to a two-person team, which was bang on when we got a break later. A patrol officer chasing drugs in Dolores found Tanita's plastic diaper and these two Polaroids hidden under some bushes." Sydowski passed around enlarged copies of two snapshots. "This material is also hold-back."

One picture showed Tanita alive, naked, being held by a man wearing no shirt. The man's head had been cut out of the picture. The second photo showed a different man with tattoos on his forearms, wearing a black hood and gloves, holding Tanita, her little eyes open wide.

Turgeon covered her mouth with her hand.

Sydowski continued.

"We're still working on the tattoos. Looks like he's done time. The man in the first picture is Wallace. His prints were on Tanita's diaper. We're certain two men were involved with Donner. Fits the profile. I suspect the diaper and picture were trophies they kept."

"Why's that?" Tippet said.

Sydowski nodded to the FBI agents. Rust answered.

"Because the killer is usually aroused by reliving or fantasizing about any aspect of the act. Look, the material is not in any residence. Our boy is smart to hide it in a public place. Makes it tough to link him to the crime. He can return to the pictures and enjoy them. He likely savored the baby's scent from the diaper, it was a clean one. The killer was the dominant team member who literally cut Wallace out of the fantasy by removing his head from the picture.''

''Didn't the guy try to set up Wallace, somehow?'' Paley said.

''Yeah, he fucked us over good,'' Sydowski said. ''Everything happened at once. Right after we found the stuff in Dolores and before we could nail Wallace, Tom Reed at the *Star* got an anonymous call saying Wallace was the killer, that we had pictures of him with the girl and that he had a record in Virginia. We figure the killer must have seen our guy find the pictures. How else would he know? Reed called Virginia, which confirmed Wallace's record for child molesting. Reed confirmed from neighbors that Wallace lived near Tanita and had her in his toddlers' Bible classes. Then he called me for confirmation that Wallace was our suspect. He got nothing, I assure you.'' Sydowski stared at Ditmire. ''Then Reed went immediately to Wallace's home, confronted him with what he had. Wallace never knew we had the pictures, the diaper, his prints, his records, until Reed told him. He denied to Reed that he was involved, then blew his brains out with a shotgun when Reed left. We never got to question Wallace hard about the diaper, the pictures, his partner.''

''We fucked up there,'' Rust jumped in. ''We were going to surveil Wallace, wire his phone, watch his mail, hoping it would lead us to the masked man. Tom Fucking Reed got in the way.''

''What about Reed's tip? Did he tape it?'' Paley asked.

''No. It was cold, out of the blue,'' Sydowski said.

''Reed's tip had to be Wallace's partner,'' Sydowski said. ''I think it was the killer. I think he panicked when he saw us discover his trophies and, fearing Wallace would finger him, tried to set him up. Something like that. Wallace's widow told us Wallace got a call about an hour before Reed arrived. The call scared him, but he refused to tell her who it was. She thought it was Reed saying he was coming over, but Reed told us he never made an advance call. Wallace and the other guy likely plotted to grab Donner for a day or two with the aim of returning her. It's been done before. But it goes wrong and she ends up in a garbage bag with her throat cut. Our tattooed guy is likely a hard-core skinner who manipulated Wallace, then trips up the case.''

''We never publicly said Wallace was a suspect?'' Paley said.

''No. Wallace was dead,'' Gonzales said. ''We want to leave his partner in the dark. So we publicly doubt Reed's story. It may not be nice, but we're chasing a child-killer.'' He paused. ''Merle, Lonnie, you got anything?''

Ditmire leafed through his notes.

''Nathan Becker is a computer systems engineer with Nor-Tec in Mountain View, head of a project for the U.S. military. The CIA told us this morning that it would not rule out a terrorist act as one plausible scenario here.''

''But we have no demands,'' Sydowski said. ''And doesn't tradition show that responsibility for acts of terrorism is usually claimed within twenty-four hours?''

''Not in every instance, Walt,'' Rust said.

Ditmire continued with the results of a VICAP check. ''Two recent child abduction-murder cases around Dallas-Fort Worth in the last three years. And for the same period, there has been one in Denver, Seattle, Detroit, Memphis, and Salt Lake City. We're getting files on them. We've got our experts trolling the kiddy porn websites and chatting on the Internet for anything that might help. We've got agents posing as kids and agents posing as pervs, baiting whatever is out there. That's it for now.''

Gonzales nodded. "Claire, any hint of cult, or human sacrifice?"

Inspector Claire Ward, an expert on cults, had been taking notes.

"Too soon to say, Lieutenant. I'd like to look at the evidence from the Donner case again."

"Walt will help you there," Gonzales said. "All right. We are going to chew up every shred we've got on this, understand? Every-fucking-thing. The heat on this one is intense." Gonzales stood up, looked at his watch, then ended the meeting. "You've got your assignments. You all know the words to the song. This is a green light. All overtime is approved. We go hard into the backgrounds. We re-create the day. We check and recheck every tip." He tucked his unlit cigar in his inside breast pocket. "Questions?"

None.

"Turgeon, please see me in my office," Gonzales said.

Papers and reports were collected as the investigators filed out of the room. Turgeon followed Gonzales to his office several doors away, where he fished through a top desk drawer, then placed her new identification in her hand.

"Sorry, Linda. I should've gotten this to you last week."

Turgeon looked at the laminated photo ID which read: Inspector Linda A. Turgeon. San Francisco Police Department. Homicide Detail. She ran her finger over the shield bearing the city's seal. It depicted a sailor, miner, and a ship passing under the Golden Gate. Above it, a phoenix rose from flames. Below was the city's Spanish motto. *Oro en paz, fierro en guerra.*

"You know our jingle," Gonzales said.

"Gold in peace. Iron in war."

Turgeon's heart swelled. Her father's gold shield was home in a jewelry box, with her favorite picture of him smiling in uniform at her. She was eight, wearing his cap, smiling up at him. She blinked several times. I did it, Dad. I did it, she thought.

"Welcome to the dark ride," Gonzales said.

"Thank you, Lieutenant."

Gonzales cleared his throat. "I knew Don in the early days."

"I didn't know."

"Yeah, we walked the Mission together. For a spell."

Turgeon nodded.

"Linda?"

"Yes."

"You done him proud, real proud."

14

Vassie Liptak, the choirmaster for Our Lady Queen of Tearful Sorrows Roman Catholic Church, tapped his baton crisply on the podium's edge, halting "The Lord Is Risen." He pushed aside his wild, maestrolike strands of ivory hair and studied his sheet music.

The North American Choir finals in San Diego were three months off. Our Lady was a contender and with God's help they could win. Victory would mean an audience with The Holy Father in Rome. Vassie lay awake nights imagining how it would be. Our Lady's singers were spiritually dedicated, but today his number-three contralto, the dwarfish spinster who cleaned the church, was off.

"Florence, dear, you are not feeling well today." He reviewed his sheet music on the dais.

Florence Schafer flushed. "Why, I'm fine, Vassie. Really."

Agnes Crawford, the choir's star soprano, put her hand on Florence's shoulder. "Are you sure, Flo? You look pale. Would you like some water? Margaret, fetch some water for little Flo.''

Florence loathed that name. Standing at four feet, six inches, she was, in the clinical sense, a dwarf.

"Please, don't bother. I'm fine.''

Vassie regarded her sternly through his fallen locks.

"I wasn't concentrating. I'm sorry.''

"Very well.'' Vassie sighed, nodding for the organist to resume. Pipes and voices resounded through the stone church, but Florence's attention wandered again.

She admired the statue of the Blessed Virgin in the alcove behind Vassie. The Queen of Heaven, in a white gown with a golden hem, arms open to embrace the suffering. She was beautiful, mourning the death of her child. As she sang, Florence recalled her own grief and the part of her that died so many years ago. Philip, the young man she was to marry, was killed in a house fire. She had wanted to die, too. The night of his death, she visited her parish priest. He helped her find the strength to live. She never loved another man. For years, she considered becoming a nun, but instead devoted herself to her church and her job as a city hall clerk before retiring after forty years.

Florence lived alone, but was not lonely. She had Buster, her budgie. And there was her hobby, true crime, mystery, and detective stories. She walked in Hammett's footsteps, Pronzini's, and others. On vacations, she took famous murder-scene tours, visiting police museums. She devoured novels and textbooks. She clipped articles, filing them meticulously. To what end, she didn't know. For each day of her life was marked by the three china cups and the three sterling silver spoons she used for tea, which she took in the morning, afternoon, and evening as she read. Three times daily, as the steam plume rose from the kettle, she pondered the meaning of her life, wondering what God's purpose was for her. It had become her eternal question.

She now knew the answer.

And this afternoon she would act on it.

After choir rehearsal, Florence prepared to clean the pews. She went to the utility room at the rear of the church and tugged on the chain of a bare bulb. The room smelled of disinfectant. It had a large janitor's sink, bottles of furniture polish, wax, rags, pails, all neatly organized. Florence closed the door, and checked inside her bag. Everything was set. If it happened again today, she was ready. She slipped on her apron, collected a rag, some polish in a pail, and went to work cleaning pews.

"And how are you this blessed afternoon, Flo? I heard the choir from the rectory. The gang sounds wonderful." Father McCreeny smiled as she gathered old church bulletins from the first pew.

"Very well thank you, Father. And you?"

"Tip top, Flo. Tip top."

You may say so, Father, but I know you're bearing a heavy cross.

Father William Melbourne McCreeny had been with Our Lady for years. A fine-looking man standing six feet, five inches tall, who at sixty-two, still maintained the litheness of his seminary days as a basketball player. With the exception of crack dealers and pimps, he was loved by everyone. McCreeny was instrumental in establishing a new soup kitchen in Our Lady's basement, using bingo proceeds to provide hot meals for the homeless. McCreeny checked his watch, then surveyed his empty church. "Five minutes before afternoon confessions. I'd best get ready." He stopped near the altar on his way to the sacristy and turned to her. "By the way, Flo, I almost forgot. This weekend I'll be asking for more help at the shelter. We're getting more clients as the word on the street goes 'round. I know you already do so much, but please consider it."

"I will, Father."

He smiled his handsome smile.

Later McCreeny emerged carrying a Bible, wearing a cassock, surplice, and purple stole. He genuflected, crossed himself before the altar. He seemed taller. Florence's heart fluttered. Seeing him like this emphasized that he was a Godly man, a human tower of strength. McCreeny lit some vigil candles at the alcove of the Virgin, then proceeded to one of the confessional booths, the rustling of his vestments echoing softly as he walked.

Overcome with fear, Florence wanted to cry out to him and gripped a pew to steady herself. Father, help me! The words wouldn't come. What was happening? She had arrived at the church that morning confident she would do what was right. Now she was consumed by doubt. McCreeny entered the confessional. She needed his guidance. Father, please, turn around! The latch clicked. The small red ornate light above the confessional went on. McCreeny was ready to perform the sacrament, ready to hear the confession of sins.

Florence went back to cleaning, touching her eyes with the back of her hand. For the next hour, she concentrated on her work. During that time nearly two dozen people trickled in and out of the church. Florence smiled at those she knew. The children held their tiny hands firmly together at their lips, prayerlike. Adults were less formal, clasping theirs loosely, letting them fall below their waists. One by one they entered the curtained side of the booth, knelt, and whispered their confessions to Father McCreeny. As she worked, Florence heard the shuffle of old tired feet, the smart snap of heels, and the squeak of sneakers as each person left the booth for an unoccupied pew where they could say their penance, some to the muted clicking of rosary beads.

Maybe it wouldn't happen today, she thought, allowing herself a degree of relief. Maybe not today. Maybe not ever again?

Florence was calmer. She had nearly finished her work. Two

more pews. Then she would go home, make some tea, and read. Moving to the last pew, she reminded herself to pick up some cream. That's when she looked up and all the blood drained from her face.

He had come.

Her hand trembled. She dropped her bottle of furniture polish. It bounced and rolled, making a terrible noise.

He stood at the back, dipped his hand in the holy water basin, and took a place in line. Florence had little time. Suddenly he glanced at her. Florence had seen him occasionally at the soup kitchen.

A crepe-sole shoe squeaked. A woman entered the confessional.

He was next

Florence collected her cleaning things into her pail, stepped into the main aisle, genuflected, crossed herself, and glanced at the huge crucifix behind the altar for inspiration. She went to the utility room, tugged on the light. She ran the faucet full force, gazing at the ventilation register near the ceiling. It was Mary Atkins who had discovered the register was part of the ductwork system for the confessionals on the other side of the wall. And that it was an excellent conductor of sound.

"It's clear as a bell. Like listening in on a telephone extension," Mary giggled to Florence one afternoon. "You should try it, Flo." Mary's eyes grew. "It's better than the soaps."

For a few months after the discovery, they secretly compared the confessions they overheard. Soon they realized the sins of their fellow churchgoers were actually minor. For Florence, the thrill wore off. And she'd always felt uneasy about what they were doing. "I just don't want to do it anymore. It's not right," Florence told Mary, who agreed, saying she felt ashamed and promised to stop. Florence tried to avoid the utility room when confessions were being heard.

Except for today.

Today she wanted to hear the confession of the man she

recognized from the shelter. She *had* to hear it. But she was paralyzed, agonizing over whether to eavesdrop on his confession. Again.

The first time was some months ago.

McCreeny was hearing confessions when she had to go in the utility room for more polish. She was certain no one was in the confessional with McCreeny at the time. She was wrong. A man was confessing to him. Florence was trying to hurry, to get out, but she could not find the polish. She kept searching, unable to avoid the voices. At first she did not understand what she was hearing. Thought it was a joke. But it wasn't. A man was begging Father McCreeny to absolve him. A chill inched up Florence's spine as she listened in horror, hearing him describe his sin in detail. She grew nauseous, and dabbed her face with cold water. The man implored Father McCreeny to swear he would honor his vow and never reveal what he was hearing. McCreeny assured him. The man hinted he would return.

During the following weeks, Florence was tortured with indecision. She couldn't tell Father McCreeny what she knew, nor any priest for that matter. She couldn't. The man would return to confess. Without warning. Once Florence saw him leaving, and made a mental note of it. He had unique tattoos on his arms.

As days passed, her conscience screamed at her: tell someone!

She did.

When the three-year-old boy was abducted from the subway, Florence called the reporter at *The San Francisco Star* who had written about Tanita Marie Donner's murder. But he didn't believe her. She knew. She couldn't blame him. But she didn't know what to do. What if the man *had* abducted the boy? She looked for answers in the steam cloud of her kettle. She found one: she needed to provide proof. God showed her the way.

Now get going.

She had a few seconds. With the water still running, Florence opened her bag, removed a miniature tape recorder she had bought a month ago, should the man ever return. Now he was here and she was ready. Florence set the volume and pressed the record button, like the clerk showed her. The red recording light glowed and she stepped up on an old file cabinet near the wall and hung the recorder by its strap from a nail above the register. Then she locked the door and shut the water off.

Voices floated through the air duct, tinny and dreamlike.

"Go ahead." McCreeny was encouraging.

Silence.

"Don't be frightened. God is present."

Silence.

"I'll help you begin. Bless me, Father—"

"It's me, Father," Tanita Marie Donner's killer said.

15

Reed spotted Ann and Zach in the *Star's* reception area.

"Could you cover for me?" Reed, standing to leave, said to Molly Wilson, who followed his attention to his wife and son.

"Sure." She was typing. "Just remember you've got the professor coming and I'm leaving soon for an FBI interview about Becker."

Passing a hand through his hair, tightening his tie, he was suddenly nervous.

"Hi, Dad." Zach leapt up. He must've sprouted another inch. He was wearing a Giants' ball cap backward, sweatshirt, jeans, Nikes, and a beaming smile.

"Hey, big guy." Reed hugged his son.

"Are you sure you've got time today? You're not too busy?" Ann observed the hectic newsroom.

"Naw." He walked them to an empty room. "You look good, Ann."

She was letting her chestnut hair grow out. Dressed in a pastel silk jacket, matching pants, and pearl necklace, she embodied a successful business woman. In her fresh-scrubbed face, her soft lips, her sculptured cheeks, and lovely brown eyes, Reed saw the woman he fell in love with—a love evinced in their son.

The glass walls of the office faced the Metro Desk and two dozen cubicles where reporters worked at their computers. The family sat at an empty round table. Reed gave Zach a brown envelope.

''What's this?''

''A present.''

Zach pulled out an action color eight-by-ten of Giants' left-fielder Barry Bonds sliding into home. ''Wow! Thanks, Dad.''

''It's nice, Tom.''

''So, Zach, tell me how you're doin'.''

''Well, I don't like getting up so early so Grandma can drive me to school. I don't like going over the bridge so much.''

''The school break's coming fast, son.''

''And I miss playing with Jeff and Gordie.''

''Meet any new friends in Berkeley?''

''Not really.''

''Zach, if there's something you want to get off your chest, then now's the time to tell us,'' Reed said.

Zach put the picture down, keeping his eyes on it. ''Know what the kids at school say?''

''Tell us what the kids at school say.''

''They say my mom left my dad because he was washed up as a reporter after making a man kill himself because of a screw up.''

Reed swallowed hard.

''That's not true,'' Ann lied.

''Is that what you think, too, Zach?'' Reed said.

Zach shrugged and met his father's gaze. With his mother's eyes, his flawless skin, he emanated innocence. ''I told them my dad found the guy who killed the little girl and the police didn't like it. I told them I am going to be a reporter, too.''

Reed was awed by his son. After all he had put him through, his love survived. Unyielding. Unconditional.

"You still got to put in more time at being a kid."

"Know what else they say?"

"What else?" Ann asked.

"They say that when your folks split and move out, they never get back together. No matter what they tell you, it never happens."

"Son, look. I know it's tough," Reed said. "But you can't put much stock in what kids say. Listen to your heart. We want to move back together, that's why we're talking about it. And that's better than not talking about it, right?"

"I guess." Zach looked at them. "But someone's in our house."

Ann touched Zach's hand. "A nice businessman from Tulsa and his wife. They are only renting. It's still our house."

Zach looked at his father. "Dad, is there another killer out there killing little kids?"

A curve ball.

"Nobody knows, but the chance of it happening to you is like being hit by a golf ball. That's why it's such a big deal. Know anybody who's been hit by a golf ball?"

"No." Zach giggled.

Ann smiled. "Didn't you have something else you wanted to ask?"

"About the *Kitty Hawk?*" Zach wanted a model of the carrier.

"No, the other thing."

"Oh, yeah. Dad, can I sit at your computer?"

"Sure, come with me."

"All right!"

* * *

Bending over his terminal, Reed typed a quick command on his keyboard, clearing his screen. Zach plopped into his father's chair and watched.

"Yo, yo, handsome." Molly Wilson glided around the cubicle and crouched beside Zach. "Haven't seen you in a while. You're getting to be a big guy. How's school?"

"Okay." Zach liked Wilson. She smelled good.

"Molly, Zach wants to hack around on the machine," Reed said. "Could you please watch him so he doesn't crash the newsroom."

"That's a pretty big assignment, but I think I can handle it, Dad." She offered her perfect-teeth smile, then stood and, while glancing toward Ann alone in the interview room, whispered, "You're looking dominated, Tom."

How dare she say that with his son present? She loved to rile him, loved to tease. "I'm going to the FBI in a few minutes," she said.

"We'll be done before then. Behave yourself and have fun, son."

"Okay."

Wilson bent over Zach, her nails clicking on the computer keyboard. "Want to surf the Internet?"

Reed returned to Ann, shutting the door behind him.

"Molly's very pretty."

"She's a flirt, Ann. And I'm a married man."

"You've lost weight."

"Well, wallowing in self-pity has its benefits."

"How's work going here?"

"I'm getting by, but they've got me on a short leash these days. How's the business?"

"We're getting more orders. My loan is almost paid off and I think I'm going to have to hire another part-time clerk."

"I brag about you to the people here who'll still talk to me."

Ann blushed a little. "Why?"

"I don't know, it's something I should have told you. I just . . . I've been doing a lot of thinking, Ann."

"Have you?"

"I realize what a jerk I've been. I was wrong about a lot of things. I can't explain it, but I know I'm not the same guy."

"How do I know that, Tom?"

"You don't." Reed stared at his hands, debating with himself as he twisted his gold wedding band. Ann still wore her diamond.

"I took a walk on the Golden Gate one night, a few weeks after you left. Let me tell you, when you're on the threshold of losing everything, when your feet are dangling over the abyss, life's priorities become clear."

"You going to kill yourself if we don't get back together, is that what you're trying to tell me?"

"No. I was speaking metaphorically."

"Were you?"

"I am not that much of a coward. I am telling you that you did the right thing, forcing me to live alone with the bad guy. Now, I . . . I want to, I am hoping we can try again."

She regarded him for a long time. "I don't know if I should believe you." She pressed her hands flat on the table.

"You damn near destroyed me. The way you treated us. It was as if we were nothing to you, like this place was the universe and you were its self-righteous, self-centered king. Never wrong. I loathed you for it. I am so confused and scared. You're telling me things, but it could be your self-pity talking. Are you still drinking?"

"Alone in my room at night. It fills the void, helps me sleep."

She wanted to believe him, he could read it in her eyes.

"We can't go on like it was before. I refuse to accept you back if nothing's changed."

"I've never stopped loving you. And this job"—Reed nodded to the newsroom—"it's no longer my life."

Ann said nothing.

"I've given a lot of thought to something you wanted me to do."

"I've wanted you to do a lot of things."

"I've been thinking that maybe I would take a leave from the paper, stay home and work on a novel."

"You're serious?"

"Yes."

They watched Zach playing on the computer.

"He misses you," she said.

"I miss both of you."

Reed looked at his wife.

"I have to think, Tom. I have to think about everything."

Reed squeezed her hand and nodded.

16

Dr. Kate Martin sat in the reception area of the *The San Francisco Star,* twisting her briefcase strap. She looked at her watch again.

Relax. Relax. Relax.

She expected to see Mandy Carmel, the *Star's* top feature writer. Her articles on SIDS babies and Bay Area children with AIDS were so well written, so compassionate.

Still, waiting here, it was difficult to put herself at ease.

Twice before coming she had picked up the phone to cancel. She didn't do it. Despite all the risks, her blatant violation of university policy and the potential harm a story could have on the volunteers, she was determined to see this through. She had tried in vain to find the funding needed to extend her research. The university, thanks to Levine, had rejected her. The state denied grant money. Corporations politely refused her. And national victims' support and lobby groups, which applauded her work, were cash strapped. Press attention was her last hope.

A sensitive article by Mandy Carmel would either save the program or bury it.

She took in the crisp current edition of the *Star* on the table before her. The latest on the kidnapping screamed from the front page: WHERE IS DANNY? She thought of his parents, of his abduction, and the questions it raised about Tanita's murder. It underscored how imperative her research was. She had to do this.

"Dr. Martin?"

She looked up. "Yes."

"Tom Reed." He held out his hand to greet her as she stood. Tom Reed!

She recognized him from the face-slapping footage which TV news stations had recently replayed. Her skin prickled with apprehension.

He was about six feet. His khaki pants, pinstripe, button-down shirt, and tie complimented his medium, firm-looking build. Mid-thirties. His tan set off his smile. His short brown hair was a little unruly. Behind wire-rimmed glasses were intense, blue eyes.

"Sorry to keep you waiting."

"I assumed I was to meet with Mandy Carmel?"

"Mandy's been on a leave in Europe and won't be back for six weeks. Your letter was passed to me."

"To you. But why? I thought—?"

"We can talk in there." He nodded to the boardroom nearby.

The room barely contained the mammoth table and leather executive chairs. The walls featured the *Star's* three Pulitzers and framed news pictures. The earthquakes, the Oakland Hills firestorm. A mother giving birth. A weeping cop cradling his dead partner.

Reed slapped his notebook on the table. Martin declined coffee.

"Be blunt, Doctor. You're upset I've been assigned to this?"

"To be blunt, yes."

"Why?"

"Your part in the Donner case and the suicide concerns me. An article about my research might be best suited for a reporter accustomed to handling sensitive issues. It involves parents who've lost children tragically. You're just a crime reporter."

"Just a crime reporter? Sensitivity is a quality alien to people like me, is that what you mean?"

"No, I mean, I—" This was not going well. "I think I've made a mistake coming here." She stood to leave.

"Your work deals with victims of tragedy, its survivors. Right?"

"It's somewhat more complex than that, but yes."

"I deal with victims, too, and probably in greater numbers than you've ever experienced. So I resent having to prove to you that I am qualified to write about your work."

"I am protective of the sensitive nature of my research."

"But the bottom line here, Doctor, is you want to manipulate us."

"Excuse me?"

"Set aside your work. You need us to keep your program afloat. That's why you're here. It's obvious from your letter. It dictates the type of story you want us to write, in accordance to the conditions you've listed." He withdrew the letter from his breast pocket, unfolded it, and read: "You may interview only the subjects I've selected and I have editorial approval." Reed stared at her. "What do you think this is, the church bulletin?"

Martin closed her eyes. Leave. Leave now, she told herself.

"I don't know who in this business you've dealt with before, but it just does not work this way." He let her letter fall on the table.

"And just how does it work, Mr. Reed?"

"If we do a story, we're going to examine your group and your research, not promote it. You say your work is valid. How do we know that? You could be with a corporation poised to

establish such programs in a chain of clinics and are looking
for a story as a source of advertising. That happens. You could
simply be seeking personal glory in your field. We don't know.
You came to us."

"I resent what you're implying. You don't know me or my
work."

"And you don't know me, or mine. You send us a blueprint
of what you want and glide in here on a cloud of academic
arrogance. You see me and your jaw drops like you've stepped
in something disgusting."

This was a disaster. Martin sat down and considered cancel-
ling everything. She had handled this poorly. The program was
doomed no matter what she did. She cupped her chin in one
hand, studied the dramatic news pictures, then Reed. He had
a dangerous, exciting air. Judging by his passion, he was likely
as committed to his work as she was to hers. She drummed
her fingers against her cheek. "Perhaps I've become too comfortable in the ivory towers of academe, Tom."

He chuckled. "If we had a couch in here . . ." Reed scanned
the room.

"Yes?"

"I'd tell you all my miserable problems. The last few weeks
have been tough ones for me, Doctor."

"Kate. Call me Kate. How about that coffee?"

"Then we'll rewind the tape and take it from the top?"

"Agreed."

Reed returned to the room with coffee in two ceramic mugs
bearing the *Star's* logo. "Today was supposed to be my day
off," he said. "I apologize for being so hard on you."

She sipped, waving away his apology. "I'm the one who
should apologize."

"I checked you out with our education reporter. I read your
biographical notes in the university directory. You're well

respected in your field and certainly didn't deserve the grilling
I gave you. Your letter hit a nerve. Being suspicious comes
automatically.''

She gave him another appraisal. Maybe he wasn't such a
self-important ass after all.

''I want to do a story about your work. I'm just not sure
what shape it will take. Tell me about it.''

Martin explained her bereavement research, what the group
was, how it functioned, and how her study differed from others
in the observations she was able to make.

Reed asked questions, and made notes.

''I'm wondering, why did you choose this field, psychiatry?''

She tugged at the cuffs of her blazer. ''That's something I'd
prefer not to discuss, if you don't mind. It's personal.''

''I see.''

''The real inspiration for the study came when I was asked
to help the two girls who found Tanita Marie Donner last year.''

''That was you?''

''Yes. It was then that I asked police if any help had been
offered to Tanita's mother. I began seeing her and the idea for
the group and the research was born.''

''What about Angela Donner? What's happened to her?''

''She's a participant in the group.''

''Really?''

Martin nodded.

''Your letter says fourteen volunteers participate in sessions.''

''Yes.''

''Are they aware of your coming to us for a story?''

''Yes. Most of them support it.''

''Tell me something about the deaths of the children here.''

Martin removed a file from her briefcase and began recounting fourteen tragedies. In some instances, the children
had been killed in front of relatives, or died in their parents'

arms, or their bodies had been discovered by them. When she finished, Reed was engrossed.

"I'd like to sit in on the next session and profile some of the parents. The program is about them. Their stories would convey the importance of your work and its impact on their tragedies."

"I'll start making calls tonight," Martin said, passing Reed a page with the time and place of the next session. "Going directly to the press, as I am doing, is a violation of the department's policy. I've put my job at the university on the line."

Reed's eyebrows shot up.

"This program is invaluable and I'm determined to save it. Not for me—for the people who are being helped by it."

"I understand."

They shook hands. Martin snapped her briefcase closed, smiled, and left. Reed sat alone in the room, thinking.

He removed his glasses, rubbed his eyes. His head ached. Yet things were brighter with Ann. And he was sure he had inadvertently found Tanita Donner's mother.

Last year, after Tanita's murder, her mother had dropped out of sight. Now, with the anniversary of Tanita's murder coming up, the press would be looking for her. In the wake of Danny Becker's kidnapping, they'd be more determined. But he knew where Angela Donner was. And soon, with a little luck, he would be talking to her. Martin's work was secondary. Angela's story, juxtaposed with Danny Becker's case, would make a great read.

And, there was more.

He had covered many of the cases Martin described, reciting the names he knew. He'd get the library files before he went to the session. The guy whose kids drowned before his eyes had to be one of the worst. Reed couldn't recall it. He'd do some digging on that one.

17

On good days, warm memories of his dead wife yielded Sydowski sufficient will to propel his life another twenty-four hours. On bad days, like this one, when he felt alone and could not accept the fact that she was gone, he contemplated his Glock.

Take the eternal sleep and find her. Be with her.

What time was it back east? The luminescent hands of his watch glowed 1:29 A.M. Three hours later where his daughters lived. Too late to call. Wearily he found his way through the darkness. He knew his house, every tick and creak of it. In the kitchen, he snapped on the light and heated some milk for cocoa.

It had been six years since he saw the monitor above Basha's hospital bed flitter, then flat line. The young doctor and nurse rushing in, telling him to leave. Battling against a killer no one could stop—not even him.

The beast slowly ravaged Basha's nervous system with muscular rigidity, condemning uncontrollable tremoring upon a gentle woman who had danced at her daughters' weddings. It consumed her by degrees, devouring her dignity a piece at a time. She could not feed herself, she could not have intelligible conversations, she could not go to the bathroom without help. Ultimately, she wore diapers. The final insult: she could not be trusted to safely hold her infant grandchildren. She watched through her tears as he cared for her. A couple of times he swore her bed was empty, she was barely visible under the rumpled sheets. Carrying her emaciated body, her fragility terrified him. She weighed nothing. She was dying in his arms.

Waiting in the hospital hallway the night they tried to save her, a strange thing happened. Sydowski heard her call his name. Once. Her voice was young, strong, wondrous. He was moored. No one else heard her. How could it be? He remembered his daughters beside him, wailing. Then the young doctor, the one with an earring in his left lobe, appeared from Basha's room and was standing before him.

"I'm very sorry, sir. She's gone. We did everything we could."

Something once indestructible cleaved inside, forcing him to hold his girls to keep from coming apart. The young doctor touched Sydowski's arm and those of his daughters.

The milk for his cocoa had come to a boil.

They would sit in the living room. She would be embroidering something beautiful for one of the babies. He'd be reading. Often he would discuss a case with her and she'd make a suggestion about an aspect he had overlooked. He respected her insights. For if he had one true partner, it was she.

Since she died, he felt uneasy being home alone. The girls' rooms were empty reminders of happier days. He shuffled around the place, chasing after her scent. It was still in the house, the fragrance of lilacs. Once he found a strand of her hair in her vacant side of their closet. His immediate reflex was to put it in an evidence bag, as if he could solve the crime of her death. Instead, he held it in his palm and wept.

He pursued death for a living: tracked it, waded into it, bagged its aftermath, and arrested the guilty. Professionally and mentally, he was prepared for every case, but nothing, not the course work, not the street time, not the scenes, prepared him for Basha. Death had turned on him and raked its claw across the web of his existence, leaving it in tatters. He could not reconnect. He had fallen into a black hole and feared he would never find his way out. Maybe he was dead, too? Maybe this was his hell? Death haunting him with the memory of his wife in the faces of corpses. The murders he could not clear. Tanita Donner. The slash across her little neck. The flies. The maggots. Her eyes. Her tiny, lifeless eyes. Open. Staring at him. Pleading. What had she seen in the last moments of her life?

Enough of this.

Get past it. He was alive. Among the living. And he was hungry. He went to the refrigerator and pulled out some egg bread, sweet butter, onion, and fresh kielbasa he bought at the Polack deli in the Mission. He'd pay dearly with heartburn later, he told himself, biting into his sandwich and sifting through the *Chronicle's* sports section. The Giants were doing well, sitting atop the division with a .651. Outperforming the A's. He'd tease the old man.

He'd never understand Johnny Sydowski's Polish stubbornness. Eighty-seven-years old, living alone by the sea in Pacifica. Why did he refuse to move in with him here? It would be easier to get to the ball games and the Polish Hall. They could share a beer and enjoy each other's company. The old man liked it where he was, so what the hell? Sydowski folded the paper, finished his sandwich, and his cocoa, put the empty plate and mug in the sink before leaving to check on his birds.

His love for breeding and showing canaries blossomed after a friend gave Basha a singing finch as a gift twenty years ago. He liked its song. It made him tranquil. He bought more birds. His collection thrived. He joined bird fanciers' societies, entered competitions, and built an aviary under the oak tree in his backyard. Basha made curtains for the windows and it looked like a tiny cottage from a fairytale. Inside, the paneled walls were adorned with ribbons, trophies, and mementos. Would he make the Seattle show next month? He pleasantly anticipated the drive up the coast. It depended. If they found Tanita Marie Donner's killer. Or Danny Becker's body.

The velvety cooing of sixty canaries soothed him as he inspected their seed and water supply. Tenderly, he picked up a nest of four fledglings, fife fancies. Seven days old and looking good. No bigger than a toddler's finger. Delicately Sydowski placed one in his hand, caressing it with his pinky knuckle while its wee beak yawned for food. He felt its warmth, its microscopic heart quivering and he thought of Tanita Marie Donner and her murderer.

Did he feel the warmth of her delicate neck, her heart pulsating?

Sydowski was exhausted, could barely keep his eyes open. He returned the fledglings, locked up the aviary, returned to the house, trudged upstairs, and went to bed, hoping to fall into a sound sleep before his heartburn started.

18

A cobra with its hood flared and fangs bared coiled around Virgil Shook's left forearm, while a broken heart engulfed in flames burned on his right. Terror and torment.

The twin forces of Shook's life were manifested in the tattoos conjured up by a killer in exchange for sex years ago in a Canadian prison. The cobra's head swayed gently, ripe to strike as Shook ladled chicken soup for the destitute shambling along the food line at the shelter of Our Lady Queen of Tearful Sorrows Roman Catholic Church on upper Market. Whispers and blessings mingled with clinking cutlery and the tap of hot food dispensed on donated plates.

If these broken, rotting burdens only knew who they were blessing. If they only knew who he really was. It was sweet. Shook inhaled the aroma of his power with that of roasted meat as one by one they came before him extending their plates, bowing their heads.

Like them, Shook haunted the city's streets and came to the kitchen often. Today he was upping the ante in his game with the priest. Today was Shook's first as a volunteer. Oh, how he loved it. Here he received sanctuary, blessings, and absolution.

He was savoring the irony of it, seeking his confessor among the crowd when he glimpsed a little treasure. A tiny temptress. Shook gauged the object of his attention. Four years fresh from the womb, he figured. She arrived before him, holding her bowl. He swam in her pure blue eyes, plunged his ladle deep into the urn. His lips stretched into a predatory grin awakening the scars on his cheeks and revealing a jagged row of pronglike teeth.

"What's your name, sunshine?"

"Daisy."

"Daisy? My, I love to pick daisies."

The little flower giggled. Accepting her bowl, her fingers brushed his. A butterfly's caress that thawed his blood. Do not flirt, short eyes. So tender. He knew what she craved. So tender. Best fly away.

Shook bit down on his lip. His migraines were hitting again. A brain-rattler had knocked him on his ass last week. The need to love again was overwhelming. It had been nearly a year since the last time. Since Tanita. Now, Danny Becker's kidnapping made it dangerous to go hunting. How much longer could he take this? He was tiring of his game with the priest. He needed to hunt, to prove the city belonged to him. Scanning the shelter, he located Daisy among the farflung tables and indulged in a bold, ravenous stare, assessing the possibilities until he was nudged by the volunteer beside him.

"You've got a customer," Florence Schafer said meekly.

Shook quickly filled the bowl for an old sod before him and was thanked with a "God bless you." Shook ignored him.

He looked down at Florence. She was familiar. Running his eyes over her miniature frame, he could smell her fear. He was curious. Why had she acted so strangely when they sent her to help him on the serving line? Not once had she turned to him. Pious little cunt. Maybe he would give her a lesson in humility.

It would be memorable. If only she knew of his power, knew who he really was.

There was only one who knew.

From time to time a knowing moment would flicker between Shook and the cold, hard eyes of those just released from Q. It was the look: con to con. But even their icy perception was never total. Only the priest knew, and he could not break the seal of the confessional. He absolved Shook of his sins, but could tell no one of his crimes. He was bound by the oath he swore to God.

Shook reveled in tormenting his confessor, reveled in spitting in the face of his God.

Who possesses the real power? Who could take his pick of San Francisco's lambs, orchestrate the Sunday school teacher's suicide, baffle the blue meanies and manipulate everyone?

The priest knew exactly who Shook was and he trembled in his knowledge.

"Hello, Florence. Lovely to see you could make it today."

Shook's ears pricked up at the sound of Father McCreeny's voice. Ah, he had arrived as expected. Grazing with the flock. Demonstrating his devotion. Standing head and shoulders above the others, dispensing God bless you's while piling his plate with food.

McCreeny stood before Shook. Emotion drained from his face and his troubled eyes feigned kindness. At last he said: "God be with you, my son. Bless you for helping us."

Shook remained silent, taking his time to scoop chicken soup into McCreeny's bowl, placing it gently in the priest's hands in a manner suggesting the reverse of the sacrament of communion.

"And God be with you, Father." Shook smiled widely, showing McCreeny his hideous teeth.

19

Wintergreen Heights was Cleve's home since his old man had walked three years ago. He lived here with Daphne, his alcoholic, welfare stepmother and half-brother, Joey, a sniveling puke. He was free of Joey today. Daphne was sober and keeping the sniveler inside because he had the flu.

Cleve kicked up his skateboard and glided to the rear of the project. He loved how the rolling of his wheels resounded off of the five towers around the courtyard. Time to sweep the neighborhood. The Heights were his and he was going on patrol to see what he could see.

Wintergreen Heights was one of the city's notorious communities. Once an island of hope, it had deteriorated into a pit of despair. Every home here had been burglarized, every person victimized. Anyone calling 9-1-1 could count on waiting ten rings before counting on police. They rarely flew the colors here, but when they came, they came by the hundreds.

Surfing down sidewalks, passing the crack houses, Cleve was on the lookout for a little of this, a little of that, and was deep into the Heights when he saw that guy with the boat again. His place looked like a shithouse. Paint blistering. Weeds and shrubs were trying to swallow the thing. His garage open. The guy was in there, working on his boat up on the trailer.

Cleve stopped.

His mind squirmed with questions: what was that guy doing with a boat like that down here? It looked like a classic. Cleve rolled up to the man.

"Nice boat."

The man looked at him and Cleve saw two distorted versions of himself in the man's sunglasses.

The man just kept on working. Cleve eyeballed him. Lot of lines on his face, looked wasted in his grease-stained T-shirt and jeans. Needed to shave. A breeze was lifting his salt-and-pepper hair like a nest of snakes. He was inside the boat, working like a surgeon on the motors. Cleve smelled gas and heard the *chink* of a wrench against metal. He stood on tiptoe and peered into the hull at the boat's massive engines, twin Mercs.

"Your craft must slash waves big time!"

The man didn't answer.

Cleve stepped back. "What's the bank on it?"

The man was silent.

"Is it like, an antique, or what? It's all wood. I thought boats these days were fiberglas, like my Cruz Missile."

The man's ratchet clicked as he replaced a spark plug. Cleve was in love with the boat. Its dark polished wood gleamed, the sun sparkled on the windshield, the chrome trim fittings, and running lights. The huge wheel was white, matching the leather seats, which had a black diamond-pattern inlay. Tiny American flags drooped from tilted chrome flag posts fixed aft.

"Seriously, man, what's the top end?"

The ratchet clicked, another plug was replaced.

"Where do you launch it?"

The man said nothing.

Rick Mofina

Cleve went to the stern, shook his head at the speed props, raised his eyebrows after reading what was written above them. In elegant, gold-reflecting script was the word: *Archangel.*

"What's the name mean? Religious or what?"

The ratchet clicked faster, then he tossed it into a toolbox and jumped out of the boat, gathered the tarpaulin, pulling it over the boat. Cleve hurried to the opposite side and helped. The man didn't object.

"The reason I came over here is because I saw some locals scoping your craft here couple of nights ago," he lied.

A rope whipped against the bow as the man tied it down quickly.

"I told them the man who owns this craft is not a man to be messed with. They said they'd be back and do a number."

The man tied down ropes at two more points.

"The way I see it is me and my buddy, we could guard it for you for a fee, which you wouldn't have to pay if anything happened."

The man stood on the trailer, stretched over the boat, and snapped down the tarp's fasteners near the windshield.

"What do you think?" Cleve said. What was that? Thought he heard a child's cry coming from the house. A little kid. Cleve knew a bawling brat when he heard one. He listened for a second cry. Nothing. Weird. Maybe a dog.

The man hopped down, walked around the boat, tying down the canvas. It took a couple of minutes.

Cleve was offended. "Hey, mister!"

The man collected his tools, wiping each one.

"This boat's going to get trashed!" Cleve knocked hard on the bow with his skateboard. Loud enough for the man to stop what he was doing. Cleve felt the air tighten, as if someone had just pulled back the hammer of a gun.

The man's face was serious as a headstone. Cleve tightened his grip on his board, seeing himself in the man's glasses.

He stood over Cleve and said, "A vigil is kept over this

vessel. Nobody *has* harmed her and nobody *will* harm her. Understand?''

Cleve nodded coolly.

The man held a finger an inch from Cleve's face. "It is not a boat," he whispered. *"It is a divine chariot!"*

Cleve nodded.

"You think twice before you try to shake me down again! Now, get your welfare-sucking ass off of my property!"

Cleve stared hard at the man before leaving.

20

Edward Keller weaved a thirty-pound, forged steel chain through the eyelets rigged to the doors of the garage beside his house, bolted it with three "burglar-proof" locks, then activated the silent alarm.

Archangel was secure, awaiting its mission.

The overgrown grass covering the scrap of yard behind the house was bordered by a fence and neglected hedge, obliterating the adjacent yards. An old alcoholic couple lived, if you could call it living, to the left. The abandoned crack house to the right was condemned by city inspectors. Police rarely showed up here where most people were too scared, stupid, or stoned to be nosy.

It was ideal for his needs.

Using a false name, Keller had bought the property for a pittance after discharging himself from the institute. Shrubs covered the barred basement windows, junk mail carpeted the barely visible front yard.

Keller's keys jingled as he unlocked the two dead bolts of

the metal door to the rear of the house. He shrugged off the neighbor kid. The nosy little criminal didn't know what he'd heard. Keller smiled. His mission was blessed. His house was his holy fortress predestined to uphold the will of God. No one could get in. And no one could get out.

Inside, he found deliverance from the sun in the cool darkness. He bolted the door, descended the creaking stairs to the basement, the cocker spaniel scampering after him. He unlocked the room. Littered with dirty plates, glasses, fast food bags and wrappers, it smelled of urine. Danny Becker was asleep on the rotting mattress.

Protector of humankind.

Keller studied his face. The dog watched as he knelt beside the boy, closed his eyes, lifted his head to heaven and gave thanks.

The angel Raphael.

He was cleansed in the light.

Sanctus. Sanctus. Sanctus.

Keller left, keeping the door open. The sleeping pills he had ground into Danny's pop would wear off soon. He had work to do. Climbing the basement stairs, he heard a noise and froze. The dog growled. What was that? A scratching coming from a darkened corner. Could it be that little punk? No. Something lurking in the dark. Something with claws. He switched on a light—suddenly the thing came out of the corner at him. A rat. A large rat, its mangy fur scraping along the wall before it disappeared into a crack in the wall.

It fascinated him. He squatted and whispered into the crack. "Vermin, if you contaminate my temple with your foul presence again, I will taste your blood."

Keller blocked the crack with a wooden milk crate.

Upstairs, he checked the front and rear doors. Each required two keys from the inside to open. Satisfied they were sealed, he went to the bathroom and showered. In his stark bedroom he put on Levi's and a sweatshirt. From his night table he lovingly withdrew the silver crucifix chain, staring at the suffering Christ.

His will be done.

Keller kissed the crucifix and slipped the chain over his neck. He went to the kitchen and made a tomato sandwich and black coffee. He gave the dog a cookie. In the living room, a bookcase stood in one corner jammed with the works of Conrad, Blake, Eliot, the Huxleys, texts on philosophy, theology, death, resurrection, and angels.

When he first held Danny Becker in his arms, Keller felt the flutter of angels' wings.

He selected the obscure work by Oberam Augustine Reingaertler, titled *Struggle for the Light: The Truth About Angels and Devils*, then sat wearily in the rocking chair. He read a passage, said to be centuries old, from a poem by a blind monk for a bereaved mother:

> *His angels first appear as disease, despair and death*
> *Yet when Heaven commands*
> *Each to remove their dark disguise*
> *Lo, we behold, the Seraphim,*
> *Cleansed by the light of one million suns,*
> *The glory of knowing the Face of God*

Keller flipped through the book, studying the seraphim, God's highest ranking angels. Isaiah had been blessed for he had looked upon their beauty, each with six wings, surrounded by flames. *Sanctus. Sanctus. Sanctus. Dominus Deus sabaoth.* Keller stopped at a passage he'd read a thousand times: *angels can be summoned for almost any imaginable emergency and for any task. . . .*

He loved his books. They confirmed the Truth. Angels come at times of desperation. Celestial fixers. It was revealed to him one night in the institute where he had sought help. The answer came in a vision: your children are waiting. The angels will help you, if you find them. But they were disguised. Wearing masks. Do not be deceived by their false identities. They belong to no one until you find them. And you will find them.

If you believed. It was the test of his faith. Keller smiled and rocked. He had found the first. Danny *Raphael* Becker. Raphael of the powers. *Healed by God.* He had still to find the others. Only then would God assist him in the transfiguration. Keller rocked in thought.

Prolonged severe grief reaction, the doctor at the institute had called it. What a fool. He could not comprehend that Keller's life had been preordained. He did not know the glory of God. So many didn't. So many had been bereft of His infinite love. If only those in anguish knew the divine truth as he did. It had been revealed to him.

If only he had spent more time with his children.

No, he had been chosen. He was the enlightened one who would demonstrate God's wonder. That was why he joined the university group. Not to obtain help, but to bestow it upon those in pain.

Keller rocked.

Maps, charts, diagrams, enlarged photographs, calendars, news clippings, and notes covered the living room walls from floor to ceiling. More papers, charts, maps, journals, and binders overflowing with notes were piled on the large computer table near the far wall.

He focused on one picture—the fading snapshot of his three dead children: Pierce, Alisha, and Joshua. Laughing, wearing colorful cone-shaped hats, a half-eaten chocolate cake before them. It was Alisha's sixth birthday. Three weeks before they drowned.

They never found the bodies.

Do not be deceived by their false identities.

Remember the will of the Creator.

* * *

The Will of the Creator.

It shone in Reverend Theodore Keller's eyes the night he watched his rural California church burn to the ground.

"It is the will of the Creator, Edward," his father said to him as the wood crackled and the flames devoured the cross atop the steeple. Edward was ten years old and took pleasure in his father's tears. No one would ever know that it was Edward who set the fire by igniting Bibles in the pulpit, an act inspired by the whippings he endured at the hands of his father in the name of God.

"Spare the rod and spoil the child!" the Reverend thundered after Edward committed sins as heinous as spilling his milk at the supper table, or failing to wash away a trace of dirt from his hands before inspection. "Edward, fetch the rod." His father would command him to get the viperlike leather strap hanging from a nail inside the study near the painting of Golgotha. Edward would tremble. He had long ago forsaken pleading for mercy. Begging was a sign of weakness, a failing to be expunged with more lashes. "Honor thy father and thy mother!" his father would yell and Edward would dutifully drop his pants, exposing his buttocks. The Reverend would twist him over his knee, raise the strap high over his head, bringing it down so swiftly it hummed slicing through the air before *thwacking* across Edward's scarred and tender flesh. The Reverend would grunt savagely, spittle flying from his mouth as he delivered each blow. Edward would bite down on a spoon to keep from screaming. His mother would hurry to another room and pray. It always ended with his father dropping a Bible on Edward's bleeding rear end, ordering him to memorize another chapter by morning. Some days, he literally limped to school, his ears ringing with the *thwack! Thwack!* of the strap.

"You are but a lamb," the Reverend bellowed the night before the fire. He was beating Edward for a crease he had found in his freshly made bed. "You are a burnt offering, a sacrifice I will not withhold from my God! I will not refuse to place you on the altar!"

That night in bed Edward writhed with fear and pain, reading the Bible. He was jolted with the realization that his father's love for his church superseded everything. Even his son's life. The crack of the strap and the Reverend's words echoed in Edward's mind. *I will not refuse to place you on the altar!*

That's when God first spoke to Edward. Cleanse your father of his piety. Save him with the fire of purification. The cracking of the strap. The crackling of the fire. Punishment for the son. Punishment for the father.

"Whoever committed this desecration shall be damned all the days of his life." Keller's father fell to his knees, sobbing as his church burned, brightly, gloriously.

Deliver us from evil. Edward grinned, flames painting his face.

Keller rocked and remembered his children.

He could hear them. Crying.

Keller rocked. *Squeak-creak. Squeak-creak.* Was there time to see it again? *Squeak-creak. Squeak-creak.*

Keller left the chair and lifted an ancient Kodak movie projector from the closet, setting it on the big table. He returned to the closet for a cardboard box of aluminum film canisters, rummaging through it until finding one marked: "Josh at Three." He threaded the film, aimed the projector at the bare wall, then hung two worn bedsheets over the windows. He pulled his chair to the projector and started the movie. The dog watched, tilting his head.

An intense white square burned on the wall, darkening and streaking as the leader flowed over the lens. A little boy's face appears, slightly out of focus. The camera pulls back. The boy is sitting on the floor of an elegant home. The Golden Gate bridge is visible through a bay window. The boy is handsome, dressed in a white shirt, vest, bow tie, and dark pants. His face is fervent with expectation. Two older children, a boy and a girl, are next to him, smiling. The little boy sits before a large gift-wrapped package. The camera tightens on a card that reads: "To Josh, Love, Daddy. P.S. Sorry I couldn't be home. I'll make it next time, PROMISE!" The camera retreats. A woman's hand comes into view, motioning to the boy. He stands and excitedly tears away the paper to get at the treasure it hides. A flowing white mane emerges. Then a saddle. The boy's eyes widen. It's a white rocking horse. He leaps upon it and begins rocking. The other children touch it. Tears sting Keller's eyes.

That day in his home office, Josh toddled in while Keller was on the phone, closing some long-forgotten deal. Josh, his arms open, Daddy, Daddy. I love my daddy. Grabbing at Keller while he was in the middle of crucial negotiations. Josh's arms struggling to hug him. Not now, damn it. I am busy. Get the hell out of here. Josh's arms struggling to hold him. Josh crying, his arms cold from the water. Hang on to Daddy. Josh slipping from his neck, vanishing into the black water. Get the hell out. *You never gave yourself to them. They only wanted you. It would have cost you nothing.*

But you paid with everything to learn that, didn't you?

The camera shakes, the picture blurs. The boy rocks and waves.

Tears stream down Keller's face. He cannot stop them.

He reduces the projector's speed to slow motion.

Joshua, his youngest child, smiles at the camera. He is a good little boy. His hair has been neatly brushed by his mother. He blinks shyly. So vulnerable. Innocent. Frame by frame the camera clicks until Keller's tears blur the picture.

Suddenly Joshua steps from the wall!

Keller's jaw drops.

A resplendent aura of ever-changing color emanates from his tiny figure as he stands in the brilliant light of the projector. The features of his face undulate ethereally, and Keller sniffs and squints as he tries to comprehend the apparition.

"Joshua? Oh, Josh. It is you! You have come!"

Keller slips from the rocking chair to his knees.

"Praise Him! Praise Him!"

Tears flow down his face. He opens his arms and inches closer to the child. It is a sign! A Divine sign! His reward!

"Praise God!" Keller's voice breaks with joy.

The film clicks faster, then slaps wildly in the take-up reel as the movie ends, trapping the squinting child in the fierce glare of the projector's light.

"I want to go home," Danny Becker pleads weakly, his chin wrinkles, and he begins sobbing. "I want my mommy and daddy."

Keller stretches out his arms and tilts his head to heaven.

"Praise Jesus. Praise Jesus! Praise Him and all the angels!"

The cocker spaniel barks.

21

Four men with droopy eyes glowered at Sydowski and Turgeon from the computer screen. Each was a Caucasian in his late forties. Bearded. Dark rumpled hair. They could have been brothers.

"Best composites I could get." Beth Ferguson's concentration was glued to the screen.

She was the police artist who helped develop the SFPD's computerized image-enhancing system for missing children, criminals, and suspects. She kept her auburn hair in a beehive, popular at the time of her wedding. Partial to Beechnut gum, she snapped it absentmindedly. Turgeon loved her earrings, tiny silver handcuffs.

Beth's office was cluttered with computers, monitors, and sketches. She could remove the face-tight masks of some suspects photographed by security cameras. Her success rate at producing likenesses was eighty-six percent. Enlarged, facially aged pictures of JFK and Elvis adorned one wall.

"Now, without beards." Beth tapped her keyboard, making

the four men clean shaven. Their heads rotated. Beth swiveled to another computer, hit some commands, and the screen showed each man's full-body composite, with her estimates of height, weight, body type, hair, and eye color.

"I put him at six feet even, 160 to 180 pounds, medium build, dark hair and dark eyes."

Beth yawned. She had put in several seventeen-hour shifts drafting sketches from witness descriptions until she saw the suspect in her dreams. And, as she had done thousands of times over the past year, she reviewed the fuzzy Polaroid of little Tanita Marie Donner, alive and naked, held by a man wearing a black hood and black gloves. It took every degree of clinical coolness Beth could muster to extract details from the fragment of tattoo visible on the man's forearm. All she could glean was a bit of flame. She was frustrated by the hood. Too loose fitting. Had the man been wearing a tight-fitting ski mask, she could have produced vital facial attributes. This morning, when she felt she had done all she could, she called Sydowski and Turgeon.

"Before I go any further," she said, "I've got bad news and worse news."

"Worst news first," Sydowski said.

"I can't compare the Donner suspect in the Polaroid with the suspect in Danny Becker's kidnapping. I've tried everything, Walt. Whether these two creeps are the same guy or not is anybody's guess."

"What's the bad news?" Turgeon said.

"Because of so many different perspectives and descriptions of Danny Becker's abductor, my composite is weak. Thirty percent accuracy tops. Watch. I'll take the most common characteristics of these fellows and give you your suspect, or fifty percent of him."

Beth typed a command, the four faces were instantly replaced on the computer screen by one. A saggy-eyed, grim-faced Caucasian with arching eyebrows in his late forties and bearded.

He was a man either haunted by remorse or devoid of it, Sydowski thought.

"Did you also take ten years off of this guy for us?" he said.

Beth sighed. "I did. Wasn't easy. Took two days. I'd rate it at thirty-five to forty percent. Here goes." Her keyboard clicked.

"Why make the guy ten years younger?" Turgeon asked.

"That's when Franklin Wallace was doing his time in Virginia."

Slowly, from top to bottom, the display terminal gave birth to a new image of the suspect. His face had fewer lines, was less heavy set. His eyes, while droopy, were somewhat more buoyant and his hair was thicker. Beth split the screen and presented two pictures of the younger suspect, one showing him bearded, and one showing him clean shaven. The printer hummed, offering crisp, perfect color pictures of both composites. "There you go."

The gold in Sydowski's teeth shined as he gathered copies of Beth's work into a file. "I owe you, Beautiful."

"Just close these cases, Walt."

Waiting for the elevator at the Hall of Justice, Turgeon studied Beth's color computer pictures. "So this is our guy?"

"One of them anyway."

"Tanita Donner's killer, or have we got two different suspects?"

"Don't know, Linda."

"We going to call a press conference? Splash the composite?"

"Nope."

"No?" Turgeon closed the folder.

"Beth only rated it thirty percent. We'd be bogged down chasing hundreds of useless leads. We'll try a few other things."

"You want me to send the younger composite to Virginia prison authorities?" They stepped onto the elevator.

"First, we'll see Rad."

Rad Zwicker was a skinny, hyperactive bachelor who worshiped computers and lived alone with his mother near the Castro. He was not only sensitive, he was the master analyst of the SFPD's computerized records. His department at the hall continually droned from the sound of huge, new, powerful data storage banks. Give him a morsel of information and he would stun you with what he could pull out. Rad annoyed many cops because he rode a perpetual caffeine high and was overeager, but he was lightning fast and brilliant, virtues the SFPD did not overstock, Sydowski thought, putting Beth's fresh composites into Rad's hands.

"You guys want a coffee, just made a fresh batch?" Rad pushed back his glasses and burrowed into the file.

"No thanks," Turgeon said.

"I'm fine, Rad," Sydowski said.

"Super! Let's get going!" Rad plopped himself before a terminal and entered Beth's calculations. He then sipped coffee from a gargantuan mug, darted to another computer, fed each of Beth's composites into it, then entered various commands. The fans to cool the computers whirred. Rad turned and smiled.

"Be ready in a few moments."

One of the computers beeped. Rad turned, telling his guests to pull up chairs beside him.

"Super! Now, here's what I'm doing. I've entered Beth's physical description of our target, with tolerances, into the California Department of Motor Vehicles drivers' and registration records data bank. I've narrowed the search to the greater Bay Area, eliminating race, sex, age, etc. That being, I would estimate a potential suspect pool of two hundred thousand.

Now if we had a suspect vehicle, it would narrow the search considerably.

"What we'll do is call in volunteer criminology students and cadets from the academy to help us sift through the pool. Here, I'll show you what we'll do. I start with our first guy here."

Rad pulled up on a large video screen the driver's license picture of an Oakland man whose age and physical description fit Beth's composite. Rad punched a command and Beth's composite of the suspect appeared in matching scale and perspective beside the Oakland man. Rad then superimposed the suspect's photo over the Oakland man.

"Not even close," Turgeon said.

"Before we get started in this needle-in-a-haystack grunt work—do we have fingerprints?" Rad asked.

"No, just the tattoo fragment," Sydowski said. "But we could be dealing with two separate suspects."

"Yes, I remember. We'll do what we did last year, run everything through NCIC and VICAP. We struck out then. Now, we have a physical description to possibly tie it to. And, for what it's worth, we'll sift through the dreaded California sex crimes registry again. And I'll rattle the Bay Area data banks."

"Anything you can do, Rad."

He ran the description through the state and federal prison systems, and the Western States Information Network. Last year, early in the Donner case, Rad had Virginia's prison records checked for the time Franklin Wallace was an inmate to see if any of his old prison buddies were with him the time of the baby's murder. "Let's try it again now that Beth's done a Dorian Gray for us."

"Dorian Gray?" Turgeon whispered to Sydowski.

"Computer aged the picture," he answered.

Rad's fingers danced over his keyboard as he entered the data bank for the federal prison system in Virginia for the years Franklin Wallace served his time for sex crimes against children. The screen showed a list of 621 male inmates Wallace could have met there. The list included social security numbers, birthdates, and file numbers from the National Crime Information Center's computers. Rad sensed Sydowski's skepticism.

"Walter, please bear in mind that data are fluid and a lot of new information has likely been entered since we last did this."

Sydowski bore it in mind.

"Although it is tempting to go with descriptions, let's go with circumstance first in narrowing our search," Rad said.

"Molesters tend to stick together on the inside," Turgeon said.

"That's right. So how many of our first number were doing time for sex crimes against children?" Rad worked the keyboard.

The list was reduced to fifty-four.

"Remove the number who were in jail when Tanita Marie Donner was taken," Sydowski said.

The list shrank to eighteen.

"How many were alive at the time of the Donner case?" Sydowski asked. Rad nodded and worked the keyboard.

The list was reduced to fourteen.

"Let's go to identifiers now," Rad said. "I'll narrow that list to Caucasians."

The computer beeped and the number now was eleven.

"How many at that time had tattoos on their right arm?" Sydowski said.

Rad prompted the computer and it answered nine.

Four tattoos had the names of women, three men had Harleys on their biceps, one had a screaming eagle, and one had a death's head. Not one had flames on their forearms.

"Shit," Sydowski muttered.

"Tattoos can be removed, Inspector," Turgeon said.

"It's only our first run, Walter, and it was quick and definitely unscientific." Rad was reaching to switch the computer off.

"Wait!" Turgeon said, startling the two men. A few clerks nearby looked up. "We forgot another aspect."

"There are thousands of possible equations to try," Rad said.

"I know. But we went through this looking for somebody to fit our suspect's description. My reading of the file is that two people were involved in Tanita Marie Donner's kidnapping and murder."

"Right. We used that last year without a description," Rad said.

"Many of these cases are partner crimes," Sydowski said.

"We know someone took the pictures in the Donner case, maybe there were other, peripheral partners?" Turgeon said. "Try this: how many of our suspects who were Virginia skinners with Franklin Wallace were living in the Bay Area at the time of the Donner abduction and murder?"

"Sure." Rad pounded in the command.

Turgeon bit her bottom lip and waited.

The computer beeped. Zero.

"Damn," she whispered.

Sydowski grunted, and checked his watch. Maybe they should pass Beth's composites to Rust and Ditmire and let the FBI play with them.

"Wait, one more thing." Turgeon had not given up. "How many of the Virginia cons are now living in the Bay Area?"

"We got zilch when we tried that last year." Rad shrugged.

"But a lot of new information has likely been entered since the last time you did this," she said.

"True," Rad said, catching Sydowski's subtle nod.

The computer bleeped and answered: one.

Turgeon's heart quickened.

Rad bolted upright. "Amazing!"

"Call him up," Sydowski said.

PERRY WILLIAM KINDHART.

His name and file appeared on the screen. Caucasian, thirty-nine, five feet, eleven inches tall, medium build, red hair, blue eyes. Death's head tattoo on left shoulder. Convicted molester. Mugs were recent. No resemblance to Beth's composites.

"Last known address?" Sydowski said.

"I'm getting it." Rad typed. The computer beeped. "SoMa. He lives South of Market. I'll print out the address. Looks current."

"Record?" Sydowski said.

Rad prompted the computer, complimenting Turgeon for her hunch.

"I don't know how we missed this guy last year," he said.

Kindhart's criminal history appeared on the screen. He had served time in the same Virginia prison as Franklin Wallace when Wallace was there. They could have met. Kindhart was convicted in Richmond of photographing children in lewd poses, and served one year. His federal sheet had charges and acquittals in half a dozen Midwestern states over the last decade. He seemed to be making his way west. His last known beef was in San Francisco. The full details of his case were only recently entered into the system, according to the data date, explaining how he was missed the first time.

"I don't believe this." Turgeon read the screen quickly.

Right about the time Tanita Marie Donner was kidnapped and murdered, Kindhart was up on charges of exciting the lust of a child in San Francisco. He supposedly took obscene pictures of two five-year-old girls he enticed into his apartment in the Mission. Evidence was shaky so the judge gave Kindhart two years probation with terms that he stay away from children, not own any type of camera, and not possess any type of pornographic material.

"This is weird." Turgeon wanted a printout.

Sydowski said nothing. His breathing grew intense, his stomach tightened, the way it tightens when a Homicide cop knows, *knows* deep in his tired gut, that he's got a solid break.

Sydowski searched Kindhart's eyes.

He knows, Sydowski felt it. He knows things about Tanita Marie Donner. About her murder. And maybe he knows about Danny, too. He knows something. And with the exception of Danny and Tanita's parents, nobody had invested more in the right to that knowledge than Sydowski had. The time had come to collect on his investment.

Calm and confidence washed over Sydowski.

"This is good," he said.

22

Lois Jensen poured water into the cafeteria-sized coffee urn and clicked her tongue at Dr. Kate Martin fussing for the third time over the spread of fruit, cheeses, and crackers.

"Don't fret, Kate, it is going to be fine."

"I need a written guarantee, Lois." Martin bit her lip.

During the year her study group had been meeting, she had always been in control. The pain exposed in this drafty old campus study room remained here, eventually evaporating like the tears that accompanied it. But that was going to change. She had relinquished command of what she cherished in order to save it.

She and Lois had arrived early to set up refreshments. Both were dressed more formally than usual—Lois in a peach, summer-knit sweater set and white skirt, and Martin in a silk blouse, hound's-tooth-check blazer and matching skirt.

"Lois, are we doing the right thing?"

"We're doing the right thing. We've all been doing well.

Even Keller. Is he coming? Is he aware the *Star* is going to be here?''

"I couldn't reach him. The number he gave me didn't work. He's never missed a session. I'll alert him at the door.''

"Most of us supported this step, Kate. It's necessary. At worst, you'll reach others who need help and they are out there. Especially now with another child kidnapped.''

"But I fear the potential damage. Some of the group didn't want to participate tonight. I'm getting cold feet.''

"We've all lost a child. Telling a reporter about it is not tantamount to the experience. If the university revokes your tenure, you can always set up your own shop, underwritten by a tissue company. I'll be your first client.''

They were still laughing when Tom Reed arrived with another man who had a camera around his neck and a bag over his shoulder.

"Right on time, Tom,'' Martin greeted them.

"Dr. Martin, this is Henry Cain, a photographer with the *Star*.''

Martin introduced Lois. They talked over coffee until others arrived, then Martin took Reed aside.

"Four have decided not to come. Three will be here, but won't speak. Six will talk and allow their names and pictures to be used.''

"Including Angela Donner?''

"Yes.''

"Is that her?'' Reed indicated a young woman, whose thighs stretched her brown slacks. Her white blouse had a large bow at the neck. Her stringy dishwater-blond hair was pinned up with two pink barrettes that looked familiar to Reed. She was at the refreshment table.

"How's she doing?''

"Good days and bad days. The Becker abduction is a setback. Coming up on Tanita's anniversary. Opens a lot of wounds, especially when the press links the cases. She still lives with her father.''

Reed contemplated Angela Donner. If he could get her story in the paper, it would break the city's heart. Tanita's case still held compelling elements: grandfather dying of cancer, while her mother copes on welfare and her killer walks free.

"Poor Angela." Martin blinked. "Tolstoy couldn't have dreamed a more tragic figure. Well, there's Edward Keller . . .''

"Oh . . . ?"

"I couldn't reach him. He doesn't know about tonight. I don't know how he'll react because—'' Martin stopped. "Off the record?"

"Sure."

"He's an eccentric."

"This is San Francisco."

"He's an eccentric's eccentric."

"I see."

"Oh, there he is. Excuse me."

Reed looked across the room at Keller. Late forties, early fifties, about six feet, firm, lean build. His beard and thick salt-and-pepper hair did not hide the lines etched in his face. Dressed in faded jeans, a navy pullover sportshirt, and a worn, gray sports jacket, Keller had an air of ardent independence, as if a dark fire raged inside. Reed recalled that the suspect in Danny Becker's kidnapping had light hair, a beard, and a slim build, according to the new composite drawings the cops were on the brink of releasing. Reed stopped himself with a warning: you are not playing that game again.

Listening to Martin, Keller was concerned and looked directly at Reed. Keller nodded, then said a few words. Martin returned.

"Edward does not want to be identified for the article."

"That's fine."

Keller took a seat, regarding Reed suspiciously.

Martin took a deep breath. "Time to get started."

She introduced Reed and Cain, reminding the group of their presence, and offering anyone who'd had a last minute change of heart to back out. Reed and Cain requested that those consenting to be identified sit together. Reed jotted down their names.

"Lois, you volunteered to go first." Martin smiled.

Lois nodded, hesitated, then laughed. "I'm sorry."

"Ease into it." Martin nodded.

Lois collected her thoughts. Her face was placid, intelligent.

"It was a gorgeous day and I was making Allan's lunch when he insisted on riding his bike to the park—you know how children can be. His friend Jerry had found a sparrow's nest. I said, you've got ten minutes. Sure, Mom, he said. I'll be right back. I'll be right back. I know he would keep his word. So after, oh I guess about half an hour, I was getting a little peeved. That's when Jerry came to my door. He was covered with dirt and looked frightened. And I thought, gee, he must've had a bad fall. I looked for Allan, but I didn't see him. Then Jerry's mouth started to move, but nothing came out. I realized that he was actually covered in blood.

"I looked for Allan. Didn't see him. I demanded that Jerry tell me where he was. Poor Jerry couldn't speak. He started to cry, pointed to the park. He got on his bike, rode to the park with me running behind him. We arrived. I saw some children standing over another child who was lying on the ground, twisted in his bike. As I ran, I knew that the bike looked like Allan's, but I couldn't see Allan among the children, so I thought that he must have run to get help for this fallen child. I was starting to mentally go through my first aid training, I still had a dish towel in my hand, when I looked down on the child, a boy. I knew he was dead, I—"

She wept. Reed made a note. Cain's camera clicked.

"I'm okay." She smiled. "When I saw that it was Allan, something happened."

Reed noticed Keller nodding emphatically.

"My child, my only child was lying there on the grass, his eyes closed as if he were asleep. He looked so at peace. He had been shot, here." Lois touched the right side of her head about an inch above her ear. "He was shot and his blood was everywhere, spreading on the ground under his head in a widening halo, a perfect halo. The most brilliant red I've ever seen. I knelt beside him. The children were saying something to me, but their voices were distant. That's when the miracle happened. Before my eyes, I saw Allan's face change. I swear it changed there as he lay on the grass, to the tiny wrinkled expression that fused with my heart the moment he was born. Then it changed to joy from the day he took his first steps, then fear from the night he was convinced a monster lived in his closet. Happiness from the Christmas Santa brought him his first bike, then shame from the day he came home from his first and only schoolyard brawl. Embarrassment on the day I saw him holding hands with a girl. Finally, it turned serene, showing perfect contentment. I cradled him in my arms, and the next thing I remember a police officer was touching my shoulder and paramedics were trying to take my boy away from me."

Lois paused.

Sniffles and coughs went around the group. Keller's head was bowed, his eyes were shut tight, his hands clasped. Praying? Reed waited for Martin's reaction. She wasn't watching Keller.

"For about a year after that I went through the motions of living. Bill and I retreated into ourselves. He didn't want to talk. I wanted counseling together. He didn't. And I couldn't go alone. I felt bitter, angry for being punished unfairly, I felt abandoned, helpless, worthless. I contemplated suicide, divorce. That's when I saw Kate's notice in the *Chronicle* about her research. I suggested to Bill that we participate. He wasn't interested. I decided to volunteer and later told Bill I had enrolled in a hobby course at the university. He thinks my 'course' has done a world of good. It has. Tonight I'll tell him what I've been doing.''

Reed knew the case. Bobby Ray Walker, a truck mechanic with a history of mental problems, was the sniper who had shot Lois's son. Walker was serving a life sentence in Folsom for the murder.

Reed asked Lois how Martin's research group had helped her.

''It's helped me come to terms with losing my child. I'm able to function now. I'm able to laugh at a good joke, eat a hearty meal, sleep through the night. I certainly don't tell every person I meet the details I've told you, but I can deal with talking about it without falling to pieces. I still feel uneasy seeing a funeral procession. I'll never fully recover from losing Allan. No parent is ever, ever the same after losing a child because a piece of you dies, too. This group has helped me survive my loss. We've all helped each other and Kate has been our guide. Some people cannot endure such a blow alone. The feelings of guilt, rage, blame, loss, futility are overwhelming, almost fatal. At times I thought I was losing my mind, hearing my son's voice at night, smelling his scent, seeing him in malls, in my dreams, feeling his kiss on my cheek.''

''How is this group different from others?''

''Some are politically motivated. Some seek vengeance. Eye for an eye. There's nothing wrong with that, if that's what you feel in your heart. I was a member of such a group during Walker's trial. At the time I was embittered. I believed Walker should have been executed. I no longer feel vengeance in my heart. Feeling that way won't bring Allan back. This group is different because it is not a public action agency. It is research. The objective is to study our bereavement, our pain and anguish with the aim of understanding it, healing. We've been helped tremendously.''

The others followed with their stories, each account as heart wrenching as the previous one. Reed's eyes burned as he listened and took notes. What was happening here? As a hardened crime reporter he had seen enough tragedy for twenty lifetimes. This was getting to him. Why? Because he'd researched most of these cases, or that he'd actually covered some? He didn't know. He questioned himself, what he did for a living. Fear of the pain he may have wrongly caused Franklin Wallace's wife and daughter gnawed at him. He thought of Ann and Zach and what he had almost lost in his own life. Self-loathing, self-doubt, and confusion haunted him in the eyes of these grieving parents.

Sitting there, Reed felt saddened. Alone. Utterly alone.

He noticed Keller staring at him as he heard Martin suggesting the group take a break.

"I think it's going well, Tom. Don't you?" Martin smiled.

He agreed, then excused himself to go to the washroom.

23

Relieved that the washroom was empty, Reed positioned himself at a urinal. Keller swung through the door and took the one next to him.

"Do you believe in God, Mr. Reed?"

Reed laughed. Given the circumstances, the question was absurd. He shook his head.

"Is that your answer?"

"Pardon?"

"Do you believe in God, Mr. Reed?"

"Look, I know it may be awkward having me here. But you should know that I appreciate the opportunity." Reed washed his hands.

"You haven't answered my question."

"What I believe is irrelevant."

"Lois Jensen believes. Some of the others are on their way." Keller bent over the adjacent sink, opening the faucets. "We try to help each other in our assemblage."

Assemblage? Was he going to break into Scripture now?

"I'm helping them spiritually through the pain. 'Through the valley of the dark sun.' "

The valley of the dark sun. Reed knew the old poem: "A Watery Death" by Ledel I. Zoran.

Keller splashed his face. "I believe you are here to test me."

"Test you? I'm sorry. I don't know what you mean."

Keller continued splashing his face. His voice had an eerie resonance as he recited: "Between the dream and the day comes the specter." Tiny water rivulets slithered down his face. "Are you the specter, sent to destroy my work?"

"Your work?" Reed was puzzled, somewhat uneasy. "No. I'm not the specter. I'm afraid I can't help you there. Excuse me." Reed tossed a crumpled paper towel into the trash.

Angela Donner spoke with a little voice, a child's voice.

"I gave birth to Tanita in the back of a bus in San Mateo. I was seventeen, living by myself. But I was going to keep my baby. My baby and me were going to make a better life for us together. I was going to finish school, be a good mother."

Angela pondered her clasped fingers and sniffled.

"When Tanita Marie was stolen from me and killed, that was the day I stopped dreaming. Everything went dark. Everything. I wanted to die." Martin passed Angela a tissue. "I bought a big bottle of sleeping pills the day before Dr. Martin came to visit. I planned to kill myself. Dr. Martin saved me. I am glad she came."

Martin smiled encouragingly at her.

"She helped me hang on, helped me think that maybe something good would come from Tanita Marie's murder. That's when this research got started and it made me feel that Tanita Marie didn't die in vain."

Angela dabbed her eyes. "But some of the bad feelings came back when Danny Becker got kidnapped in Balboa. It woke up my pain. Someone's out there stealing children. I pray every night for Danny Becker's mother and father. I saw them on TV. I pray their son will be returned safe, that the police find the person who took him and the person who murdered my baby.''

Reed paused a moment before asking her a few soft questions about the group. Afterward, she agreed to be interviewed later at her home, then Reed turned to a fresh page in his notebook.

Keller wanted to go next. ''I think it's appropriate, I give my testimony now,'' he said.

''Certainly, Edward,'' Martin said.

Keller looked at Reed. ''I remind you, I do not wish to be identified in any way in your newspaper, but I believe what I have to say is crucial.''

''That's not a problem,'' Reed said.

Keller studied Reed for several moments before beginning with a recitation: '' 'All that he was, all that he had been, looked back from the still water.' ''

Keller allowed the words to be absorbed. Martin put a hand to her temple as if anticipating disaster.

''You know those lines, Mr. Reed?''

Zoran again. Reed nodded. '' 'A Watery Death,' I think.''

''My children drowned.''

Reed hadn't found any clippings in the newspaper's library about Keller's case. ''I understand,'' he said.

''You understand?''

''Yes.''

''Have you ever lost a child?''

''No.''

''You have children?''

''A son, Zach. He's nine.''

Keller pondered this information. ''My eldest boy was nine when he died. It was a boating accident.'' Keller's eyes were cold, dry.

Reed prompted him. ''You lost all of your children?''

''Yes. All three of my children. Pierce was nine, Alisha six, and Joshua three. I was with them. Just the four of us. I rented a boat to the Farallons. A storm hit as we neared the islands.''

Keller stopped cold. Reed looked at Martin for a cue. She shrugged. Lois Jensen and Angela Donner were sniffling.

"What happened?"

"It hit us hard. Rain, thunder, violent winds, wild swells cresting at seven, maybe eight feet. We were tossed like a toy. A whale came up under us and split the hull. We took on water. I failed to get life jackets on the children. We ended up in the ocean. Stay near me, I told them. It was impossible. They drowned calling for me. I survived. They never found their bodies. My wife blamed me and left shortly after.''

Keller stared at Reed. "It was God's will. I was being punished.''

"For what?"

"Living a lie.''

"You believe this is the reason your children drowned?"

"I *know* it's the reason.''

"I see. What do you mean by that—you were living a lie?"

"I can't tell you.''

"Why not?"

"It's complicated.''

Reed said nothing.

"What my valiant brothers and sisters here have tried to convey tonight is the universal truth that when your child dies, you die, too. You become something else.''

Reed waited for the religious kicker.

"When my children died, I died, but was born again.''

Bingo.

"I didn't realize it at the time. It was a very slow process. It was an awakening followed by a revelation.''

"Tell me about it.''

Keller's eyes went to Martin, then to Reed.

"With all due respect to the professor's fine work, she has only touched the surface. The truth is that if a parent comes to terms, accepts their child's death, they are destroyed. They have lost.''

Martin leaned forward slightly. Reed sensed she was hearing this for the first time. Keller continued.

''They must accept the divine truth. It was revealed to me.''

''What is the 'divine truth'?'' Reed said.

''We will be with our children again if we are true believers. If we don't accept the divine truth, our children are lost forever. You can rescue them if you truly believe you can.''

Looney tunes, Reed thought, making notes to hide his reaction.

''Lois Jensen witnessed God's work on the face of her son. I told her she is on the brink of her revelation. That is why I participate. To help the group realize the divine truth.''

''You say you can rescue your children. From where?'' Reed said.

Keller closed his eyes. ''I know that soon I will be with my children again. That I will deliver them from purgatory. God in His infinite mercy has revealed this to me. Every day I give Him thanks and praise Him. And every day, I wage war against doubt in preparation for my blessed reunion.''

What the hell was going on here? Was this some sort of bizarre grief cult? Reed knew stranger things had happened in San Francisco. But why would Martin want publicity? No, it had to be that Keller was one sandwich short of a picnic. How could Martin tolerate him? Something about him was out of sync. Reed couldn't put his finger on it, but it troubled him.

''You don't believe a word I've spoken, do you?'' Keller said.

''I believe you believe that what you've experienced is true,'' Reed said. ''How long ago did the accident happen?''

''Look at you. Sitting there, so smug. I've read your stories about Danny Becker and about Angela's little girl.''

Reed sighed.

''It's devil's work, what you do!''

Reed closed his notebook.

"You've got all the answers, don't you?" Keller said.

Martin intervened. "Edward. Edward, please. Tom's our guest."

"I *know* why he's here." Keller stood.

"Mr. Keller, I apologize if my being here upsets you."

"I think I've said enough." Keller headed for the door.

"Edward, please, don't leave," Martin pleaded.

"Good night, everyone," Keller said over his shoulder as he left.

"I feared this would happen." Martin was deflated. "I'm sorry he reacted to your presence the way he did, Tom, Henry."

They waved it off.

"If no one minds, I'd like to end the session. It's been memorable," Martin said. "Thanks, everyone. And thanks Tom and Henry. We look forward to the article."

"Thank you," Reed said.

As group members collected jackets and tidied up, Martin took Reed aside. She was concerned about Keller.

"It was a disaster with Edward. Is he going to be in the story?"

"I don't know."

"I should have prevented him from talking."

"Why?"

"The anniversary of the drownings is coming up." She smiled across the room at Angela, waiting in a chair, twisting her hair. "That, along with Christmas and birthdays, is an extremely bad time."

"No promises. His words were on the record, but I'll keep this in mind, okay?"

"Okay."

Reed approached Angela. "Thanks for waiting," he said.

24

Keller returned to his house in Wintergreen Heights, deactivated the alarm, unlocked the locks, went to his bedroom, took the silver crucifix from his nightstand, and slipped it around his neck. In the living room, from the cluttered worktable, he removed a huge worn Bible. It was two centuries old. The pastor at his children's memorial service had given it to him.

"God's love never dies. Accept it and your children shall always be with you."

He plopped in his rocking chair, Bible on his lap, and read, reflecting on his clash with Tom Reed. The fool. Mocking his revelation. But it didn't matter. He had succeeded in battle. Passed another test, abided in the Lord, and emerged triumphant. It was the Will of the Creator.

Not the Reverend Theodore Keller's version, but The true Divine Will revealed in the purifying flames of his burning church. God had pulled back the curtain of Edward's destiny that night, whispering revelations in his young ears.

His father's congregation couldn't afford to rebuild, forcing the Reverend to move down the highway and down in stature to a smaller California town where they existed on handouts from the faithful. It was humiliating for Edward, going to school, knowing the clothes he wore and the lunch he brought were not provided by God, but by farmers, merchants, widows—the parents of his classmates.

Edward's loathing for his father festered and he vowed not to follow his impoverished, sanctimonious life. At seventeen, he discarded his parents, and up and left. He hitchhiked to San Francisco and he put himself through college, working nights at a bookstore, weekends at a contracting firm in North Beach. He studied philosophy and business, graduating near the top of his class, not knowing what he would do with his life.

One day he returned to the overgrown site of his father's razed church. Amid the weed-entombed foundation, he realized his ambition. He would build churches. Many of California's churches were aging. A market existed.

Keller obtained a loan and was soon offering poor parishes new churches with long-term payment plans. His pitches were attractive. His knowledge of theology, philosophy, and his son-of-a-preacher approach ingratiated him with church leaders.

It also captivated Joan Webster, the only daughter of a minister in Philo. She astounded him, distracting him during his first meeting with Reverend Webster. She possessed a celibate air of fresh-scrubbed wholesomeness. He wanted to be with her. He gave her father a ridiculously good deal and personally supervised the construction of the new church so he could be near her.

Joan thought he was intelligent, handsome, unlike any of the local young men. He was a builder, a dreamer who could sweep her away from dusty old Philo to the lights of San Francisco.

They courted for a year, then married and moved to a bungalow in Oakland. Joan was loving, fulfilling her role as dutybound wife and mother, bearing them Pierce, Alisha, and Joshua.

Keller's business flourished, becoming one of the state's largest church-building firms. They bought a huge Victorian in San Francisco with a postcard view of the Golden Gate bridge. There, they lived behind a deteriorating veneer of happiness. Keller preoccupied himself with making money, renegotiating contracts, making most congregations beholden to him for decades. He was addicted to the power. His passion for his business overshadowed his love for his family.

Whenever Joan tried talking to him, he stifled her with a Biblical proverb. As time passed, she urged him to take one of the children with him on business trips. He rejected the idea. They would be in the way. Jeopardize a contract. Their discussions evolved into prolonged, late-night arguments, with Joan insisting he spend more time with the children, or there was no point in maintaining the facade of a family. She would leave him.

Resentfully, Keller acquiesced.

One at a time, he took the children on business trips, but he was so stern with their conduct that they dreaded going with him. Joan knew he was uncomfortable having the children with him, but she believed she was rescuing her family from disaster. Clinging to the hope he was a loving father imprisoned by his work, she suggested he spend a day alone with the children, away from the business. Renting a boat to go birdwatching and picnicking at the Farallons would be a memorable outing.

That weekend, he loaded Pierce, Alisha, and Joshua into the Cadillac and drove down the peninsula to Half Moon Bay.

Keller rocked in his chair, Bible in his lap, stroking his beard. *Squeak-creak. Squeak-creak.*

That weekend.

His children. The storm. The whale. Sinking. Darkness swallowing the children. His children.

Dawn, hugging a rock. Someone lifting him. Warmth. A motor droning. Antiseptic hospital smells. Someone calling him. Joan's face. Edward! Where are the children? Telling Joan what happened. Her face. Breaking. Her broken face seared into his soul.

My angels! My angels! Edward, where are my children, please!

Squeak-creak. Squeak-creak.

Keller set the Bible aside.

Time to resume his work. He went to the basement.

"Home. I want my mommy and daddy," Danny Becker moaned from the floor where he was scribbling with crayons in a fat coloring book. The dog sat dutifully at his side. The room was foul. Danny's clothes were soiled. He had wet himself. Keller went upstairs, ran a hot bath, pouring Mr. Bubble into the water.

A watery death.

Keller knelt at the tub. The cocker spaniel padded into the room, then Danny appeared, gazing longingly at the water. It was a sign. Keller smiled, began removing Danny's clothes, then hoisted him into the water. He unwrapped a bar of soap. Danny was docile, enjoying the warm water and bubbles. Noticing Keller's silver crucifix, he reached up and held it in his tiny hand for inspection.

Jesus said to his disciples: You shall not despise any one of these little ones, for I say to you that in Heaven their angels see the face of my Father.

Keller cleared a circle of water in the bubbles, cupped the back of Danny's neck, and immersed his entire head. Fear leapt onto Danny's face. Underwater his eyes widened. His hand shot up, seizing Keller's crucifix in a panic-stricken grasp and he pulled. Keller closed his eyes and smiled.

For since by mankind came death, by mankind came too the resurrection of the dead.

"Pull, Raphael! Pull, sweet healing angel! I beseech you! Will you pull my Josh from the watery purgatory into which I cast him?" The crucifix chain sank deep into Keller's neck. Danny's breath escaped in a wild underwater scream boiling to the surface. Clutching the crucifix in a white-knuckled grip, he raised himself from the water, coughing, gasping for air. The dog yelped. Danny rubbed his eyes, his tiny body shaking as he cried.

It was wondrous, like the sound of a newborn. Keller covered Danny with a towel, and lifted him from the tub. He had baptized him, readied him for the transfiguration. "It will be done! It will be done! Oh thank you, Raphael! Thank you!" Keller's voice trembled. He was tingling with exultation, eyes brimming with tears. He carried Danny to his bedroom and opened the closet. It was crammed with cardboard boxes.

"I want my mommy and daddy." Danny wiped his eyes, watching Keller slide a box before him.

"Joshua" was written on the box in neat feminine script. It was jammed with children's clothing—boy's summer items, neatly folded and smelling powerfully of mothballs. Danny coughed. Rummaging, Keller found a set of pajamas, powder blue, dotted with tiny fire trucks.

"These will be your new clothes." Keller put the pajamas on Danny. "And there's a special set for the transfiguration."

Danny didn't understand.

"It's time for a story," Keller said.

Back in the living room, Keller selected a blue binder from the table. The dog followed them. Keller sat in his rocking chair with Danny on his lap and sighed.

"Later, can I go home, please?" Danny said.

Squeak-creak. Squeak-creak.

The chair rocked. The binder, marked "Daniel Raphael Becker/Joshua," cracked when Keller opened it.

"This is the story of a little boy named Josh who has gone away."

Keller turned to the first laminated page. It was a color portrait of the little boy Danny saw the other night riding the rocking horse in the movie on the wall. In the picture, the boy's eyes danced with happiness. His hair was parted neatly, his hands were clasped together in his lap in a well-directed studio pose.

"Who's that?" Danny touched the page.

Keller hesitated.

"My Josh. He's waiting in a cold dark place for me to get him. Only you can go there. That's why you're here. I sent for you. And this is how I found you." He turned the page to a photocopy of a microfilmed newspaper clipping of a birth announcement. It was placed under the words: IT'S A BOY! and a graphic of a smiling stork, wings extended, a baby suspended in a bundle swinging from its beak.

Keller read aloud:

> "BECKER Magdalene and Nathan are proud to
> announce the birth of their first child,
> Daniel Raphael, who arrived March 14,
> weighing 8 lbs., 7 oz."

Raphael and the month were circled in red. Joshua Keller had been born in March.

Keller turned to an enlarged shot of Danny chasing the swans at the pond behind his house, then to a section of a city map with the Beckers' street circled. Next, there was a photocopy from the San Francisco city directory listing Magdalene and Nathan Becker, their Jordan Park address, and Nathan's job as an engineer with Nor-Tec, then the Beckers' municipal tax and land title records. The next pages were printouts of data on the Beckers and their property taken from municipal, county, state, and federal websites. Keller then reviewed some pages of the Beckers' family history that he had purchased from a genealogy service on the Internet. Then he turned to credit card bills, bank statements, a wedding invitation, a doctor's appointment notice for Danny, a grocery list, telephone bills, utility bills, and community newsletters. All were stained, creased, and torn. Keller had retrieved them from the Beckers' garbage. Then there were some snapshots of Danny's home, taken from the front, sides, and rear.

"That's my house!" Danny slapped the pages.

Pictures of Maggie Becker walking with Danny, helping Danny from the car in their driveway, were on the next page. Then pictures of Nathan walking with Danny in the neighborhood, in the BMW, Nathan entering Nor-Tec, then at Candlestick, and walking in Golden Gate Park.

Then came Keller's notes.

FATHER: Mon to Fri, 6–6:30 a.m., goes downtown and catches CalTrain for Mountain View. Home by 7–9 p.m. MOTHER: 7 a.m., rises with A. Breakfast. Morning errands. Groceries on Thursday. Mon-Wed-Fri afternoon paints in studio loft while child is in local day care. WEEKENDS: SAT: father takes A on Sat. outing. Eves. parents go out and sitter watches A at Becker home. SUN: mother and child attend church in morn. AFT: all three go for excursion.

The notes were meticulous, his work precise. He had reaped success.

He had prepared, responded, and prevailed. He followed the signs and was rewarded.

Poor Nathan Becker. Surely, his heart was broken. But he had let Danny wander on the train that day, had rested in the devil's arms, cloaked in the shadow of a deadly sin: avarice. His failure to be vigilant over Danny was testament to the value he placed in his worldly pursuits. But that was not Keller's concern. His work was his concern. And so much remained.

The Angel would help him.

It was preordained. Raphael was his name.

Keller closed the binder and looked upon the Angel, shifting drowsily on his lap. He had arrived the same month Josh was born and was the same age as Josh when he was lost. Keller had recognized the signs. The Truth was revealed to him. His children were not dead. They were waiting to be reborn in celestial light.

Squeak-creak. Squeak creak.

Only God's Angels could rescue them, transfigure them.

Raphael was first. One of the Powers. Chief of the guardian angels. Guardian of mankind. Protector of children.

Keller reached for a second binder, a thick pink one bearing the title "Gabrielle Michelle Nunn/Alisha." He turned to a portrait of a six-year-old girl. Her shimmering chestnut hair was a halo in French braids. Her radiant eyes. Her emerald velvet dress, delicate lace trim ... "Alisha. My beautiful Alisha." Keller caressed the picture, sniffed, and turned to another birth announcement:

NUNN Paul and Nancy are thrilled to welcome their second bundle of joy, a little sister for Alexander. Gabrielle Michelle was born 4:12 p.m., April 12, weighing 6 lbs., 9 oz. Thanks to Dr. Cook and the nurses at Metro Hospital.

Gabrielle and the month were circled in red.

Gabrielle. Gabriel.

Gabriel. God's ambassador to the world. The Angel who heralded Christ's birth.

He had found Gabriel. He turned the page to a recent color photograph of Gabrielle Nunn smiling, soaring on a park swing near her home. He smiled back, then flipped to a picture of Gabrielle hugging her dog, Jackson. Opposite, was Jackson's missing-reward poster. Keller reached down to Jackson sitting at his feet, patted his head, and sighed as he flipped through pages of documents, detailed information, notes, and photographs of the Nunns and Gabrielle. She was going to turn six very soon. Alisha was six. Born in June.

It was time. It was time.

Keller closed the binder.

Long into the night he rocked with Danny Becker sleeping on his lap. Drifting to sleep himself, he recalled the lines of Doris White's long-forgotten poem, "My Angel." "Their coffins were opened and all were set free, behold my Angel with the jeweled key."

25

Sunrise. Fog shrouded the city.

Inspector Linda Turgeon came out of her neat house on upper Market and deposited herself into Sydowski's unmarked Caprice Classic.

"Good morning." She yawned, accepting the steaming 7-Eleven coffee cup he handed her. "Thanks."

"Sleep well?"

"Not a wink." She placed her copy of Perry William Kindhart's file with his on the seat between them.

Traffic was light on Market, which would take them directly to SoMa, Kindhart's most recent address.

"What's your take on Kindhart?" Sydowski said.

"He's our best potential connection to Donner. A molester who did time with Wallace in Virginia. We know Wallace did not act alone and that Kindhart was in San Francisco during the time of Donner's abduction and death."

"But in the picture, the hooded guy holding Donner has a tattoo. Kindhart doesn't."

"Mr. Tattoo is the only guy we know of, right now. Maybe others are involved. Maybe Kindhart had nothing to do with it, but he may know something. Like who the tattoo is. I think we'd be remiss if we didn't give Kindhart a good shake to see what falls out."

Sydowski nodded approvingly.

Turgeon was pleased. They were on the same frequency. Partners.

The fog was lifting when they glided into downtown. At the edge of the Tenderloin, the streets were strewn with used condoms and hypodermic needles. A few hookers were still working. One hiked her skirt, squatted, then urinated on the sidewalk at Market and Larkin.

"Will you look at that," Sydowski shook his head. "Somebody otta call a cop."

Turgeon burst out laughing. "So you do have a sense of humor," she said.

"Damn right. I'm a fun guy. Ask anybody."

"I did."

"Did a little background checking, did you?"

"Mm-mmm."

"What'd you come up with?"

"You live alone in Parkside. You raise birds. You've cleared more files than anyone else in the detail's history. You've refused promotions because the job's in your blood. The Donner case haunts you and you probably won't retire until you close it."

"Anything else?"

"People tell me you're an arrogant Polack hard-ass."

"I should put that on a T-shirt."

"They also say that after Brooks, you're the finest Homicide dick the Golden State's ever seen."

"I should put that on a T-shirt, to remind Leo."

"But there's a disturbing side to you I am curious about."

"I may take the Fifth, here."

"Is it true you killed a guy, shot him?"

Sydowski grew pensive. "It was during the war. I was a kid."

"What happened?"

He gazed out the driver's window. "I'll tell you another time?"

"Sure."

"What about you? I don't see a ring—you married?"

Turgeon peered into her coffee cup. "Came close."

"Yeah?"

"An architect."

"An architect?"

"Met him after his house in the Marina was burglarized."

"Thank God for criminals."

"We lived together for a year, talked about kids, the future. Everything was rosy. We set a date. You know the tune."

"This where the violins come in?"

"Wanted me to leave the job. It was too dangerous for him. He wanted me to quit the force, stay home, look after the cats. He was asking too much. To quit would be denying what I am."

"And what's that, Linda?"

She looked at him. "A cop. I'm a cop like you, Walter."

"Like your old man, you mean."

"Yeah. I mean, my biological clock is ticking down and I still want to get married, have kids. But it's just that when my dad was murdered, I vowed to be a cop and now I am one. I can't give it up."

They left it at that as they rolled into SoMa, South of Market.

"They used to call this 'south of the slot' for the cable car line that ran through here," Sydowski said.

"You're betraying your age, Walt."

"Used to be a helluva neighborhood."

SoMa was now the realm of machine shops, warehouses, Vietnamese restaurants, and gay bars. Latinos who fled Central

America's bloodbaths made their home here in decaying tene-
ment houses, which were the quarry of visionary developers
who bitched over cell phones about San Francisco's sunshine
codes and zoning laws. Red tape kept SoMa on life support.
They wanted to pronounce last rites.

Kindhart's building had risen from the rubble of the 1906
quake and fire, a small hotel that evolved into a bordello, a
shooting gallery, then a fleabag apartment complex. All it
offered now was a view of the James Lick Skyway, Interstate
80, the Bay Bridge, and Oakland.

Sydowski and Turgeon climbed the creaking stairs to the
third floor and pounded on Kindhart's door. It was 5:45 A.M.
No answer. Sydowski pounded again, harder.

"Mr. Kindhart?" he called loudly.

Sydowski continued pounding. Down the hall a door opened
and a one-armed man stepped from his apartment.

"Knock off the shit," he growled.

Sydowski flashed his shield. "Mind your own business."

"Fucking pigs." The man's door slammed.

Sydowski resumed pounding.

"Who the fuck is it?" a deep voice snarled from Kindhart's
unit.

"Police, Mr. Kindhart, we'd like to talk to you."

"Fuck off. I won't talk to you."

"We're investigating a case. Won't look good if you refuse
to cooperate, Mr. Kindhart."

There came a string of unintelligible cursing, a mattress
squeaked, empty bottles clinked, then more cursing, locks were
rattled, and the door opened. Shirtless, unshaven, and barefoot,
Kindhart stood just over six feet. His unbuttoned, torn Levi's
yielded to his pot belly. He held the door defensively, reeking
of alcohol, assessing Sydowski, then Turgeon.

"May we come in?" Sydowski said. "We'd like to talk to
you."

"What about?" One of Kindhart's lower front teeth was missing, the survivors were rotting.

"Franklin Wallace," Turgeon said.

"Franklin Wallace?" Kindhart scratched his whiskers. "Franklin Wallace?"

"Prison. Virginia. Think hard," Sydowski said.

Lying was futile. Kindhart surrendered his door, went to the kitchen of his studio apartment, put on a kettle for coffee, sat at his tiny kitchen table, and lit a Lucky Strike.

"Hurry it up, I gotta go to work." He exhaled, rubbing his eyes.

Turgeon looked around. Sydowski joined Kindhart at the table.

"What kind of job you have, Perry?"

"You know the fucking answer to that. So why are you here?"

A handful of pornographic magazines dropped on the table-top contained color pictures of naked children in obscene poses with men.

"This is a violation of your parole," Turgeon said.

"That's unlawful seizure, I know my fucking rights, hon."

"You have rights." Sydowski casually slipped on his bifocals, wet his thumb, and flipped leisurely through his notebook. "You're a carpenter's apprentice at Hunters Point, Perry?"

"What the fuck does that have to do with anything?"

"Work with lots of other guys, family men with children." Sydowski turned to Turgeon. "I think they'd understand the term 'predatory pedophile,' don't you, Inspector?"

"We could always show them a picture of one."

Sydowski smiled.

Kindhart's kettle piped. He made black coffee for himself only.

"Tell us about the last time you saw Wallace," Sydowski said.

"Why should I? You're just going to report me."

"We are going to report you, but whether we tell the judge you helped us with our investigation, or obstructed it, is up to you."

Kindhart squinted through a pall of smoke and slurped his coffee. "I shared a cell with Wallace in Virginia and looked him up when I got here. Being a Sunday school teacher he was plugged in, figured he could help me get a job. I saved his ass inside. He owed me."

"A real job, or something in the trade?" Turgeon asked.

"Look, I just take pictures, that's all I do."

"What about the three cousins, the little girls in Richmond, Virginia?" Turgeon said.

"I just took pictures. They wanted me to."

"And the two five-year-old girls last year in the Mission?"

"I told you I just take pictures when they want me to. They love to have their pictures taken. I don't date them like Wallace did. I don't know anything about that shit with that little Donner girl last year and why he offed himself. I had nothing to do with it."

"We never suggested you did," Sydowski said.

"Right. Like I don't know why you're here." Kindhart shook his head. "Ever since that boy got grabbed, it's been all over the news again. I just take pictures, that's all I do. I don't date them." Kindhart dragged hard on his cigarette, then pounded the magazines with his forefinger. "Besides, they're all little prostitutes anyway. They know exactly what they're doing. Always coming on to the people who know. Wallace and his friend had terrific insights into them."

"What's his friend's name?" Sydowski asked.

Kindhart shook his head and took a pull from his cigarette. "Only met him once or twice. I think he was from Montana or North Dakota. Some far-off place like that."

"Describe him."

"Describe him?"

"Race?"

"White. A white guy."

"Height?"

"Just under six, average."

"Age?"

"Late forties, I'd say."

"Anything specific you remember about him?"

"No . . ." Kindhart stubbed out his cigarette. "Yeah. Tattoos. He had tattoos. Snakes and fire, or something, here." Kindhart brushed his forearms.

"Where does he live? Where does he work?" Sydowski said.

"Don't know."

"How did you know him?"

"Through Wallace. He was Wallace's friend."

"He do time in Virginia, too?"

"I don't remember him, but he was a con."

"How do you know?"

"Walked the walk. Talked the talk."

"Where'd he do his time?"

Kindhart shrugged.

"Where'd you meet him?"

"Bookstore off Romolo. I was there with Wallace when he came in and they started talking."

"He like to date children?"

"Wallace said he did."

"Ever take his picture while he was on a date?"

"No fucking way. I hardly knew the guy."

Sydowski dropped a print of the Polaroid showing Tanita Marie Donner sitting on the lap of the hooded man with the tattoos. "Who's that man?" Sydowski asked.

Kindhart picked it up. Examined it, then put it down. "That's Wallace's friend."

"How do you know?"

"The tattoos."

"Who took that snapshot?"

Kindhart shrugged.

"You used a Polaroid last year with the little girls in the Mission, didn't you, Perry?"

Kindhart didn't remember.

"Tell you what"—Sydowski closed his notebook and smiled—"you better come over to the Hall with us while we get a warrant to tidy up your place here."

"I told you I had nothing to do with Wallace and that girl."

"I'm sure you're being truthful and won't mind telling us again after we wire you to a polygraph?"

"A fucking lie-detector?"

"You have a problem with that, Perry?" Sydowski asked.

"I want to call my lawyer."

Sydowski slowly folded his glasses, tucked them into his breast pocket, and stood. "You know what I find interesting?" He towered over Kindhart. "I find it interesting how an innocent man with nothing to hide never thinks of calling a lawyer. Now why would you need a lawyer, Perry?"

He didn't answer.

Sydowski leaned down and whispered into his ear: "Did Tanita Marie Donner get to call a lawyer?"

Kindhart said nothing.

"Did Danny Raphael Becker get to call a lawyer, Perry?"

Sydowski clamped his massive hand firmly around the back of Kindhart's neck and squeezed until it started hurting.

"Don't worry, *voychik*. You can talk to your lawyer about the big bad SFPD and your right to prey on children. And I'll talk to the construction workers at Hunters Point about baby fuckers, skinners, and all-round pieces of shit. Sound good?"

The gold in Sydowski's teeth glinted as he smiled. "Good. Now, if you don't mind. I think we should be on our way."

26

BOY'S ABDUCTION HAUNTS MOTHER OF KIDNAPPED-MURDERED
BABY GIRL

The head of *The San Francisco Star's* lead item skylined
above the fold across six columns, over a four-column color
shot of Angela Donner in Tanita Marie's room, hugging a
teddy bear. A large familiar poster of Tanita dominated the
background with REWARD emblazoned above Tanita's face.
"Murder" was, by chance, at Angela's eye level. Photos of
Tanita and Danny Becker accompanied the story by Tom Reed.
It began:

> Angela Donner can't stop her tears as she hugs her dead
> child's teddy bear and prays for Danny Becker who was
> abducted in the same area where her daughter Tanita
> Marie was kidnapped and later murdered a year ago.

> "I pray Danny Becker will come home alive, that his
> mom and dad won't have to go through what I've gone

through, and live with every day. And I pray my baby's
murderer is brought to justice." Angela, 21, cries softly
in the first interview she's given since her two-year-old
daughter's slaying shocked The City. . . .

Not bad, Reed thought, taking a hit of coffee at his desk in
the newsroom after reading his package of stories. His lead
piece turned to page two and keyed to his feature on Martin's
group, the anchor piece on the front of the Metro section.

He had beaten both the *Chronicle* and *Examiner*. Mixed with
the satisfaction of scooping the competition and owning today's
Star was Reed's sympathy for Angela Donner. She was an
obese, homely young woman who kept apologizing for her
home, a dilapidated apartment permeated with a pungent odor.
Her father was in his chair before a General Electric fan that
oscillated atop a TV supported by a wooden fruit crate. He was
shrouded in a white bedsheet. From time to time, his wrinkled
hand would slither from under it to gather ice chips from a
plastic bowl. His skeletal jaw worked slowly on the ice.

"Earth to Tom. Did you hear me?"

"Sorry. What?" Reed looked up from his paper and over
his computer terminal at Molly Wilson, typing feverishly.

"I said, how much longer are you going to admire your work?
You're worse than a summer cub with journalistic narcissism."

All morning, Reed had accepted compliments on his stories.

"You know," Wilson said, "I half expect you to start dusting
your awards and telling me about your glory days."

"This is how it is with us old guys, Molly. It's rare for us
to get it up. But when we do, the sensation is indescribable."

Wilson halted her typing. "I wouldn't know, Tom."

Reed turned to the Metro section and the feature on Martin's
group. Whatever was happening here with Wilson did not sit
right. What did she want? A relationship? Sex? It didn't matter.
"Ann and I are trying to get back together."

Wilson had a pen clamped in her teeth. She typed aggressively for several moments before removing it. "Would you go over this for me?" She was all business now.

Reed turned to his computer and called up her work on his screen.

"It's all the notes for my piece on the FBI's psychological profile of the guy who kidnapped Danny Becker," she said.

"When is it going?"

"Tomorrow. I just can't find a lead."

Wilson's notes were a transcription of her interview with FBI Special Agent Merle Rust. Reed caught phrases like: "Deeply scarred individual—traumatized by cataclysmic event involving children—lives in fantasy world—stimulated by alcohol, drugs or even religious delusions—appears normal—will most likely re-offend."

He chuckled. "Sounds like Ed Keller."

"Who?"

"One of the parents in the bereavement group. A religious nut I left out of my piece because he was a goof—" He touched a finger to a line on his screen. "Here's your lead."

Wilson glided around their workstation to join him as he typed: "Danny Becker's kidnapper is likely a psychologically traumatized man with the potential to abduct another child, says an FBI profile obtained by the *Star*, blah blah blah."

"That's it. Thanks." Wilson returned to her desk.

"Reed?"

It was Jebb Harker, the metro assignment editor. His tie was loosened, and he held a rolled paper in one hand. "You hear anything about a suspect being arrested this morning in the Becker case?"

"No. Nothing." Reed sat upright, concerned.

"Just got off the phone with Mumford in circulation. Seems this morning one of our drivers was filling a box near the Hall of Justice when he saw two plainclothes cops bring in a guy in cuffs."

"Big deal. They arrest people every day."

"The driver recognized one of the cops. Swears it was this guy."

Harker unfurled the newspaper to a small photo of an SFPD inspector talking to reporters on the steps of Danny Becker's Jordan Park home on the day Danny was abducted.

"Holy shit!" Wilson snatched the paper from Harker. "That's Walt Sydowski, one of the lead dicks on the Becker and Donner cases! Something must have popped. What do you think, Tom? Tom?"

Reed didn't hear her. He was at the far end of the newsroom, jabbing the elevator button.

The Hall of Justice on Bryant Street had a polished stone lobby and a metal detector all visitors must pass through. Fucking Checkpoint Charlie, Reed thought, grabbing his keys from the basket once he was cleared. He caught the UP elevator as its doors were closing, ascended to the fourth floor and Room 450, the Homicide Detail, nearly bumping into Inspector Swanson Smith, a soft-spoken man of linebacker proportions, who glared at him from the file he was studying.

"I ain't buyin' no damn subscription today, Reed."

"I came to buy you coffee."

"Get your damn nose out of my ass, I'm too busy for sex."

"Sydowski in?"

"Why would you insult a great man like that with your presence?"

Reed said nothing.

"Cool your engines, newsman." Smith turned to summon Sydowski, his handcuffs knocking against the beeper clipped to his hip.

Reed sat, bouncing his knee. Come on. Come on.

Sydowski appeared, a file in his hand.

Reed was relieved to see him. "Inspector. Did you bring somebody to the hall this morning in cuffs?"

"Yes."

"You did?" Reed opened his notebook. "For Becker or Donner?"

"Those are the priority files right now."

"Is that a yes, Inspector?"

"Thomas, put your notebook away."

"Why?"

"Because I want to explain something to you."

"I don't want to hear anything I can't use."

"Well you better leave then. It's up to you."

Reed stared at him. "All right," he said, tucking his notebook in his jacket. "Probably going to see it in the *Chronicle* or *Examiner,* anyway. Seems every time I play by the rules, I get screwed."

"You've got one hell of an attitude," Sydowski said.

"Wonder how I got it."

"Sit down." Sydowski nodded to the wooden chairs lining the detail's small reception area. "We brought a guy in this morning who we think may have known somebody we remotely suspect in one of the files. That's all I can tell you. Sit tight, we may have more later."

"Sure, I'll read all about it in the *Chronicle* or *Examiner.*"

"I don't have time for your wounded pride."

"The shit I went through over Wallace was a little more than wounded pride, Walt."

"Nothing I can do about history."

"You know I was right about Wallace."

"Maybe. Maybe not. You fucked up, *voychik.* Using me as confirmation when I didn't give you anything. I told you to sit on what you had. Going to Wallace with your tip before we could talk to him so he could do himself, do you know what that cost us?"

"Do you know what it cost me?"

"Your problem is, you're too stupid to realize when someone is being nice to you."

"And you can't stand it when someone like me digs something up. Let's talk about wounded pride. Yours."

Sydowski stood. "Look, I've got one murdered child, maybe two." He bent down, his face so close Reed could smell the coffee and garlic on his breath. "You better quit playing amateur detective and stay the fuck out of my way, understand?"

"Thanks for all your help, Walt," Reed stood. "Next time I get a piece of information about a case, I'll wipe my ass with it."

Reed slammed the door behind him, thumbed the elevator button with all of his weight, then snapped through his notebook for a clean page. Calm down, he told himself. Okay, he could try a few other sources. Sure. He had so many these days. Damn it, what was he going to write? That they brought in a guy they think may know a suspect. It was thin.

While searching his notebook for an answer, anything, Reed saw his notes from Martin's bereavement group. Edward Keller's stuff.

". . . Zoran. A watery death . . . I was being punished for living a lie . . . When my children died, I died but was born again . . . The revelation . . . The Divine Truth . . . I will be with my children again . . . You can only rescue them if you truly believe you can . . . Every day I prepare for my blessed reunion . . . I've read your stories about Danny Becker . . ."

The FBI's profile, "traumatized by cataclysmic event involving children . . . stimulated by . . . religious delusion" fit Keller like a glove.

Yes it did. But why did he have such a weird feeling about Keller? He did fit the general description of Danny Becker's kidnapper, but so did thousands of bearded Caucasians in the Bay Area. But why couldn't he find any old stories about Keller's case in the news library? Not one. He went back ten years. It was puzzling that he couldn't find a single item about a businessman losing his three children in a boating accident near the Farallons. Maybe he missed it? He should look again. Maybe use the Net.

Outside, on the steps of the hall, Reed thought he'd better cool the Keller theory. Get a grip. He would never admit that in a dark corner of his heart he nurtured doubts that Franklin Wallace was Tanita Donner's killer. Now, in the span of minutes, he'd got some poor grief-stricken born-again pegged as a child-killer. Why?

Because he loathed religious extremists? Or was it the gleam of self-righteousness in Keller's eyes? Because he was pissed at Sydowski? Because he was anxious about getting back together with Ann? Who knew? But there was something about Keller. Reed wondered about Keller's story. Was his tragedy true? Why would he lie about it? If it was true, it would make a great read, especially with the anniversary of the drownings coming up. Sliding behind the wheel of his Comet, studying his notes, Reed decided to do some discreet digging on Keller, to see where it went.

27

Padding to the porch for her morning paper, Nancy Nunn looked for Jackson. Where was that dog? Reaching for her paper, she surveyed the street for her five-year-old daughter's cocker spaniel, hoping to spot him, snout to the ground, sniffing his way home. Gabrielle yearned for him. She and Jackson had been inseparable since the Christmas morning she found the blond, long-eared pup under the tree. Then one night last month he vanished from the backyard.

Gabrielle was shattered.

The next day the family plastered missing-reward posters throughout the neighborhood. Nancy and Ryan, Gabrielle's older brother, knocked on doors. Paul, Gabrielle's dad, drove for blocks, with Gabrielle calling for Jackson from the car. Where was Jackson? Paul was not convinced he ran off. But what else could have happened? Whatever, it didn't matter. They had to do something. Certain Jackson was not coming back, Nancy and Paul planned to surprise Gabrielle with a new pup for her sixth birthday in two weeks.

No fog this morning.

Nancy checked the street once more for Jackson, groaning at *The San Francisco Star's* headline. It was CHILD ABDUCTOR MAY STRIKE AGAIN, FBI FEARS with the kicker, "Man Who Took Danny Psychologically Scarred." She bolted her door and went to the kitchen.

Nancy rarely read news stories. Taking care of her husband, a firefighter, and their two children while holding down a part-time job left her no time to digest the pound of information slapped on her doorstep each morning. She took the *Star* for the coupons.

Danny Becker's kidnapping had made Nancy vigilant, especially when Paul was at work. She looked in on Gabrielle and Ryan frequently while they slept, rechecked the locks of their house, reminding herself the Sunset was a safe neighborhood, the best place in the city to raise kids. She was coping as rationally as could be expected, remembering how earlier, talking to Paul about it, she sought something positive in Danny Becker's abduction.

"Maybe now police will catch the killer. Maybe this new case gives them a lead and they'll find Danny safe."

"Police?" Paul scoffed. "Like with the Zodiac, Nance? The cops never caught him. Don't hold your breath for the police to stop this guy. A .45 in the head is what it's going to take. And it won't come from the cops, it'll be some kid's old man."

Nancy was grateful Paul restrained himself from displaying his Remington, out of respect for her abhorrence of guns. While the Sunset was largely unscathed by crime, she now found comfort in the fact her husband, a former U.S. Marine sergeant, still kept his gun.

This morning, in her kitchen, Nancy read the latest news about the abduction. Offer more reward money, she thought. Somebody in this city knows where Danny Becker is.

The kitchen phone rang. She got it.

"Hey there, Nance!" Wendy Sloane, her neighbor and best friend.

"Hey yourself."

"They still haven't caught the creep yet. The *Chron* figures he's a parolee from a prison for child molesters. What's the *Star* say?"

"He's playing some kind of fantasy in his head and he'll strike again. Hi, handsome." Ryan, Gabrielle's eight-year-old brother, came yawning into the kitchen, pajama clad, and hugged her. "Can you start your own breakfast while Mom's on the phone?"

He pulled a box of cornflakes from the cupboard.

"Paul home?" Wendy asked.

"No. He's working. What are your two up to, with no school today?"

Wendy had two girls. Charlotte was nine and Elaine was seven.

"Fretting about the birthday parties coming up. Joannie Tyson's is in a few days and then Gabrielle's. They're excited about Gabrielle's because they think she is prettier than Joannie and Joannie's party is going to be so big."

"Lady, your daughters are cruel."

"They're running around deeply concerned about what to wear and who's going to be there to impress."

"You're raising a pair of debs. How proud you must be."

Both women laughed.

"Nancy, you're still taking Gabrielle to Joannie's party, right? You're not going to overreact to this kidnapping crap?"

"I considered not going, but I don't want to scare the kids. Besides it would be rude not to go to Joannie's party, then expect her to come to Gabrielle's."

"There you go, girl."

Nancy could hear Wendy's smile and it warmed her to know

they were friends. They had met at the Better Food Value Mart in Stonestown, where they were part-time cashiers. When they learned they lived near each other in the Sunset, they became pals. Wendy was a big-hearted Texan from Austin who adored country music and joked about writing her own tune, "Livin' 'n' Lovin' in the Fogbelt." Her husband, Rod, was a welder who drank a bit. But he did have two saving graces. He brought home a regular paycheck and he could two-step. "I'll hang on to him. Until a better dancer with a bigger paycheck comes along."

Nancy and Wendy chatted every day on the phone and routinely packed juice, snacks, a thermos of coffee, the kids, and walked the few blocks to the playground between Moraga and Lawton. They gossiped while their children played. Today was a playground day.

"Meet you there in an hour," Nancy said.

"You got it."

"Wendy . . . ?"

"Yes?"

"Bring your copy of today's *Chronicle?*"

"Oh, you old worrywart! Sure, I'll bring it."

Don't give in to a siege mentality, Nancy told herself. Be realistic. Keep an eye on Gabrielle and Ryan. That's all she had to do.

In the living room, Nancy inspected the new flower-print dress she had made for Gabrielle's birthday party. She stayed up late to finish it. It was draped over a sofa chair. Tracing her fingers over her fine needlework, she smiled, then returned to the kitchen where Ryan was starting on a second bowl of cornflakes.

"Can I join scouts today, Mom?"

"We'll talk about it later, okay? Get dressed when you're done. We're going to the playground." She kissed the top of Ryan's head.

After showering, Nancy slipped on a pair of old Levi's and a Blue Jays T-shirt. She pulled her hair back into a ponytail while her full-length mirror reflected a figure women envied and men enjoyed.

Gabrielle's room was the freshest smelling room in the house. At times Nancy was certain she detected the lingering fragrance of baby powder. Were her senses deceiving her? Or, was it merely part of the bittersweet experience of watching her daughter grow up, knowing that one day she would be gone? Nearly six years old and already peering over the edge of the nest. Recently, a poster of Leonardo DiCaprio had replaced one of Big Bird. Taped to the wall above Gabrielle's nightstand was a snapshot of her hugging Jackson. It broke Nancy's heart.

Sensing a presence, Gabrielle stirred, then woke.

"Hi, sleepyhead."

Gabrielle rubbed her eyes.

"Time to get up. We're going to the playground."

"Know what, mom?"

"What?"

"I dreamed Jackson was in my bed, licking my face!"

"You'll always have him in your dreams, sweetheart."

"I know. But it's not the same as for real."

"We're going to see Letty and Elaine, so rise and shine."

Wendy waved from their usual park bench. "Good morning, Nunns!"

The children called to each other.

"Boy, the joint's jumping this morning." Nancy deposited herself beside her friend and unscrewed the coffee thermos. "I remember the days when we used to have the place to ourselves."

"You sound like an old bag lady."

The children scampered to the swings. Charlotte, Gabrielle, and Elaine held hands. Ryan trotted behind them. The women enjoyed their coffee and watched a pair of teenage lovebirds snuggling on a bench to their left. A few yards away, on a tattered blanket under a tree, a scrawny man wearing wire-rimmed glasses, a Haight castaway, was reading. To their right, a bearded man in sunglasses and a fedora sat alone with his newspaper. He caught Nancy's glance, and nodded. She smiled back. She didn't know him. He went back to his newspaper, which reminded her of something.

"Did you bring your *Chronicle?*"

Wendy produced her rolled edition from her bag.

Nancy began reading, gasping at the speculation that Danny Becker's kidnapper was a paroled pervert. She slapped the paper on the bench, looked over at Ryan and Gabrielle. If anything ever happened to them, it would kill her.

"How can you be so calm about it?"

"Look at it logically. A zillion people live in the Bay Area. Look at the odds. You'd win the lottery before this guy came after your kids."

Nancy considered it. "What would I do without your Texas common sense?"

"You'd go crackbrained and lock yourself up with the kids. Oprah would do a live show on your lawn. 'Mrs. Nunn, it's been twenty years since the Bay Beast last struck—are you willing to let your grown children out of the house now?'"

They laughed, poured more coffee, then discussed Joannie Tyson's seventh birthday party at the Children's Playground in Golden Gate Park. Of all places, they groaned. Well, it was a huge park and still a beautiful choice for a little girl's giant birthday party, they agreed. Thirty kids. Wendy was saying something about Joannie's mom going overboard when they heard the scream. A child's scream. They took instant head counts. All children were accounted for. All standing. None bleeding. Gabrielle was screaming. Nancy caught her breath, realizing Gabrielle was not hurt.

"A puppy! A puppy! Look, Mommy, a puppy, just like Jackson!"

A teenage girl with a cocker spaniel tugging at a leash in front of her rushed near them. Gabrielle was poised to run to the dog.

The bearded man on the bench to their right looked up from his newspaper at Nancy calming her daughter.

"Shh-shh, honey. He's a nice puppy, just like Jackson, but he's not Jackson. You have to try to stop thinking about him. It's hard, but you have to try."

Nancy arched an eyebrow, a signal for Wendy's help.

"Tell me, princess," Wendy chirped, "are you all set for Joannie's monster birthday party?"

Gabrielle's fawn eyes could melt an iceberg. "Letty and Elaine and me are going to ride the carousel and have birthday cake."

Gabrielle then skipped back to the others.

"Thanks, pal." Nancy slapped Wendy's shoulder.

"What are you guys going to do about her puppy-dog blues?"

"We're surprising her with a new pup on her birthday."

"Might be the cure."

As they talked, the bearded man eavesdropped, appearing to be completing the crossword puzzle of his carefully folded newspaper. In fact, he was making notes—notes about Gabrielle Nunn, who would be six soon, about Jackson, her missing cocker spaniel, and Joannie Tyson's upcoming birthday party at Golden Gate Park. It would be a large party with thirty children. Chaos. The man made precise notes about the time and location.

Then Edward Keller put the pencil stub in his breast pocket. He loved today's news, the part about religious delusions. How could mortals distinguish between delusion and divine revelation? Keller strolled from the playground, tapping his folded newspaper against his leg. Behind him he heard the Angel Gabriel's laughter and he was bathed in the light of truth.

Sanctus, sanctus, sanctus. Dominus Deus sabaoth.

Keller praised God for his help.

28

Gabrielle Nunn joined the chorus of shrieking girls spinning in the tub of the carousel. Its ancient organ huffed a mazurka and Gabrielle was the happiest she had been in weeks, almost forgetting that her dog Jackson had disappeared.

It was Saturday. Joannie Tyson's seventh birthday party at the Children's Playground in Golden Gate Park. A monster bash. Thirty-two kids. A tiny Be-In. The summer of cake and ice cream.

Gabrielle was wearing the flowered print dress her mother made especially for her sixth birthday, a few days away, but Gabrielle had pleaded to wear it today. Her mother gave in. Then Nancy Nunn plaited her daughter's auburn hair into French braids, Gabrielle's favorite. Now, whirling and laughing with her friends Tracey Tanner, Millie Palmer, and Rhonda King, whom everybody called Help-Me Rhonda, Gabrielle was having a perfect day.

A dream day.

Round and round she went. Her stomach tingling as if an

ecstatic butterfly were fluttering inside. She wanted to ride the carousel forever. But when they finished their third successive tour, Nancy Nunn, who was watching the girls, feared a fourth ride would be risky, given the amount of cake and ice cream they downed earlier.

"Can we catch up with the others now?" Millie Palmer asked.

Between the cake eating and the present opening, the party had separated into small groups, each chaperoned by an adult. Some had gone to the Troll Bridge, some to the Mouse Tower. Wendy Sloane had taken Letty, Elaine, and three other girls to the Farmyard.

"Can we go to the Mouse Tower, Mrs. Nunn?" Tracey Tanner asked.

"No, the Farmyard!" Rhonda King said.

"Before we go anywhere, ladies, who has to go to the washroom?"

Millie and Rhonda shot up their hands.

Nancy herded her foursome to the nearest washroom. Millie and Rhonda each found a stall. Nancy put Gabrielle and Tracey before the mirrors to check their hair. Soon Millie came out of her stall to wash her hands. Minutes passed. Rhonda was taking a long time.

"Rhonda?" Nancy called, trying the stall door. It was locked.

"Oh, Mrs. Nunn, I don't feel good," Rhonda moaned. The other girls looked at each other. "I feel like I'm going to—"

Rhonda retched and vomited. The girls grimaced.

Rhonda coughed violently.

At Nancy's insistence, Millie, the group's smallest member, scooted under the stall and unlocked the door. Rhonda was on the toilet in tears, her panties around her ankles. Humiliated. Nancy held her trembling hand, dabbed her tears with a crumpled tissue, brushed her hair from her eyes.

"Oh, sweetheart, don't worry."

"Gross," Tracey said.

"It's going to be fine, dear," Nancy assured Rhonda. "Tracey, please get me some paper towels soaked in cold water and some dry ones. Girls, stay by me while we help Rhonda."

"But Mom, it's so gross!" Gabrielle complained.

"Stay here, Gabrielle," Nancy ordered over her shoulder while helping Rhonda pull up her underwear. "Rhonda sweetie, this happens to every little girl, so don't you worry."

Tracey gave Nancy the paper towels. None of the girls teased Rhonda about her nickname as Nancy cleaned her up. They stood by for support, except for Gabrielle. The acrid odor overwhelmed her.

Gabrielle did not want to be sick herself. Lured by the carousel's organ puffing a new polka, she took it upon herself to wait outside the washroom. She stood alone, watching the revolving animals, the dreamy horses, the chariots, the rocker, the turning tub. Mom should be pleased. After all, she was a big girl. A smile was blooming on Gabrielle's face when suddenly a shadow fell over her.

"You are Gabrielle?"

A tall man with a beard, dark glasses, and a ball cap smiled down at her. She didn't know him, but he had a friendly, soft voice. Had to be one of the dads for the party, she guessed.

"You are Gabrielle Nunn whose dad is Paul, a firefighter, and your mom is Nancy."

Gabrielle didn't realize she was nodding.

"Let's talk over here." The man took her aside, glancing at the snapshot in his hand, giving it to her. "This would be your pup?"

Gabrielle's eyes widened and her jaw dropped open.

"Yes! It's my dog, Jackson! Where is he?"

"In my truck." The man nodded down the hill toward the parking lot. "Your folks wanted me to bring him to you for your birthday surprise. Happy birthday, Gabrielle."

"But it's Joannie's birthday today. Mine is in a few days."

"Boy did I mess up. I'm sorry, Gabrielle. Please don't tell

anybody. Please." He looked around. Everyone near them was watching the carousel. "I gotta go before anyone sees me," he said, holding out his hand for the snapshot.

"Gabrielle!" her mother called from the washroom.

"Just waiting by the door, Mom. I feel better here."

Gabrielle pulled the picture to her chest.

She was disarmed. Whatever innate shield she had against strangers evaporated as she thrilled not with doubt but delight in the belief Jackson was nearby. If she could just hold him again.

"Wait, mister. Can't I just see him? Please?"

The man rubbed his beard thoughtfully.

"I won't tell anybody. I promise. Please."

"Just a quick secret peek?"

"Yes. A secret peek."

"Gabrielle!" Her mother's voice echoed from the washroom along with Rhonda's whimpering.

"I'm okay, Mom, I'm just waiting outside the door!" Gabrielle called. Then to the man she whispered breathlessly: "Oh please, let's hurry!"

"Okay. Count to ten, then follow me quickly to my truck. Don't let anybody see you. Just a quick, secret peek."

The man walked away.

Counting to ten, Gabrielle heard Rhonda retch. Her mother was going to take forever in there. She could cuddle Jackson in secret and be back before her mother missed her, if she hurried.

Gabrielle followed the man from the carousel, down the hill to the parking lot.

29

Behold the Seraph's face.

The Angel appeared in the distance. A celestial vision.

Edward Keller stood at his truck, the driver's door open, Gabriel nearing him. Smiling. Empowered by God. The Angel-child. Immortal. All-knowing. Radiant with the glory and the calm.

I am cleansed in the light of the Lord!

Keller was overcome, blinking back tears.

From inside the truck's cab, Jackson saw Gabrielle approaching and barked. The rope around his neck was knotted to the passenger door's arm rest. Keller had long ago removed the door's inside handle and lock button. The passenger door could not be opened from the inside.

Gabrielle ran to the truck.

Keller stepped aside, leaving a clear path to Jackson.

Gabrielle hesitated, a tiny wave of unease rippling through her. She wanted to hold Jackson so badly it hurt, yet something was out of place. She didn't know what it was. Like the time she glimpsed a solitary tuft of black mingled with Santa's white hair at the Stonestown Mall. She didn't know what to do, so she kept it secret. What about now? She was not worried about the kidnapper, like her mom, because this man was her dad's friend. She was sure about that because Jackson was right there. She just didn't want to get the man, or herself, in trouble. She glanced back at the carousel.

"Maybe I should tell my mom?"

"I suppose, but it would ruin the surprise."

Jackson yapped, and wagged his tail. He was so cute.

"My other door's broken there. Won't open. Go on in this way and see your pup. Never seen a dog in a more fierce need of a hug."

Jackson panted, moving as close to her as the rope permitted.

"Okay, a quick hug, then I'll go back and keep it secret."

She crawled into the cab along the bench seat and embraced Jackson, nuzzling his face, giggling as he licked hers.

"I missed you so much. You naughty doggie running away from me!"

Leaving the door open, Keller slipped in behind the wheel, and casually kneaded the dog's neck.

"My name's Ned Jenkins. I live on the other side of the park. I found your little fella in my garage the other day."

"In your garage?"

"Yes ma'am. Seems he got himself pinned under a pile of junk. Luckily there was a big old bag of dog cereal I had left there. My old dog Fred died awhile ago." Keller saw little traffic in this corner of the lot. "This fella's got lots of spark. He tore into the cereal, kept himself alive. Seems like a real nice little guy and he's no worse for wear."

Gabrielle gave Jackson a bone-crushing hug.

"Thanks for letting me in on the surprise, Mr. Jenkins. I better get back now. It's going to be hard waiting for my birthday, but I promise to keep our secret."

Keller didn't move. He produced a worn copy of Jackson's missing-reward poster the Nunns had put up weeks ago.

"Your notice here says there's a reward?"

"Yes. Fifty dollars. It's at home at my house."

Keller thought. "Well since Jackson's return is no surprise anymore I might as well get my reward. What the heck?"

Gabrielle didn't understand.

"But it's at my house and Dad and Ryan went to Coit Tower."

"I'm sorry, Gabrielle, I forgot to tell you that your dad was meeting me at your house. I told you I know him from the station."

But wasn't this supposed to stay a surprise?

"Look, we'll drive to your place, tell your dad about my screwup. It will be all right, don't worry. Paul will get a laugh, I'm always messing up at the station. Then I'll get my reward and your dad will drive you back to the party here."

Gabrielle looked toward the carousel.

"You were telling the truth about the reward, weren't you?"

She nodded, hugging Jackson to her chest.

"I want to pick it up now because I'm going out of town on business tonight and I'll be gone for a long time."

Keller slammed his door, started the engine, surprising Gabrielle, flooding her mind with confusion. Before she knew what was happening, the truck rolled out of the lot and down Kezar Drive.

"This will only take a second. You're safe with me."

"But I just don't know." In a whisper, more to herself than to Keller, Gabrielle said, "I don't want to get into trouble." She buried her face in Jackson's neck, squeezing him until he yelped. She caressed him as they left Golden Gate Park.

I don't want to get into trouble.

30

"Gabrielle!"

All the saliva in Nancy Nunn's mouth dried up as fear slithered down her throat.

"*GABRIELLE!*"

Nancy came out of the washroom with Rhonda, Tracey, and Millie expecting to find Gabrielle at the entrance. But she wasn't there. She was gone.

Again Nancy took a speed-of-light inventory of the area. No sign of Gabrielle. Nothing.

"Maybe she went to the Troll Bridge, Mrs. Nunn?" Tracey said.

"Maybe she went to see the others?" Millie said.

Not my kid. My kid knows better to wander from me like this.

Nancy grabbed Millie's hand, then Rhonda's. She made Tracey jump when she ordered her to take Rhonda's free hand. Nancy's terrified heart was on the verge of bursting through her chest. She scoured the carousel. The organ was playing a funeral march, the revolving animals mocking her with accusing silence.

Why weren't you watching your child?

"Mrs. Nunn, you're squeezing my hand too tight. It hurts!"

Nancy questioned people nearby. "Have you seen a little girl in a flowered dress?"

Puzzled stares. Heads shaking.

"She was standing here! You must have seen her!"

Eyes stared at her as if she were insane.

"My little girl is missing, somebody help me please!"

"Nancy, what's going on?" It was Wendy Sloane. Worried. Her group of girls huddled around Nancy and the others. Smiles dying on their faces.

"Nancy!"

"G-Gabrielle's gone."

"What?"

"She's missing. We were in the washroom together. She wandered out ahead of us. A few seconds ahead. She's gone. Wendy, I don't know—"

"Nancy, she can't have gone far."

"I-I don't . . . I should have been watching. If anything. Oh God."

"Stop it." Wendy grabbed Nancy's shoulders. "We'll find—"

Two teenage girls stood awkwardly next to Nancy, uncomfortable, not comprehending exactly what was happening.

"We saw a little girl in a flowered dress near the washroom."

"Where is she?" Nancy barked.

One of the girls flinched.

"She was talking to a man—"

Nancy's stomach heaved. "Where did she go! Where!"

"Well, I think—"

"Hurry up!" Nancy's voice was breaking.

"The man went that way." One of the girl's pointed toward

the parking lot. "Then the little girl followed him. Two minutes ago."

Nancy jumped as if something had exploded under her feet, running to the parking lot. Breathless, she went to the first person she saw in the lot. A man wearing a green John Deere ball cap, in his early seventies, was shutting the driver's door on his camper.

"Please help me. My little girl's missing. She came this way, wearing a flowered dress. Have you seen her?"

"I don't think so. We just got here, right, Mother?"

Seeing Nancy distraught, the white-haired woman on the other side of the camper approached her and took her arm.

"What's wrong, dear?"

"My daughter's been abducted. A man led her this way a few minutes ago. Oh, help me."

"Arthur, quick, find a policeman!"

The man headed dutifully to a pay phone.

Nancy searched parked cars, frantically screaming Gabrielle's name. The woman followed helplessly. Across the lot, a tall, well-dressed man stepped from a Mercedes and jogged to Nancy.

"Lady, what's wrong?"

"My daughter's been abducted by a man who brought her this way. Please, have you seen her!"

"I did see a little girl walking around here a few minutes ago."

"Yes!"

"Hair braided, her dress kind of pinkish?"

"That's her! Where did she go? Tell me, please!"

He looked intently over Nancy's head at the lot and Kezar Drive. He had been in his car, talking business over his phone.

"I saw the girl talking to a man at a battered old pickup truck. There was a little blond dog inside the truck."

"What?"

Nancy covered her mouth with both hands, her mind reeling

with a thousand horrors. Jackson. Jackson was a little blond dog. Remembering Paul believing Jackson didn't run away. Somebody stole him. I don't know why but I know for damn sure he didn't run away.

Apprehension swept over the man's face as he steeled himself.

"She got into the truck with the man and he drove off."

Nancy's head spun. The woman caught her, steadying her.

The man realized he could do something. "I've got a phone, I'll call 9-1-1! I'll drive around after the truck, lady, wait here!"

Nancy fell to her knees, seeing nothing, hearing nothing, feeling nothing, not even the strange older woman whose strong arms held her so tightly they kept her from falling off the earth.

31

Standing at the living room window of her stucco bungalow, Eva Blair was curious about the strange truck that had stopped in front of the Walker place across the street. Nobody got out of the truck. The engine was idling. Looked like a man and— Eva could just make out a little head—a child. A bearded man talking, no, arguing, with a child. It was none of her business. She was being an old busybody.

But something strange was going on.

Eva could just make out part of the truck's rear plate. California. "B" or "8" or "E." It was a battered old pickup. A Ford, according to the tailgate. The man seemed angry. There was a glint of metal in the cab. A knife? Did the man have a knife? Goodness! What in the world was he doing? Now he was tossing something out the window. She should call the police. The truck was filthy, neglected, a disgrace.

The engine growled and the truck sped away.

An ominous feeling came over Eva and she decided, for good measure, to jot down what she could remember of the truck. She slipped on her bifocals, left her house by the front door, and started across the street toward the spot where the truck had stopped. Something was on the sidewalk.

Eva gasped. A mound. A small fluffy, heap of ... hair. Human hair, beautiful chestnut hair. She bent over to examine it closely, gasping before hurrying back to her house to call the police.

The hair was dotted with fresh blood.

32

God be praised.

Keller had left Golden Gate Park without a hitch. Gabrielle was as quiet as a lamb, hugging her pathetic mutt.

"You are a radiant Angel." He could not take his eyes from her.

"Thank you, Mr. Jenkins."

Keller had been checking his rearview mirror every few seconds since they left the park. No hint of trouble. Time to shift things into higher gear. "Say, Gabrielle, it's pretty hot. Want a soda?"

"Yes, please!"

Keller fished through a canvass knapsack behind the seat, producing a can. "I'll open it for you."

"Thank you." Gabrielle took the can from him, gulped a huge swallow. It was cold. She let Jackson lick some from her hand. "Bad doggie." She wagged a warning finger at him. "Don't you ever run away from me again!"

"I bet you believe in God, say your prayers every night?"

She nodded as the truck jerked over a pothole.

"Goodness. You spilled some on your dress. We'll have to stop so I can clean it for you."

Gabrielle looked at her dress and saw no stain. "I don't think I spilled any, Mr. Jenkins."

"Yes, you did. I'll get it for you, as soon as I find a safe place to stop. Up there looks good."

Keller spotted a house with a FOR SALE sign. It looked empty. Neighborhood was quiet. He had to do this now, couldn't wait any longer. It was still several miles to Wintergreen Heights. He stopped in front of the house and left the engine running.

"I really didn't spill any, Mr. Jenkins. Honest. I looked."

"You spilled some down your chin." Keller grunted, reaching into the knapsack and pulling out a plastic bag with a damp face cloth inside, reeking of medicine.

Gabrielle touched her chin. It was dry, but before she could do anything, the stinky wet cloth was over her mouth, forcing her to breathe through her nose. She struggled, kicked, and tried to scream. Jackson barked. Gabrielle dropped her Coke. It spilled and hissed on the floor. Keller held the cloth firmly against her face, staring into her fluttering eyes as she fell asleep.

Jackson barked fiercely.

"Shut up!" Keller said, removing Gabrielle's dress and leotards, stuffing them into the knapsack. Rummaging in the pack, he pulled out a pair of child's shorts and a Forty-niners' T-shirt. In seconds, he had slipped them on Gabrielle, along with a ball cap.

Then he pulled a pair of scissors from the knapsack, leaned Gabrielle forward, and began snipping off her chestnut braids.

The dog growled, leaping at Keller, biting at his hands. Damn! Keller caught his forefinger between the razor-sharp blades, and most of the hair in his hand went out the window. The wound was deep.

Damn it!

At that instant, Keller saw an old woman watching from her living room window. What did she see?

Keller stomped on the gas, the engine roared, tires peeled, stones flew in anger. How could he have been so careless! He pounded the steering wheel, driving his rage like a rocket. Try to relax.

His heart thumped. It was happening. As it had been prophesied. To the ignorant, the girl was a little boy who'd fallen asleep. But he knew the truth. The Divine Truth.

Slow down to the limit before you attract more attention, he told himself. Come on. The old woman saw nothing. What was there to see from her angle across the wide street? Nothing. She saw nothing: a man stopping to look at a house that was for sale. Nothing.

But the hair? What if she called the police?

Was he doubting his mission? His revelation?

He was cleansed in the light of the Lord. He must never cease believing he was blessed. That's right. He had put more than a dozen blocks behind him now and was beginning to relax, focusing on his route to Wintergreen. The Angel was sleeping. Good. Keller looked at the dog. The mutt could lead the police to him. He could sacrifice it with the scissors. He could do it right now. He could pull into a back alley. It would take three seconds, then he—

Traffic had come to a dead halt. The rear bumper of the Honda in front of Keller rushed at him. He hit the brakes in time to avoid crashing. The two lanes ahead were merging into one. Cars inching along. What was happening? He saw a flash of red emergency lights.

Police! A roadblock?

Keller's tongue swelled. He began sweating. The rearview mirror reflected a clogged river of vehicles, a virtual parking lot. He could try escaping by driving along the sidewalk. No, that would guarantee a pursuit.

He was trapped. Keller squeezed the wheel. No. Not this way.

You promised to help me. Do not forsake me.

The Angel was sleeping.

"Got the number two song in the Bay Area coming up, but this just in from the newsroom." The radio in the convertible VW Golf creeping alongside Keller was cranked to distortion. The young redhead alone behind the wheel was oblivious as she puffed on her cigarette. "A five-year-old girl was reportedly abducted less than thirty minutes ago from the children's playground at Golden Park. Her name is Gabrielle Nunn. She has brown, braided hair and is wearing a flowered dress. Police say she may have been taken by a man." The radio faded away.

No. Not this way. Stay calm. He reached under the seat between his legs for the Smith & Wesson, purchased last year from a crack dealer in the Mission.

Numbers filed. Untraceable, like the wind, my man. Two C's.

Keller slipped the gun casually under his left leg. He thought of the phony license he got on the street, along with fake birth certificates, credit cards, library cards. When he required it, he could be anybody he wanted. God will provide, his father would say.

Ahead, a charter bus belched black smoke, its big diesel rattled as it crawled, clearing a line of sight. Keller first saw an SFPD black-and-white blocking one lane, then another. Then the ambulance and a mangled car flipped on its roof. He saw the firefighters with the jaws of life clattering like a ravenous metal-eater to get at the bloodied person trapped inside. An accident. Okay. Keller sighed.

Suddenly a cop stood before him on the road, directing traffic.

"You!" The officer pointed at him. His motorcycle was nearby. A Harley Davidson. Impossible to outrun. He was an imposing traffic bull in dark aviator glasses, leather jacket,

leather boots, and a leather utility belt with a holstered gun.
"Hold it right there!"

Keller eyed the officer as he approached.

Not this way. He refused to let it end here. He felt the hard
barrel of the gun under his leg, and kept both hands on the
wheel. The cop made leathery squeaks as he walked. His stern
face telegraphed a clear message: Do not fuck with me, sir.

The dog barked and Gabrielle stirred. Her eyelids flickered.
Do not forsake me. A droplet of sweat rolled down Keller's
back between his shoulder blades.

"What's the problem, officer?"

"Sir, are you aware your left front tire is underinflated?"

"No, I wasn't aware."

Just then the officer's portable radio crackled with something
unclear. He snatched it, and requested a repeat of the transmission. Keller slid his hand under his left leg, fingering the gun.

I am cleansed in the light of the Lord.

Again, the officer could not make out the radio message.

"Been crapping out like this all day," he complained, cursing
city bureaucrats. "Sorry, sir. Get that tire pumped."

"No trouble, officer."

The cop gave Keller a polite salute and waved him through.

It went according to his prayers. According to the prophesy.
Thank God! Praise Him! He gazed upon the sleeping Angel.
Behold the Seraph. Behold Gabriel. God's messenger now
belonged to him.

Sanctus, sanctus, sanctus.

33

The highway curled breathtakingly close to the cliff edges above the Pacific, its cresting cobalt waves pummeling the rocks while embracing the beaches below.

The view soothed Sydowski whenever he drove to Pacifica and today he needed soothing. His visit with his old man left him with souvenirs. He flipped down the visor mirror again. The cuts on his freshly shaved face had coagulated. He winced, pulling at the bits of tissue paper. The things a son will do to make his old man happy.

Sydowski had found his father sitting on his bed in his shoebox bungalow at Sea Breeze Villas, staring sadly at the Pacific.

"What's the matter, Pop?" he asked in Polish.

"They won't let me cut hair anymore. They say I'm too old." Tears streamed down his cheeks.

"Is that so? Where's your kit?"

"The old whore took it."

"Pop, don't call Mrs. Doran an old whore."

"Well, she's not a young one."

Sydowski marched to the carpeted, lilac-scented office of Mrs. Doran, Sea Breeze's chief administrator. A kind, attractive woman in her fifties, Elsa Doran managed her "camp for golden kids" with the sternness of a drill sergeant. Always happy to see Sydowski, her eyes sparkled and she loved calling him "Inspector." But the sparkle vanished when he asked her for his old man's barber's kit.

"Mr. Sydowksi, your father's senility is a concern. I can't allow him to cut hair and give straight-razor shaves. He trembles. He could injure someone. We'd be sued."

Sydowski made it clear to Elsa Doran that he would not lose an argument with her over his father's scissors and razor.

"Give me his kit, or I pull him out."

She sighed, and retrieved the kit from a locked desk drawer. He thanked her and returned to his old man.

"How about a trim and a shave, Pop?"

John Sydowski's eighty-one-year-old face brightened and he sat his son before his dresser mirror, draping a towel around his shoulders. They talked sports, birds, politics, crime, and vegetables as he cut his hair, then lathered his face for a shave. Sydowski loved how his father's unit smelled of aftershave, like his old three-chair shop in North Beach. He loved the feel of his old man's comb through his hair, the clip of the scissors. For a warm moment he was a kid again. But when his old man neared him with the razor in his shaking hand, Sydowski's stomach quaked. No way out of it, so he closed his eyes, feeling the blade jerk into his skin again and again as his father scraped it across his face.

"See. Only a nick or two." His old man beamed when it was over, removing the towel stained with Sydowski's blood before slapping on the Old Spice. Sydowski damn near passed out from the sting.

"Thanks, Pop," he managed through gritted teeth, going to the bathroom to put toilet paper on his wounds.

They talked over tea, then his old man grew drowsy and fell asleep. Sydowski covered him with a blanket, kissed his head, gathered the kit, and returned to Elsa Doran's office. She stared at Sydowski's face in disbelief.

"Don't ever give him his kit again," he ordered, handing it to her. "If he fusses about it, call me."

Elsa Doran understood, locked the kit in her desk drawer, and smiled up at Sydowski as he left. "What you did for John was very tender, Inspector." Her eyes sparkled. "Very tender."

Now, returning to San Francisco on the Pacific Coastal Highway, Sydowski reflected on the case. He and Turgeon had squeezed a lead from Perry Kindhart. After they got a warrant, they tossed his apartment, but found nothing tying him to Tanita Marie Donner or Danny Becker. Then IDENT dissected it. Zip. No prints, hairs, or fibers. Nothing, until they checked Kindhart's Polaroid camera and came up with a latent belonging to Franklin Wallace. The camera had been wiped, but one print was missed—a lost right-thumb print screaming to be found. It didn't prove a thing, but it was leverage.

"Let me get this straight, Perry," Turgeon said. "You had absolutely nothing to do with Tanita Marie Donner or Danny Becker?"

"That's right." Kindhart stubbed his tenth Lucky Strike in the ashtray of the Homicide interview room at the Hall of Justice. Turgeon and Sydowski went at Kindhart, who played the relaxed con, wise to the program. He knew they could hold him for seventy-two hours before having to charge or release him. Earlier, on the drive to the hall, Kindhart decided against a lawyer. "You're right, I've got nothing to hide. Some guys can't function in the morning."

Sydowski sat across from Kindhart in the interview room, letting Turgeon do most of the asking. Kindhart was taken with her, she'd struck a rapport with him, letting him believe he had the upper hand, was controlling the information. Like a practiced snake charmer, she skillfully coaxed his tongue from his mouth and let him wrap it around his own throat. Kindhart would roll over—all he needed was a little nudge. When the rumblings of Kindhart's empty stomach grew distracting, Sydowski began talking about his passion for cheeseburgers from Hamburger Mary's. Hunger was a powerful motivator.

"How 'bout I send out for a couple of cheeseburgers and some fries, Perry?" Sydowski offered. Kindhart accepted. Enthusiastically.

Sydowski and Turgeon left. When they returned, Sydowski had his nose in the report from the search of Kindhart's apartment.

"Sorry, Perry, we got sidetracked. We'll order those burgers soon as we clear something up here." Sydowski kept his face in the file, sifting papers.

"What's to clear up?"

"Perry, we found Franklin Wallace's prints on your camera."

"That's a fucking lie." Kindhart looked at Turgeon.

"And," Sydowski continued, with a bluff, "the lab reports aren't back yet, but the snapshots you saw of Tanita with Wallace and the hooded tattooed man, were likely taken with your Polaroid."

"Bull-fucking-shit."

"And there's the note," Sydowski threw out another bluff.

"What note?"

"Wallace's suicide note."

"What does it say?"

"It's not good, Perry. That's all we can tell you. I'm sorry."

Kindhart was dead silent.

Sydowski locked his eyes on him and waited. Kindhart looked at Turgeon, at her beautiful, patient face. She waited. Kindhart's stomach grumbled. He lit another Lucky Strike and blinked thoughtfully. The wheels were turning.

Here it comes, Sydowski knew.

"Did that little fuck try to implicate me? After what I did for him in Virginia? Is that what this is all about?"

"Where were you on the Saturday Danny Becker was kidnapped from his father off BART?" Turgeon sat down.

"Modesto. I told you."

"Can you prove it?"

"People saw me there."

"Where were you last year when Tanita Marie Donner was abducted, then found in Golden Gate?" Sydowski asked.

"I can't remember. I think I was in town." Kindhart dragged hard on his cigarette, squinting.

"Uh-hh." Sydowski slipped on his glasses and studied the file. He let a minute of silence pass, then said, "Before we go on here, Perry, there are certain rights we have to advise you of. I am sure you know them." The gold in Sydowski's teeth glinted as he continued in a friendly tone. "You have the right to remain silent—"

"Hold every-fucking-thing."

Sydowski stopped. "Are you waiving your Miranda rights?"

Kindhart nodded. Sydowski wanted him to speak because the room was wired, they were recording the interview.

"We have to be clear, Perry. Are you waiving your rights?"

"I'm waiving my fucking rights because I was not involved with those kids. I don't know what you think you got on me, but it's not what you think. It's not the truth."

"Then tell us the truth, Perry," Turgeon said.

Kindhart's breathing quickened and he eyed both of them. "Franklin wanted me to join a party. Just the three of us. Me him and his new friend. He said they were going to pick up a little date, play for a day, then let her go."

"When was this?" Turgeon asked.

"Around the time the Donner kid went missing."

"What was the date?" Sydowski asked.

"I don't know. I figure it was the Donner kid."

"Why?"

"Franklin said it would be a little one who couldn't ID anybody."

"What happened?" Sydowski asked.

"I never went."

"Why?"

"I had to see my parole officer that day."

"What day?" Turgeon asked.

"The day Tanita Donner went missing. I know you can check it out. I know from the news reports the time she was grabbed, and I was with my parole officer."

"Convenient, Perry," Sydowski said. "Ever call a guy by the name of Tom Reed?"

"Who's that?"

"You just said you follow the news reports."

"I'm supposed to know this guy?"

"How do we know you weren't involved?" Turgeon said.

"Because I wasn't. Franklin came to me that night and asked me if I wanted to come to their party. I said no. I didn't like his friend. He scared me. An iceman."

"The friend came to your place, too, that night?" Sydowski said.

"No."

"So what happened?" Turgeon asked.

"I let Franklin borrow my camera, which was stupid. He dropped it off the next day and that was the last time I ever saw him. After the news on the girl and Franklin's suicide, I wiped my camera clean."

"Where were they holding her?" Sydowski said.

"All he said was that it was a safe place."

"What about the mystery man, Mr. Tattoo?" Turgeon asked.

"I only met him the one time at the bookstore about a month before it happened. I swear."

"Why didn't you tell police this last year?" Sydowski said.

"Because with my record, I was afraid. And I was afraid Franklin's friend might come after me."

"Can you tell us anything more about Franklin's mystery friend?"

"All I know, and I swear to you this is all I remember, is that he is a skinner con from Canada and Franklin once called him 'Verge.' "

They released Kindhart, put him under surveillance, then called the Royal Canadian Mounted Police and the Correctional Service of Canada. It was a government holiday in Canada, and with only a first name as an identifier, it was going to take several hours before the Canadians could run checks and start faxing files on possible suspects. Sydowski used the break to see his old man.

Sydowski was optimistic about the lead. It could be the turning point. Usually he dismissed the mysterious-person-did-it alibi, but there *was* a mystery man involved in this. Kindhart was in Modesto when Becker was grabbed, that checked out. And Kindhart didn't fit the suspect's description. No tattoo. Not even close. Sydowski was driving north, passing Sharp Park when his cell phone rang.

Maybe the Canadian faxes had arrived. "Sydowski."

"Walt, it's bad," Turgeon said. "We've got another abduction."

"Another one!"

"Five-year-old girl, from her mother in Golden Gate Park. A man in a pickup. Bearded. Fits with the Becker case."

"I'm on my way."

Sydowski hit his emergency lights and siren.

34

"Gabrielle. The little girl's name is Gabrielle. Her mother kept screaming her name," seventy-three-year-old Fay Osborne from Ottumwa, Iowa, said as Tom Reed wrote quickly in his notepad.

He had taken Fay and Arthur, her seventy-five-year-old husband, a retired farmer, aside.

"This is a son-of-a-bitchin' thing to do to a little girl." Arthur repositioned his John Deere ball cap each time he patted his sweating forehead with his handkerchief. Reed hid the Osbornes from the other reporters who swarmed Golden Gate Park.

The *Star* had sent Reed, Molly Wilson, and two photographers to the park. Other staff were en route. Wilson was at the carousel with the two teenage girls who saw the kidnapper, getting their accounts just before police took them away for statements.

Reed was having trouble hearing Fay and Jack Osborne over the TV news helicopters and satellite trucks roaring into the

parking lot. Local stations were taking the story live. Shielding
her eyes, Fay regarded a hovering chopper. The cradle-to-grave
tribulations of a life bound to Iowa soil were written in her
face, eyes, and sturdy hands. Probably attended church every
Sunday, Reed figured.

"Her mother kept saying that it was all her fault for not
watching her daughter more closely," Fay said.

"You see anything strange in the parking lot before the
mother ran up to you?"

"No. But this man approached us after seeing her upset."

"Where is he now?"

"Gone. After helping the mother, he ran back to his car
phone, called the police, then drove off, trying to follow the
pickup truck."

"Did he say anything before he left?" Writing furiously,
Reed stopped looking at the Osbornes.

"He had been talking on his car phone when he saw a little
girl come into the lot, and trot up to a parked pickup truck,
and talk to a man who had a dog in the cab. They only talked
a few seconds, then she got in and they drove off."

Reed never took his eyes from his notes as he wrote. "Did
he get the truck's plate number?"

"I don't think so."

"What did he say this man in the pickup looked like?"

"He said he had a beard, light-colored hair. In his forties or
fifties."

Reed froze, and stared at the Osbornes. "A beard and light
hair?"

Fay Osborne nodded. Reed's mind spun with suspicion.

Beard. Light hair. Like the guy who took Danny Becker.
Like the born-again kook from Martin's bereavement group.
He had a beard and light hair. Right. And so did 100,000 other
men in the Bay Area. Slow down. Why did he think he was a
detective? Didn't he learn from the Franklin Wallace fiasco
last year?

Reed finished with the Osbornes, went to the carousel, and took Wilson aside. "What'd you get?" he asked.

"Great stuff." She flipped through her notes. "Her name is Gabrielle Nunn. From the description I got from two girls who saw her talking to a man before she went missing, I'd say he's the same creep who grabbed Danny Becker from BART."

"Me, too."

"Gabrielle was here for a friend's birthday party, a huge one, something like thirty kids. She's waiting alone outside the washroom when she talks to this man in a ball cap and dark glasses. Nobody remembers the guy's face, only that he was bearded with blondish hair."

"Just like Becker on BART. Ball cap and dark glasses."

"Gabrielle talks to the man, follows him to the lot. Her mom, Nancy Nunn, comes out minutes later. Can't find her. The teens tell her about the man. Mom runs frantically to the lot. And get this! The whole thing may have been caught on amateur video!"

"No shit?" Reed checked to ensure no other reporters were eavesdropping. "How did you find out?"

"I overhead a guy tell a detective that he was videotaping his kids on the carousel about the same time. He said maybe he caught the guy on tape."

"He give the tape to the detective?"

"Yes. He took off before I could interview him."

"Good stuff. See if we can get a print from it. My guess is they'll release it anyway."

"Right. You get anything?"

Reed told her about Fay Osborne and the businessman who followed the pickup. Suddenly, Wilson remembered something and reached excitedly into her purse, pulling out a snapshot.

"One of the mothers from the party gave me this picture of Gabrielle. Taken an hour ago. What an angel. Five years old. Her birthday is next week. Her mother was freaked over Becker's kidnapping, and with Donner being found here, she was afraid to bring Gabrielle to the party today. Her mother made that dress. What a little angel, huh?''

"She's cute all right. Anybody say anything about a dog?"

"Yeah, hold on." Wilson handed Reed the snapshot and flipped through her notes. "Here, Jackson. Gabrielle's cocker spaniel pup. Ran off or something from their home about a month ago."

"It fits."

"What fits?"

"That this could've been premeditated. The guy took her dog, then uses it today to lure her away."

"Yeah, that would work."

"Call the desk. We should send someone to the Nunn house in the Sunset, talk to the neighbors."

"Your house is in the Sunset, Tom."

"Yeah, but I never heard of this family."

"Excuse me!" A grim-faced SFPD officer was unreeling a taut yellow police line around the carousel area, as other officers cleared people from the scene. The plastic ribbon sealed off the carousel enclosure, then stretched along the path Gabrielle had taken to the parking lot, encompassing the lot itself, protecting the entire scene.

"Shit, Tom. They usually do this for homicides."

"Likely a grid search, in case the bad guy dropped something."

Drew Chapman, one of the *Star's* photographers, joined them, clicking off a dozen frames.

"Chappy. Where you been?" Wilson said.

"Deep in the west end. A group of suits were poking around the scene where they found the murdered baby last year. The *Examiner* and *Merc* were there, too. Not bad for pix."

"Cops put on the white gloves?" Reed asked.

Drew shook his head. "I don't think they found dick." Drew nodded to a group of detectives nearing the area and raised a camera to his face. "Those guys there."

Reed recognized Rust and Ditmire, along with Turgeon and Sydowski, walking outside the tape at the far side, stopping to talk with the uniforms, instructing them to do something.

Drew fired off a few frames. ''We overheard them say something about a press conference at the hall later. I don't know about you guys, but I think it is all linked. I think we got some twisted, fucking, serial child-killer.''

Maybe, Reed thought, considering the names as a connection. Danny Raphael Becker. Gabrielle Nunn. *What an angel.* Raphael. Gabrielle. The Angel Gabrielle. Gabriel. Raphael. Angels.

35

In Room 400 at the Hall of Justice, a funereal mood descended upon those watching Gabrielle Nunn's abduction over and over again. In color, slow motion and reverse. They saw it on the same big-screen TV the homicide dicks used to watch ball games, *Dirty Harry* movies, and *Dragnet* reruns.

Vaughan Kreuger, a mechanic from Buffalo, was videotaping his four-year-old twins on the carousel with their mother when Gabrielle was taken from the playground. He volunteered his tape to a detective at the scene. Given the circumstances, the Kreugers didn't want it.

Nancy Nunn wept. For her, it was a perverse ballet—the horses, the rocker, the chariots carrying laughing children, safe children.

Nancy's husband, Paul, and her friend Wendy Sloane watched with her. Sharon Cook and Brenda Grayson, the two teens who saw Gabrielle talking to a stranger, were also there. Watching beside them was Janice Mason, a lip reader from Gold Bay Institute for the Hearing Impaired. Next to her, Beth

Ferguson, the sketch artist, was making notes and outlines. Turgeon, Rust, Ditmire, Gonzales, Mikelson from General Works, Kennedy from Investigations, Chief of Inspectors Roselli, and a guy from the district attorney's office were among the group, hoping for a break.

Give us a lead, something. Anything.

Kreuger and his camera were at the opposite side of the carousel from Gabrielle and the stranger. It was difficult to see anything except the strobelike glimpses of swimming, formless color.

"Wait! I see her!" Gabrielle's mother pinpointed the spot on the screen. The officer operating the VCR halted the tape, reversed it in freeze-frame mode, one frame at a time. Thirty seconds went by. Nothing but blurry people. Two grandmothers. Then strobe-style nothingness. Dark-light-dark-light-dark-light

"I don't see anything," one detective said.

"I saw her! She's there!" Nancy said just as Gabrielle Nunn appeared on the screen.

"Freeze it, Tucker!" Kennedy sat upright.

Nancy gasped, choking on her tears, pressing her fingers to the screen. It was not a clear frame, it did not betray details of her face, mouth, or eyes, but it was Gabrielle. No question. A grainy, static-filled jerky frame of the soon-to-be six-year-old standing alone in the dress her mother had made for her birthday.

Sydowski studied the color Polaroids of Gabrielle taken at the party. Paul Nunn helped Nancy sit down and the tape continued in slow motion. Gabrielle vanished. The camera's angle changed, and caught her again, but she disappeared. Dark-light-dark-light-dark-light. She reappeared completely in focus as a shadow fell over her. A man. It was a man's back. The image was jittery. A profile appeared, snowy, out of focus, void of details, but for a beard, ball cap, sunglasses.

"That's him!" Sharon Cook, one of the teens, pointed at the TV.

"Definitely!" Brenda Grayson said.

The Nunns could not identify the man trapped by Kreuger's video camera for one second of real time. The stranger had something in his right hand and was showing it to Gabrielle before he was cut out of the frame. A postcard, or picture. Miraculously, Gabrielle's face focused as she tilted her head, accepted the picture, and spoke.

" 'Jackson! Where is he?' " Janice Mason from the institute read Gabrielle's lips, just as the tape ended.

Sydowski saw the veins in Paul Nunn's reddened neck pulsating. He exploded. "He stole the dog for this! Planned it! Sonofabitch! I'll kill him!" Nunn buried his face in his large hands.

Earlier, Paul Nunn told the detectives he suspected Gabrielle's pup was stolen from their backyard a month ago because he found the gate open and bits of raw hamburger in the pen. Now, more evidence mocked them from the big screen. They were hustling an IDENT unit to comb the Nunn's yard, Sydowski thought as Officer Tucker cued up the best frame of the kidnapper for Beth Ferguson to sketch. Sydowski caught her attention. She gave her head a subtle negative shake that told him she had few attributes from the footage for a composite. Sydowski knew it. So did the others. A fuzzy rear to near profile of a baseball cap, dark glasses, and a beard wasn't much to work with. But it was something, and if anyone could extract more physical detail about the guy from the teens, Beth could.

Sydowski turned to his copy of the telex from the Royal Canadian Mounted Police, apologizing for the delay getting a file and photo of the one possible suspect from the Canadian prison system. His name was Virgil Shook, which fit with the "Verge" reference from Kindhart. Shook had the right kind of tattoos in the right spots. But they didn't have his file, sheet, or pictures yet. They had absolutely nothing on Shook. It was a national holiday in Canada and the Mounties were having computer problems. Rust was urged to use the FBI and State Department's pull and call the U.S. Embassy in Ottawa for action.

Sydowski studied the grainy contours of Gabrielle's abductor on the TV screen, weighing and measuring every dancing photo-electron composing his image. His heartburn flared; fear and anger raged in the pit of his stomach. Was he now closer to the thing he had been hunting, the thing that had scarred him? The tape clicked and whirred. The stranger with Gabrielle was just a man. Flesh and blood. Fallible. Conquerable. The suspect's ghostly image on the video was a solid break, but it came at a high price. He looked upon Gabrielle Nunn's mother and father being escorted away with the teens to help Beth with a composite.

"We've got a shitload of work to do and no time to do it," Leo Gonzales told the detectives at the table. Alerts had gone out statewide, a grid-search of the playground at Golden Gate was underway, and exhaustive background checks with the Nunns, Beckers, and Angela Donner to find a common thread, anything that might link the families. And they'd go back to them on Virgil Shook, once they had his damn file. Until then, absolutely nothing was to be made public about Shook. Not yet. He might run. But they would find him. The FBI would dissect his crimes and compare them with the San Francisco cases. They would find his friends, climb his family tree, lean hard on Kindhart. Phone taps, mail monitoring, and surveillance for the Nunn home, canvass their Sunset neighborhood—they knew the drill. They would hold a news conference, release the blurry footage, details of the kidnapping, and make a public appeal for help.

"You all know what's at stake here. Do whatever it takes," Gonzales vowed to the group.

36

Why? Why? Why? Why? Why? Why?

Nancy Nunn was overwhelmed. Where was Gabrielle? What was he doing to her? Oh God. Please watch over her.

All my fault. It's all my fault. Why wasn't I watching her? What was he going to do to her? Oh God, would she ever see her again? Golden Gate Park. That's where they found that baby girl last year. Murdered. Oh God. The accusing eyes of the carousel horses.

I'm okay Mom, I'm just waiting at the door.

The man was a Caucasian, late forties to mid-fifties. He had a full beard, bushy blondish hair, medium build, about 170-190 pounds, six feet to six feet, two inches tall, Beth Ferguson estimated as she worked in a nose, ears, and mouth that might match those of the man the teens had seen. He wore a long-sleeved shirt; the girls couldn't see any tattoos. They kept repeating, reciting details. Nancy and Paul sat with them, studying the sketch, struggling to remember if they had ever encountered the man who took Gabrielle. Nancy prayed.

God please help me. Please don't harm her. She's just a little girl, an innocent little girl. We should be looking for her. My child has been abducted. Why didn't the world stand still? Why wasn't everyone looking for her? I have to find her—

Nancy bolted to the hall, where she was stopped by the throng of detectives leaving the conference room, running square into one of them. He was calm, compassionate. She felt his large, strong hands steady her shoulders gently. He smelled of a trace of Old Spice. Nancy's father wore Old Spice. The hall fell silent except for Nancy's sobbing as she looked up at the detective, her voice breaking.

"Bring her home to me. Please bring her home to me."

Sydowski's blue eyes watered with understanding. He knew her suffering—he would carry it with him as a crusader carries an amulet. It was his solemn promise. She read it in his face, the face of a good man. He embodied her hope. Her only hope.

"I promise you, Mrs. Nunn, we will do everything we can on this earth to find Gabrielle."

Tears rolled down Nancy's face as her husband took her in his arms, comforting her. "If he asks for money, we will pay it," Paul Nunn said. "Whatever he asks for. We'll sell the house."

Sydowski nodded.

Two other detectives ushered the Nunns away for more questioning before taking them home.

Turgeon and Sydowski said nothing in the elevator or during the walk to the car. Nothing anyone could say would be worth a damn. They were alone with their thoughts and the case. Turgeon started the Caprice, had slipped the transmission into reverse when Gord Mikelson ran up to them.

"CHIPS just locked on to a truck, could be our guy."

"What?"

"Bearded man driving a battered pickup with a girl about six or seven wearing a dress. They have a dog in the cab. Near the Presidio, northbound towards the bridge. CHIPS bird has got him and Marin County's rolling. The guy hasn't made us yet!''

"Punch it, Linda!" Sydowski switched on the police radio.

The Chev roared, leaving fifty feet of smoldering rubber at the hall, emergency lights wigwagging and siren screaming.

37

San Francisco's skyscrapers and the surging whitecaps of the Bay wheeled slowly under the California Highway Patrol chopper approaching the south end of the Golden Gate Bridge near the Presidio.

It had been assisting the San Francisco police in the abduction investigation, hovering over Golden Gate Park, the Sunset, and Richmond districts. It had returned to its Oakland base to refuel when its radio crackled. An off-duty CHIPS patrol car spotted a pickup matching the description in the Nunn kidnapping, northbound on 101 near the Palace of Fine Arts. The chopper lifted off within forty-five seconds of the call.

The suspect truck was a Ford, the driver Caucasian, bearded. Passenger was a girl, five to eight years old, her head barely visible from the rear. A small dog was in the cab. The cruiser couldn't get closer for the truck's tag without being noticed.

Traffic on 101 near the Golden Gate looked like a set of toy cars from the air. The CHIPs chopper was nearly invisible, lingering a quarter mile or so south. The spotter locked onto the pickup through high-powered binoculars. The truck was now on the bridge.

Police radios sizzled with dispatches as cars from several jurisdictions headed to the area. No stop would be made on the bridge. Too risky. It would happen at the viewpoint exit on the north side. The suspect was considered dangerous and possibly armed.

They would hold him for the SFPD.

Weaving through traffic on the Golden Gate, Turgeon and Sydowski monitored the takedown on their radio.

"Yeah, we've got him," huffed a CHIPs officer. "No, problem here. No weapons."

Turgeon and Sydowski arrived minutes after the arrest, with Turgeon blasting the siren, jolting slow moving rubberneckers out of their way. Half a dozen officers were at the scene, four cruisers with front doors open, emergency lights pulsating, surrounded the pickup, radio calls competing with the chopper above.

An officer was talking to a man in the backseat of one car. In the front seat of another car an officer talked with a little girl, while a blond dog panted in the rear seat behind the cage. Motorists slowed to gawk. A few tourists nearby watched with worried, puzzled faces as officers searched the interior of the pickup's cab. Sydowski clipped his shield to his jacket and groaned. Also watching were TV news crews and newspaper photographers. Reporters were talking to people, taking notes.

"Those guys are fast." Turgeon shook her head.

The Chev's Michelin radials screeched as they skidded to a halt next to the pickup. Sydowski had his door open before the car stopped and a highway patrol officer glanced at his shield.

"San Francisco PD?" the officer shouted over the chopper.

"That's right," Sydowski said, noticing the stripes and the name plate of Sergeant Marvin Miller.

"This is Inspector Turgeon," Sydowski said. "Mind if we talk to these people?" Turgeon went to the car holding the driver. Sydowski went to the car with the little girl, opened the cruiser's passenger door, and squatted beside the girl. She was terrified.

"Excuse me, officer." Sydowski did not take his eyes from the girl. "Hi there. I'm Inspector Sydowski. I'm a police officer, too."

She nodded.

"I bet this has got you pretty scared, sweetheart?"

She nodded. Her chestnut brown hair was in a neat ponytail, tied with a pink bow. Her face darkened. "Was Daddy driving too fast? He says police will stop you if you drive too fast."

"Well, that's true," Sydowski said. "People shouldn't drive too fast. You're a pretty smart girl to know that. Can you tell me your name and how old you are?"

"My name is Jennifer Corliss. I'm seven years old and I live at 7077 Brownlington Gardens. Where's my daddy?"

The dog barked. A retriever pup.

"This your dog, Jennifer?" Sydowski asked, reaching into his jacket for the Polaroids of Gabrielle Nunn.

"His name is Sonny Corliss. He lives with me and my daddy and mommy and my little brother, Ethan. Where's Daddy? We have to go now. Mommy and Ethan are waiting at the cabin."

Sydowski held up that morning's birthday party snapshot of Gabrielle for Miller. Not even close.

"Daddy's right over there, Jennifer." Sydowski nodded to his left. "We're going to take you to him in a minute. Meanwhile, why don't we let you sit in with Sonny, while we talk to your daddy, okay?"

"Okay."

Sydowski and Miller started for the second cruiser where Jennifer's father was being questioned.

"Say, you Sydowski, from Homicide?"

"Yup."

A smile grew on Miller's face. "The legend himself. I thought I'd recognized you from the news."

Turgeon stopped Sydowski before he got to the car.

"I don't think he's our boy, Walt."

"Uh-huh. Well that's not Gabrielle Nunn back there."

Turgeon's face was taut. "Mr. Corliss is not thrilled with all this attention. He's pissed off." Turgeon looked at a business card. "Thoren J. Corliss, executive with a downtown invest-ment group."

Sydowski saw Corliss several yards away, out of earshot outside the police car leaning against its front right fender, arms folded resolutely across his chest, ignoring the officer talking to him. Corliss was in his late thirties, early forties. Trim build, thick sandy hair, and a beard, tanned chiseled cheeks. Faded jeans and a navy Ralph Lauren polo shirt. Way-farers hung from his neck. A man who was always in charge. A man who sealed deals on squash courts, knew his way around most foreign capitals. A guy who carried a phone with him everywhere. Likely called his lawyer already, Sydowski thought.

"He's demanding to speak to somebody in charge," Turgeon said.

"Oh, is that right?" Sydowski said.

"We ran his name and made some calls," Miller said. "He's clean. Checks out. Just picked up his seven-year-old daughter, Jennifer, from school and they're on their way to the mother and son at their cottage at Bel Marin. That's their dog, too, a retriever. They fit the damn description circulated. We told him that. Told him the situation."

Sydowski rubbed his chin, told Miller his people made the right call, then nodded to the reporters.

"Marvin, anybody here talk to the press yet?"

"No. It's your show."

Sydowski turned to Turgeon. "You up to it, Linda?"

"What have you got in mind?"

"Talk to those guys and set the record straight. Tell them we stopped a subject matching the description in the Nunn kidnapping. Don't give Corliss's name or any details about the abduction. We'll give them more at the press conference later."

"And what are you going to do?"

"Talk to the old man here. Send him on his way."

Turgeon was uneasy. A few minutes ago, Sydowski was holding Gabrielle Nunn's traumatized mother, staring into her eyes. She didn't like the way his jaw was fixed, the way he regarded Corliss.

"Don't rough him up, Walt," she joked.

Sydowski shoved a Tums into his mouth.

Thoren J. Corliss drew himself to his full height, standing nearly eye to eye with Sydowski.

"And who the hell are you?" Corliss snapped.

Sydowski handed him his badge and identification.

"Homicide?" Corliss stared at Sydowski. "What is this?"

"We're investigating the recent abduction of a little girl, Mr. Corliss. Unfortunately your truck, with yourself, your daughter, and your dog, fit the description of the suspect's vehicle."

"I can't believe this!"

"I can only offer you our apology. You are free to leave now."

"I cannot believe this has happened!" Corliss threw up his hands. "Is this assuring police work? Arresting innocent people?"

He tossed Sydowski's shield back at him. "I'm not leaving until I speak to my lawyer."

"Why? You haven't been charged with anything."

"I've just been arrested. My rights have been violated."

"You have been inconvenienced, sir. That is all. Again, I thank you for your cooperation and understanding of the gravity of the situation. Please, Mr. Corliss, I suggest you leave."

"Oh, you'd like that wouldn't you? I'm going to lodge a formal complaint over this matter. I'll go to the media, and I'll sue."

Sydowski said nothing.

"Four police cars pounced on us. My daughter saw her father forced at gunpoint to step out of our truck with my hands in the air and lie on the ground. Like a low-life criminal. We were publicly humiliated. There was a goddamn helicopter hovering over our heads for Christ's sake. We're innocent people. I'm a law-abiding taxpayer and I won't stand for this kind of harassment."

Sydowski had enough and stepped closer to Corliss, invading his personal space. "I've eaten about as much of this as I can stand, sir. A few hours ago a little girl, about the same age as your daughter, was kidnapped from her mother by a man with a beard, like yours, driving a pickup truck, like yours. He used a dog, like yours, to lure the girl away. A few days ago, a man kidnapped a boy from his father on the subway. These children are gone. Their parents are crazy with fear. The last time this happened, we found the child, a two-year-old girl. She was stuffed in a garbage bag." Sydowski moved closer to Corliss. "Her throat was cut. I know. I held her corpse."

Corliss blinked.

"Now, why don't you just trot over there to the press and tell them how outraged you are. Tell them what a terrible injustice this has been for you. I'm sure the parents of the kidnapped children will thank you. And think what a hero you'll be to everyone who knows you."

Corliss's adam's apple bobbed as he absorbed Sydowski's advice.

They heard a child's voice and saw Jennifer Corliss.

"Daddy!"

Corliss picked her up in a crushing hug.

"The police said it was a false alarm. We can go now, Dad."

Corliss studied his daughter's face, kissed her, then he turned to Sydowski. "Then I guess we'll be on our way."

38

Four hours after Gabrielle Nunn was kidnapped, scores of reporters crammed into the Hall of Justice cafeteria, which was serving as a press room. Flanked by a number of SFPD brass, detectives, and officers from various jurisdictions, the chief took his seat and prepared to tell San Franciscans a monster was preying on their children. He sipped some water, cleared his throat, and leaned into the microphones heaped on the table before him.

"Five-year-old Gabrielle Nunn of San Francisco was abducted by a man a short time ago while at a birthday party at the Children's Playground in Golden Gate Park. The suspect drove away with her in a pickup truck, a battered, dark-colored Ford, late 1970s, plate beginning with a 'B' or 'E' or '8.' We suspect the same man also kidnapped three-year-old Daniel Becker from his father on BART near Balboa Park and are investigating any link to last year's kidnapping and murder of two-year-old Tanita Marie Donner."

Blazing TV lights accentuated the chief's green eyes. Speed winders whirred with sporadic camera flashes.

"We have some aspects of Gabrielle Nunn's abduction we will make public. A month ago, the Nunns' blond cocker spaniel pup, Jackson, disappeared from their home in the Sunset. We believe the dog was taken by Gabrielle's kidnapper, who used it today to entice her to go with him.

"Another vital lead comes from a family who was videotaping their outing at Golden Gate Park today when Gabrielle Nunn was lured away. They recorded Gabrielle's abductor. We've enhanced the tape and will show it to you. We have since produced a composite of the suspect. Everyone will be given copies of the video, the composite, pictures of Gabrielle Nunn, and her dog.

"We've expanded our investigation into these crimes by establishing a formal task force consisting of the SFPD, FBI, state, and other agencies. We have a dedicated tip line for any information on these crimes. And the mayor's office has increased the reward for information leading to an arrest in any or all of the cases to $200,000. Anyone with any information should call us."

The chief nodded to an officer. Suddenly, an enlarged color picture of Gabrielle Nunn stared at reporters from the screen overhead. It was one of the Polaroids taken at the party. Gabrielle, eyes bright, and oblivious to the horror looming.

"What a cute child," said a reporter near Tom Reed.

An angel. That's what Wilson had called her.

Suddenly the computer enhanced face of Gabrielle's abductor emerged beside her. A Caucasian, in his late forties, early fifties, bearded, with snakelike strands of blondish hair writhing from under a ball cap. His mouth was a slit. Large, dark glasses hid his eyes, concealing whatever force propelled him to hunt her, take her, and ram another stake into San Francisco's heart.

Seeing his face next to Gabrielle's was chilling.

Reed examined the composite.

Something was familiar. What was it?

Two officers rolled a large monitor and VCR to the front.

The chief said, "Now, we'll show you the videotape. The sequence we've edited lasts about twenty seconds. We've removed the sound, isolated Gabrielle and the suspect with identifying circles."

It was incredible. A hissing snowstorm filled the monitor before the dark-light strobe revolutions of the carousel appeared and the abduction of Gabrielle Nunn was carried out, in slow motion.

It was surreal.

Reed took notes.

The footage was blurry, jittery. Gabrielle and her kidnapper were trapped in halos. It was still difficult to discern the man under the ball cap, glasses, and beard. The tape vibrated, was out of focus. Even in slow motion, his face was indistinct. When he turned, the camera captured his slightly distorted profile. It froze.

The rapid-fire clicking of the still cameras broke the silence.

"That's our best image of Gabrielle's abductor," the chief said.

Reed examined the monitor. Something gnawed at him. The screen was glowing with the suspect's computer composite.

Then the video monitor.

The composite.

The monitor.

He swallowed. Hard.

The man. His beard, his nose, the shape of his head, his build.

Edward Keller.

He resembled Edward Keller, the religious nut from the bereavement group. Reed never forgot the people he clashed with. Keller was irrational, telling him how he had lost his three children in a boating accident. But Reed could not find any news clippings of Keller's tragedy. Why? Was Keller a liar? An eccentric? Quoting ancient poetry and Scripture, babbling about his "divine revelation," and his "blessed reunion with his children."

Didn't the FBI's profile say Danny Becker's kidnapper was traumatized by a cataclysmic event involving children?

His blessed reunion with his children.

Children.

Are you the specter sent to destroy my work?

You can rescue them if you truly believe you can.

Reed found Sydowski among the stone-faced dicks lining the wall. Should he put him on to Keller? But what if he is wrong? What if Keller was just a nut, sick with grief, and Reed sicced the police on him. Especially now? Didn't Dr. Martin say the anniversary of the tragedy was approaching, always a difficult time for grieving parents? The last time Reed had galloped after a hunch, a man committed suicide, and Ann and Zach left him. Reed tapped his pen against his pad. But two children had been stolen.

The chief was taking questions. Reed had missed most of them, coming out of his thoughts to catch a stunner.

". . . you found a bloodied body part in the Sunset and it belonged to Gabrielle. Is that true, Chief?"

The chief was not pleased. "Your information is inaccurate. We found some of Gabrielle's hair. We believe her abductor cut it to alter her appearance. It is not uncommon in abduction cases."

"What about the blood?"

"We haven't determined if it's the abductor's or Gabrielle's. And I can't disclose details on the hair."

"Chief, what about the stop made on the Golden Gate?"

"False alarm. Somebody who resembled the description."

"There's a rumor that a fugitive child-killer from Canada is a suspect and is under surveillance."

"We have a number of people we're checking out. We have no Canadian fugitives under surveillance."

"Did you arrest a suspect and let him go?"

"No. We brought in a few people known to us for questioning."

"Do you have any leads on the suspect in the video?"

"None."

"Any ransom calls, demands, or contact from the kidnapper?"

"Nothing."

"What about the Becker case, any contact?"

"Nothing."

"Do you think the children have been murdered? Are you dealing with a serial child-killer?"

"We have no evidence to suggest any homicides. Until then, we work on the assumption they are being held somewhere."

"Why do you think the cases are linked?"

"The similar patterns. Bold, daylight, stranger abductions in each of them. And in the Becker and Nunn cases, the suspect's description is very similar."

"Any theories on the motive behind the cases?"

The chief turned to FBI Special Agent Merle Rust, who took the question. "Our psychological profile suggests the suspect's motivation stems from a traumatic event in his life involving children, abuse, a tragedy."

"Sexual abuse?"

"Possibly."

"Chief, anything linked to cult or Satanic involvement? What about a terrorist link to Nathan Becker's defense contract computer research?"

"Nothing on all counts."

"What do the abducted children have in common? How does this man come to chose Danny Becker and Gabrielle Nunn?"

"We have some leads, but we can't reveal them. Now, before we close here, I just want the people of the Bay Area to know the dangerous situation we're facing here. Parents should be vigilant with their families at all times and report anything suspicious. Thank you for coming." The chief was peppered with questions as he made his way out.

Reed broke from the pack and caught up to Sydowski. "You got a moment, Walt?"

Sydowski led him down the hall until he found an empty office.

"Make it quick." Sydowski closed the door behind them.

"That footage really the guy?"

"It's him. We showed it to Danny Becker's father."

"Is it the same guy in Tanita Marie Donner's murder?"

"Don't know."

"What about the guy you brought in the other day?"

"I told you, he was a shit-rat who gave us a lead to check."

"What's his name?"

"Can't tell you. We're still checking."

"Do you think Danny Becker and Gabrielle Nunn are dead?"

"I don't know."

"What have you got, Walt? What've you really got?"

"Not much. A fuzzy description. Gabrielle's hair."

"You think this guy's going to strike again?"

"Off the record? This entire conversation never happened?"

"What conversation?"

"I think he will strike again. We're trying to track him, anticipate his next move. But we've got dick to work with."

Reed nodded, and mulled his next thought.

"I got to go," Sydowski said.

"Wait, Walt." Reed swallowed. "What if I recognized this guy?"

Sydowski's face grew into astonished anger. "Don't fuck with me!" He stabbed Reed's chest with a finger. "Has this fucker been calling you?"

"No. No. Nothing like that."

"What are you talking about, then?"

"His beard. He looks like someone I met once, but I'm not sure."

"You're not sure." Sydowski bristled. "Let me tell you something. If you know this guy, if you have any information about him, then you'd better tell me now."

"Well, it's just—"

Sydowski held a warning finger under Reed's nose. "Because if you're sitting on information just for the sake of a goddamn story, we'll come after you harder than we did on Donner. And this time I'll be leading the fucking charge."

"He just looked familiar, vaguely familiar. Like somebody I may have met once, but I just can't place him," Reed lied and backed off.

"His description fits any one of about two hundred and fifty thousand men in the Bay Area."

"I was just trying to get some background on the investigation. This is such a huge story."

Sydowski shook his head incredulously, his face reddening.

"You're wasting my time. We've got a child murder and two stolen children and to you guys it's just a game, just a huge story."

Sydowski was seething. "It's so easy for the press, isn't it? You get us up there, hit us with questions that make us look asinine, no matter how we answer. You do your stories and you go home. Not us. We have to find this fucker, have to breathe, eat, and sleep with what he's done and may do again. It gets personal for us, so don't come around me playing your smart-ass give-and-take games."

"We're affected by this as much as you."

"Ever see a murdered baby's corpse? You know what that does to you? You ever have to escort a mother to the morgue to identify the rotting remains of her two-year-old daughter? Then hold her as she cries so hard you swear she's breaking apart in your arms?"

Sydowski's eyes were glistening. "Do you know this asshole, Tom?"

"I guess not."

"All right. Then unless you've got something substantial to tell me, don't bother me anymore." Sydowski left the room.

Reed went to the window and stared at the city.

39

The San Francisco Star's afternoon meeting broke and weekend editor Blake MacCrimmon carried his note-filled yellow legal pad across the newsroom.

The city's psychopath had stolen another child.

MacCrimmon had called in six reporters on overtime for the story. The *Star* was coming out with a huge package— MacCrimmon had cleared four inside pages. Deadline was two hours away, but that was not the source of his unease. It was the story. When he saw the shaky footage of Gabrielle Nunn's abduction, his skin stung; something that hadn't happened to him since he covered Vietnam. He had four grandchildren who lived near Golden Gate Park. He stopped at Tom Reed's desk.

"Your story is going to be our main news hit on front. Lead off with something like: 'Fears that a serial killer is stalking children after a man abducted a five-year-old girl Saturday, days after a three-year-old boy was kidnapped.' "

"How long can I run with it?"

"Forty, fifty inches. Put the footage of the bad guy up high."

"No problem."

"I've got Molly camped out on the Nunns' doorstep tonight, in case of a ransom call, or the family talks to the press. We'll send the night guy to relieve her later."

"What else have we got going?"

"A Jack Thorne column. It captures the mood: nervous parents keeping their children close, city sharing the Beckers' and Nunns' anguish. Color on Gabrielle, her family, the dog connection, the suspect's psych profile, a summary of the three cases, that sort of thing." MacCrimmon adjusted his glasses. "Anything you think we should add?"

Reed noticed a back issue nearby with his feature on the bereavement group. Again, he thought of Edward Keller. Maybe he should tell MacCrimmon about his hunch, ask to be freed to quietly investigate Keller. Then again, maybe not.

"You have something on your mind, Tom?"

"No. Sounds like a solid package."

"Story's drawing global interest. Other papers in Britain, Japan, and Canada are sending staff here." MacCrimmon checked his watch, then patted Reed's shoulder. "Better get busy."

Reed's story came together smoothly. After proofing it, he sent it to MacCrimmon's computer desk.

Reed massaged his neck and looked at Molly Wilson's empty chair. Tomorrow was going to be another long day with follow-up stories. The mayor was holding a don't-worry-the-city-is-safe press conference. Exhausted but satisfied, Reed considered leaving to get some sleep, but adrenaline was still coursing through his system. Something hideous had hit the city and he was part of it, secretly experiencing the macabre thrill every crime reporter knew, loathed, and would never truly comprehend. From Salinas to Ukiah, wherever the *Star* went, people would devour his work, gasp and shake their heads—in office towers, restaurants, airports, malls, schools and kitchens.

Reed knew this and it excited him. It always did.

Reed checked his watch. It was not that late. He should call Ann and Zach just to hear their voices. They hadn't been together since their lunch in Berkeley. Reed smiled at how Zach was giddy with the good news.

"Soooo?" Zach's eyes ping-ponged between his parents as he sucked up the last of his strawberry shake. "What's taking so long?"

"What are you talking about, son?" Reed said.

"Us getting back together. I told Gordie we're moving back."

Reed exchanged a glance and a smile with Ann.

"We haven't heard back from Mr. Tilley," she said.

"You mean the Okie guy who's renting our house with his wife?"

"Watch your manners, Zach," Reed said.

"The nice businessman from Tulsa."

"It's going to take some time for Mr. Tilley to arrange to find another place before we can move in," Ann said.

"A couple of months at least," Reed added.

"A couple of months? Well, okay." Zach burped. "Excuse me."

"And you are going with me on my business trip to Chicago," Ann said.

They were putting the pieces back together. Once they returned to their house, regrouped as a family, he would request a leave and take a crack at his novel and they would put what had happened behind them. It was all they could do. For the rest of their lunch, he stole glances at Ann and Zach, loving them and wondering if the fractures would ever fade. That was a few days ago.

Tilley told them moving out of their house wouldn't be a problem. He was supposed to get back to Ann with a date.

Reed picked up the phone to call her, but it was late. Zach was likely asleep. He snapped off his computer, slipped on his jacket, and waved to the night desk. Leaving the newsroom, he decided to call Ann and Zach tomorrow. Maybe they'd get together after his shift. He could put some distance between himself and the story.

Reed would be in his lonely bed and asleep within forty-five minutes, and without the help of Jack Daniel's. He hadn't touched the booze for five nights now. He did it by focusing on his priorities, Ann and Zach. That's all he had to do, he told himself, stopping at the bank of reporters' mail slots, where he found something in his box. What's this? An ancient *Star* article taken from a microfilmed back issue with a note from Lillian Freeman, the newsroom librarian. The article was short. No byline. The head was:

THREE S.F. CHILDREN DROWN IN BOATING ACCIDENT

The was a note with the article:

"Tom: I know you wanted this a long time ago but I just found it. Apparently this happened twenty years ago, not ten. Hence the delay. We had little on it. You could check the *Chron* and the *Exam*. I left some material marked for you in the reading corner. Hope it still helps. Lillian."

Reed read the story of how Edward Keller's children drowned in the Pacific. He was transfixed. He got a steaming mug of black coffee and headed for the newsroom library.

40

Two hours after she had given an emotional news conference on her front lawn, Nancy Nunn was in her bedroom, sedated. Turgeon was still on the phone. Sydowski set his coffee aside, as he steadied himself to see Gabrielle's brother, Ryan, after somebody told him the eight-year-old had questions.

Ryan was downstairs with Nancy Nunn's friend Wendy Sloane and her daughters, Charlotte and Elaine. The family room had the requisite paneling and indoor-outdoor carpeting. A small bar with three swivel stools stood empty at one end, with a Giants' pennant and a neon beer sign glowing from the wall behind it. Closed tonight. There was a well-worn couch and loveseat set before a big-screen TV. It was a room where a family could snuggle up in front of a movie, or play monopoly, or laugh, or be happy, or anything safe and mundane.

But not tonight.

Tonight it was a sanctuary for the three children huddled on the floor watching a movie. The children were sitting on sleeping bags. Plastic bowls overflowing with popcorn were next to them, untouched. Wendy Sloane was on the sofa, dabbing her face with a crumpled tissue. She saw Sydowski, then looked away. She had seen enough of police to last her the rest of her life; moreover, she would never forgive herself for teasing Nancy about her fears.

Sydowski grunted amicably as he sat with the children on the floor, introduced himself, and invited them to ask any questions that might be on their minds.

The girls were silent, watching the movie.

Ryan turned to Sydowski, his eyes cold and dry.

"Is my little sister dead?"

"We don't know, Ryan. We just don't know."

"How come? You're a detective, right? You're supposed to know."

"We haven't found anything, not a single piece of anything you could think of that would prove Gabrielle has been hurt."

"But the news said you found her hair and stuff?"

"We think the stranger cut her hair so people wouldn't recognize her from her picture. We're going to make a new picture of her. It doesn't mean she has been hurt."

Ryan's face brightened a bit. "That means she could still be all right somewhere?"

"Exactly, but with shorter hair."

"And that's really why there's going to be more searching tomorrow with a helicopter and dogs and everything? Not because you're looking for her dead body, like the TV news said?"

"That's right. We're looking everywhere for your sister and for anything to help us figure out what happened to her, so that we can find her. So far, no matter what anybody else tells you, there is nothing to prove Gabrielle has been hurt. You got that straight from me. That's my word as a San Francisco Police Inspector. Okay?"

"Okay."

"Excuse me, Walt." Special Agent Merle Rust took Sydowski aside. "IDENT's finished with her bedroom. Came up with nothing, zip. We should give it a quick once-over."

Sydowski agreed, patted Ryan's shoulder, then left with Rust.

It was like walking into the bedroom of a doll's house. The two men dwarfed it, casting huge shadows on the walls.

Rust squatted, examining the contents of Gabrielle's dresser, while Sydowski sat on her bed. Soft pastel, patterned wallpaper with tiny bouquets covered the walls. The ceiling borders were painted a lilac shade. Beautiful, Sydowski thought. A framed piece of embroidery reading: "Gabrielle's Room" hung above the bed. A multicolored crayon drawing of Jackson, Gabrielle's puppy, hung on one wall. This was the room of a happy child, like the rooms of Tanita and Danny.

As Rust sifted gingerly through Gabrielle's dresser drawers, Sydowski ran his fingers over the flowers printed on her comforter. She had been here hours ago. Sleeping, dreaming. Safe. He touched her pillow, traced the frills of the cotton pillow case, and picked up a stuffed pink bear.

"Snuffles," Rust said.

"Huh?"

"Snuffles, Walt. According to her dad, it's her favorite possession, after her pup."

Sydowski touched Snuffles to his nose, inhaling a sweet child's scent. Rust opened Gabrielle's closet, crouched down, and inspected the items jammed into it, starting with Gabrielle's shoes.

"Why in hell are you doing that?" Paul Nunn asked from the doorway. "What could you possibly hope to find?"

Rust and Sydowski exchanged looks.

Nunn's eyes were still wet and he was exhausted from having endured hours of police interviews. Rust stopped, but remained crouched.

"Paul," Sydowski began, "everybody has secrets. Even children."

"Secrets? What secrets?"

"Gabrielle may have been approached by her abductor before. He may have tricked her into keeping it secret. He may have given her something, a little gift." Sydowski nodded to Gabrielle's crayon drawing of her dog. "Maybe she hid a drawing, or wrote something."

Nunn absorbed Sydowski's rationale. "But we've told her and Ryan never to talk to strangers."

"He may not have been a stranger to her. He may have learned something about you and Nancy to trick her. If he took her dog, then he's working from a plan."

Nunn rubbed his stubble, then the back of his neck.

"She's a good girl, she always tells us everything."

"You don't know that," Rust said.

"What about her hair? You found her braids and there was blood."

"Well," Sydowski said, "it's exactly like we've said. We suspect he cut her braids off to change her appearance. She may have struggled and he likely cut himself. If he tossed her hair in the street like he did, it means he was likely in a hurry or afraid he was being watched. It is common for the stranger to want to alter the child's appearance right away."

"Why didn't you tell the press about the suspect?"

"What suspect?" Sydowski said.

"Virgil Shook. I heard some of the detectives talking tonight."

"He's a loser we want to check out. We're waiting for his file from Canada—that's where he's from. We're checking out a lot of people as fast as we can. You should keep his name to yourself."

"Why? If he's got my daughter, you should tell the whole world and splash his face across the news."

"We need every edge we can get. We don't want the kidnapper to know what we may find out about him. It could blow up in our faces."

"That what happened in the Donner case last year with that guy who committed suicide?"

"Something like that, yes."

"Is this Shook guy connected to that baby's murder and my girl?"

"There are similarities in all three cases. That's all we know."

Paul took a deep breath, his shining gaze going around the room tenderly. His little girl's room, where he tucked her in, read her stories, brushed away her fears, promising to keep her safe. And now his little girl's room was somehow violated by the presence of these men—these men who'd looked upon corpses of children, and into the faces of killers. These men who'd touched death, touched evil, were now touching his little girl's private things. They had invaded a hallowed region and somehow fouled it.

"Do what you have to do." Nunn left, bumping into Inspector Turgeon, who smiled at him before entering and closing the door.

"What's the latest, Linda?" Sydowski said.

"IDENT picked up the prints of a pervert from one of the stalls in the girls' bathroom at the Children's Playground. Belong to Donald Barrons. He doesn't look like the composite. We've got two people who can put him there about one hour before the abduction. Vice is grabbing him. Barrons likes to expose himself to little girls."

"I thought somebody checked him clean on Donner and Becker," Sydowski said.

"Maybe we should be more thorough this time," Turgeon said.

"Shook's file arrive yet?" Rust asked.

"The Mounties promise it by tonight."

Rust cursed.

"That it?" Sydowski said.

"IDENT's back at daybreak to do the yard and the neighborhood. More searches with volunteers at Golden Gate. DMV's still working up a pool of suspect vehicles based on the partial plate.''

"What about the tip line?'' Sydowski said.

"I called them. Hundreds of calls, kooks, crazies. They're checking out everything, but there aren't enough bodies, so it's going to take awhile.''

Sydowski nodded. No one spoke.

The room became quiet, except for Rust sifting delicately through Gabrielle's clothes. They had nothing. Two children stolen from their parents in broad daylight and they had nothing to give them a degree of hope. Sydowski slipped a Tums into his mouth.

41

The whipping of the chopper over Golden Gate Park thundered on the TV, then faded as the somber voice of *Metro-TV News* reporter Vince Vincent described the kidnapping and hunt for Gabrielle Nunn.

Squeak-creak. Squeak-creak.

"And tonight, at their Sunset home, Gabrielle Nunn's mother, Nancy, made a heart-stopping plea to her daughter's abductor . . ."

The story cut from the carousel at the park to Nancy and Paul.

Squeak-creak. Squeak-creak..

Keller yawned as Vincent summarized the case, how police linked it to Danny Becker's kidnapping and the unsolved abduction and murder of Tanita Marie Donner last year. The composite of Keller flashed on the screen followed by the dramatic, blurry home-video footage of Gabrielle talking to Keller.

Keller stopped rocking.

There was a description of Keller's truck, then the missing

poster of Gabrielle's dog, details of her severed braids, a picture showing how she would look with shorter hair. Clips of police going door to door in the neighborhood where they found the hair.

"I saw this man stop and he seemed to be struggling with a child in his truck. I thought it was so strange," Eva Blair recounted to reporters what she had witnessed near the Walker place that afternoon. "It was unusual, so I called the police."

Forensic experts searched for clues in the spot where Gabrielle was taken, in the parking lot, and in the secluded area where they found Tanita Donner. Police were in Dolores Park where evidence in the Donner case was found last year. Someone in a pickup was stopped at the Golden Gate Bridge. Garbage collection was halted in Golden Gate Park and around the Sunset. Trash bins were emptied, their contents prodded by officers in overalls and surgical masks. Scores of volunteers, mothers and fathers with their children, walked across sections of Golden Gate Park searching for clues. Police officers and cadets went door to door with pictures of Tanita Donner, Danny Becker, Gabrielle Nunn, and the suspect's composite. The reward for good tips on the cases was raised to $200,000, and the SFPD and FBI had formed a multiagency task force to investigate.

A task force?

Keller swallowed. His throat was dry. Almost raw.

So be it. His mission was sanctified.

Squeak-creak. Squeak-creak.

The abductions have shaken the Bay Area to its very core.

"It's every parent's nightmare," Charlene Munro told reporters as she, along with her ten-year-old daughter and twelve-year-old son, combed Golden Gate Park's wooded areas. "We helped in the search for Danny Becker. I'm a mother, too." Charlene swept aside some grass with a stick, then called her children, who had ambled a few yards from her. "Stay close to me, guys! I just hope this works out for the best."

Squeak-creak. Squeak-creak.

Vince Vincent went on about the intense investigation, the rumors about a psychic being called and contacts with police who faced serial child murder cases in Atlanta, New York, and British Columbia.

Keller switched his set off. Scattered around him were the early editions of the major Bay papers. He had read every word, studied every picture, graphics, locator maps, everything on the case.

Let them search.

It was late, but he was not tired. He went to the worktable, looked through the heap of journals, binders and notes, stopping to study the time-worn snapshot of his three children: Pierce, Alisha and Joshua. Laughing. A few weeks before they drowned.

They never found the bodies.

So let them search. For Raphael. For Gabriel.

They'll never find the bodies. The Truth was revealed to him. His children were not dead. They were waiting to be reborn in celestial light. Only God's Angels could rescue them, transfigure them. Then together they would walk in The Kingdom of God. How could police know his Divine Mission? They were mortals. How could they comprehend what was preordained?

They could never know the Divine Truth as he did.

It had been revealed to him. He had been chosen. He was the enlightened one who would show the world God's wonder. Edward Keller had been ordained; he was the light beyond sorrow, the light beyond the veil of death, destined to fulfill a Holy Mission.

He was cleansed in the light of the Lord.

Soon everyone would know God's love, His name, His glory. *Sanctus, sanctus, sanctus. Dominus Deus sabaoth.*

The Angels, soldiers of God's merciful love, were sent to him.

Keller smiled, for it was true. He had found the first.

Danny Raphael Becker. Raphael of the Powers. Healed by God, Chief of the Guardian Angels. Guardian of Mankind. Protector of Children.

And he had found the second, concealed as Gabrielle Nunn. Gabrielle. Gabriel. God's ambassador to earth. The Angel who heralded the coming of the Messiah. Gabriel had come to him. She was the messenger. She was his.

She was in the basement with Raphael.

It went according to his prayers.

Thanks be to God. Praise Him.

Keller found the silver crucifix and slipped it around his neck. Then he reached for the binder with the names of his eldest son, Pierce, and the third Angel, caressing his meticulous notes inside. One more Angel to complete the choir. One more to complete his Holy Mission. One more and God would initiate the transfiguration. He would find his children. Be with them. Bring them back. Nothing could keep him from his holy destiny now. Nothing. He held his crucifix in a white-knuckled grip. He'd come too far, endured too much pain. Nothing must go wrong now. Suddenly he heard something—

Screaming? Yes. Screaming.

Hysterical screaming from the basement where the angels were.

42

Something as big as an elephant was inside Gabrielle's head beating to get out. It hurt.

She tasted something horrible in her mouth, like vinegar and medicine. Open your eyes. Can't. They're too heavy. Maybe they're stuck shut. Lying on something soft. A bed? Where is she? It didn't smell like her room. Her house. It's smelly here, like something rotten, like a scary place. Where is she?

Squeak-creak.

Where is she? What happened? The party. Joannie Tyson's birthday party at the park. The carousel. Butterflies in her stomach. Rhonda King throwing up. Gross! The man outside the bathroom. Jackson. He found Jackson. A quick secret peek in his truck. Want a soda? You spilled some but—the wet cloth—can't breathe—Jackson barking the cloth dripping medicine—fighting—kicking.

Squeak-creak. Squeak. Creak.

Don't open your eyes!

Something—someone touched her cheek. A soft, warm hand. Small.

Please. Please. Please. Don't hurt me.

She had to open her eyes. Had to. Okay. A little boy. On his knees looking down at her. A boy who was smaller than she was, staring at her. She blinked at him and sniffed. The boy looked sad.

"Who are you?" he said.

"Gabrielle Nunn. Who are you?"

"Danny."

"Where am I? Have you seen my dog, Jackson?"

Danny didn't answer.

"Where's Mr. Jenkins? He knows my dad."

Danny just stared at her.

"Where is this place?"

Danny said nothing.

Gabrielle sat up and looked at him until a tiny light of recognition glimmered on her face. "You're the little boy on TV, the one who got kidnapped—you are!"

"Where's my daddy?" Danny said. "Can I go home now?"

Newspapers covered the basement window. It looked dark outside. Were those bars, like jail? A dim bulb hung from the ceiling, like in Gabrielle's dad's garage, painting the grungy, cracked walls in a pale light. Where's the TV? Were there people here who can take her home? Where was Jackson? Where was Mr. Jenkins? She was confused. She didn't like this place. There were three mattresses, ripped, with stuff coming out of them. They smelled. Why three? The door was closed. Garbage and stuff plastered the floor. Yech!

"Danny," she asked, "who lives in this place?"

He just sat there, his face dirty and white, like he was sick or sleepy or something.

"I don't like this place. I want to go home now," she said.

Danny offered her a chocolate-covered, vanilla cream cookie.

"It's got a bite already." She didn't touch it.

Rick Mofina

Danny bit into the cookie.

Gabrielle knew she was with the boy who got kidnapped and had his picture on TV everywhere. The boy everybody was looking for all over the place. Suddenly she realized a terrible thing.

She was kidnapped, too!

"Danny, where is this place?"

He just stared.

"What's going to happen to us now?" she asked.

Danny's fingers were sticky from the cookie. He was really littler than she was. His chin crumpled and his eyes clamped shut and he began crying in a ragged voice like he had been crying forever. Gabrielle wanted to cry, too, but something inside took over. Big kids look after little kids, they told you in school. Gabrielle put her arm around him.

"Don't cry, Danny." She sniffed. "My daddy will take us home."

"I want to go home, now!"

"Me, too. I wonder who lives in this place?"

Danny pointed a tiny finger to the door. "The man who took me."

Squeak-creak. Squeak-creak. He was out there!

Gabrielle's stomach bounced. Gooseflesh crawled along her arms.

Squeak-creak. Squeak-creak.

She hated Mr. Jenkins, whoever he was. He had tricked her. He lied. Where was Jackson? He must have stolen Jackson from her. He was a bad man. She was in trouble now. Her mommy and daddy told her never talk to strangers. No matter what. But he had Jackson and said he knew Daddy. *No matter what.* She broke the rules and it was all her fault. Mom and Dad were going to be mad. She had to tell them she was sorry she broke the rules. They would come and get her if she told them everything. Maybe she wouldn't be in too much trouble.

Gabrielle knew what she had to do. She had to tell her mom
and dad. But how?

Telephone.

If you ever get lost, Gabrielle, just call home.

She would call home right now.

"Where is the phone, Danny?"

He pointed to the door. "Out there."

Squeak-creak. Squeak-creak..

She was scared. She looked around the room again.

"Danny, you sure there's no phone in this room?"

"Out there."

Gabrielle stood, she was a little dizzy. Maybe she should
just sit here and wait. No! She had to do it. She had to, so she
wouldn't be in trouble. She had to phone home. And she had
to pee.

Squeak-creak. Squeak-creak.

The grease-stained burger boxes and bags crumpled as she
moved to the door. What if the man was watching from a spy
hole, ready to come in at any second? The wrappers, napkins,
empty drink cups, boxes, and bags rustled. Something squished.
Yuck. A half-eaten burger. Stale ketchup bled under her shoe.
In the far corner some wrappers were moving.

By themselves!

Gabrielle froze.

The bags moved a little, trembling like something was gnawing on them. Gabrielle watched. Maybe it was Jackson? What
else could it be? It had to be Jackson. Gabrielle cut a path to
the corner.

"Here, pup," she cooed, lifting a large bag just as a giant
rat with ketchup dripping from its mouth flew at her, coming
so close she felt its tail slap against her palm!

Gabrielle screamed, jumped back, falling.

A vanilla cream cookie whizzed by the rat's head.

"Go away!" Danny shouted, reaching into his bag for
another.

Gabrielle scurried to Danny. Together they fired cookies at the rat. It had touched her. She was scared.

The door swung open.

Mr. Jenkins. Only, he didn't look so friendly now. A big silver cross was swinging from his neck. He spotted the rat, disappeared, and returned with a baseball bat.

"Vermin!" he screamed, bringing the bat down swiftly, missing the rat. It squealed, the bat went *clunk* and garbage scattered.

He yelled, swinging the bat down again.

The fierceness of the man's attack frightened the children more than the rat did. His eyes were huge, popping out of his head, the white parts as big as eggs. His hair wild like a nest of angry snakes. Spittle clung to his beard.

Keller swung again, making a wet, squishing sound. He laughed, his bat dripping with the blood of the rat. Gabrielle screamed. Keller looked at her.

"It is done," he said, moving toward the children.

Keller's expression changed. Raphael and Gabriel were before him. He saw their auras.

The light of one million suns shone upon him.

His rage was replaced by rapture. Like a victorious battle-weary soldier, he laid his foe at the throne. The bloodied, pulpy carcass, fur and mangled intestines, lay inches from Gabrielle and Danny. Gabrielle stifled her sobs, trying not to look.

"W-We want to go home, now. Please, Mr. Jenkins," she pleaded.

Keller did not hear her.

"You have come, Gabriel. God's emissary. You have come to me!"

"Please, Mr. Jenkins! Let me phone my mommy and daddy!"

Remembering the bat, Keller lifted it to his face, examining the blood with fascination.

"I am cleansed in the light of the Lord. I have tasted the

blood of my enemies. None shall defeat me, for my mission is divine and I am truly invincible.'' He moved his fingers over the blood-slicked club. ''I am cleansed in the light—I have tasted the blood of my enemies.

''My mission is divine. I am truly invincible.''

Gabrielle pulled Danny tight to her.

Keller went upstairs to the bathroom and ran the bath water.

God had answered his prayers.

One more angel and the choir would be complete.

Then the tranfiguration would begin.

Wiping the tears from his face, he stood and kissed his crucifix.

It was time for the second baptism.

43

If Virgil Shook worshiped anything in this world beyond himself it was the Zodiac, the personification of power.

The Zodiac was the hooded executioner who had murdered five people in the Bay Area during the late 1960s and mocked police in the cryptic letters he wrote to newspapers. His cunning eclipsed the best minds of the SFPD and the FBI. He owned the city, mastered its fear, yanking it by a leash at his leisure. The Zodiac was a visionary, a seer who knew that when he died, his victims would be his slaves and he would be a king in paradise.

They had never captured him. Shook sighed.

For a time last year, like the Zodiac, he had sipped from the cup of power. He had enjoyed Tanita, the little prostitute. Loved her to death and forced the city to tremble in the wake of his omnipotence. He had manipulated Franklin Wallace, outsmarted police, and taunted the priest with his confessions, spitting in the face of his God, compelling him to genuflect to the power of The One.

That was then. Now the city was under the spell of another. A new player was reaping the harvest of Shook's work and Shook was enraged.

Who did this new fuck think he was?

Shook snapped off the late-night TV news after absorbing the reports of Gabrielle Nunn's abduction in Golden Gate Park. The horror in Nancy Nunn's face had seared him. Her pain should have been his to relish. Yet he watched mournfully from afar, like a starving wolf contending with the mark of a new predator.

Shook paced his dirty flophouse room, oblivious to the opera of sirens piercing the foul night air of the Tenderloin. If he was going to be immortalized like the Zodiac, it was time to up the ante. Time to teach the challenger a lesson in a way even more thrilling than it had been with poor little Franklin Wallace, when he plucked him like a harp, savoring the danger of it to the point of arousal.

Franklin? It's me.

Oh Lord, don't call me at home like this. Lord don't!

They know, Franklin, he lied. They know about Tanita. Me. You.

NO!

They know everything. And the press knows, too.

No!

They found the pictures of you with her in Dolores Park. They are coming for you soon. You know what that means.

No!

Remember our pact, Wallace. We must pay for our sins. We both know that.

But, Virgil, I—

Think of your family, the insurance. They won't pay if you're connected to anything criminal, Franklin. They are coming for you.

Wallace was sobbing, a sickly, man-child kind of weeping.
Virgil, please! I don't know what to do.

You do know. *We both know. Good-bye, Franklin.*

Virgil—No, wait.

May God have mercy on you, Wallace.

Shook fired the blank from the .22, dropping it with the phone on the floor. Wallace screamed through the earpiece, his voice tiny, distant. An hour later, Shook stood safely out of sight near Franklin's house, smiling to himself when that fool he called at the Star *appeared on Franklin's doorstep, like an obedient lapdog.*

Everything flowed. Beautifully. The Zodiac would applaud him.

Time to move on. Time to teach a new, painful lesson, one that would transcend his work with Franklin, one tempered with rage for the new fuck.

Shook pulled on a pair of gloves and went to the corner newspaper box, returning with two fresh editions of the *Star*.

He went to his bed, a huge steel-framed monstrosity from a St. Louis hospital that had burned down. He unscrewed the middle hollow bar from the head and carefully tapped out several rolled-up Polaroid snapshots of himself with Tanita Donner. No one had seen these pictures. And no one knew of the tantalizing clue he had left police before he dispatched the little prostitute to paradise.

Shook traced gloved fingers tenderly over the photos before selecting two. He ripped the Nunn abduction story from the first newspaper and scrawled a note over the text, using a blue felt-tip pen, like the Zodiac. He folded the clipping, put it in a plain, brown envelope, along with one of the Polaroids. He sealed the envelope, scanned the phone book, then addressed the envelope to Paul Nunn.

He made an identical envelope and addressed it to Danny Becker's family. Then Shook left his room, taking the subway to Oakland, where he would drop the two letters in a mailbox. Another yank on the leash.

44

The Ayatollah Khomeini glowered at Reed.

EYE OF THE HURRICANE. AMERICANS HELD HOSTAGE AT THE
U.S. EMBASSY IN TEHRAN. EL SALVADOR TEETERING. MOUNT
ST. HELENS SPEWING ASH AND ROCK. SOVIET INTERVENTION IN
AFGHANISTAN. All there in black-and-white, bleeding on the
front page.

1980.

All there except for Keller's tragedy. Wrong page? Reed
checked the skyline. Wrong date. He hit the advance button
on the Minolta and whisked through time along a microfilm
torrent of photographs, headlines, and advertisements. The take-
up reel buzzed. It was late.

He stayed at the paper after reading the old *Star* clip on
Edward Keller's boating tragedy. Alone in the news library,
searching the past. Reels of microfilm newspapers and opened
news indices were piled next to him, signposts to Keller's case.
The *Star's* clippings were a start. He was also going through
the *Chronicle* and the *Examiner* for their takes, looking for

something extra, any vital piece of information that would . . . what? Connect Keller to the kidnappings?

He had a beard and looked like the guy in the fuzzy home-video footage. And there was something strange about Keller, something that just didn't sit right.

Be careful, Reed. This ain't no movie. Hunches are mean, wild horses. You rode one last year and ended up with your ass getting stomped. The memory of Wallace's widow slapping his face still stung. Wallace's little girl clinging to her father's leg hours before he put his mouth around a double-barreled 12-gauge.

"Leave my daddy alone!"

You'd better be damned careful. The reel clicked and stopped. This is it. BILL RODGERS WINS THE BOSTON MARATHON. MOUNT ST. HELENS ERUPTS. Photos of an anguished President Carter and the wreckage of U.S. helicopters in the desert where eight Americans died in the failed rescue of the hostages. And Keller's story. A small item, inconspicuous. Below the fold:

BUILDER'S 3 CHILDREN LOST IN FARALLONS TRAGEDY

Three children are missing and feared dead after a family sight-seeing excursion ended in tragedy yesterday near the Farallon Islands.

Nine-year-old Pierce Keller, his sister, Alisha, 6, and their brother, Joshua, 3, are presumed drowned after the small boat chartered from Half Moon Bay by their father, Edward Keller of San Francisco, capsized in a storm southeast of the islands.

"The search for the children will continue through the night and tomorrow," a U.S. Coast Guard official said. The chances of finding them alive were "remote," he said.

"The weather was severe and none of the children had

life jackets. We found the father on a buoy, suffering from extreme exhaustion and hypothermia."

Keller is recovering in San Francisco General Hospital. He is the owner of Resurrection Building Inc., one of northern California's largest contracting firms, specializing in the construction of churches. An official with the company was too distraught to comment when reached by the Chronicle.

No other details were available.

Resurrection Building? Churches? Keller built churches? Interesting. Explained his religious ranting. Reed punched the photocopy button. As the Minolta hummed, he searched the San Francisco phone book and the current state directory of companies for a listing for Resurrection Building. Nothing. He searched the phone book and city directory for Edward Keller's listing. Nothing.

He pulled the story from the copy tray and read it again. Then he snapped through his notes from his interview with Keller.

"I know that soon I will be with my children again. That I will deliver them from purgatory. God in His infinite mercy has revealed this to me. Every day I give Him thanks and praise Him. And every day I wage war against doubt in preparation for my blessed reunion."

Reed went over the passages several times.

He removed his glasses, chewing thoughtfully on one earpiece.

"I will be with my children again."

He sifted through his papers for Molly's article on the FBI's psychological profile of Danny Becker's kidnapper. The quotes leaped from the page: "—traumatized by cataclysmic event involving children—lives in fantasy world stimulated by alcohol, drugs or religious delusions . . ." Religious delusions.

And there was another key about the suspect, the FBI had

told Molly. Reed scanned her story. Here it was. Yes. They always followed the news coverage of their cases to learn what police knew and to enjoy feelings of invincibility, superiority.

Keller told Reed that he had read his stories about Danny Becker and Tanita Marie Donner.

Reed rubbed his tired, burning eyes.

"You know you are crazy to be here at this hour, Reed." Molly Wilson's bracelets chimed as she breezed over to him, brandishing a first-edition copy of that day's *Star*.

"Let me see that." Reed took the paper, still warm and moist from the Metroliner presses.

"You should be in a bar, Reed. We own the front page."

The double-deck forty-point headline screamed:

SERIAL CHILD-KILLER STEALS SECOND CHILD

"I didn't believe the night desk when they said you were working in here. What the hell are you up to at this hour?"

Wilson bent over behind Reed, her hair playing against his shoulder. He caught a trace of her Obsession.

"Let's go have a beer. Photo guys are saving a table at Lou's."

"I'll pass."

"You'll pass? Why? What's so important here?"

Reed looked at Wilson. Deciding to confide in her, he got up and shut the library door.

"This is between you and me. It doesn't leave this room, Molly."

He returned to his chair. Wilson sat on the table.

"Remember, I joked to you about this Keller guy from the bereavement group when you were doing up the FBI profile?"

"Yeah."

"Before I go any further, read this." He handed her his notes from Keller, the old clippings from the tragedy twenty years ago, and her article on the psych profile. It took less than two minutes for her to ingest everything. Next Reed handed her working prints of the police composite and a still from the blurry home-video footage of the suspect in Golden Gate, then Henry Cain's contact sheet of the pictures he shot of Dr. Martin's bereavement group. Although Edward Keller didn't want his picture taken, Cain took it. Secretly. Most photographers would have. It's an unwritten rule in the business. You never know when you'll need a photo of a certain person. Like now. Wilson held the contacts up to the light and squinted through a loupe at the one-inch-square shot of Keller.

"Holy fuck, Tom. Put dark glasses on Keller and he looks just like the composite. What do you think?"

"He's got to be a suspect. There's got to be something there."

Wilson pulled up a chair, sat next to Reed, and began picking through the papers. "What do you think is going on?"

"I think he could never come to terms with the drowning of his three children. Something snapped inside and he grabbed Danny Becker and Gabrielle Nunn as surrogates."

"What about the Donner case? Where does it fit in?"

"I'm not sure. So far it's different. I mean in that case a body was found. Maybe something went wrong with that one, or it's not related. I don't know anymore."

"Look at this!" Wilson underlined the ages of Keller's children when they drowned, then drew a line on a blank piece of paper, writing three-year-old Joshua Keller's name on one side of the line. Opposite Joshua's name she wrote, "Danny Raphael Becker, 3." Under Joshua, she wrote, "Alisha Keller, 6." Across the line she wrote "Gabrielle Michelle Nunn, 5."

"Look at the old stories Tom. Gabrielle will be six by the anniversary of the tragedy, the twenty-first."

"That's right."

"Something else. These names"—Wilson circled Raphael and Gabrielle—"these are angels' names."

"I thought that, too. Are you sure?"

"I'm a lapsed Catholic. I wrote a high school paper on angels."

Reed studied the names, thinking.

"Angels. Maybe to him the kids are angels or something?"

"Maybe guardian angels?"

"Maybe. It would fit with the profile. I mean we've got him on the traumatic cataclysmic event with children."

"Right, the drownings."

"And we've got him on religious delusions."

"Church building, Scripture spewing, grief-stricken nut who is stealing kids with angel names who are the same age as his dead children." Wilson shook her head.

"What?"

"I don't know, Tom. It's just so incredible."

"Not really, Molly. Look, remember I did that feature on the woman who posed as a maternity nurse and walked out of an East Bay hospital with a newborn?"

"It was a good piece."

"Well, the FBI's research showed that a key motivator for child abductors—and it's mostly women who do newborn hospital abductions—is the need to replace a child. So it's not unreal. And I'm thinking, this could be the same thing Keller is going through."

"Yeah, but for twenty years, Tom? We're making a leap here."

"Stranger things have happened."

"Okay, so it fits. So why not go to the police? Why not tell Sydowski about your theory? Let him check it out."

Reed stared at her, saying nothing. Her suggestion made perfect sense, but he couldn't do it. Wilson knew.

"It's because of what happened last time you played your hunch, right? You're a little gun-shy?"

"Something like that. What if I tell Sydowski, and he goes to Keller and it turns out he's not the bad guy at all? Keller's in a counseling group, the anniversary of his kids' deaths is coming. What if the police spook him and he loses it or—''

Reed couldn't finish the thought.

''You don't want another suicide.''

Tom rubbed his face. ''I may have been wrong about Franklin Wallace, Molly. It's been haunting me. I just don't know.''

''I don't think you were wrong there. Wallace had something to do with Tanita's murder. Maybe it was a partner crime.''

''Okay, say I was right about Wallace. But I went through so much shit with that. It cost me so much. I'm torn up with this.''

''But what if Keller is the one? There's so much at stake here. The kids could be alive.''

''I know.'' Exhausted, he placed his face in his hands.

Wilson bit her lip and blinked. Her bracelets tinkled as she brushed her hair aside. She tapped a finger on the table thoughtfully before turning to him.

''I'll help you, Tom.''

''What are you talking about?''

''There's only one thing you can do.''

''What?''

''Check Keller out yourself, quietly. Take a few days, dig up everything you can about him, then decide whether or not to pass it to the police. That's what you're thinking, isn't it?''

''It would be risky. The paper would fire my ass if it found out what I was doing.''

''Nobody would have to know. I'll cover for you. I'll help you.''

45

Sydowski was wide awake. The numbers of his clock radio blazed 3:12 A.M. from his night table. He tugged on his robe, made coffee, and shuffled to the aviary to be with the birds.

He deposited himself into his rocker, a Father's Day gift from the girls, running a hand over his face, feeling his whiskers as he sat in the dark, listening to the soft chirping.

Turgeon had volunteered to stay with Mikelson, Ditmire, and the crew keeping an all-night watch at the Nunn home. For all the sleep he was getting, he might as well have stayed, too. He fingered his beeper. Linda would page him if anything popped.

Damn. This was a ballbreaker.

The out-of-focus video footage was good, but it wasn't enough. They had squat. No good calls. No solid leads. Virgil Shook's file was supposed to arrive today. That should help. They had zip on Becker and Nunn. DMV was working up a list of all Ford pickups and the California partial tag. They were certain the severed braids they found were Gabrielle's.

Beyond that and the footage, they had no physical evidence on **Becker** and Nunn.

IDENT would hit the Nunn house and neighborhood at daybreak, concentrating on the dog's pen, comb it for anything. More than two dozen detectives were dissecting each family's background for a common denominator. Why were these children selected? Was it random? Becker was stalked; Nunn was lured in a calculated plan. But the guy risked getting caught. If he was fearless, he was on a mission, and when there was a mission, delusion fueled it. What kind? Nothing surfaced to lead them to terrorists. Nothing to lead them to a cult, or human sacrifice, according to Claire Ward with Special Investigations. The familys' religious backgrounds varied. Angela Donner was Baptist, the Beckers were Protestant, the Nunns, Anglican. No common thread, except their Christianity. And those faces.

Angels' faces.

Tanita Marie Donner. Peering into that bag. What he did to her was inhuman. Was it Shook? Was he their boy? Was he now out of control? Tanita may have been stalked. Taken in broad daylight. But he killed her, left a corpse, left pictures, left his mark, and called the press. Why? To mock the police? Was he just practicing with Tanita?

Practice makes perfect.

Sydowski was alert now. Might as well go to the hall.

In the shower, he thought of the children. What about their birth months? Signs of the Zodiac. The Zodiac? He patted Old Spice on his face after shaving, pulled a fresh pair of pants over his Fruit of the Looms. He chose the shirt with the fewest wrinkles, a blue Arrow button-down, plopped on his bed, and laced up his leather shoes. The Zodiac had taunted police with his mission. Sydowski took a navy tie from his rack, knotted it, then strapped on his shoulder holster, unlocked his Glock from the safe on the top closet shelf. He checked it, slipping it into his holster. He hated the thing, it was so uncomfortable. He put on a gray sports coat, rolled his shoulders. Gave his

hair a couple of rakes with a brush, reached for the leather-
encased shield, gazing at his laminated ID picture and his badge.
A lifetime on the job. Twenty-six years of staring at corpses.
He looked at the gold-framed pictures on his dresser—his
girls, his grandchildren, his wedding picture. Basha's smile.
He slipped the case into his breast pocket and left.

On the way to the hall, he stopped at his neighborhood all-
night donut shop. A few nighthawks huddled over coffee. Jennie, the manager, was wiping the counter with an energy that,
at 4:30 A.M., was painful to witness. Her face told him he
looked bad. "You're working too hard, Walt. You getting
enough sleep? A growing boy needs his sleep." She poured
coffee into a large take-out cup. "You need a woman to take
care of you." She spooned in sugar, a couple of drips of cream,
snapped on a lid.

"You think so?"

"I know so. You're early today. Bert ain't made no chocolate
yet. I've got some fresh old fashions though. Warm from the
oven."

"Fine."

She dropped four plain donuts into a bag. Rang up the order.
"It's a shame about them kids, Walt."

A moment of understanding passed between them.

"You'll crack it, Walt. You're a wily old flatfoot."

Sydowski slid a five toward her. "Keep the change, Jennie."

At the Hall of Justice, in the fourth-floor Homicide detail,
three faces watching him from the mobile blackboard in the
middle of the room stopped Sydowski in his tracks. Poster-size
blowups of Tanita Marie Donner, Danny Raphael Becker, and
Gabrielle Michelle Nunn.

Score: Three to fucking zero.

A couple of weary inspectors were on the phone, pumping
sources on the abductions. Files and reports were stacked next

to stained coffee mugs. The *Star's* morning edition was splayed
on the floor, the front-page headline blaring at him. The
enlarged, city case map at one end of the room now contained
a third series of pins, yellow ones, for Gabrielle Nunn. Someone
was shouting in one of the interview rooms. A door slammed
and a massive slab of Irish-American righteousness with a
handlebar mustache, in vogue for turn-of-the-century beat cops,
stepped out: Inspector Bob Murphy.

"Who you got in there, Bobby?"

Murphy had been up for nearly twenty-four hours. He slapped
a file into Sydowski's hand. Sydowski put on his bifocals and
began reading.

Donald Arthur Barrons, age forty-three. Five feet, three
inches tall, about one hundred pounds. Red hair. No tattoos.
No beard. Nowhere near the description of the suspect. He was
the flasher pervert whose prints were lifted from one of the
stalls in the girls' washroom at the Children's Playground after
the abduction. Witnesses put Barrons at the park earlier that
morning.

"Accomplice?" Murphy anticipated the question of description. Barrons had molestation convictions. Worked downtown.
Parking lot attendant.

"Vice picked him up about midnight at his apartment."

"And?"

"We got zip. Sweet dick, Walt. I jumped him too soon."

"Why's that?"

"He admitted right off to being there. Said he goes there to
play with himself in the girls' can. But he's alibied solid. Was
working his lot well before Nunn was grabbed. It checks. He's
got clock-punched parking receipts. Witnesses. And a hot dog
vendor remembers selling him a cheesedog. So, nothing."

Sydowski went back to the file. Barrons worked for EE-Z-
PARK, a company that owned several small lots in prime
downtown locations, "Do you know if the Beckers and Nunns
ever parked at his lot?"

"No."

"Ask them. If they can't be sure, get the company to show you records. I know they computerize tag numbers of all cars. Check the Ford and the partial tag with them, too. May be a common factor there."

Sydowski slapped Murphy on the back and handed him the file. "I'd kick Barrons loose, go home, and get some sleep."

Murphy nodded. He was a good cop. The boys in Vice did jump Barrons too soon, Sydowski thought, starting a fresh pot of coffee in the coffee room. He stared at the fading poster above the counter. A .38 Smith & Wesson with a steel lock through the action—"Keep it locked at home." They may have blown it with Barrons. Damn. Too many divorced, heart-broken cops thinking like fathers instead of detectives here.

Notice of a case status meeting was scrawled on the black-board: 8:30 A.M. Sydowski eyed the fax machine. Nothing from Canada. He sipped coffee and flipped through a basket of the most recent tips and leads that had been checked, or dismissed. He went through the E-mail printouts. Lots of advice on how to conduct an investigation. Cyber advice from around the world pointing them to suspicious websites and kiddie porn stuff. Most of the tips came from crazies. Most of it was plain useless stuff. Sightings across the Bay Area of a man fitting the general description. "Suspect spotted on BART last year, caller can't remember when." Impossible to check. Psychics and anonymous kooks such as: "Caller says she heard suspect confess to God that he killed Tanita Donner. Caller says she was instructed to inform police by the Lord." Sydowski shook his head.

One dismissed report came with a cassette recording. Sydow-ski rummaged through his desk for his machine, inserted the tape, rewound it to the beginning, put on a headset, and pressed the play button.

"We've been in love for more than a year. . . ."

The words hung in the air like a bizarre smell. It was difficult to determine the speaker's gender.

"Danny is with me now. It's better this way. He loves me. He's always loved me. Our first meeting was so beautiful, so innocent. I think it was preordained. Shall I tell you about it?"

Sydowski checked the accompanying report. The caller had phoned in on the task force line, which was wired to record calls.

"I was walking through the park when we saw each other. Our eyes met, he smiled. Have you seen his eyes? So expressive, I'm looking at them now. He is so captivating. I won't tell you how we made contact, that's my little secret, but I will say he communicated his love to me intuitively. A pure, virtuous, absolute love . . ." The voice wept, rambling for five minutes until the line went dead.

Sydowski removed his headset, went over the accompanying report. The caller was Chris Lorenzo Hollis, a forty-year-old psychiatric patient who called from his hospital room. The staff said he'd been mesmerized with the Becker kidnapping, and fantasized about being Danny Becker's mother. He watched TV news reports, read the newspaper stories faithfully. He hadn't left the hospital in sixty days.

Sydowski went to another cleared report, opening a thin legal-size file folder containing a single sheet of paper sealed in clear plastic and a two-page assessment. The piece of paper was left that night on the counter of the SFPD station in Balboa Park. Nothing on the person who delivered it. It was in a blank, white letter-size envelope. No markings. Sydowski read the document.

Re: Kidnapping of Danny Becker and Gabrielle Nunn
  Dear Sirs: This material was channeled spiritually so it is open to interpretation. The kidnapper is Elwood X. Suratz, born Jan. 18, 1954. He is a pedophile who was in the city recently for counseling. He cancelled his

appointment when he became overwhelmed by his urges. While in a semipsychotic state, he went XXXXXX hunting for prey on the subway where he abducted Danny Becker. . . .

The letter graphically described assaults on Danny, then detailed biographical material on Suratz. The accompanying two-page report dismissed the tip as bogus. No such person existed. Every claim in the letter has been double-checked. Not one item could be verified. The letter was typed on the same portable Olympia manual that was used for ten other similar letters sent to police on ten different high-profile cases. Police suspected the letters came from somebody who thought they had psychic abilities. They didn't.

Sydowski gulped his coffee just as the fax machine began humming. The first of twenty-six pages, via the FBI liaison in Ottawa, on the Canadian police, prison, and psych records of Virgil Lee Shook were arriving, including copies of the most recent mugs of Shook. He was a forty-eight-year-old Caucasian, six feet tall, one hundred eighty pounds. He had light-colored hair. Put a beard on him and he fit the description in the Becker-Nunn cases. His tattoos matched those of the hooded man in the Polaroids with Tanita Marie Donner.

Sydowski felt his gut tighten and popped a Tums.

Shook was born in Dallas and drifted to Canada after he was under suspicion of assaulting a four-year-old boy near La Grange, Texas. In Canada, he achieved a staggering record of sexual assaults on children. In one instance, he claimed to be a relative and lured a seven-year-old boy and his five-year-old sister from their parents at a large park near Montreal. Shook kept the children captive for five days in a suburban motel room, where he tied them to the room's beds, donned a hood, and repeatedly assaulted them. He took pictures of the children and kept a journal detailing how he satisfied his fantasies before abandoning them alive.

Shook was arrested two years later in Toronto after three university students caught him molesting a five-year-old boy in a secluded wooded area. Shook had abducted the boy from his inattentive grandfather hours earlier off the Toronto subway. In court, Shook detailed his attacks on scores of children over the years. His actions were born out of his own misery. He said he was sexually abused when he was a nine-year-old altar boy by his parish priest. Shook was ten when his father died. His mother remarried and he was beaten by his stepfather. Shook grew up envying and loathing ''normal'' children. He would never overcome his need to exact a toll, ''inflict damage'' on them. After earning parole three years ago, he had vanished.

A wolf among the lambs.

Sydowski sat down and reread the entire file.

Trauma as a child. Religious overtones. Need to re-offend. Fantasy fulfillment. A pattern of crime that fit with the Donner-Becker-Nunn cases. Shook was lighting up the FBI profile like a Christmas tree. Sydowski reached for his phone and punched the number for Turgeon's cell. They would bring the task force up to speed on Shook at the eight-thirty meeting.

''Turgeon.''

''It's Walt, Linda.''

''You're up early.''

''Get down here to 450 as soon as possible. We've got Shook's file.''

''Is it him, Walt?''

''It's him, Linda, and guess who his hero is?''

''I couldn't begin.''

''The Zodiac.''

46

At dawn, a white van squeaked to a stop at Gabrielle Nunn's home and four sober-faced members of the San Francisco Police Department's IDENT detail got out. Dressed in dark coveralls, they talked softly, yawning, finishing off coffee, and tossing their cups into the truck. A second van arrived with six more officers. They went to homes on either side of the Nunns', waking owners, showing them search warrants. Yellow plastic tape was stretched the length of seven houses, sealing front and backyards with the message: POLICE LINE — DO NOT CROSS. The Nunn home was the middle house. Before the day's end, every inch in the sectioned-off area would be sifted, searched, and prodded for anything connected to the case.

It was no ordinary Sunday morning here. Something had been defiled in the inner Sunset, where less than twenty-four hours earlier Gabrielle had skipped off to Joannie Tyson's birthday party, radiant in her new dress.

Her neighbors knew the nightmare.

They had seen the news crews, gasped for reporters, watched

TV, and read the papers. This morning, they stared from their doors and windows, shaking their heads, hushing their children, drawing their curtains. "I hope they find her. Her poor parents." Something had been violated, something terrifying had left its mark, now manifest in yellow police tape—America's flag of tragedy and death.

Ngen Poovong knew death intimately. But you couldn't tell by looking at the shy eleven-year-old, standing at the tape with the usual cluster of gawkers and children. The horrors of Ngen's life were not evident in his face, his T-shirt, shorts, and sneakers. His secrets never left his home, which was two doors from Gabrielle's. Ngen did not know Gabrielle and Ryan well. He had difficulty making friends, his English was so poor. His family had been in San Francisco a short time. He watched the men in coveralls. Police. Never talk to police. He knew what the excitement was all about, but he was frightened. He glanced over his shoulder to his house and saw Psoong watching him from the window.

Do not tell them what you know.

Ngen said nothing. Just as he had done last night when police came to their door, followed by the TV people. He remembered Psoong peeking through the curtains, then turning to Ngen and his older sister, Min. "Something is wrong," Psoong told them in their own tongue. "Police are going to every door."

Ngen and Min had not seen him this worried since the black days when they were all crammed on the boat, drifting hopelessly in the South China Sea. "They are going to every house taking notes. They will be here soon."

"Maybe they know?" Min said, pulling Ngen close.

"We must make no mistakes. Remember the rules."

The rules were simple: Listen to everything. Watch everything. Know everything. Say nothing. You are ignorant. Trust no one. Without the rules there was no survival. And Psoong Li, and Min and Ngen Poovong were survivors.

Their families had met on a smuggler's trawler, crammed

with one hundred other people who paid 1,000 U.S. dollars a person for safe passage from Laos to Manila. Four days out, pirates attacked. Ngen's father and mother were killed. So were Psoong's parents. Min was raped. Psoong was stabbed, but survived. Ngen wanted to jump to the sharks. Min became mute and stared at the sea. Psoong comforted the survivors, organizing the rationing of the little fresh water and rice that were left. He was especially kind to Min and Ngen, urging them to be strong to honor the memory of their families, to believe in their rescue. Psoong, Min, and Ngen became friends, forming a small family, and Psoong shared the secret that his father had wisely sent his savings to Psoong's uncle in California, who had written that the best candidates for immigration to the United States were families with relatives living there. Psoong had a plan.

He proposed that Min act as his wife and Ngen as their son. Psoong was thirty-one, Min was twenty. With no documentation on their ages, they would lie to make it work. Afterward, they could go their separate ways, if they chose, but for now it was a matter of survival. Min stared at the sea and agreed. There was no other choice.

"Good," Psoong said. "No one will ever learn the truth if we follow our rules." Failure would mean deportation and death.

"Remember the rules," Psoong whispered to Min and Ngen three days later when a Hawaii-bound Swedish freighter picked them up. After eleven months in a refugee camp, an American official granted them life when he stamped his approval on their applications to enter the United States.

In San Francisco, they lived in the basement of Psoong's uncle's house for several months, maintaining their secret, remaining family. Then they bought an old two-story house in the Sunset with Psoong's father's savings and the money they earned as office cleaners. They lived quietly in fear—fear that intensified when police came to them last night.

Remember the rules. We cannot go back. No one must know.

The two detectives, who were not in uniform, flashed their badges and Psoong let them in. They did not stay long after Psoong explained in faltering English that they knew nothing about the missing little American girl. When the detectives left, Psoong thought that was the end of it and managed a smile. His relief vanished less than an hour later when one of the officers returned with an Asian woman. She was fluent in five Asian languages, including theirs.

She was a pretty, young, university language professor from Berkeley who could not be fooled. Right off she explained how the police were not the slightest bit interested in them, only their help, which they could give confidentially. After listening to her warm, friendly assurances, Ngen immediately wanted to tell her what he had seen.

The woman asked if they remembered seeing anything odd in the last month or so. Psoong and Min shook their heads. The woman showed them a picture of Gabrielle. Yes, Ngen knew her and talked to her once or twice. She was a friendly little girl who loved her dog.

"How do you know she loved her dog?" the detective said.

The professor translated.

Ngen shot a glance at Psoong. Remember the rules. The professor caught the communication and placed herself on the couch between Psoong and Ngen, showing Ngen an enhanced picture of Gabrielle's kidnapper. For a microsecond, recognition flickered in his eyes.

"Have you seen anyone like this man around here before?"

Ngen swallowed and shook his head.

The professor knew the truth. "Are you certain? Nothing will happen to you if you think you know something." Her pretty eyes held him prisoner. She would not let him look at Psoong.

"No," Ngen lied.

The woman asked Min and Psoong a few more questions,

then cards were left and requests made for calls if anything was remembered. This was a very serious case. A little girl's life was in danger. Ngen noticed how the tall detective searched his eyes for something.

Now, watching the police scrutinizing Gabrielle's yard, Ngen struggled to understand what was happening. More than twenty officers in coveralls, with radios crackling, were investigating the neighborhood. The enormity of Gabrielle's disappearance hit Ngen. He could no longer stand it. He hurried home and pleaded with Min to allow him to tell the police what he had seen. What if the kidnapper had stolen him? Wouldn't Min and Psoong want help? This was the United States, people helped people here. Min called Psoong, who was at work. He came home, worry etched in his face.

"I, too, have thought about the matter. It is true that I could not bear another tragedy, if this abductor were to take Ngen. We must help police catch him. But first we need assurances."

Psoong called the number on the professor's card and she arrived with two new officers—Sydowski, a big man with gold in his mouth and his associate, a dark-haired young woman, Turgeon. Min made tea. The professor assured them the police were only interested in the kidnapping of the little girl who lived two doors away.

"The little girl's dog did not run away a month ago," Ngen began.

"What happened?" Sydowski asked as Turgeon made notes. The professor translated.

"A man took the dog in the night."

How did Ngen know?

"I saw him from my bedroom window," the professor repeated.

Sydowski asked to see Ngen's upstairs bedroom. They saw the small telescope on Ngen's nightstand at the window. They remained calm. The bedroom's large corner windows overlooked the Nunns' backyard. Sydowski could see two IDENT people kneeling in the dog's kennel.

"Tell the officers everything," the professor said.

Ngen loved to look at the stars and moon. They were his hope when they were adrift at sea, and now his communion with his dead mother and father. The night the man came there was a three-quarter moon. It was about two A.M. because he had set his alarm to get the best view. All was tranquil in the neighborhood. Ngen could hear the Nunns' air conditioner humming. He was studying the moon when he saw a man walking down the back alley. He focused his telescope on him. He looked like the man in the police picture. He unwrapped some meat and fed it to the dog, then walked away with the dog to his truck, which was parked down the alley, and drove away.

Sydowski and Turgeon absorbed Ngen's account.

"Did he get a license plate?"

The professor translated and the boy said something at length, reaching for the star journal he kept, flipping through pages.

He kept a journal! Sydowski couldn't believe it.

At school they taught you to take license numbers if you ever saw anything bad. But he didn't get the entire plate.

"The first three characters: B75," the professor translated.

"Was it a California plate?"

"Yes."

"What kind of truck was it?"

Ngen didn't know trucks.

"If we showed him pictures?" Turgeon asked, while taking notes.

The professor explained. Ngen nodded. "Yes, that would help."

Sydowski wanted to know what kind of meat the man gave the dog, and did Ngen see a store's logo on any wrapping or package?

The professor translated. Ngen thought for a moment. It was hamburger in a white tray with transparent wrap.

"What sorts of things does Ngen write in his star journal?" The professor asked Ngen.

"Dates and times of everything he saw in the night."

"Did Ngen make such notes the night he saw the man take the dog?"

Yes, he did because it was so unusual.

"May we borrow the journal?" Turgeon asked.

The professor made the request. Ngen looked to Psoong, who nodded.

One more time, because this was so important, Sydowski wanted to know what happened when the man approached the Nunns' yard.

Ngen said the man threw some hamburger into the dog's kennel and the dog ate it without making a sound. Then the man opened the gate and the dog ate more from his hand. Then the man picked up the dog, took him under his arm, and walked to his truck and drove off.

"Did the man throw the wrapper away?"

Ngen thought. Yes, he tossed it aside.

"Where?"

Somewhere in the alley near the yard.

"Again, what did it look like?"

The woman explained, then said something to Min, who left the room. She returned with three packs of frozen meat. Ngen touched a package of sausages, packed on a white foam meat tray with clear plastic wrapping and a producer's label with a bar code on one corner, with the date, weight, cost, and a product code.

Turgeon made notes. Sydowski reached for his radio and summoned the head of the IDENT unit to Ngen's room. The man arrived, his eyes darting to the boy, the meat, Sydowski, then Turgeon.

"This is what we're looking for, Carl," Sydowski said.

Captain Carl Gray turned the package over in his hands.

"Sausages?"

"A meat tray and wrapper just like this one," Turgeon said.

"The guy lured the dog away with wrapped hamburger," Sydowski said. "If we could find the wrapping, label, and product code—"

"Right." Gray came up to speed. "Then we could narrow where and when he bought it." Gray reached for his radio. "I'll call my team for a briefing. But it'll be a needle in a haystack, Walt."

"I know. It's been nearly a month."

Gray left, and while they thanked Ngen and his family, something ate at Sydowski, something he needed to know, so he told the professor to ask.

"Why didn't you come forward yesterday?" the woman said.

Ngen looked at Psoong, at Min, and the professor, who immediately knew the answer. They were scared.

Sydowski nodded.

Then Ngen looked directly at Sydowski, and in a little boy's voice that was awash with emotion, spoke spontaneously, rapidly, forcing the professor to struggle to keep up with him.

"They were scared that police would send them back, but he loved this country, it was his home and did not want to make trouble because he knew that people who make trouble are punished. The day after the dog was taken, Ngen saw the little girl and how sad she was. He saw the signs in the neighborhood with the dog's picture and heard her calling him every night. He wanted to tell her that he saw a man steal her dog, but was afraid."

Ngen began crying. Min comforted him.

"His heart ached for the little girl who loved her dog so much. Ngen knew what it was like to love someone and lose them. The girl is gone and he is terrified. It is all his fault. Had he spoken earlier, maybe she would be safe. And now that he has spoken, maybe the kidnapper will come for him? Please do not punish his family. He is sorry. Please forgive him! Please!''

The professor dabbed her eyes with a tissue.

Sydowski and Turgeon exchanged glances.

47

By Monday afternoon, Reed was atop Russian Hill, approaching a Victorian mansion overlooking the Golden Gate Bridge. A gabled roof topped its three stories, twin turrets, and colossal windows. The open front porch was edged with ornate spindled railing, and the clipped lawn was rimmed by a wrought-iron, spear-tipped fence.

Would he find answers here? Anything that would bring him closer to Keller? So far, the house was the only lead he and Wilson came up with after digging all of Sunday and this morning. No matter what they tried, quietly using their sources in a number of agencies, scouring the Internet, they could not nail a good address for Keller. He was invisible.

Even Professor Martin provided little help. Coincidentally, she popped by the *Star* that morning to thank Reed over coffee in the cafeteria for the feature on her group. Reed made time for her because he wanted to know more about Keller, but he was careful not to tell her about his suspicions. And if Martin had any, she kept them to herself.

"Tom, I just want to thank you. After your article ran, we received pledges of support and calls from bereaved parents searching for help. I thought your reporting and writing was sensitive."

"Don't thank me. Say, what did Keller think?" Reed was casual.

"I don't know. He is so private. Why do you ask?"

Reed shrugged. "No reason. I mean, he really didn't like me."

She was wearing a summer dress and sandals. Almost no makeup. She was attractive, Reed thought. "I'm glad you left him out of your story. He has a lot of pain to deal with right now."

"Don't we all, Kate?"

Reed's cell phone rang. He had to go.

Standing to leave, he asked Kate to put him in touch with Keller again. He wanted to apologize. She would, only she did not have a number or address for him. It was curious. Maybe she had taken his number down incorrectly, or there was a mix-up. Anyway, none of the others knew him or where he lived. And something strange had happened.

"He stopped coming to the sessions after you visited the group."

"Really? It was because of me?"

"I don't know. It could have been a number of things. I mean, I don't know much about him beyond his loss of his three children. And I'm worried because the anniversary is coming up. I've been trying to find him. I believe he gave me a phony number to protect his privacy. If I locate him, I'll let him know you would like to see him. I owe you."

It was Molly Wilson who called Reed. She had tried finding Keller's wife, Joan Keller. Joan Webster, if she was using her maiden name. She checked the DMV, voters' registration, everything she could think of. Nothing.

As for Keller, only a San Francisco post office box and two other addresses surfaced from all of their checking. One was for the bungalow that the Kellers rented for a couple of years in Oakland during the late 1960s. Wilson knocked on some doors, went through old directories, trying to find old neighbors, see if Keller kept in touch with anybody. Nothing.

They were missing something obvious. What the hell was it? Reed reflected, coming to the last address, their last hope for a lead: the mansion on Russian Hill. He pushed open the unlocked gate, entered the yard, and gazed at the house where Keller had lived with his wife and children twenty years ago. Before their lives were destroyed.

No one answered the bell. Reed waited. Rang again. He heard the clank of metal on stone and went around to the side, where a woman was on her knees, tending a rosebush. Property records showed the owners were Lyndon and Eloise Bamford, who bought it from Carlos Allende, who bought it from Keller about a year after the tragedy. The robust woman appraising Reed appeared to be in her sixties. She had the attractive, intelligent face of a lady who was not easily intimidated.

"May I help you?" She patted a trowel against a gloved hand.

"I'm looking for Eloise Bamford?"

"You found her. Who are you?"

"Tom Reed, a reporter with *The San Francisco Star.*"

"A reporter?" She stood and accepted his card.

"Sorry to interrupt you. I was hoping you could help me."

Sensing something behind him, Reed turned and faced an uneasy Doberman. "I have identification if you would care to see it?"

Eloise Bamford smiled.

"No, you look the part. Go away, Larry," she ordered the dog. "We'll go to the back porch. I've just made lemonade."

They sat in exquisite cane chairs and Reed admired the Bamfords' backyard. It was a sloping garden, with an oasis of large trees, dells of ferns, and fiery-red rhododendrons, pathways lined with rose-covered, stone retaining walls.

Reed sipped pink lemonade and told Mrs. Bamford—who insisted on being called Eloise—about the bereavement group feature and his hunt for Keller. He did not reveal his fears about Keller, keeping his urgency out of the conversation, hoping Eloise might jump in.

She didn't.

As he continued, Reed was drawing the conclusion he had hit another dead end. He showed Eloise the articles of Keller's tragedy. She read them while he absorbed the garden's tranquility.

"Yes, I remember the case and the Allendes." She gave the clippings back to him. "They were from Argentina. Sold the house to us after a year. Couldn't stand to live here anymore. Sad."

"Why was that?"

"Too many ghosts."

Reed nodded.

"Of course, you know how Joan Keller died?"

She was dead? "I was trying to find out."

"Suicide. Here. Not long after the children drowned."

He had never found any stories about that, nor an obit.

"Joan Keller's death was what led the Allendes to sell. They didn't know the Kellers' history until someone around here mentioned it. Mrs. Allende couldn't bear to stay in the house. They sold it. Moved back to Argentina. I think he was a diplomat."

"The tragic history of the house didn't bother you?"

"Not really."

Eloise wanted to know why Reed would come to the house looking for Keller when he hadn't lived in it for such a long time.

"It's because I can't find him. I know it's a long shot, but I thought you might have a current address for him. Do you know him?"

"Not at all."

"I see." Reed was at a loss. "I just thought coming here might help me find him. After the story on the university's research, Keller seemed to vanish."

"Like a ghost himself."

"I suppose." Reed thanked her for her lemonade and time.

"Why do you need to find him?"

"I need to talk to him about his tragedy. The twenty-year anniversary is coming up. The *Star* wanted a memorial feature."

"Mmmmm . . ." Eloise kept turning Reed's card over.

"I'm curious," Reed said.

"It's part of your job."

"How did Joan Keller die?"

Eloise sipped her lemonade and looked out at the garden for a moment, watching a pair of swallows preening in the birdbath.

"She hung herself in the attic sometime after her children drowned. She was a tormented young woman."

How would she know? Reed nodded. A sweet-scented breeze caressed them as Eloise tapped his card in her hand.

"Some of the family's things are still up there."

"Things?"

"In boxes. The Allendes never touched them. I don't think they ever used the attic. We just shoved the stuff into a corner, thinking somebody would claim it one day. We tried to locate Edward Keller ourselves years ago. No luck."

Reed understood.

"Would you like to look at it? It might help you?"

The air in the attic was stifling.

Stained-glass octagonal windows filtered dusty beams of light to a crumpled tarp in a dark corner. The floorboards creaked. Eloise stopped under an overhead joist bearing a faded "X."

"The insurance people or police marked the spot where she tied the rope and stepped from a chair."

Reed paused. He could have reached the beam if he wanted.

"And over here"—Eloise pulled back the tarp, stirring up a dust storm that made Reed sneeze—"is what Edward Keller abandoned. All this was theirs."

It was a small warehouse of boxes, crates, and furniture. Reed opened a trunk. A chill passed through him. It was filled with children's toys. He found a valise filled with papers and sifted through them. Mostly bills and invoices for the house. Eloise went to a small desk, rummaged through a drawer, and pulled out a thick leather-bound book with yellowing edges. It smelled musty.

"This was her diary. You've never known such abject sadness."

Her handwriting was elegant, clear, from a fountain pen. He flipped the pages. The secrets of her life. It began on her sixteenth birthday. Her small-town-girl disappointments and dreams. Her exciting first meeting with Edward Keller. "Deliciously handsome tycoon from San Francisco," she wrote. "What a catch he would make!" Reed flipped to their marriage, the children. Joan's concerns evolving into frustration and anger at how Edward never had time for the children, missing birthdays, holidays. The mansion was a gilded cage. Their marriage was strained. Edward had become intoxicated with success. She begged him to make time for the children.

They needed more of their father, not more money.

Reed thought of Ann and Zach.

He flipped ahead to the tragedy, and was stunned by her final entry.

"I can no longer live. The investigators say the children never had life jackets on, that Edward took them out, despite being warned of a storm coming. I blame him. I can never forgive him. Never. It should have been a joy for him, not a chore. He killed them! And he killed me! I hate myself for not realizing how vile he is, for trusting him with my children. They were never his! The bastard should have drowned, not them. It should have been him. Not my children. They are gone. They never found their tiny bodies. He promises to bring them back. Rescue them. The fool. All his money cannot bring them back. I can't live without my children. Pierce. Alisha. Joshua. I must be with them. I will be with them. I love you, my little darlings!''

Those were her last words. Probably written in the attic.

Reed closed the book. Stunned. It was Gothic.

They never found their tiny bodies.

He promises to bring them back.

''Is the material helpful, Tom?''

Eloise was sitting in a chair, patting her moist brow, drinking lemonade. Half in shadow, half in light, she looked like some kind of soothsayer oracle. Reed had been too engrossed to notice the half hour that had passed. ''Uhm, sorry, yes! Eloise. It's very helpful. Sorry, to take so much of your time.'' He stood.

''Glad this old stuff is of use to someone.''

''May I borrow this diary?''

She cast her hand about the Kellers' belongings. ''Take whatever you need and just call me if you want to look at anything again.''

In thanking her, Reed gave her another business card. They laughed. He jotted down her number and left, clutching the book.

Joan Keller's diary contained a few revelations that could lead him to Keller. But it wouldn't be easy and there wasn't much time to work on them. The anniversary of the drownings was only days away.

Once out of sight of the mansion, he trotted to his old Comet.

48

Keller was following the path of his exalted mission.

Pursuing the third angel. The conqueror of Satan.

Sanctus, sanctus, sanctus. Snip. Snip. Snip.

The doubters were closing in. Snip. Snip. And he still faced many obstacles in his final step to the transfiguration.

He remained calm.

I am cleansed in the light of the Lord.

The time has come to transform himself. Snip. The doubters had photographed his face and were searching for him. But he did not worry, trimming his hair, his beard, lathering his face. Soon all would know him as the enlightened one, the chosen one, anointed to reveal the celestial promise of reunion with his children.

Along his glorious path, he never challenged the mysterious ways of deified love. Michael Jason Faraday was the third angel, or so he thought, until the nine-year-old Oakland boy had moved to London with his family a few months ago. At first Keller could not understand it. He was certain Faraday was the third angel. The signs were correct. His age, his birthday. Keller had studied him, kept a vigil. But before he could make contact, he was gone.

On the eve of the transfiguration, the third angel vanished.

What was the message?

It had to be a divine test of faith.

Keller had remained steadfast. Like Christ in the desert. He did not succumb to temptation, to doubt. God would light his path to destiny.

And he did.

A couple of weeks from the transfiguration, the mortal identity of the true third angel was revealed to him. It took Keller some time to absorb the holy sign. It became crystalline a few days ago, during his morning reading of the Scriptures. He now knew who the third angel was. He had little time to find him.

Keller finished shaving, then made a few phone calls, talking politely, jotting down notes. He put on a white shirt, tie, and suit, checked his old leather briefcase. It was empty except for one business card—that of Frank Trent, of Golden Bay Mutual Insurance. Trent was the man who had handled the death claims for his children twenty years ago. Keller tucked the card in his breast pocket and took the briefcase with him before looking in on Gabriel and Raphael.

Midafternoon. They were sufficiently sedated. He locked the basement door, then the house, and walked into the brilliant sunlight, a well-dressed, respectable-looking businessman on a Holy Mission. After twelve blocks, he hailed a cab.

Veronica Tilley yearned for her family and friends in Tulsa.

"I am a fish out of water here. A stranger in a strange land," she would tell her husband, Lester.

His face would crease into a smile. "Now, now, Ronnie. Just make an effort to experience the city, gather some memories. It's only for two years. Hang on."

"Of course, I'll hang on, Lester. What choice do I have? I am just telling you I miss Oklahoma. It doesn't shake like California."

Lester's eyes twinkled. "We'll be back home soon."

Veronica had agreed to Lester's two-year transfer to San Francisco because she realized he had to satisfy some deep-seated manly need. He'd devoted twenty-three years to his company, all of them in Tulsa. The boys had gone off to college, and the middle-age jitters were getting to him. Younger managers did well by taking out-of-state postings. Lester had to prove he could run with the youngbloods.

But Veronica was lonely in San Francisco. She missed her position as secretary-treasurer of Tulsa's Historical Society. She longed for their house in Mapleridge, hated that they had to lease it and rent in San Francisco. For her, coming here was like going to outer space. Earthquakes. Weirdos. The other day on the Mission Street cable car, a man wearing a print dress, pearls, and rouge on his cheeks, sat beside her.

Gawd. And now this. She puffed her cheeks and exhaled.

Veronica was miffed. The couple who owned the house they were renting had just informed them that they were going to move back after ninety days. Ninety days! People didn't do things like this in Tulsa. After just settling in, she and Lester had to find another house to rent. And in this market! Here she was running around, checking with agencies, newspapers, searching for a suitable place. Oh, she was glad the young couple had reconciled. There was a little boy involved. But Veronica was also ticked. She told Lester they should talk to a lawyer, but he insisted it would be best if they found another place and let the young couple get on with their lives.

Veronica circled one of her choices in the classifieds: "Furnished. Alamo Sq. Restored 12rm Vict. Hot tub. View antiques. 3 frplcs." Must be heavenly because it sure was expensive—$3900.

The doorbell rang.

Veronica peeked through a curtain. A salesman of some sort was standing on her doorstep. He seemed harmless. She opened the door.

"Good afternoon. I'm Frank Trent from Golden Bay Mutual."

"Yes . . . ?"

"I'm here for Mrs. Ann Reed."

"Ann Reed? Boy they don't waste time."

"I beg your pardon?"

"Talking to myself. Sorry, they haven't moved back yet."

"I'm confused. This is the address for Ann Reed?" Keller knew the family had moved. And he knew the Lord would help locate the third angel. "The policies for her and her son, Zachary have lapsed."

"Life insurance?"

"I'm a new agent. I've yet to meet her and it's imperative I get her signature today on clause changes." He tapped his briefcase.

"We're only renting their house. They're moving back in ninety days. Why don't I take your card and have her call you?"

"That's kind of you, but I will be out of town on business for three weeks by this afternoon and I fear I may miss her. It's vital that I get her signature today."

Veronica studied the stranger. He seemed okay.

"Do you have a card?"

Keller reached into his breast pocket and handed her Frank Trent's card. Veronica held it thoughtfully.

"Come in."

She went to the telephone table in the hall, flipped through her address book, punched in a number. The line rang and rang, unanswered.

"Nobody's home," she said.

"Well I just don't know what I am going to do." Keller frowned.

Veronica didn't really want to give out Ann Reed's address in Berkeley, but she didn't exactly feel beholden to her either. What the hell? She copied Ann Reed's address and number from her book.

"There you go. Maybe you can reach her yourself, Mr. Trent."

Keller accepted the piece of paper and looked at it for the longest time. Strange, Veronica thought, the way he just stared at it, like it was a winning lottery ticket. Finally, he looked her in the eye and smiled with disturbing intensity.

"God bless you," he said. "God bless you."

49

Florence Schafer sat alone at her kitchen table, reading the morning papers. Her face turned ashen.

The families, friends, and supporters of Danny Becker and Gabrielle Nunn displayed yellow ribbons across the city on doors, car antennas, in shop windows, on trees, billboards, and in schools. Volunteers who answered phone tips and went door to door with MISSING-REWARD flyers wore them as arm bands. When they came to her house, Florence agreed to hang one from her mailbox. A group of mountain climbers affixed a giant yellow bow on the south spire of the Golden Gate. It was the manifestation of collective anguish and hope the children would come home alive. Consequently, the San Francisco press called the investigation "The Yellow Ribbon Task Force."

Days after Gabrielle's kidnapping, the case remained front-page news and the lead or second item of every local newscast. And when the President and First Lady offered sympathy to the families of "San Francisco's tragedy," during a presidential visit to the city, Tanita Marie Donner, Danny Becker, and

Gabrielle Nunn became household names across the country. The national press gave the story strong play.

Florence placed *The San Francisco Star* flat on the table and sighed. Her reading glasses fell from her face, catching on her chain, and she massaged her temples. The kettle screamed to a boil. Feeling the weight of the world on her shoulders, she made a fresh cup of Earl Grey tea. What was she going to do? She had to do something. The faces of Tanita Donner, Danny Becker, and Gabrielle Nunn beckoned from the paper. Buster, her budgie, chirped from his perch in his cage by the kitchen window.

"What should I do, Buster? I've called the police three times and no one has come to see me."

What had she done wrong? She had told the police she heard Tanita Donner's killer confess to God that he murdered her. She left her name and number. The last officer she talked to was like the others. He didn't believe her, she could tell. He kept asking how old she was, did she live alone, and as a devout Catholic how often did she go to church, what kind of medication did she use? He thought she was an old kook. She knew. He doubted her because she wouldn't give him details or proof she heard the killer confess.

Now she had proof.

Florence's Royal Doulton teacup rattled on the saucer as she carried it into her book-lined living room. She found comfort in this room where she enjoyed her crime books, but nothing in them had ever prepared her for this. The real thing. She was scared.

Time to check it, once more. She could only stand to hear a little bit. Florence picked up the cassette recorder, and pushed the play button. The tape hissed, then Father McCreeny cleared his throat.

"How long has it been since your last confession?" he urged the person in the confessional.

"It's me again," the killer said.

"Why haven't you turned yourself in? I implore you."

The killer said nothing.

"Are you also responsible for the kidnappings of Danny Becker and Gabrielle Nunn?"

Silence.

"I beseech you not to harm the children, turn yourself in now."

"Absolve me, priest."

"I cannot."

"You took an oath. You are bound. Absolve me."

"You are not repentant. This is a perverted game for you. I do not believe you are truly sorry. There can be no benediction."

Silence. A long moment passed. When the killer spoke again, his voice was softer. "Father, if I am truly repentant, will I receive absolution and the grace of Jesus?"

McCreeny said nothing.

"I need to know, Father. Please."

Silence.

"Father, you don't understand. I had to kill her. I had to. She was an evil little prostitute. I had to do the things I did to her and the others. Their faces haunt me, but it is God's work that I do. Franklin helped me with Tanita. He was a Sunday school teacher. He knew the magnitude of my work. That's why he helped me."

"God does not condone your actions. You misinterpret His message and that is what brought you here. Please, I beg you, surrender yourself. The Lord Jesus Christ will help you conquer your sins and prepare you for life everlasting."

"We had to cleanse the little harlot of her impurities. We took her to a secret spot I know. Oh how she screamed. Then we—"

Florence snapped the machine off and clasped her shaking hands in her lap. She couldn't bear another word. She had heard every horrifying detail before. She knew what she had to do now.

She went to her clipping file and retrieved the year-old articles of Tanita Marie Donner's case, staring at one of the news photos of SFPD Inspector Walt Sydowski. He was in the TV news footage yesterday, a member of the Yellow Ribbon Task Force. His face was warm, friendly, intelligent. He was a man who would understand. A man who knew Tanita's case, knew people. A man she could trust. She went to the phone and this time, instead of calling the Task Force Hotline, she called the San Francisco Homicide Detail and asked for Sydowski.

"He's out now. Like to leave a message?" some hurried inspector told Florence, taking her name, address, and telephone number.

"Tell him I have crucial evidence in one of his major cases."

"Which case? What kind of evidence?"

"I will only talk to Inspector Sydowski."

Florence enjoyed a measure of satisfaction at being in control of her information. At last, she was taken seriously.

"He'll get your message."

She sat in her living room, staring at the tape and sipping her tea. Again, she studied the news pictures of the children, their cherub faces. Florence now understood the purpose of her life and no longer felt alone.

50

"They are mine, just like Tanita is mine in paradise. My little NUMBER ONE." The printed words bled in blue felt-tip pen across a news feature on the Nunn-Becker-Donner case torn from *The San Francisco Star.* "MY LITTLE NUMBER TWO," covered the article's photo of Danny; "MY LITTLE NUMBER THREE," obscured Gabrielle's face. The note was signed "SON OF THE ZODIAC" and was accompanied by a Polaroid of the tattooed, hooded man with Tanita Marie Donner on his lap. A picture no one had seen before.

The items were sealed in a plastic evidence bag which Special FBI Agent Merle Rust slid to Sydowski at the top of the emergency task force meeting at the Hall of Justice.

Sydowski slipped on his glasses; his stomach was churning.

"It was intercepted this morning by U.S. Postal inspectors," Rust said. "We just got word they caught an identical one for Nunn's parents an hour ago."

"We're lucky the families haven't seen these," Turgeon said.

"He send copies to the press?" Inspector Gord Mikelson said.

"We suspect he hasn't," Special FBI Agent Lonnie Ditmire said. "No confirmation calls."

Rust watched Sydowski crunching on a Tums tablet.

"What do you make of it, Walt? You know the file—is it him?"

"It's him."

"What makes you certain?" Ditmire said.

"The hold-back is a neatly folded note in blue felt-tip pen that he left in Tanita Marie Donner's mouth. I told nobody about it."

"Gonna tell us what it said, Walt?" Rust opened his notebook.

" 'My little number one.' "

Someone at the table muttered: "Fucking serial."

"Any trace evidence on the note, Walt?" Rust asked.

The note was clean.

"Tanita Donner's mother get one of these Son of Zodiac things?" Lieutenant Leo Gonzales unwrapped a cigar.

"So far, no," Ditmire said. "It was mailed three days ago at a box near the BART station at the Coliseum in Oakland."

"Ain't that a fucking coincidence?" Gonzales lit his cigar.

"We'll send this stuff to the lab for prints and saliva." Rust tapped his Skoal canister on the table. "I would say it's Virgil Shook. We've all read his Canadian file. His history gives him a pattern and he matches the profile. You agree, Walt?"

Sydowski nodded. The new Polaroid, the reference to "MY LITTLE NUMBER ONE," the article from the *Star*. It was Shook.

"Why haven't we found him?" Nick Roselli, chief of Inspectors, closed his folder of Shook's file.

"We've got people on that; we're pushing street sources hard. We'll get him, Nick." Gonzales clamped hard on his cigar.

"Better be goddamned now, Leo. The mayor's office and the commission are chewing new assholes for us." Roselli's gaze went round the table. "If he grabs another kid before we have him, this city will never forgive us."

"Why don't we splash him? Call a news conference and splash Shook's face to the world," Ditmire suggested.

"He'll disappear if we do that," Sydowski said. "He wants to play games like his hero. He's going to stick around to see what we do. If we can buy a few days, just a few days to find him—I've got a few hopeful leads."

Turgeon, already angry at Sydowski for not telling her about the hold-back note, barely concealed her surprise.

"All right." Roselli gritted his teeth. "We'll give it a couple days and make a full court press on the street to find Shook. We'll freeze every undercover operation possible and we'll hammer the streets until the fucker pops up. But if he goes to the press with this shit"—he nodded to the intercepted note— "we're fucked."

"What's the status on everything else?" Roselli said.

"We like Shook for Donner, but we have nothing to put him to Becker and Nunn, except for the stuff today," Mikelson said. "Nothing back yet on the blood on Nunn's severed braids. Shook also matches the general description of the suspect in Becker and Nunn. But it's not enough."

Inspector Randy Baker, a young, bright Berkeley graduate, said they were using the bar code from the meat wrapper found at the Nunn home to pinpoint the store where the hamburger used to lure Gabrielle's dog was purchased.

"And we're using the partial tag we have on the suspect pickup, cross-referencing it with owner's registration, driver's license pictures, and specifics to create a suspect pool," Gonzales said.

"If that's it"—Roselli rolled up his file on Shook and slapped it against the table—"then make a goddamn arrest and clear this file."

* * *

Turgeon was silent leaving the meeting. She didn't utter a word, walking to the parking lot with Sydowski. But once he started the unmarked Chevy, something inside her ignited.

"Why, Walt?"

"I'm sorry, Linda."

"But why? Do you know how humiliating that was? Do you have any idea? I thought we were partners. I requested to work with you."

"You weren't my partner then. At the time, I was pretty well working Donner alone. I had to protect the integrity of the case. I never meant to hurt you."

"But you could've told me about the note in her mouth."

Sydowski said nothing. What could he say? He was an arrogant Polish cocksucker and he knew it.

Turgeon turned away from him, letting the street and the minutes roll by. "What the hell are your 'hopeful leads,' Walt?"

"Well, I'm still hoping for them."

Turgeon smiled. "You are a son of a bitch."

"I am."

"Where you taking me, you prick?"

"We're going to visit Kindhart, on the job in Hunter's Point."

"Think we can squeeze anything more from him?"

"Maybe. If you offer him sex, he might give us Virgil Shook."

She rolled her eyes.

Kindhart was not happy to have two Homicide detectives questioning him at his job. He told them that Shook may be living in a Tenderloin flophouse and hanging out at a shelter somewhere. Then he threatened to call a lawyer if they didn't stop harassing him.

"Either charge me, or stay the fuck out of my face."

Sydowski and Turgeon returned to the Homicide Detail. The Royal Canadian Mounted Police had called with the names of two of Shook's associates in the Bay Area. They were new names that weren't on his file. They came from a relative in Toronto.

As Sydowski talked on the phone with the mountie from Ottawa, Turgeon read their messages. She went through them quickly. Routine stuff, so she set the batch down and opened Shook's file. But something niggled at her. Did one message say something about evidence? Turgeon shuffled them again. Here it was, from a Florence Schafer. Gaines had taken the call.

"Schafer says she has crucial evidence in one of your major cases, Walt," Gaines wrote. He ran Schafer's name through the Task Force hotline. Schafer had called three times before, according to the caller history printout Gaines attached to the latest note.

"Nutcase?" Gaines scrawled on the printout, underlining the passage where Schafer claims she heard Tanita Marie Donner's killer confess to God at Our Lady Queen Of Tearful Sorrows Roman Catholic Church on Upper Market.

Hadn't they just built a new soup kitchen there? Turgeon remembered something about it in the papers. She tapped Sydowski's shoulder. And Catholics confess their sins. She should know. Turgeon tapped harder. And the FBI's profile said the killer lived in a fantasy world that could be stimulated by religious delusions. Turgeon was now pounding Sydowski's shoulder, forcing him to cover the telephone's mouthpiece.

"Jeez, Linda, what is it?"

She held Florence Schafer's messages before his face.

"Walt, I think we've got our lead."

51

The yellow ribbon affixed to Florence Schafer's mailbox quivered in the Pacific breezes sweeping up the rolling streets of Upper Market and over her frame house. Turgeon pressed the buzzer. They waited. When the door opened, their gaze dropped to a child-sized, bespectacled woman in her sixties.

"Florence Schafer?" Turgeon said.

"Yes."

"I'm Inspector Turgeon." She nodded to Sydowski. "This is Inspector Sydowski. San Francisco Police. You have information for us on a case?"

"May I see your identification?" Florence said. She saw their unmarked car parked on the street. None of her neighbors appeared at the windows. Florence inspected their badges.

"Please come in."

Turgeon took in the living room, raising her eyebrows at Florence's books. All were about crime. Sydowski went to Buster, who was chirping on his perch, preening his olive green plumage.

"He's a beautiful Scotch fancy," he complimented Florence, accepting a china cup of tea and joining her on the sofa. She sat on the edge so her feet could reach the floor.

"You know something about canaries, Inspector?"

"I breed them for showing, mostly Fifes."

"It must be a relaxing hobby for a man in your line of work."

"It can be."

Turgeon took the nearby chair. The room had the fragrance of guest soap, reminding her of childhood visits to her grandmother's home. Doilies under everything, even the King James Bible on the coffee table. Turgeon kept her tea on her lap. "Excuse me, Florence. I'm curious. Why so many crime books?" she said.

"Oh yes, well crime is my hobby." She smiled at Sydowski. "May I please see your shield again, Inspector?"

Sydowski obliged her. It was obvious Florence was happy to have company. Too happy, maybe. Turgeon and Sydowski exchanged quick glances. They'd give this nutbar another five minutes.

Florence admired the shield with the city's seal and motto in Spanish. *Oro en paz, fierro en guerra.* "Gold in peace. Iron in war," Florence said. "I know the city's crest and motto. I'm a retired city tax clerk."

"Florence," Turgeon interrupted her reverie. "You called Homicide and said you heard Tanita Marie Donner's killer confess?"

"Yes, I did." She returned Sydowski's ID.

"You said you have evidence of that confession?" Sydowski said.

"Yes."

"What sort?" Turgeon produced her notebook, but didn't open it.

"He must never know it came from me. I'm afraid."

"Who must never know?" Sydowski said.

"The killer."

"We'll keep it confidential," he said. "What is your evidence?"

"It's on tape. I taped him confessing."

Sydowski and Turgeon looked at each other.

"It's on tape?" Sydowski was incredulous.

"I'll play it for you. I have it ready." Florence left the room to get it.

"Walt?" Turgeon whispered.

"I don't fucking believe this."

Florence returned with a micro-cassette tape recorder. She set it next to the Bible, turned the volume to maximum and pressed the play button. Sydowski and Turgeon leaned forward as it played, the voices sounding otherworldly, echoing through the church's air ventilation system. For the first few minutes the priest argued with the confessor, saying that he could not absolve him because he was not convinced he was truly sorry, that if he was sorry, he should go to police and give himself up.

The killer remained lost in his own fantasy world.

". . . We took her to a secret spot I know in the Tenderloin. Oh how she screamed. . . . Then we took her . . ."

Turgeon struggled with her composure as the killer cheerfully detailed what he did to Tanita. She kept her head down, taking notes, bile seeping up the back of her throat.

The priest was gasping, begging the killer to surrender.

Florence was dabbing her eyes with a tissue.

Sydowski was certain they were hearing Tanita Marie Donner's killer, because the killer was the only person who knew the details the confessor was reciting. Sydowski listened with clinical detachment to the recounting of a two-year-old girl's abduction, rape, murder, and disposal. Like the missing pieces of a shattered glass doll, every aspect came together, matching the unknowns. This lead broke the case. But it came at a price. The killer's references to "the others" made him shudder. Did this guy kill Gabrielle Nunn and Danny Becker? What about the intercepted notes to the families?

MY LITTLE NUMBER ONE.
MY LITTLE NUMBER TWO.
MY LITTLE NUMBER THREE.

Was it a countdown? Were they going to find more little corpses?

The images of Tanita Marie Donner whirled through him, her eyes, her empty beautiful eyes piercing him, boring through the years of cynicism that had ossified into armor, touching him in a place he thought was impenetrable.

In death, she had become his child.

But sitting there in Florence Schafer's living room, his face was a portrait of indifference, never flinching, never betraying his broken heart. Dealing with the dead taught you how to bury the things that kept you alive. The tape ended.

"Florence, can you identify the man on this tape?" he said.

"I know his name is Virgil. I don't know his last name."

Turgeon was writing everything down.

"He has tattoos." Florence touched her arms. "A snake and flames. A white man, mid-forties, about six feet, medium build, salt-and-pepper beard, and bushy hair."

"Where does he live?" Sydowski said.

"I don't know." Florence looked at Turgeon taking notes, then at Sydowski. Realizing the gravity of her situation, she said, "Please, please, he must never know I've spoken to you. I'm afraid of him."

"It will be okay, Florence," Sydowski said. "Now, is there anything else you can remember that will help us get in touch with Virgil? Where he goes, what he does, who he does it with?"

Florence blinked thoughtfully. "He comes to the church almost daily, to the shelter."

"At the shelter, does he mention the children, Danny Becker, Gabrielle Nunn? Talk about the news, that kind of thing?"

"Oh no."

"Is he friends with anyone at the shelter?"

"Not really. He keeps to himself." Florence sniffed. "Inspector, what if he has the other children with him? I pray for them. You have to catch him before it's too late. You have to catch him." She squeezed her tissue. "I saw him at the shelter two days ago. He should be around again soon."

Sydowski touched Florence's hand. "Calling us was the right thing to do."

Florence nodded. She was terrified.

"You are a good detective, Florence," he whispered.

A warm, calm sensation came over her. Her search for the meaning and purpose of her life had ended.

Buster chirped.

"May I use your phone?" Sydowski said.

52

Some twenty-five miles south of San Francisco along Highway 1, Reed pulled into Half Moon Bay, a drowsy hamlet caressed by the sea and sheltered by rolling green hills, where farmers harvested pumpkins, artichokes, and lettuce. A brochure for heaven, Reed thought, stepping from his Comet at the marina, the gulls shrieking in the briny air.

He strolled the docks, showing photocopied clippings of Keller's tragedy to locals. They looked at them, then shrugged and scratched their heads. It was a long time ago. Nobody was around then. After half an hour, he decided to try the local paper, when a young, tanned woman he had talked to earlier jogged up to him.

"Try Reimer," she said.

"Who?"

"He's a relic. Been here so long, he ran charter for dinosaurs. If anyone would remember that story, Reimer would."

"Where do I find him?"

She glanced at her watch.

"Gloria's on Main Street. Go there and ask for him."

"Thanks."

Reed was optimistic. He had to be on to something with Keller. His instincts kept nudging him to keep digging. Before coming to Half Moon Bay, he had driven to Philo, where Keller's wife, Joan, had grown up. After checking the old Keller mansion on Russian Hill and reading Joan's diary, he figured it was a logical place to go. But no one he talked to in town remembered her and he didn't have the time to dig further. While eating a club sandwich at a Philo diner, it struck him that before heading for Half Moon Bay, he should stop at the cemetery. Maybe Joan was buried there.

The groundskeeper was a helpful gum-snapping university student. He listened to Reed's request, then invited him into the dusty office. "Keller, Keller, Keller." The student's fingers skipped through the cards of the plot index box. Except for Nirvana throbbing from his CD headset, it was quiet and soothingly cool. "All right." He pulled a card, bobbing his head to his music and mumbling. "Section B, row two, plot eight. Far northwest edge, lots of shade."

Keeping a vigil at the Keller gravesite was a huge white marble angel. Its face was a sculpture of compassion, its outstretched wings protecting the polished granite headstone. Over Joan's name and those of her children Pierce, Alisha and Joshua, their birth and death dates, the epitaph read:

> If angels fall,
> I shall deliver them
> And together we will
> Ascend to Heaven

An icy shiver coiled up Reed's spine. Inscribed next to Joan and the children's names was Edward Keller's. His death date remained open. A fresh bunch of scarlet roses rested at the base of the headstone with a note reading: "Forever, love, Dad."

Reed swallowed.

The ages of Danny Raphael Becker and Gabrielle Nunn matched the ages of Joshua and Alisha Keller when they drowned.

Raphael and Gabriel were angel names.

If angels fall, I shall deliver them and together we will ascend to Heaven.

This supported Molly's theory. Had Keller carved his plan in their headstone? Did Keller think Danny and Gabrielle were surrogates he required for some twisted mission?

If he could just find Keller. Talk to him. Size up his place. He grabbed his cell phone and punched Molly Wilson's extension in the newsroom. He got her voice mail. He left a message.

They had to find Keller. And they didn't have much time. Reed traced the gravesite roses to a Philo flower shop, which placed them there on behalf of a San Francisco shop where Keller paid for them. He was pulling up to Jack's on Main Street in Half Moon Bay when his phone rang. It was Wilson.

"Tommy, where the hell are you?"

"Half Moon Bay. Trying to find a guy who may know Keller. You have any luck locating Keller?"

"Zero. You'd better get back soon—something's up on the case."

"What?"

"Nobody knows. It's just the buzz going 'round."

"Okay. Listen, I've got a small lead on Keller. He bought flowers a few weeks ago for his family plot in Philo. He bought them through Elegant Florists in San Francisco. See if you can get an address for him from the shop. Do it now, we've got to find him."

"Sure, Tom. But you'd better get back here at warp speed.

The boss is wondering what you're up to and I don't think I can cover for you much longer."

"I'll be back in a couple of hours."

Gloria's was a postcard-perfect seaside diner. Red-checked gingham covered the tables, the aroma of home cooking filled the air. Only a handful of customers: two women, real estate agents judging from their blazers, examined listings over coffee at one table; and a young couple ate hamburgers at another. Reed took the rumpled old salt, reading a newspaper alone at a window table, to be Reimer.

"Excuse me." He stood before the man, keeping his voice low. "I'm looking for a gentleman named Reimer, who runs charter."

"You found him." Reimer had a friendly face. Reed handed him his card, and explained that he needed help with an old drowning case. He showed the old clippings to Reimer just as the waitress set a mushroom-smothered steak sandwich and fries before him. After reading the articles, Reimer removed his grease-stained cap and ran a hand through his wispy white hair. "I'm listening, lad." Reimer cut into his dinner.

Reed sat and was careful not to mention the abductions, telling Reimer how he met Keller for the bereavement group piece, and that it was vital he find him again for another story he was researching.

" 'Fraid I can't help you."

"You don't know this case?"

"Oh, I know it." Reimer chewed. "Was here when it happened. Terrible thing. They never found the children's bodies and old Ed Keller never got over it. Wife killed herself, you know."

"How do you know that he never got over it?"

"Well"—Reimer chewed some more—"he comes here and

hires me couple times a year to run him to the Farallons, the spot where they drowned.''

''When's the last time you saw him?''

Reimer thought. ''Couple months ago.''

''He say anything to you?''

''Never speaks.''

''Got any credit card receipts from him?''

''Always pays cash.''

''How long has he been doing this?''

''Ever since it happened.''

''You know where he lives?''

Reimer shook his head.

''What does he do out there, when you get to the spot?''

''He drops a wreath of flowers and mutters to himself, things like how he's going to bring them back. It's sad.''

''What do you make of it all?''

Reimer scratched his salt-and-pepper stubble, his leathery, weather-weary face creased. ''Tom, I've run charter in the Pacific all my life and I've seen a lot of strange things. But I never seen anything like Ed. Can't let go of the past, can't accept that what's done is done and ain't nothing he can do. But you know something?''

''What's that?''

''He thinks otherwise. Thinks he can change history. I think he's got some kind of plan percolating in his mind.''

''What makes you believe that?'' Reed's cellular phone trilled. ''Excuse me.'' He fished it from his pocket.

''Tom, hustle your ass back here!''

''Molly, did you get Keller's address?''

''I'll tell you when you get back—something's up!''

''Tell me now, Molly. Did you get an address?''

''He bought the flowers with a check through a Fargo bank. I'm outside the branch across from the paper. I went in, said I was his daughter, making a fifty-dollar deposit into his account for his birthday. They took the money. I asked if their records

showed his 'new' address. Teller said the address they had was
a P.O. box.''

''Nice try.''

''Wait, the teller said I should check with Keller's branch,
which is near Wintergreen Heights. At least we can put him
there. But it might not matter now.''

''Why?''

''Rumors are flying that the task force has a suspect.''

''Is it our guy, Molly?''

''Damned if I know. No one has a name or anything. Just
get back here! Something's going to break on this, I can just
feel it!''

''Okay, I'm on my way.''

''One more thing, your wife called from Chicago. She and
Zach are arriving earlier then she planned. She wants you to
pick them up. American, ten A.M., tomorrow.''

''Thanks.''

Reed thanked Reimer as he slipped the phone into his pocket
and stood to leave. Then he remembered something. He reached
into his breast pocket for two small stills of the blurry home
video of the suspect in Gabrielle Nunn's abduction.

''You recognize that guy?''

''These are from those kidnappings in the city. Seen 'em on
TV.''

''Look like anybody you know?''

Reimer studied the pictures, shaking his head.

''Does it look like Keller?''

''Could be anybody.''

Reed nodded and took the pictures back. ''I'm sorry, you
mentioned something about Keller having a plan?''

''Right, well, Ed is drowning in his grief and guilt. It's
obvious. Well, when we returned from the charter, he told me
the time had come to buy his own boat.''

''Why?''

Reimer sucked through his teeth and shrugged. ''I figured

it was so he could take himself out there whenever he wanted, like I told him. You know, he's never driven a boat since that night.''

"That it?''

"I guess. 'Cept he kept muttering about destiny.''

"Destiny?''

"Yup. Said he needed a boat for destiny.''

"That's all he said?''

Reimer nodded, staring hard at Reed. ''You think he grabbed those kids from the city, don't you?''

Reed put two five-dollar bills on the table. "Who knows? Thanks for your time. I've got to get going.''

Reed barely noticed the drive to downtown San Francisco. The epitaph from the Kellers' headstone was stuck in his head, like a children's rhyme . . . *If angels fall.*

53

Molly Wilson stood at *The San Francisco Star* Building's side entrance, tapping her notebook against her thigh, watching the parking lot until she spotted Reed and ran to him.

"Tom! Don't go upstairs! It's Benson."

"What about him?"

"I've never seen him like this. He's pissed at you."

"Where's the news in that? The man hates me."

"He's white hot like he was last year over Donner."

Reed stared at her. "What's going on up there, Molly?"

"He wants to know what you're working on, where you are."

"You didn't tell him, did you?"

"No. I did the best I could to cover. I told him you were checking a lead on a suspect in the kidnappings. It seemed to work. He never asked about you after that. That was yesterday."

"You didn't mention Keller?"

"No, I told you."

"Okay, then what?"

''Today the rumors are flying from the hall that the task force definitely has a suspect and Benson asked me about it. I didn't know anything, nobody at our place knew anything. You know anything?''

Reed knew nothing new. He was busy chasing Edward Keller.

''When I told Benson we didn't know about the suspect rumors, he went ballistic. He was furious that no one knew where you were. He tried to find you, started calling people. When he got nowhere, it was straitjacket time. He wants to see you.''

Reed swallowed.

''Tom, I did the best I could. I'm sorry.''

''Where are you going now?''

''He's kicked me over to the hall to chase the suspect rumors.''

Wilson removed her keys from her bag, then touched Reed's shoulder. ''Remember, Tom, he's not like us. He's not human. Keep repeating that to yourself and don't let him get to you.''

Reed glanced up at the building. ''He wants me fired, Molly.''

Myron Benson gestured sharply at Reed through the glass walls of his office. He wanted Reed to enter.

''Shut the door,'' Benson said.

Reed sat at the round polished table across from Benson. The table, like Benson's office, was clutter free. He was studying a file, his clean-shaven face was like silly putty, and his fine web of vanishing hair accentuated his huge ears. The edges of his mouth curled into a smirk as his rodentlike eyes fixed on Reed.

''Your recent personnel file is a horror story. You are just not the reporter you used to be, Tom.''

Benson's condescending tone brushed over Reed's pent-up animosity, like a hair caressing a detonator.

Benson was bureaucratic ballast who, years ago, walked into the *Star* off the street, passing himself off as an up-and-coming reporter to an old editor, who hired him and died two weeks later. Benson had to ask other reporters how to spell words like "sheep," "equal," and "idiot." One day he could not find Seattle on a U.S. map and wondered aloud if anyone knew San Francisco's area code.

Facts that could never be confirmed began surfacing in Benson's copy. When he learned the paper was going to fire him, he stole a tip called in for another reporter and broke a major story about police corruption, to which other reporters were assigned to help. The *Star*'s publisher, Amos Tellwood, congratulated Benson personally on his "fine, fine work." Benson parlayed the old man's favor and was soon a regular guest at the Tellwood estate in Marin County. He began dating Tellwood's only child and heiress, his daughter, Judith. She was an awkward woman, so neglected by her family that she immediately fell in love with Benson. He acknowledged her existence and she guaranteed his at the *Star* by marrying him. He had three children and several promotions by her.

Every newsroom has at least one Myron Benson, an editor who not only knows little of what is happening on the streets of his city, but would be lost on them. Benson rarely read his own product; it taxed his attention. Often, he suggested story ideas he unconsciously took from overheard newsroom conversations about pieces the *Star* had already run. And when he came up with an original story angle, it was a jaw dropper.

Life for Benson was a daily commute in his Mercedes from his seven-bedroom home in Marin, across the Golden Gate, to the paper.

The only thing looming over his blissful existence was the *Star*'s shame over the Tanita Donner-Franklin Wallace story. That shame was embodied in Tom Reed, but to fire him over Wallace would be public admission that Benson had mismanaged the matter and that the *Star*'s story was wrong. It would be detrimental to the paper's credibility. But to fire Reed for another reason, one solid enough for which he had no grounds for a wrongful dismissal suit, would eliminate the storm clouds over Benson's sunny life and please the old man.

In the few seconds Benson eyed Reed, he realized that he might finally have him by the balls.

"Where have you been for the last two days, Tom?"

"Researching the Becker-Nunn kidnappings."

"Have you?"

"You assigned me to it. You wanted to see where 'the abduction thing was going,' remember?"

"I did. And I specifically said I wanted straight-up reporting from you. So where have you been and what kind of research have you been doing?"

"Chasing down leads."

Benson looked at Reed, letting the seconds pass.

"I understand that you've been all over Northern California on the paper's time following a tip."

"Yes. That's what you pay me for."

"Is it the suspect the task force has in its sights?"

"I don't know."

"You don't know because you haven't been around."

"I believe the lead I have is solid."

"Do you? Then why didn't you tell me about it?"

"I needed to check a few things first."

"Sounds like you were enterprising, Tom, following a theory."

"No, I just needed to check—"

Benson's fist came down on the table. "Enough bullshit!"

A few people near enough to hear stopped working, staring briefly at Benson's office.

"I told you that I don't give a good goddamn about your hunches on this story!"

Reed said nothing.

"I told you I want nothing more from you than straight-up

reporting, yet you go off like some rogue contravening my orders. Now tell me right now why I should not fire you!''

Reed did not answer him.

"We know what happened the last time you followed one of your goddamned theories on an unsolved case, don't we? It cost this paper a quarter of a million fucking dollars! You are just not worth it, Reed. Now tell me why I should not fire you.''

"Because I think I know who took Danny Becker and Gabrielle Nunn.''

"You think you know?'' Benson rolled his eyes. "Just like you knew who murdered little Juanita Donner.''

"Tanita.''

"Who?''

"Her name was Tanita Marie Donner.''

"What the fuck do you know, then? Who is your suspect, Reed? Tell me!''

"I'm not absolutely certain yet that he's the—''

"Tell me now, or I'll fire you on the spot!''

Reed digested the threat.

He was tired. So tired. Tired from driving to Philo and Half Moon Bay. Tired of fighting the Bensons in this world. Tired of the business. Tired of his life. He reached into his worn briefcase and pulled out his dog-eared file on Edward Keller. He told Benson everything he knew about Keller and showed him the photos the paper secretly took at the bereavement group. Benson compared them to the blurry stills from the home video at Gabrielle Nunn's Golden Gate party. After Benson took in everything, he leaned back in his chair and set his plan in motion.

"Give me a story saying Edward Keller is the prime suspect.''

"What?''

"I want it today.''

"You can't be serious. We're still trying to find him.''

Benson was not listening. "We've got those grief group pictures. We'll run them against those blurry police-suspect photos. It'll be dramatic for readers."

"But those pictures were taken surreptitiously."

"What the fuck do we care? You've got him pegged as a child-killer. For all we know, he's the prime target of the task force."

"But I need more time."

"You've wasted enough. Now get busy. I want thirty inches. You send the story to me and see me before you leave. Is that understood?"

"I think this is wrong."

"You don't think. You do what I fucking tell you."

He struggled to keep from telling Benson what a worthless little man he was. The words seethed on his tongue, but he clamped his jaw firmly and left the office.

Resign, he told himself.

Reed sat before his computer terminal and logged on. *Quit on the spot.* Benson was making him walk the plank, setting him up to be fired. *End it all now.* But conflicting emotions pinballed in his brain. Keller was the guy, wasn't he? What about the two abducted children? Maybe he should call Sydowski. Right, if he needed more abuse, Sydowski was the man to call. Reed kicked everything to the back of his mind and began writing what Benson ordered.

Two hours later, he knocked on Benson's open office door. Benson was on the phone and clamped his hand over the mouthpiece.

"Done?"

"You have it on your desk now."

"Wait right there, I've got Wilson at the Hall of Justice."

Reed waited.

"Okay, Molly, yes . . ." Benson scribbled on a notepad. "Yes, anything beyond that? . . . Uh-huh. Okay good, keep us posted."

Benson hung up. "Wilson's sources at the hall say the task force has a prime suspect under surveillance somewhere right now."

"You want me to help?"

"No. I want you to get the hell out of here and don't come back until I call you personally. You are now on indefinite suspension."

Reed said nothing, and turned to leave.

"By the way," Benson said. "Your employment here hinges on the integrity of the story you just wrote."

Walking to his old Comet in the parking lot, it occurred to Reed that he had a few things to be grateful for. Edward Keller did not have a widow to slap Reed's face, nor any children to scowl at him.

On his way to his rooming house at Sea Park, he would stop at Harry's Liquor Store for a bottle of Jack Daniel's Tennessee Sipping Whiskey.

He realized he had just been fired.

54

The smell of hot food wafted from the basement windows of Our Lady Queen of Tearful Sorrows Roman Catholic Church on Upper Market. Turgeon was talking on her cellular phone to an SFPD dispatcher who was directing four marked radio cars to the area.

"Tell them to take up compass points a block back, out of sight of the church." She trailed Sydowski and Florence Schafer down the stairs through a rear metal door.

They came upon the kitchen, steamy and noisy with a dozen volunteers grappling trays of food, dodging each other.

"Louey!" Florence called over the din. "He's the kitchen boss." Louey wiped a cleaver on his stained apron. He was in his thirties, had a three-day growth of beard, and the bleary eyes of an A.A. candidate. Florence introduced the inspectors, saying they were looking for somebody and everything was fine.

"How many exits to the basement here, Louey?" Sydowski said.

"Three: the back, the front"—Louey pointed to a far corner with the cleaver—"and that stairway to the sacristy."

"Thanks."

"Anybody I know?" Louey said.

"Who?"

"The guy you're looking for."

Sydowski glanced at Florence, who put her hand on Louey's arm.

"You don't know him. He's one of my old friends. The inspectors just want his help."

"Yeah? For what?"

"We'll let you in on it a little later," Sydowski told him. Louey went back to work.

Sydowski went to the kitchen door to check the layout. It was like a bingo hall with two sections of row upon row of long tables divided by a middle aisle. A fire marshal's certificate near the door put the capacity at four hundred. Supper had begun. Less than two dozen people were seated and eating. A few hundred more were queued at the serving tables at the kitchen end of the hall. Volunteers dished up meals and encouragement.

Sydowski decided to give it some time. He and Turgeon knew Virgil Shook's general description and his tattoos. In a few minutes, they would join the volunteers casually walking the hall.

"If he's out there today, we'll have the uniforms cover the exits. Linda and I will take him quietly while he's eating." Sydowski removed his tie and suggested Turgeon let her hair down. "We don't want to look too obvious."

Barney Tucker, a retired diesel mechanic and devout Catholic, greeted the shelter's "guests" at the door, his stomach expanding the words: JESUS IS LOVE on his T-shirt. Barney clasped his big hand warmly over Virgil Shook's as Shook passed by with the others making their way to the serving table.

"Nice to see you, friend," Barney said.

Shook ignored him, breathing in the aroma of turkey, beef, peas, corn, tomato soup, baked potatoes, fresh buns, and coffee. Sustenance, sanctuary, and pity from the pious. The God bless yous blended with the tinkling of cutlery as the holy ones tended their miserable flock. Contempt slowly painted Shook's face. He battled the urge to scream: *Do you know who I am?* If they knew, they would bend their knees.

Shook's migraines had started again. Cranium quakes. Aching in his head, his groin. Fuck, it hurt. He needed to love again. It had been so long. So long. He searched the hall for someone. Maybe that little temptress from Nevada? Daisy of the incredible blue eyes. He couldn't find her. Fuck. The food line passed the cardboard donation box and he deposited a nickel.

Turgeon patroled the far aisle, carrying a plate of fresh buns, wishing she were in jeans and a sweatshirt instead of a blazer-skirt combo. She did her best, smiling, scouring exposed arms for tattoos and faces for features matching Shook's composite.

She stifled a yawn. She had not been sleeping well. At night, lying alone in bed, she was attacked by fear for Gabrielle Nunn and Danny Becker. She could not switch off Shook's confession. They had to bring this all to an end. Were they too late?

A possibility jumped at Sydowski as he went from table to table, topping glasses with a pewter pitcher of milk. If they spotted Shook, spotted him clean without Shook making them, then maybe they could hold off grabbing him so they could surveil him. He might lead them to the children. If they were still alive. He might lead them to evidence. They could also lose him. He could abduct another child. It was a risk Sydowski weighed, studying the line that reached from the serving table to the door, searching for tattoos, the right body type and face. He constantly checked to be sure his sports jacket was buttoned so his gun was unseen. He concentrated, taking stock of the hall, the exits. How fast could he make them if Shook bolted? What would he do?

Florence's scalp tingled. She saw the flames. The broken heart. And the cobra curled around Virgil Shook's left forearm.

It was him. In line, making his way to the serving table.

"Whatzamatter, Florence? You look like you seen a ghost."

"Huh?"

"Something catch your eye, there?" Marty, an ancient, bottle-and-can collector, smiled at her from his plate of food, then followed her gaze across the hall to the long line of people waiting to be served.

"Oh. No, Marty. I'm sorry." Florence distracted him by putting her hand on his frail shoulder. "Ran off with my thoughts, I guess. Say, how about some gravy for that turkey?"

"Well, I don't want nobody goin' out of their way." A toothless smile came out from hiding in Marty's grizzled beard.

"No trouble for a handsome man like you."

Florence stole another glimpse of Shook. Their eyes locked, charging her with raw panic. She looked away, struggling to conceal it, squeezing Marty's shoulder.

"Gravy. Coming right up, Marty."

Lord Jesus, please help me! Was she running to the kitchen? She didn't know, or care. She was numb with fear and ordered herself to be strong. Be calm for the children.

"Careful!"

She nearly ran into a volunteer carrying an urn of hot soup inside the kitchen door. She leaned against a wall, gasping.

Louey came to her. "Florence, you okay? What the hell is going on?"

What the fuck was it with that little bitch? Why was she gawking at him like that? Like she knew something about him. Shook couldn't place her. Fuck it. Let it simmer. He had enough to think about right now, like the letters. It had been a week. Nothing had surfaced in the news. Nothing to help him get off. The blue meanies kept a lid on it, denying him the pleasure of increasing San Francisco's pain. What would the Zodiac do? Send the letters to the press, threaten harm if they weren't published.

Slices of turkey and roast beef were heaped on Shook's plate next to a mountain range of mashed potatoes.

"Welcome, friend," a young woman volunteer said.

Shook was cold to her kindness. Moving down the serving table, he grimaced. His pain was nearly unbearable, his need to love again was overwhelming and this other player, New Fuck, made it too hot to hunt. The letters, the game with the priest were poor substitutes for the real thing. He couldn't stand it any longer. He had to do something.

Kindhart.

They could hunt together. Shook could plan something like he did with Wallace. Grab a little prostitute, enjoy her, and turn up the heat. It would be rapturous. But where was Kindhart these days? He seemed to be scarce. Fuck him. Shook could do it himself. He grabbed a couple of buns and it hit him again. Who was that twitching dwarf gaping at him back there? She was familiar, yet he couldn't place her. Why had she acted so strange? Pious little cunt. Maybe he would give her a lesson in humility.

Shook bit savagely into a bun and headed for a solitary table.

* * *

Florence was hysterical.

"It's him! It's him! Sweet Lord, he saw me!"

"Listen to me, Florence! Take a deep breath!" Sydowski said.

Turgeon was on the cellular phone. "Have the units move in to the church exits now! No lights, no screamers!"

Florence was sobbing. Sydowski was bent over, holding her shoulders in his big hands, comforting her. Turgeon pinpointed Shook from the kitchen door.

"I've got him, Walt. Doesn't look like he suspects anything yet—yes." Turgeon described Shook over the phone, "Caucasian, white T-shirt, beard."

"Good work, Florence. It will be over soon."

Curious kitchen staff had gathered in a circle.

"Folks, this is San Francisco Police business. It is a matter of life and death that you tell no one we are here." Sydowski flashed his shield. "Please. It's important that you carry on."

"What exactly is going on, officer?" one man asked.

"Sir, we will tell you later. Please. Your help is vital now."

"Walt, dispatch called the TAC Team."

"We'll sit on him until they get here."

"And if he runs, Walt?"

Sydowski didn't answer. He went to the door for a look at Shook.

He sat alone, back close to the wall, stabbing at his food with his right hand, his left forearm draped defensively around his plate, displaying his tattoos, letting the world know he was a motherfucker. He scanned the hall continuously, trusting nothing. It was the way you ate inside. Old habits died hard. But he never faced trouble here. It was one of the things he liked about Our Lady. That, and the fact it was clean. The hall was clean and the church was clean, smelling of candle wax and lemon furniture polish. Pure and clean.

That was it.

Shook stopped chewing.

She cleaned upstairs. Polished the pews. And she was always there when he visited the priest! He had a clear line to the kitchen door as a thin young man carrying a tub of dirty dishes entered. In the half second the door opened, Shook saw a professional-looking woman in a blazer talking on a phone. And he saw that little slut talking to a man in a suit, with gray hair, tanned face—he recognized him from TV news.

He was a fucking cop!

Shook's pulse rate exploded. The little bitch was telling them about him!

They had come for him!

Shook heard the squeak of brakes, an engine idling. Through a cracked basement window, he saw the car's rocker panels, its black-and-white paint scheme. The window was too small to get through.

Fuck! Fuck! Fuck!

Uniformed officer Gary Crockett joined Sydowski and Turgeon in the kitchen, a radio in his hand.

"Use your earpiece," Sydowski demanded. "Tell the others."

Crockett relayed the order through his radio.

"You got bodies at all the exits?" Turgeon asked him.

Crockett nodded. "Who've we got?"

"Suspect in the child abductions—shit!"

Sydowski saw the Channel 5 Live News van pull up to the rear.

"Crockett, have somebody keep the press back!"

"TAC is rolling, Walt," Turgeon said from her phone. "Yes. Patch him through—Walt, it's Lieutenant Gonzales."

He took the phone. "Leo. It's our boy." His eyes were on Shook.

"We need him, Walt. Sit on him 'til TAC gets there."

"I know my job, Leo."

"I'm ten minutes from you. Rust and Ditmire are on their way."

"Jesus!" Sydowski tossed the phone to Crockett. "He's made us. Linda, come on! Crockett have your people move in when I shout."

Shook rose, walking calmly to the door. He heard their footsteps on the hardwood floor behind him.

"One moment please!" It was the male pig.

Shook's stomach tightened. He kept walking. He was not going back inside. Never going back. He reached down into his boot. "Police! Stop right there!"

The economy had cost Dolores Lopez her job cleaning toilets in the office towers of the financial district. Her boss, Mr. Weems, was a born-again Christian who cried when he let Dolores go. She was a single mother with four children. She didn't know what she was going to do. In one month, she would lose her apartment on Potrero Hill. Every day she prayed to the Virgin who smiled upon her. They had found Our Lady's shelter last week and Mr. Weems had arranged a job interview tomorrow with a cleaning firm in Oakland. Dolores was telling her children to never abandon hope, to always pay homage to the Mother of Jesus, when she felt her hair being torn from her head, as she was lifted by an arm crushing her neck.

The steel point of a knife was pressed solidly below her eye. She heard shouting, but did not scream.

"Mama! Mama!" Carla, her three-year-old daughter, ran to her. Someone pushed her back. Dolores pulled weakly at the arm around her throat. And she prayed because she knew she was going to die.

Please, Holy Mother, watch over my children.

Sydowski pulled his Glock from his hip holster. Turgeon had her Smith & Wesson trained on Shook's head.

"Drop the knife, now!" Sydowski was ten feet away. Turgeon moved to Shook's side. Shook glanced at her and said nothing.

"Everybody on the floor!" Sydowski locked eyes with Shook. "Don't be stupid! Release the woman! We want to talk!"

Two uniformed officers entered the doorway, guns drawn. Sydowski noticed the eye of a TV news camera peeking through one of the basement windows. His fingers were sweating on the trigger of his gun. He hated this. Christ, did he hate this. Shook was encircled, four guns aimed at him. Sydowski ordered the officers into a pattern to avert crossfire.

"You can leave here dead, or you can leave here alive. But you are not leaving with the woman. Drop the knife now and release her."

"Let me out of here or she dies and it's on you!"

Shook cut Dolores with the knife, blood spurted down her cheek. Her children screamed.

"Officer!" Sydowski was talking to the uniform fifteen feet from Shook's right shoulder. "Do you have a clear head shot?"

"Yes, sir!"

"Don't fucking try it, pig! You'll hit her! Let me outta here. I ain't going back in the fuckin' hole!"

"We just want to talk, Virgil."

"I ain't going back!"

Dolores's face was a half mask of blood. Shook twisted the knife.

Sydowski holstered his gun, raised his open hands, and eased forward. "We want to talk, Virgil. Please, let her go."

When Shook relaxed his arm to reposition it across Dolores's throat, she bit into his bicep and stomped on his foot. Shook winced, and she broke away grabbing Sydowski's outstretched hand, flinching when she heard two shots.

They were deafening. The first bullet hit Shook in the lower neck shredding his internal and external jugulars, exiting into the ceiling. The next destroyed his trachea and spleen before lodging in his stomach. The knife went flying. He dropped to the floor.

The uniformed officer was frozen, his gun still extended. There were screams, sirens, and the smell of gun powder. Police radios crackled. Turgeon called for an ambulance. Dolores Lopez embraced her children.

Shook was on his back, making gurgling noises, blood and vomit oozing from his mouth. His white T-shirt was glistening crimson. Sydowski was on his knees, trying to obtain a dying declaration. Turgeon was there with him, listening.

"What is your name?" Sydowski said.

Shook made unintelligible noises.

"Where are the children, Virgil?"

Shook's mouth moved. Sydowski placed his ear over it. Nothing.

"Did you take Danny Becker and Gabrielle Nunn?"

Nothing.

Sydowski touched his fingers to Shook's neck. Was there a pulse?

Gonzales rushed in. "How bad is it?"

Turgeon shook her head. Sydowski bent over Shook's mouth again.

Special FBI Agents Rust and Ditmire arrived.

"Oh this is beautiful," Ditmire said. "Fucking beautiful."

Shook was still making noises when paramedics began working on him. "It's bad. We're losing him," one of them said.

Sydowski stood, and ran his hand over his face. Walking away, he grabbed a chair, smashing it against the wall under the quotation:

IT IS IN DYING THAT WE ARE BORN TO ETERNAL LIFE.

55

The new note taped to Reed's door was scrawled in unforgiving block letters: "WHERE IS RENT? NO RENT, NO ROOM. L. Onescu."

Reed had broken too many promises to Lila. His key didn't work. She had changed the lock. He set down the paper bag containing his supper: Two bottles of Jack Daniel's and potato chips. He searched his wallet. Thirty-five bucks. His checkbook was in the room. Damn.

He walked the two blocks uphill to Lila's building, entered the lobby, and leaned on the buzzer to her condo. No answer.

"She's not home, Reed," a man's voice echoed through the intercom. "Hey, I'm surprised you're not at work tonight."

Reed looked into the security camera.

"Long story. I'd rather not talk about it now, Mickey."

"Sure."

"Where's Lila? She leave a key for me? I have money for her."

"Gone to visit a nephew in Tahoe. No key. Sorry, pal."

Reed walked back, got his supper, sat in his car in front of Lila's Edwardian rooming house, overlooking the Marina District, the Golden Gate, and the Pacific. It was night. He thought of bunking with the other tenants, or driving to a motel. He was exhausted. Maybe he would call some of the guys at the paper, ask for a couch. He took a hard hit from the bottle. Staring at San Francisco's blinking lights, he searched for the answer to one question: "How the hell did he get here?"

He was seething. It kept him awake, made him thirsty. What had happened? He was a professional, married to an exceptional woman, blessed with a fine son. They had a good life. They were fighting to save it. They owned a good house in a good neighborhood. He had never intended to hurt anyone in this world. He worked hard. He worked honestly. Didn't that count for anything? Didn't it? It had to. If it counted for something, then why the fuck was he in the street, swilling whiskey in the back seat of a 1977 Comet, watching the thread holding his job and his sanity slowly unravel?

Wallowing in alcoholic self-pity, he looked at his situation for what it was: circumstances. Benson had thrown a fit, Reed forgot to pay his rent, and was too drunk now to go somewhere for the night. No one was to blame. He chose the car. Quit sucking on the bottle. Call it a bad day and go to sleep. Deal with it in the morning.

An engine revved rudely.

The sun pried Reed's eyes open.

It took a moment before he realized where he was and why.

His head was shooting with lightning strikes of pain and the stench in his mouth was overpowering. The bottle was half gone, the other untouched. He saw the greasy, half-eaten bag of potato chips, and nearly puked. He had to piss.

He needed a shower, a shave, a new life.

Reed spotted a kid walking by, delivering the *Examiner*.

"Buddy, can you spare a paper?"

The lanky teen stopped, taken aback by someone in Reed's shape crawling out of a car in Sea Park.

"I have exactly enough for my route."

Reed fumbled through his wallet.

"Here's five bucks, just give me one, and buy another one."

The kid eyed the bill, then gave him a crisply folded copy.

Reed sat on the hood of his car, letting the sun warm him, and unfolded the paper. His mind reeled, the headline screamed:

KIDNAPPING SUSPECT SHOT BY COPS IN CHURCH.

It stretched six columns over a huge color photo of a man bleeding on a stretcher. There was an inset mug of him, file photos of Tanita Donner, Danny Becker, and Gabrielle Nunn. The guy was shot in a hostage taking yesterday at a soup kitchen in an Upper Market church. He was pegged as the man behind Tanita's murder and the two abductions.

Virgil Shook? Who the hell was Virgil Shook?

Reed devoured the story and the sidebars. Never heard of Virgil Shook. The *Examiner* had nothing on Edward Keller. They got this guy in a church in the Upper Market? Didn't he get a call from a woman connected to a church there, a woman claiming she heard the killer confess? Yes, and he had written her off as a nut.

Reed went inside, upstairs to the bathroom down the hall from his locked room. He remembered that old Jake on the third floor subscribed to the *Star*. Reed flushed, then took the stairs two at a time, and banged on the door until Jake said, "Go away."

"Jake. It's Tom, Tom Reed from downstairs. It's important."

Jake didn't answer.

"Jake did you get *The San Francisco Star* today? I just want to look at it, please! It's important!"

Reed heard shuffling, the locks turned. Jake was wearing

over-sized boxers, a T-shirt dotted with coffee stains, and a frown. He practically threw a wrinkled copy of *The Star* at Reed.

"Have it! Criminals are ruining this great lady of a city!"

Reed hurried to his room with Jake calling after him: "Why don't you guys accentuate the positive of San Francisco!"

Out of habit, Reed had his key in the door to his room before remembering it wouldn't work. Damn. His phone rang. Once, twice, three times. The machine clicked on.

"Reed, this is Benson. Your employment with *The San Francisco Star* is terminated today. You disobeyed my instructions. Yesterday's hostage taking proved that your story about Edward Keller was erroneous. It was a virtual fabrication that would have left us open to a lawsuit. Personnel will mail your severance papers and payment. No letter of recommendation will be provided."

Reed slammed his back to the door, slid to the floor, burying his face in his hands.

He couldn't think. He was free falling. He was fired! Terminated! Blown away.

His phone rang again, but the caller hung up.

What was happening to him?

The other bottle was in the car. Untouched. Reed wiped his mouth with the back of his hand, feeling his stubble, realizing he still had *The Star* in his hand. He read the articles about the hostage taking with Virgil Shook, the pedophile ex-con from Canada. Molly wrote most of them. Zero about Edward Keller.

The phone rang three times. The machine clicked.

"Where the hell are you?" Molly said. "I need your help here, Reed. Haven't you heard, all hell's broken loose. It's not Edward Keller, it's some pervert from Canada. Call me! They've started looking for the bodies! Get your ass in here!"

Yeah, right.

Reed sat there, his eyes closed. He was drowning. Floundering in the awful truth.

He heard his phone ringing again. The machine got it.

"Tom, what happened?" His wife was angry. "We waited at the airport for over an hour."

Airport? He was supposed to pick up Ann and Zack this morning.

"We're at Mom's. Call me." The temperature of her voice dropped. "If you have the time."

56

The new white minivan parked in the shade of a eucalyptus grove on Fulton in Berkeley near the university was a rental from San Jose. For two days now it had been an innocuous fixture across the street, three doors down from Doris Crane's home. Her two-story house was framed perfectly in the van's rearview and driver's side mirrors.

Edward Keller watched it with the vigilance of a statue.

Occasionally he would study his reflection. He hardly recognized himself—clean shaven, his pale skin was tanning. The dye he had selected worked well, darkening his short, neat hair. He no longer saw himself. He had been transformed. He had been ordained, enlightened to show the world the wonder of God's Love.

I am cleansed in the light of the Lord.

After his divine work in obtaining the address from the hillbilly living in the Angel's house in San Francisco, Keller went to the public library, and scoured the directories and other registries, learning much about Doris Crane in a short time.

She was widowed in 1966 and lived alone in the house, working part-time as a secretary in Berkeley's law department. Doris had one daughter, Ann, who had one son. He was nine years old.

Pierce Keller was nine years old.

Ann owned three children's clothing stores in the Bay Area. Keller suspected her marriage was troubled, because she and the Angel were renting their home and living with Doris Crane. A blessing that kept her loathsome, arrogant husband out of the way.

Keller had already met him.

Thomas the doubter.

The oaf could not grasp the meaning of his mission: helping the bereaved through the valley of the dark sun. At first, Keller did not know Reed's role, believing he was sent to destroy his work.

But the truth was revealed.

It was destined that they should meet.

Reed was the signpost to the third Angel. It was revealed to him in Zach Reed's birth announcement. Keller found it in the public library's newspaper archives. Zachary Michael Reed.

It was destined. His middle name was Michael. He was Zachary Michael Reed. Zachary, father of John the Baptist, whose birth was foretold to him by an Angel. John the martyred prophet who baptized Christ.

Michael the Archangel.

Finding Michael was challenging. For the past two days, Keller saw nothing at the house, except for Doris Crane's comings and goings. Although he tried to remain calm and trust in the Lord, he worried. So last night he took Doris Crane's garbage. He probed it, finding a copy of a travel company's itinerary for Ann Reed. She had two round-trip plane tickets to Chicago. The tickets were for A. and Z. Reed. She was attending a conference at the Marriott. They were scheduled to return this morning. Keller checked his watch. The plane had landed in San Francisco two hours ago. He was convinced he would see the third Angel today. For Heaven continued to shower him with protection.

Virgil Shook was the latest miracle. His arrest and shooting had dominated the front pages of this morning's papers. Shot him dead, some reports said.

In a church. It was preordained.

Sanctus. Sanctus. Sanctus. Keller's mission was divine.

He was invincible.

Soon police would learn that the repulsive child abuser was not the enlightened one. The incident was divine intervention, designed to shield Keller long enough to complete his work. He was so close to the transfiguration.

Keller's body tensed.

A cab stopped in front of Doris Crane's house.

A woman got out of the rear passenger's side, while the driver unloaded luggage from the trunk. The woman was in her early thirties, attractive, very businesslike.

Ann Reed.

She was tired, angry, as she rummaged through her wallet and called into the cab.

"Come on, Zach, wake up, we're home."

Keller held his breath.

Michael. The third Angel.

The drowsy boy dragged himself out of the car. He was wearing a Chicago Bulls T-shirt, baggy jeans, new sneakers. As his mother slapped bills into the cabby's hand, the boy wearily grabbed a canvas travel bag and trudged into the house.

Keller watched.

His heart nearly tore free from his body.

Sanctus, sanctus, sanctus. Dominus Deus sabaoth.

Michael.

Commader of Heaven's army! Conqueror of Lucifer!

Behold!

A prince in God's celestial court.

Michael! He had found the true Michael!

Keller had gazed upon Michael the Archangel.

And he shone with the light of one million suns.

He was overwhelmed in the presence of divine majesty. Soon, he would realize his exalted mission.

The transfiguration.

The reunification with his lost children.

It was his destiny.

Keller clasped his hands together tightly, bowed his head, touching his lips to his whitened knuckles.

57

Sydowski kept his promise.

Angela Donner cradled twelve white sweetheart roses in her arms, as if carrying a baby. Sydowski pushed her father, John, in his squeaking wheelchair along the pebbled paths of the cemetery to Tanita Marie's headstone. Sydowski had vowed to make a pilgrimage to Tanita's grave with her mother and grandfather once her murder had been solved. It had. Her death had been avenged. Her killer killed.

When they stopped at Tanita's marker, the early morning sun was hitting the polished granite. It was emblazoned in light. The grounds were silent but for the distant traffic and John's soft moans. Sydowski patted his shoulder.

Angela knelt, setting the flowers at the foot of the stone, kissing it as a breeze rolled through the oaks sheltering Tanita's plot. Tears streaked her face as she caressed the epitaph, tracing the sun-warmed letters of her daughter's name. "You know, Inspector, I've been part of the university bereavement group."

"I know."

"I have come to accept that my baby was a lamb sacrificed for the sins of this world."

Sydowski nodded. Angela continued.

"I see her everywhere in the faces of children. I ache when I see mothers hug their daughters. I know my baby is with God. Probably making Him laugh. I have to carry that in my heart to survive."

"I understand."

"Thank you for working so hard. I know you really cared. I just hope with all my heart you find the other children. Alive."

Sydowski swallowed hard and closed his eyes. Would there be two more deaths? Two more funerals with little coffins? He needed a lead. Something. Anything. Sydowski's pager bleated.

Clamping his teeth on his unlit cigar, Lieutenant Leo Gonzales grunted angrily, seating himself with the detectives at the table in Room 400 at the hall. By the grave way he was rearranging the fresh pages in his hands, it was a safe bet something was fucked. Badly. This was the first status meeting of the Yellow Ribbon Task Force since Virgil Lee Shook was pronounced dead at San Francisco General sixteen hours ago. Papers and reports went round the table. The cork and chalk boards bearing maps, notes, and photos of Tanita, Danny, and Gabrielle, Shook, the suspect's composite, and a blurry still of him from the home video, were again wheeled to one end of the room.

"Listen up. It's just like we figured. No way is this over. We've got the serology tests. From the saliva on the envelopes of the intercepted letters to the families, we got an O-positive blood type. From the semen in Tanita Donner's homicide, we got an O positive. Shook is O positive. And we've got one of Shook's latents on the knife used in Donner. We put the lab stuff, along with Shook's identification through his tattoos, the

Polaroids, his taped confession, and we've got him for Donner, with Franklin Wallace as accomplice. DNA will nail it.''

''What's the problem?'' Lonnie Ditmire wondered.

Gonzales halted the question with his hand. ''Let me finish.'' He shuffled his papers. ''The blood-typing tests on Gabrielle Nunn's severed braids found in the Sunset were redone. We just got the results. Gabrielle is A positive. Shook, O positive. The problem is, the blood on her hair is B positive, a male Caucasian.''

''Just like we feared, we've still got another player out there,'' Turgeon said.

''Exactly.'' Gonzales dropped the pages, as the impact sank in.

''Could we have some kind of pedophile ring going here?'' asked Bill Kennedy, deputy chief of Investigations.

''Could be,'' Gonzales said.

''What about Shook's friend, Perry William Kindhart?'' Nick Roselli, chief of Inspectors, asked. ''Have we leaned on him, Walt?''

''We've leaned hard. He's got a lawyer now. We've got nothing on him. No leverage. He's under surveillance.''

''What about the taped confessions, Florence Schafer and the priest, people at the shelter, Shook's past?'' Roselli said.

''Nothing substantial beyond what we've already got.''

''What about Shook's place in the Tenderloin?'' Gonzales said.

Sydowski, Turgeon, Ditmire, Rust, and several others from the task force had scoured Shook's room overnight and into the early morning hours.

''More pictures of Shook with Tanita,'' Rust said. ''A diary detailing his desires. He mentions Wallace, taunting the priest with confessions, and he wrote that whoever took Becker and Nunn was making it hard for him to 'go hunting.' At this point, it looks like Donner and the recent abductions are unrelated.''

''What about Kindhart?'' Roselli said. ''Is he mentioned?''

"In passing," Sydowski said. "Other than the camera link to Donner, we've got nothing that puts him with any of the cases."

"Claire"—Gonzales turned to Inspector Claire Ward, the expert on cults—"you went to Shook's place. Anything there to suggest a cult connection?"

"Other than the fact we maybe have a minimum of three people involved in the abductions, absolutely nothing."

Kennedy loosened his tie. "So what have we got on Mr. B Positive? We've got a blurry video of him stalking Gabrielle Nunn in Golden Gate. We have a composite, but it is still too vague. What else we got?"

"We know he stalked Gabrielle and took her dog, which he used later to lure her away," Turgeon said.

"Right, and we've got a partial plate on the truck, an old Ford with a California tag beginning with "B" or "8," something like that."

"And there's the meat tray found near the yard," Ditmire added.

"How's Rad Zwicker doing in Records with that pool based on the partial?" Roselli wanted to know. "Anything that ties Shook to the truck or any vehicle?"

"Nothing yet." Gonzales flipped through his reports. "We don't have a specific year on the truck. We do have the first three characters on the tag: 'B75.' That gives us a pool, of what? Something over a thousand. They're being checked individually."

Sydowski had an idea. "Did we check parking tickets for all Ford pickups with the partial at Golden Gate the day Gabrielle was taken?"

Gonzales nodded. "Zwicker did that, through traffic. Zip, Walt."

Turgeon thought of something else. "Did we check for tickets for all pickups with that partial in and around the Nunn home in the Sunset prior to her abduction, say for the past six months? Because if he was stalking her, he would have spent time in her neighborhood.''

"I don't think we did it specifically with that partial tag, Linda. Hang on.'' Gonzales reached for a phone and punched Zwicker's extension, and ordered the check done immediately, then hung up. "He'll get back to us,'' he said.

Roselli rolled up his sleeves. "We could try running down names of all Caucasian males with B-positive blood between thirty and sixty years old in mental institutions and Bay Area hospitals. We could do the same with recent releases from county, state, and federal jails. Garrett and Malloy, you take that.'' Notes were made.

Using the bar code from the meat wrapper, Inspector Marty Baker came up with a list of eighty stores where the meat could have been purchased. He narrowed the purchase time line to four days prior to the dog snatching.

Kennedy liked that lead. "Work up a hot info sheet. We'll get uniforms and anyone we can spare to canvas the stores and the 'hoods.''

Gonzales turned to Inspectors Gord Mikelson and Hal Zolm from General Works. After Shook died, they went to the parents of Danny Becker and Gabrielle Nunn to assure them no concrete evidence had surfaced suggesting Danny and Gabrielle had been harmed, that police suspected Shook was involved in the abductions only because he claimed he was. It was not unusual for people like Shook to make such claims. The task force was working to verify their validity.

"How did it go, Gord?''

"Not good.''

"The parents believe their children are dead and they blame us for not keeping Shook alive to get information.''

Gonzales nodded. He had no quarrel with the families' right to be outraged.

The meeting stretched into a two-hour affair.

"We should check every death—criminal, accidental, or

natural, involving children of the same age and gender as Danny and Gabrielle,'' Sydowski said. ''Call Sacramento and do it through vital statistics.''

''How far back?''

Sydowski did some quick math. ''Twenty years, say.''

''Do you know how many you're talking about for the entire state?'' Ditmire said.

''Narrow it to the Bay Area. If he's taking kids from here, the tragedy likely happened here,'' Sydowski said.

''Could check with mental hospitals, private clinics, and psychiatric associations for any cases that might fit with what we've got here,'' Rust said, tapping his canister of chewing tobacco on his chin.

Kennedy wanted the streets sifted for anything on new kiddie porn operations in the west. Rust pledged the FBI's help on that front.

Roselli and Kennedy decided on releasing a short press statement saying they believed Virgil Lee Shook was responsible for the murder of Tanita Marie Donner, but they had nothing to confirm he is linked to the Becker-Nunn kidnappings, only that vigorous investigations by the task force are ongoing. It would go out at three that afternoon.

The meeting was ending when the phone rang for Gonzales. Gonzales said nothing, took notes, then slammed the phone down with a grin.

''Son-of-a-bitch! We got a hit on a 1978 Ford pickup tagged for parking near a hydrant three blocks from the Nunn home in the Sunset. It was one week before the dog vanished. Brilliant work, Turgeon! The old Son of Sam parking ticket probe. Son of a fucking bitch!''

Kennedy looked at the address Gonzales had taken for the pickup. ''Let's move on this now!''

58

Sitting on Grandma's front porch steps, Zach Reed could hear his mom on the phone to his grandmother. She was pissed, big time.

"I refuse to accept him treating us like this—Mom—no." Grandma was working at the university. "I am not taking any more of this!"

Hearing his mom talk this way hurt. Everything was breaking, spoiling his dream of living together again in their home.

"Mom, I've given him a lifetime of chances—No! He was supposed to pick us up this morning at the airport. He wasn't there. No sign of him. Not a word. I know it's a little thing but it always starts with the little things!"

His mother listened, then said: "I checked with the airline message center, our hotel in Chicago, and his place. Absolutely no word from him. This is how he treats us! This is how committed he is!"

Zach hated this. Just chill, Mom, he pleaded silently from the steps, driving his chin into his forearms which rested on his knees. He stared at his sneakers, new Vans, Tempers. He had tried to calm Mom down at the airport, where she sat steaming for an hour. Maybe Dad was on a story because of the missing kids?

"I don't care, Zach," she hissed as they waited on an airport bench. "That's not the point. The point is he is supposed to be here! A promise is a promise." That was how you measured a person's worth, by the number of promises they broke, she said, blowing her nose into a tissue.

A few hours earlier on the plane, everything was great. Mom was happy, telling him the surprise: Dad was picking them up at the airport. Maybe they would have lunch, talk about being together again, maybe drive by their house. Man, it was heaven. Soon he would be back with Jeff and Gordie, catch up on things.

But it all fell apart when they came down at San Francisco International. No trace of Dad. Mom had him paged. Three times.

Now, sitting on Grandma's porch, with everything breaking into a million pieces, he didn't know what to do. He fished for his father's business card from his rear pocket. It read: TOM REED, STAFF WRITER, THE SAN FRANCISCO STAR, and bore an address, fax number, and his direct extension. It was a cherished possession. One Zach carried everywhere. He studied the blue lettering, stroking the embossed characters, as if the card were a talisman that could summon his dad.

Zach hated this separation cooling off crap. He hoped his friends were wrong about your folks never getting back together once they split. Please be wrong. He looked hopefully up and down the street. Traffic was light. All he saw was some doof by a white van a few doors down. Was he staring at him? Zach wasn't sure. The guy was checking the air pressure on the tires.

The rumbling of a broken muffler cued him to his father's old green monster stopping in front of the house.

"Mom! It's Dad!"

Zach catapulted to the driver's door, and gripped the handle. "Hey, son!"

"Dad, Chicago was a blast! We went up in the Sears Tower and I got to go in the cockpit on the flight home! Are we gonna drive by our house? Are we gonna have lunch? And look, Mom got me new Vans, Tempers!" Zach opened the door for his dad.

"Hold on there, sport." Reed climbed out of the car.

Zach threw his arms around his father, his smile melting when he smelled a familiar evil odor. Zach stepped back, noticing his dad's reddened eyes, his whiskers, and the lines carved into his face.

"Guess you've been working pretty hard on the big kidnapper story, that's why you missed us at the airport, huh?"

Reed looked into his son's eyes for a long moment,

"Something like that, Zach."

"Well Mom's pretty pissed at you."

"She has every right to be."

Reed saw Ann's silhouette in the doorway, put his hand on his son's shoulder. As they went inside, Zach saw the white van drive off.

In the house, Zach did as his mother told him and went upstairs to his room and closed the door. Loud enough for his parents to hear. Then he quietly opened it, lay on the floor, and listened.

"Where the hell were you, Tom?"

"Ann, I don't blame you for—"

"You promised us you would be there."

"I know, but something came up on the kidnappings, I—"

How many times had he hurt her by starting with "but something came up." Her face reddened under her tousled hair, her brown eyes narrowed. She had removed her shoes, her silk blouse had come slightly untucked from her skirt. Jesus, she was going to explode on him.

"You look like shit and you reek," she said.

"It's complicated. I can expla—"

"Were you with Molly Wilson, a last fling?"

"What? I don't believe this!"

"You've been drinking again."

"I never told you I quit. I never lied."

"That's right. You were always honest about your priorities." Her eyes burned with contempt. She thrust her face into her hands, collapsing on the sofa. "Tom, I can't take this anymore. I won't take this anymore." Her voice sank to a whisper. "You told me you had changed, but you lied. Nothing's changed."

That wasn't true. He wanted to tell her, but all he could manage was: "Ann, I love you and Zach with all my heart."

"Stop it!" She spat, pounding her fists on her knees. "Your words are cheap. They're for sale any day of the week to anyone with fifty cents! But one thing you can't do with them is hold a family together!"

Ann stood, grabbing a copy of that morning's *Star* from the coffee table, the one with Virgil Shook's shooting splashed on the front. "It can't be done see!" She ripped up the paper, tearing Shook on the stretcher in half, tossing the pieces aside. "You can't hold anything together with paper."

Ann sat again, her face in her hands.

He was stunned.

She had reduced him to nothing.

A zero.

Everything he had struggled to be, the thing by which he defined himself was demolished. His eyes went round the room, noticing their unpacked bags as he ingested the truth. Ann despised him not so much for his trespasses, but truly for what he was. He searched in vain for an answer. He wanted to tell her he had been fired, tell her everything. How he was haunted by the accusing eyes of a dead man's little girl. How he was falling and needed to hang on to something. Someone. But he didn't know what to say, how to begin.

"Okay," he said softly. "Okay. I understand."

He turned and left.

Watching from his bedroom window, Zach saw his father's car disappear down the street, the Comet's grumbling muffler underscoring that promises had been broken. Tears rolled down Zach's face.

59

Dust and pebbles pelted acting Calaveras County Sheriff Greg Brader as he watched the four helicopters descend one after the other, his shirt flapping angrily against his back.

It was supposed to be his day off. He was painting his garage at his home in San Andreas when his wife had called him to the phone. It was his dispatcher: The SFPD and FBI were flying out immediately because of a possible county connection to the kidnapping case in the Bay Area. Brader had less than an hour to prepare.

While some small town cops may have gotten jittery at the prospect of a profile case popping up in their yard, Brader was cool. Before coming to the county eight years ago, he had put in twelve years with the LAPD, six of them in Homicide. Without changing his torn jeans and stained T-shirt, he kissed his wife and got in his marked Suburban. He made calls over the radio and cellular while driving directly to West Point, a sleepy village forty minutes away.

Brader and two deputies cordoned off the ball diamond and

its parking lot, turning it into a landing zone for the San Francisco FBI's new MacDonnell Douglas 450-NOTAR and larger Huey, which carried the FBI's SWAT team. Sydowski, Turgeon, and a handful of others from the task force landed next in the two CHIPs choppers.

Special Agent Merle Rust and SFPD Inspector Walt Sydowski were the contact people, along with FBI SWAT Team Leader Langford Shaw. Brader introduced himself, shouting over the noise of the rotor blades.

"You fellas best ride with me. My guys will bring the others." As requested, he had obtained a school bus for the SWAT Team and its equipment. Other task force members rode with Brader's deputies as they roared off in a convoy of three police cars and the bus.

"We'll be there in under twenty minutes," Brader said after making a radio call to his deputies at the property. "I've had two people sitting back on the house since you called."

"What have you got?" Rust asked.

"As you know, the pickup is currently registered to a Warren Urlich. He's a sixty-eight-year-old recluse, a pensioner. Makes extra cash fixing cars and trucks; sells them, too. Neighbors say he never talks to anybody and he's got so many vehicles on his property, they never know when he's home."

"What about the kids?"

"Like I told you when you were flying out, Urlich's nearest neighbor thinks she saw two kids on the place that maybe arrived recently. A little boy and girl. She was only sure they weren't living there before."

Rust and Sydowski exchanged glances.

Stands of pine, cedar, and sequoias blurred by the Suburban as it ate up the paved ribbon snaking through the Sierras of Cavaleras County. This was where prospectors flocked during the gold rush in 1849. It was home to Twain's celebrated jumping frog, clear lakes, streams, tranquility, and people who wanted to be left alone.

Cars and pickups in various stages of disrepair, junk, a yapping dog on a long chain, and ramshackle outbuildings dotted Warren Urlich's land, a three-acre hilly site with an abundance of trees.

The FBI SWAT team set up a perimeter around the rickety house, while the county deputies and some task force members formed an outer perimeter. Brader's Suburban and the bus, which was the command post, were virtually out of sight about one hundred yards from the house.

From the hood of Brader's truck, Sydowski glimpsed a broken toilet and a pit bull with a bloodied rabbit carcass in its jaws, as he swept the property with Brader's binoculars. He chewed a Tums tablet—his second since they landed—and steadied himself for the worst. He feared another deadly shootout like the one with Shook. He prayed for the children to be alive, but if they were in this shit hole, they were ninety-nine percent for sure dead.

He passed the binoculars to Turgeon. She rolled the focus wheel slightly, bit her lip, then handed the glasses to Brader.

Sydowski studied her protectively for a moment.

Inside the bus, SWAT Team Leader Langford Shaw made radio checks with his people. Everybody was in position. Fred Wheeler, the unit's hostage negotiator, called the house over the FBI's satellite phone.

Someone answered.

"Mr. Warren Urlich?"

"Yup."

"Mr. Urlich, this is Fred Wheeler, I'm a special agent with the Federal Bureau of Investigation. We'd like to talk to you, sir. We have heavily armed people positioned around your home and would like you to please walk slowly out the front door with your hands in the air now."

Wheeler was answered with silence.

"Mr. Urlich, Warren?"

Nothing.

"Did you hear me, sir?"

"I heard you, I just don't believe you. This a joke?"

"We'll sound a police siren now."

Wheeler nodded to Shaw, who signaled Brader and the Suburban's siren yelped.

"What do you want to talk about?"

"We'll discuss everything when you come out."

As Urlich and Wheeler talked, SWAT team members tightened on the house, peeking inside windows with miniature dental mirrors. A girl of about seven or eight was playing with a doll near the back door. In a heartbeat, an agent grabbed her, clasping his hand over her mouth, removing her to the outer perimeter.

Shaw, listening on his headset radio, nodded, and whispered to Wheeler, "We have a girl removed safely. She says it's just the man and a boy inside now and the man has lots of guns and bullets."

On the phone, Urlich—who did not know the girl was gone—had not decided to cooperate with Wheeler.

"You make me kinda nervous," Urlich said. "Can't we just talk on the line here? 'Cause if it's about them kids, I don't know nothin'. That's Norm's business and I ain't a part of it."

"It would be much better, Warren, if we could talk face to face."

Shaw had more information.

"The girl says she and the boy were brought to the property a couple of weeks ago."

Urlich was getting impatient. "I told you I don't know nothing about nothing."

"I didn't say you did. We just want to talk, maybe you can help us on a serious matter. Maybe this is all a misunderstanding. Please come out now, sir. Help us clear things up, so we can be on our way."

Several seconds passed before Urlich said, "I'm coming out."

Wheeler told Shaw, who alerted the unit. Nearly a dozen FBI guns were trained on Urlich's front door. It cracked open. A long, riflelike object slowly extended from it. A white dishrag was tied to what turned out to be a broom. A weathered man in his sixties, dressed in stained overalls crept out.

"Please put the object down, Warren." A loudspeaker ordered.

He obeyed, looking around for the source as his pit bull howled, leaping at his chain toward him in a futile attempt to warn him of the SWAT member who stepped from the front of the house and forced Urlich to his knees, frisking and hand-cuffing him before escorting him to the command post.

Rust, Sydowski, Ditmire, Turgeon, Brader, and Shaw took Urlich aside. Urlich's eyes went round the group. He seemed indifferent. Rust and Sydowski began asking questions. Urlich answered them, and before long they realized they were on the right track, but at the wrong address. The children, a five-year-old boy and his seven-year-old sister, were Urlich's grand-children, his son Norman's kids. Norman had lost a custody fight, and last month he had abducted them from his "ex-bitch Marcie" in Dayton, Ohio, and brought them here.

"This is what this show is all about, ain't it?"

Inside the shack, they found two kids' video-movie member-ship cards for a store in Dayton and two juvenile library cards for Dayton. Calls made to the store, the library, and Dayton PD were further confirmation of a parental abduction, contrary to a court custody order. The children would be returned imme-diately to Mom in Ohio.

Meanwhile, two agents who checked every wreck on the grounds approached Rust. "No pickup, sir," one agent said.

Rust turned to Urlich. "According to California's Depart-ment of Motor Vehicles, you own a 1978 Ford pickup, license 'B754T3.' Where is it?"

Rust held an information sheet before Urlich's face. He

leaned forward, hands still cuffed behind his back, squinting
at the page.

"I can't see. My glasses are in my bib here."

Urlich was uncuffed. He slipped on his glasses, studied the
page.

"Well, shit, I sold that thing months ago to some fella from
San Francisco. For cash. Got a bill of sale in the house."

"Why is this truck currently registered to you?" Sydowski
said.

"Guess the registration never got changed like it was supposed to."

"What's the buyer's name?" Rust asked.

"I got it in the house, in my office."

Urlich's office was a cracked rolltop desk buried under
mounds of auto magazines, newspapers, brochures, junk mail,
notes, and phone books. Amazingly he reached into the heap
and pulled out a slip of paper, smudged with engine grease.
The pickup's bill of sale.

Rust looked at it, cursed, and gave it to Sydowski.

John Smith had bought the truck.

"Says here he also bought a boat and trailer from you."

"Yes. Northcraft with twin Mercs. Paid nine thousand for
the whole shooting match."

"He said he was from San Francisco?" Sydowski was taking
notes.

"Yes."

"Why come out here to buy a truck and boat?"

Urlich shrugged. "I only advertised the truck."

"You advertised? In what?"

Urlich reached into the pile again, retrieving an automotive
buy-and-sell magazine. "I put all my stock in here." He licked
a finger, casually browsing through the pictures of cars and
trucks, each bearing an information caption. "Goes all over
Northern California. Here it is." He tapped the picture.

Rust and Sydowski stared at a profile photo of the Ford

pickup truck used in the abduction of Gabrielle Nunn from the Children's Playground at Golden Gate Park.

"You got a picture of the boat and trailer?" Sydowski said.

Urlich indicated his paper pile. "In there somewheres."

"You got any of the nine thousand he gave you left?" Rust said.

"Yup, why?"

"Can we see it?"

Urlich fished a jingling key chain from his coveralls and unlocked a drawer, then a metal strong box containing several envelopes filled with cash. "Some is deposits on my stock." He handed Rust an envelope containing several fifty-and hundred-dollar notes. They were fresh-from-the-mint bills with sequential serial numbers. They could yield the suspect's prints. And the Secret Service and Treasury people might be able to give the task force a point-of-circulation bank.

"Can you remember what this man looked like?" Sydowski said.

Urlich scratched his chin.

"Any distinguishing scars, tattoos, any memorable speech patterns?"

No, Urlich said, before giving a vague, useless description.

"He come with anybody?"

Urlich shook his head. "Said he hitchhiked."

"Hitchhiked?" Sydowski took a note. "Any idea at all where he lived? Worked? His phone number?"

Urlich shook his head. "Nope. I see quite a few people and it was a long time ago."

"Anything about him that sticks in your mind?" Turgeon said.

Urlich couldn't recall anything.

"He say what he needed the truck for?" Ditmire said.

"Nope."

"What about the boat?" Sydowski wondered. "He say anything about that? He came for a truck and leaves with a truck and boat.''

"Now that you mention it, he was something of a holy man about the boat.''

"A holy man?'' Ditmire said.

"Yes, he came for the truck and fell in love with the boat. He said it was destiny that he should find such a boat.''

"Destiny?''

"Destiny or fate, as I recall.''

"In what way?'' Sydowski said.

"Well I never advertised the boat. It was just sitting here, not really for sale and he spots it and starts on some Bible mumbo jumbo.''

"You remember any of it?''

"Just that it was about life and death, resurrection.''

"Resurrection?'' Sydowski said. "He sees this boat and talks about resurrection?''

"Guess it had something to do with why he needed the boat.''

"He say why he needed that boat?'' Rust asked.

"Well . . . after that he sort of clammed up, it was like he was talking to himself and suddenly remembered I was there.''

"Did he say why he needed the boat?'' Sydowski pushed.

Urlich appraised Sydowski, Rust, and the others, chuckling at his memory before sharing it. "Said he needed it to find his children.''

To find his children?

The law men stared at each other, bewildered.

During the return flight to San Francisco, several intense calls were made to the Hall of Justice and Golden Gate Avenue. The entire task force was to meet within ninety minutes.

60

Zach forced himself to quit bawling like some sort of candy-ass wuss. Jeff and Gordie would laugh at him, but it hurt. Everything was coming apart. His folks were really splitting. The kids at school were right. When your folks split and move out, they never get back together, no matter what they tell you.

Right after the big blowup with Dad, Mom went to her room, and slammed the door. He heard her crying, wailing like he had never heard before. It scared him. Her sobbing tore at his heart.

He didn't know what to do. But he had to do something, had to grow up and do something.

He opened his school backpack and was shoving stuff in it. He had made a decision. He was going to Gordie's. He'd stay with his pal. He'd get away.

He stuffed his CD player, Batman comics, Swiss army knife, penlight, Walkman, some underwear, and balled up some pants, socks, shirts, and a jacket into his pack. He dropped to his knees and carefully slid out the envelope he kept hidden under the big dresser in his room. It contained his life's savings: $117.14.

Zach hoisted the bag on his back, slipped out of the house, and trotted off, growing angrier and more determined with each step he took along Fulton.

Mom and Dad were breaking a promise.

This was how you measured a person's worth, by the number of promises they broke.

It just wasn't fair.

He headed toward Center. He knew the way to BART. He'd take it to San Francisco and then take a cab to Gordie's house. They could call Jeff and catch up on stuff, talk about old times. Maybe he could move in with Gordie. Maybe there was some way he and Gordie could become brothers. Maybe sign some court papers or something. Gordie's mother and father never fought. Gordie's dad was an accountant and was always home.

It was kind of nice being on his own. Before he got on BART, he'd stop at that hobby store along the way and buy that monster-size model of the U.S.S. *Kitty Hawk.* He could take it with him to Gordie's and he could help him put it together. That would be cool!

He was on his own now. They didn't need him around in Berkeley anymore. Zach sniffed as he waited for the light to change at an intersection. He glanced over his shoulder and noticed a white van a few car lengths away. Funny.

Looks like the same doof that was hangin' out near his grandma's place earlier. So what? Zach shrugged off his curiosity.

61

One cherry had tumbled into place.

Two more and they had a jackpot.

Sydowski loosened his tie as everyone settled around the conference table in Room 400 at the hall. Most had to stand. Gonzales wheeled a new chalkboard into place, in front of its predecessor bearing the blown-up faces of Tanita Marie Donner, Danny Becker and Gabrielle Nunn, and the map with its color locator pins. The new board had enlarged color photos of the Ford pickup, the boat, and trailer.

They were on the bad guy's trail.

The next cherry would be his identity.

And the next would be finding him with the kids. Sydowski sipped his coffee, bit into his chicken sandwich. He and the others had returned from Calaveras in time to grab stale food from the cafeteria before the meeting. The pickup truck lead kicked it all into overdrive. More people had been brought in.

''We've got new information, so listen up, we'll be handing out assignments.'' Gonzales stood at the new board, examining the new material in his file folder. "The ident team left behind in Calaveras just lifted two latents from the new bills left over in the buy of the suspect pickup. They match the single latent we found on the wrapping of the hamburger used to lure Gabrielle Nunn's dog. We pumped them through the system. Zilch.

"We are also checking all prints of anyone who has ever been bonded in the state—private investigators, armored car guards, state and federal workers, just to make sure we've covered everything."

Adam McCurdy, chief of Investigations, interjected. "The chief will hold a press conference this afternoon to make a public appeal for information on the pickup and the boat and trailer, reiterating the reward. He will say that we believe Virgil Lee Shook is responsible for the murder of Tanita Marie Donner, but that we have nothing linking him to the abductions of Becker and Nunn. He will state that the suspect in those kidnappings is still at large. We'll add whatever new information is pertinent."

Gonzales nodded.

"We're sending out alerts on the truck and the boat, targeting marinas." Gonzales flipped through his file. "Treasury's still working on the serial numbers of the new bills to determine point of circulation. So far they have narrowed it to a San Francisco bank. And, on the hamburger . . ." Gonzales found another data sheet. "A brick wall. Because the label was damaged, we could only confirm it as a purchase in the city. And, on the boat and trailer: same as the pickup, no change in registration. Still comes up to Urlich."

As Gonzales summarized the case, Sydowski finished his sandwich, slipped on his glasses, and made notes, his theories and hunches percolating, extracting the essence of a vital angle he knew he had overlooked. It tried to surface during the chopper flight back from West Point, flailing in his subconscious as the patchwork of vineyards, pastureland, orchards, towns, and urban sprawl rolled below. It was difficult to converse through the helicopter's intercom, leaving each person alone with his thoughts as they thundered back to San Francisco. Now, sitting in Room 400, Sydowski replayed them, trying again to catch the key, hidden aspect that had been gnawing at him.

It had been so long since he had talked with his daughters. He was consumed with the case. It was national news. The girls called him regularly, the red message light blinking at him from his machine almost every night when he got home. "Saw you on TV, Dad, hope you're taking care of yourself." Geneva, his firstborn daughter, sounded like her mother.

Then came his second daughter, Irene, forever the baby of the family. "Hey, Pop, I know you're busy, call us when you get a chance. Oh, Louise wants to leave a message, go ahead, honey."

"Hi, Grandpa! I saw you on TV, I love you."

It was always too late for him to call back. He rarely had a free moment to check on his old man. And he was likely going to miss the Seattle bird show.

Sydowski glimpsed Turgeon taking notes intensely. She was wearing a powder-blue pullover sports shirt, navy Dockers, and glasses. Her hair was up in a bun, accentuating her pretty face, her youth. She could pass for a Berkeley grad at a lecture. But she was a veteran cop, a good investigator with good instincts, and although he hadn't known her very long, he was glad she was his partner. He found a degree of paternal comfort in her presence.

Sydowski chided himself for drifting. The key aspect escaping him stemmed from the Donner file . . . a common denominator with Donner . . . Christ, it was at the forefront of his memory, sitting there slightly out of focus. Something Angela Donner had told him.

Gonzales moved the review along. "Now I'll turn it over to Bob Hill of the FBI's Behavioral Science Unit in Quantico, Virginia. He flew in this morning. Bob."

A self-conscious smile of acknowledgment flashed across the long face of the lanky soft-spoken supervisory agent. Hill was in his late forties and had a gently cerebral air about him.

"As you know, I've been assisting on the profile in this case since Danny Becker's abduction, when the unit was contacted. I'd like to caution you about putting all your eggs in one psychological basket. The profile is only a tool, as you know." Hill was acutely aware many case-hardened investigators viewed psychological profiling as mumbo jumbo. "But each development helps us sharpen it. May I use the board, Lieutenant?"

Gonzales helped reposition the board so everyone could see. Then Hill took a finger of chalk, and summarized the profile.

"Based on our reading of everything so far, you have a profoundly wounded Caucasian, late forties, early fifties, traumatized by some horrible life-altering event involving children. He either caused it, witnessed it, or was close enough to it to be affected. We could assume it involved his children. And given his age and the ages of the kidnap victims, it likely happened twenty to twenty-five years ago. He has likely sought some kind of therapy, or help which failed to ease whatever psychological pain he has suffered."

A detective had a question. "Could this guy have been sexually abused as a child, and is grabbing the children as a form of payback?"

"Traditionally, that is the case in abduction-sexual-homicides with children. In fact, based on what we know of the Donner-Shook matter, I would say that's what happened there. Predatory pedophiles usually seize their prey when no one is watching. Tanita Donner was stolen from her home when nobody was around to see. But what you have with Becker and Nunn is rare, bold daylight abductions of young children from their parents in crowded, public places. Your guy is on a mission, he feels protected. He's so far gone in his fantasy that he thinks nothing can touch him. Andrei Chikatilo, the Russian serial killer who murdered fifty-three boys, girls, and young women between 1978–1980, told police after his arrest that during his killing spree, he felt at times that 'he was concealed from other people by a black hood.' Well, I believe our guy here is similar in that he thinks he is on a righteous mission.''

"What kind of mission?" someone asked.

"A religious one.''

"What makes you think so?''

"A couple of things. What we heard today from the man who sold him the pickup and boat.'' Hill glanced at his file folder of notes. ''Mr. Urlich described the buyer as a 'holy man' who muttered about it being 'destiny' that he found the boat, and rambled about 'life, death and resurrection.' That he needed the boat to 'find his children.' ''

The room fell quiet.

"And there is one other element that may or may not be another indicator of your guy being driven by a religious fantasy and that's found in the full legal names of the children.'' Hill printed them on the chalkboard: Daniel Raphael Becker and Gabrielle Michelle Nunn. ''Raphael and Gabrielle, if spelled this way''—Hill printed ''Gabriel'' on the board—''are the names of angels.''

"Angels?'' someone repeated.

Hill heard the comment as he placed the chalk in the tray.

"In Christian theology, angels are supernatural intercessors for God. Our guy may think the children are angels of some sort. I believe he looked for these children because they have 'angel' names, that his mission is directly connected to his personal tragedy, which he has either relived or plans to relive with Becker and Nunn.''

Hill brushed chalk dust from his hand.

"If you find out who this guy is and learn his background, you have a shot at learning what he has done, or plans to do.''

At that moment the elusive lead hit Sydowski full force.

You know, Inspector, I've been participating in the university bereavement group.

Reed wrote about it in the *Star*. And Reed came to him after the press conference on Gabrielle's abduction, after seeing the blurry video!

Wait what if I recognize this guy? He looks like someone I met.

Reed had met Angela Donner's study group, but no one in the task force had thought to investigate those people—people who had suffered traumatic psychological pain involving children!

62

"Zach?"

Why didn't he answer her? Ann Reed pulled herself together, taking stock of the woman staring back from her dresser mirror. Tousled hair, tearstained eyes, the lines of her face.

"Zachary?"

She concentrated on hearing a response. Nothing. Give it time.

What a pathetic sight she was. A grown thirty-three-year-old woman, mother of a nine-year-old son, a university graduate with her own business. And where was she? Living in the same room where she played with Barbie dolls, looking into the same mirror she looked into when she was a child, dreaming of how perfect her life would be.

How had this happened? How had it all turned to shit?

"Zach, please come in here, we have to talk."

No answer. Must be angry at her and his father. Could she blame him? They had put him through hell. Maybe he was jet lagged after this morning's flight from Chicago and was nap-ping. That was fine. She craved sleep herself. But she had too much to do. She had to put this mess on a back burner and check her stores. She needed a shower.

Her mother was right, she thought, as the hot water soothed her. She came down hard on Tom. She had overreacted. He was working hard. The kidnappings were a big story, out of the ordinary. And the paper putting him on probation didn't make it any easier for him.

The taps squeaked as she turned off the water.

Tom must be in agony.

Let him stew for a while. She would call him tonight and they would decide where to go from here. She still loved him and was willing to attempt a salvage operation. If he was.

"Zachary?"

Ann pulled on a pair of blue jeans, a fresh T-shirt, brushed her hair, then knocked softly on her son's bedroom door.

No answer. Ann opened the door.

"Zach—" Ann stopped dead. He was gone. "Where is he?"

Calling his name, she searched upstairs, the bathrooms, the other bedrooms. Not a trace. Strange. He must've slipped downstairs. "Zachary!" Where the hell could he be?

Ann stomped through the house. "Zachary Michael Reed!" He hated his middle name. She only used it to telegraph anger to him. No Zach.

She went outside, slamming the door behind her. He was starting to piss her off. Didn't she tell him to go upstairs and stay in his room? She checked the garage. His bicycle was untouched. The front and backyards. Nothing. Hands on her hips, she exhaled her irritation. She didn't need this. Not now.

Zach wasn't in the street, or at the corner store with the pinball machines he loved, or in the small vacant lot where the neighborhood kids played a half-block away. Two boys there, about twelve, clothes streaked with grease, were struggling to replace a chain on an overturned bike. "Hi fellas."

They traded glances, then sized her like she was an invader.

Parents never entered this realm looking for kids. Beckoning was done by little sibling messengers. Reading Ann's face, defense shields went up. Whoever Zach was, he was in serious shit. One of the pair moved his foot stealthily, nudging a pack of Lucky Strikes under a jacket lying on the ground. Ann pretended she didn't notice.

"You sure you haven't seen him a little while ago, guys? His name is Zach Reed. He's nine years old, blondish hair, wears new sneakers, uh, Vans, and a Giants ball cap, uhmm—"

"Zach? The little kid from across the Bay living with Granny down the street?" asked the bigger kid. He possessed the aura of a bully.

"That's right! Did you see him?"

"Yesterday, but not today"

She studied these boys—strangers to her but known to her son, realizing she had opened a secret door to Zach's life, that she no longer knew every detail of the child she had brought into this world. Nine years old and he knew older boys who smoked, boys who were practiced liars. It scared the hell out of her.

The smaller boy squinted up at her. "Is he in big trouble?"

Ann covered her mouth with her hand, eyes watering.

"No. I just want to find him."

After calling his name and searching a three-block radius around the house, it enveloped her: the cold fear that Zach was missing.

Ann grabbed the phone and began punching the numbers for her mother at the library. No. She sniffed and hung up. He didn't know his way on campus. But maybe he did? But Mom would call if he suddenly materialized. Ann returned to his room. Maybe he was back?

"Zachary?"

His room was empty.

Defeated, she sat on his bed, shaking as she wept. *Where are you? Why are you doing this to me?* Zach's black nylon travel bag yawned from the foot of the bed, opened, but not unpacked. It appeared as if he started unpacking, and took a few things out before changing his mind. She looked around his room. Where was his portable computer game? His CD player? His little knife? He treasured those things. She went to the dresser and lifted it slightly. His stash of cash, savings from his allowance, was gone. She looked around again. So were his jacket and school backpack. *He's run away.*

She called Tom's place, letting the phone ring. His machine clicked on. She left a message, urging him to call her immediately. She hung up and dialed another number. She had an idea.

"*San Francisco Star* newsroom," said a hurried voice.

"I'd like to page Tom Reed. This is his wife. It's urgent."

Her request was met with an unusually long silence.

"Hello?" Ann said.

"I'm sorry, Mrs. Reed, I can't do that."

"Why not?"

"Well, uh. Tom was, uh—" the voice dropped to a confidential whisper. "He . . . as of yesterday, he no longer works here. I'm sorry."

She hung up and sat down. That was what he was trying to tell her. It explained why he missed them at the airport, why he had been drinking. He was fired. She buried her face in her hands.

Time to get it in gear, Annie. Where was the most likely place Zach would go? To his father's.

Okay. She would drive across the Bay to Tom's rooming house. She stood. Wait! What if Zach returns? She should wait here.

She brushed her tears away, grabbed the phone, and punched Tom's number again, letting it ring and ring and ring.

She would keep calling until she broke that freaking machine.

63

God was present.

Edward Keller felt the intoxicating heat of His love. It was overpowering—he was swirling in it, as he hurried through Berkeley for San Francisco, delighting in the celestial trumpeting that melted into horn honking, waking him to the fact that his rental van was drifting toward oncoming traffic. Keller shrugged it off.

He had found Michael the Archangel. He had gazed upon him.

Sanctus, sanctus, sanctus.

The transfiguration was near, brushing against his fingers. All he had to do was obtain Michael, the last angel.

The Lord would illuminate the way.

For God will send His angels to watch over them. And they shall embrace them and carry them to Heaven.

Waiting for the light to change at an intersection west of the campus along Center, Keller feasted obsessively on a thumbnail. He was planning his route to the Bay Bridge, when a miracle blazed like a prophet's comet before his eyes.

"Sweet Jesus!" He couldn't believe it! It was Michael!

Heaven's warrior!

Keller managed only a glimpse, a mind-searing glimpse of nine-year-old Zachary Michael Reed, wearing a bulging back-pack and crossing Center. He was walking.

He was alone.

Alone!

Keller drove ahead for a block and tucked his van into a parking space ahead of a larger cargo truck, out of sight. He adjusted his passenger-side mirror, catching Michael's distant reflection.

And behold the earth shook and God's angel descended from the skies. His eyes were like lightning, and any who opposed him were struck dead.

The boy's image grew with each step, quickening Keller's pulse. He was sweating. What should he do? What if Michael spotted him and became suspicious? He had to remain calm. In control, as he was with the others.

I am cleansed in the light of the Lord.

The final challenge.

Michael stopped at a store, less than three car lengths away. Had he noticed the van? He couldn't have. Keller adjusted the mirror again. It looked like a hobby store. Michael peered into the window, then went inside. Where were the adults? Was he allowed to go to the store alone? Keller waited. No one else appeared. The boy was alone.

It was a sign.

He must act on it.

Dominus Deus sabaoth.

Keller scurried to the back of the van, watching the storefront from its tinted rear windows. He quickly changed into a shirt, tie, dress pants, and suit jacket. The same outfit he used for his insurance man. He knotted the tie, combed his hair neatly, and slid on a pair of dark aviator glasses.

The van's side door rolled open.

Anyone watching with a modicum of interest would have seen a very serious, professional-looking man of authority stepping from his new van to attend to an important business matter. If they guessed he was a cop, they would be right, Keller would tell them confidently if pressed. For in his breast pocket he carried the leather-cased laminated photo ID and shield of Randall Lamont, special investigator for the State of California, a personality he had created after sending fifteen bucks to a mail-order house that advertised in the back of a detective magazine.

But Keller knew no one was watching, or cared.

Except God.

And He was lighting the way.

64

"Inspector Turgeon? Inspector Sydowski?"

"Yes," Turgeon said.

Professor Kate Martin stepped from the door of her condo, indicating two sofas facing each other over a glass-and-rattan coffee table, the centerpieces of her living room overlooking the Golden Gate and Pacific. A hint of hyacinths lingered.

Although she was barefoot in Levi's and a long-sleeved, ratty flannel shirt, Martin moved with the swanlike elegance of a self-assured woman. But Sydowski's deeper reading picked up the unease in her eyes. Her hair, pulled back with a navy barrette, was loosening. She corraled the wild strands slipping in front of her face, revealing bright white flecks on her hands. She folded her arms across her chest. "I was painting a bookcase when you called."

Turgeon and Sydowski saw the file folders stacked on the coffee table. Martin had obviously stopped painting to scour through them.

"Sit down, please. Be comfortable. I've made some raspberry tea. Would you care for some? I have coffee, too, if you like?''

"Tea would be fine," Turgeon said.

"And Inspector Sy-DOW-ski? I hope I'm pronouncing it correctly?''

"You are. No tea for me, thanks." Then he thought of something as she started for the kitchen. "Dr. Martin?"

She stopped and smiled.

"By chance, would you have any Tums?''

"I'm sorry, no. I do have Alka-Seltzer.''

"That'll do, thanks.''

The chicken sandwich Sydowski had inhaled during the briefing was jitterbugging through his system. It nearly burned a hole in his stomach during the drive over as Turgeon read aloud, for the second time, every word of the article the *Star* had recently published on Martin's bereavement research study.

The Homicide Detail's secretary had clipped the story, "as per the lieutenant's instructions." Leo was a pain that way about the local papers. Anything with the word "murder" in it activated her scissors. But what with the Yellow Ribbon Task Force working a green light, Gonzales never got around to reading this one. And Sydowski, a scrupulous reader of crime stories, missed it. When he approached Gonzales immediately after the FBI's profiler went on about the bad guy suffering psychological pain involving children, Gonzales ordered the secretary to get the story.

It was written by Tom Reed.

"First he fucks us up on the Donner file—what the hell is it with this guy? Flora, can you make some copies of this please?''

Leo's eyes narrowed and his jaw tightened on his unlit cigar as Sydowski told him how Reed had tiptoed up to him after the news conference on the Nunn abduction, after seeing the fuzzy video and composite. How he hinted about recognizing the bad guy.

"This is a huge goddamn lead, Walt! You and Linda find the prof and see if anyone in her group fits the FBI's profile."

Sunlight probed the prismatic crystal glass of fizzing antacid Martin set before him. When she offered imported Scottish shortbread cookies, Sydowski had to restrain himself from unloading on her about the gravity of their visit. Lady, this ain't a fucking tea party.

Martin had priceless information and Sydowski wanted it. With two children missing, and most likely dead, he and their parents had a right to it. He was here to claim it. He swallowed some Alka-Seltzer, gritted his teeth, and nodded to the files.

"Are you prepared to help us, Doctor?"

Turgeon left her tea untouched and produced her notepad.

"Yes. After we talked on the phone, I reviewed the files of my research subjects and I think, uhmm, I think . . . uhm, I think one man may, uhm . . . I'm sorry."

Martin was coming apart. She stared mournfully at the files, gripping her knees. Her eyes were glistening when she tried to speak again. She was stunned with embarrassment. Fear.

"I'm concerned about patient-client confidentiality."

"But you're not their doctor?" Turgeon said.

"Yes, but I entered into an agreement with each subject for the research. They all volunteered."

"Doctor, does the profile suggested by the FBI fit one of your subjects?" Sydowski tapped the files. "We can get a warrant."

Martin looked at Turgeon and Sydowski, her eyes drowning in the whirlpool that engulfs a person once they learn that a dark force dwells under the skin of a person they thought they knew. Sydowski had seen that look break on the faces of a killer's family as they struggled with shame, remorse.

It was heartbroken, pleading:

Please don't judge us.

How could we have missed it?

What could we have done?

Their anguish consumed them as if they had helped plunge the knife, squeeze the trigger, or tighten the ligature. They were yoked with blame and pain, becoming the murderer and the victim, condemned to die a piece at a time for the rest of their lives.

Eyes downcast, Martin cleared her throat, touched her face with the back of her hand. She grasped the top file, retrospectively flipping through the yellow pages of her handwritten notes.

"This is my file on Edward Keller. He participated in my research. He was a walk-in. His is the most unusual case of prolonged grief reaction I've ever experienced, evolving into stages of delusion."

"Doctor, please," Sydowski said. "Does the profile fit him?"

Martin swallowed. "Like a tailor-made suit."

It only took a few minutes for her to recount Keller's case history and everything she knew about him: his fantasies, his religious delusions, how he reacted suspiciously to Tom Reed when he arrived to write on the bereavement group, how Keller demanded not to be photographed or identified before ultimately storming out.

Turgeon took notes. Sydowski steepled his fingers and listened.

"You ever fear he would act out his delusions?" Sydowski said.

Martin shook her head, burying her face in her hands. "I've read the papers, watched the TV news on the abductions. I've seen the grainy video of the suspect, the composite sketch. Once, for a second, I thought there was a resemblance to

Edward, but I dismissed it. I never thought in those terms. I never thought, I—''

''Don't beat yourself up.'' Sydowski began reading Keller's file.

''It's subconscious denial. I counsel people who do this.''

''Where do we find him?'' Sydowski asked.

''I don't know. The number and address he gave me are invalid.'' Martin fished Keller's personal information sheet from the file for Sydowski. ''I just never made the connection, never grew suspicious. The signs were evident. I knew he needed extensive help. I suggested it to him. How did I miss . . . how could I . . . the people I am studying have lost children . . . I never—''

Turgeon clasped Martin's shoulder. ''No one could have known. Stop thinking about yourself and start thinking about everything you can tell us about Edward Keller. I'll have Bob Hill, the FBI's psychological profiler, come here immediately to consult with you.''

''Certainly.''

''May I use your phone?'' Sydowski stood, grasping Keller's file.

Martin nodded toward the kitchen.

When he was alone dialing Leo's direct line, Sydowski belched. He felt much better. The line rang once.

''Homicide. Gonzales.''

''Leo, it's Sydowski. I got a name.'' He was browsing through Keller's file.

''So do I, Walt.''

''How's that?''

''We just got a hit on the prints from the new bills in the truck buy and the meat tray from the Nunn home. Belong to an Edward Keller. Seems twenty-odd, nearly thirty years ago, he was bonded as a night security guard for a warehouse in the city. Got his blood type, too. It matches the trace we found on Nunn's severed braids. We don't have a good address for

Keller yet. We've put the entire task force on him. What name do you have?''

"Same one: Edward Keller."

"No shit! You got an address for him, Walt?"

"Not yet, but get this: he lost his three children in a boating accident twenty years ago. Two boys and a girl. The ages of Danny Becker and Gabrielle Nunn match the ages of two of them."

"That's two. That means he's got to take a third kid."

"Right. A boy, age nine."

"And he was in that group Reed wrote about?"

"Yes, Leo."

"Shit. Walt, get ahold of Tom Reed. See if the *Star* has pictures, an address on Keller, anything."

65

The hobby shop was small, its two rows of shelves were crammed with model ships, racing cars, fighters, rockets, trains, landscapes, paints, and brushes. An eagle-sized P-51 Mustang was suspended in a dive by fishing line tacked to the ceiling. Soaring near it was a British Spitfire, a Japanese Zero, and a Messerschmitt. The air was pungent with plastic, balsa wood, and airplane glue.

A sixty-year-old man, with thick sideburns drifting to his jaw, a Caesar's crown of white hair, and horn-rimmed bifocals, was hunched over the glass counter, tinkering with a dragster. The two inches of ash on the Marlboro hanging from his pursed lips was dangling perilously over the cockpit. His bowling-ball gut strained the buttons on his stained shirt when he straightened to eye the ID and shield of Randall Lamont.

"I'm looking for a boy, about ten years old, blond hair, backpack, sneakers. He was seen in this area within the last half hour." Keller's face was somber behind his dark glasses.

The old man dragged hard, squinted through a smoky cloud

and nodded to the corner. "Could be the fella you want, drooling over the *Kitty Hawk* there. He just came in." The man coughed. "Anything to do with that gang shooting in Oakland?"

"I'm not at liberty to discuss the matter." Keller snapped his ID shut. He went to the boy, who was kneeling before the bottom shelf and a huge boxed model of an aircraft carrier.

Keller crouched next to him. "Are you Zachary Michael Reed?"

Zach's gaze darted over him, blinking before he nodded.

"Your mother is Ann Reed and your father is Tom?"

Zach was suspicious. What was this? Who was this guy? Was this because he ran away? Was he one of those school cops Dad used to tell him about, the kind that chased runaway kids?

"It's all right. I'm Randall Lamont, a state detective." The man reached inside his jacket and showed him his badge.

A detective?

"I'm a friend of your dad's. He's a reporter with the *Star*. We're friends from way back. I live in Berkeley."

"Am I in trouble?"

"Not at all." Keller dropped his voice to a confidential tone. "Zach, your dad sent me to find you. We've got a problem."

"A problem?"

"It's your mom." Keller put his hand on Zach's shoulder. "She's had an accident."

"What? So fast? How could—I just left."

"Your dad went with her in the ambulance. I live nearby and he called me to find you."

"Wha—I—what happened?" His voice was trembling. "Is she—"

"Tell you on the way. You have to come with me to the hospital."

Zach grabbed his pack. "Is she going to be okay?"

"I'll tell you all I know on the way, son."

They left the store, hurrying to Keller's rental van. Zach

froze when he recognized it. It was the same van he had seen parked near his grandma's for the past couple of days. The guy unlocked the passenger door and swung it open. Zach didn't like those sunglasses. Wasn't he the guy he had seen hanging around down the street? Something didn't feel right. But didn't he say he lived down the street? Still something didn't feel right.

"Why didn't my grandma come find me?"

"She's on her way to the hospital, Zach."

"Well, how did you know where to find me?"

"I saw the direction you left in just before your dad called me."

A distant siren sounded his dad's warnings about strangers.

Never go with a stranger, no matter how smooth their line is. They may say I'm hurt, or Mom's hurt, or there's some emergency. They can make it sound real bad. And they'll be the nicest people—they won't look like creeps. Trust your instincts. If you don't know the person then don't go, Zach. Don't go!

"Are you scared because you don't know me, Zach?"

That was it. But Zach didn't know how to say the truth. He looked at his feet, agonizing about his mom.

The man removed his sunglasses and smiled. A friendly smile.

"Tell you what, son, we can go back to the store, call the hospital and leave word for your dad or grandmother to come for you. I'll wait with you if you like?"

Zach looked at him. "All right."

Keller patted Zach's head and they started back to the store. No problems, no protest, which led Zach to conclude, this guy was for real. A bad guy would not take you back. He'd try some scam to get you in to his car while he had you on the street. He'd never take you back.

Zach stopped. "I changed my mind."

"You're sure, son?"

He nodded. "Tell me what happened."

Keller bent down, eye to eye with him.

"It may be her heart. She collapsed after you left. I guess she managed to get hold of your dad."

Zach's chin crumpled. "A heart attack?"

Keller put his hand on his shoulder. "I don't know. Your dad didn't tell me any more than that. We should get to the hospital, if you still want me to take you."

He did.

"I think it's my fault," Zach mumbled, bowing his head to sob as he let Keller help him into the van and buckle his seatbelt. "The whole thing with my mom and dad is my fault."

Keller climbed behind the wheel, slipped on his dark glasses, turned the ignition, felt the engine come to life with glorious victory, and pulled away.

Zach had drawn his knees to his chest, hiding his face on them under his arms, crying softly. Keller stole glimpses as he drove south on Interstate 80 to Oakland.

He radiates with the light of one million suns.

His face buried, Zach did not know where they were traveling. "Is she going to die?" He sniffled from under his arms.

Keller did not answer. They approached the Bay Bridge.

"Mister, is my mom going to die?"

The new van hummed silently, save for the tires—rhythmically clicking along the freeway. Keller touched Zach's shoulder.

Heaven's warrior.

Keller kept his eyes forward. "What is it like to look upon the face of God?"

Zach recoiled.

"Serpent slayer, chief of Heaven's army."

Zach's mind gathered speed, his eardrums pounded in time with his beating heart, for suddenly he knew. He knew what had happened.

Kidnapped. He had been kidnapped by a psycho.

"You are my light and my salvation." Keller smiled. "I praise you, beloved of God."

As the van moved west along the upper deck of the spectacular bridge to San Francisco, Keller reached under his seat for the plastic bag and the chloroform-soaked cloth.

66

Some days, when the midafternoon sun hit it just right, the Bay Bridge glowed like a portal to paradise. For an instant, its majestic span and spires changed from flat silver to a surreal white against the blue-green waters of the Bay a few hundred feet below.

Today, its beauty was lost on Tom Reed. For him, the bridge had become a tangible span of despair between everything he had done wrong and the futility of his future. It was his third crossing, and with each trip, his emotional freight increased, unraveling the worn thread by which his life was swinging. Reed was rushing east on the lower deck and wondering how much more crap a man was supposed to stomach in one day.

His marriage lay in ruin, he was fired from his job, he was an alcoholic, or on his way to becoming one. He had caused the suicide of an innocent man and very nearly accused another. And now Zach pulls a first and runs away. Nine years old and he takes off.

Could it get any worse?

Sunlight strobed through the bridge's steel girders. Reed glanced over his left shoulder at San Francisco's skyline, then at the mesmerizing whitecaps below. Why not end it all? He had considered it when he arrived at his room in Sea Park after the blowup with Ann. It was a dumb-ass notion, supplanted by his need to get into his room and reacquaint himself with Jack Daniel's. Lila had not returned. So, he kicked the door. It opened with little damage on his second try. He'd pay for that move when Lila got back.

Reed collapsed in the sofa chair, his head pulsating. What was he going to do? Leave town? Chicago? He had some buddies at the *Tribune* and the *Sun-Times*. He could beg for a job. He could see Molly tonight after she finished her shift. She wasn't the answer and he knew it.

Reed decided to take care of his immediate needs: shaving, showering, and changing into better-smelling clothes, ignoring the flashing red light of his telephone answering machine until he finished, which was half an hour later.

The first call he played back was the most recent one.

"Reed, Walt Sydowski. Give me a call as soon as you can." He left his cell phone and pager numbers.

Sydowski? Reed sneered. Likely found out he had been fired and wanted to relay condolences from the Homicide Detail. Sure, I'll get right back to you, Walt.

Next, came a panicked message from Ann: "Tom, is Zach with you? I can't find him! I think he's—"

The phone rang. Reed stopped the machine and grabbed the call.

"Tom, do you have Zach?" Ann was hysterical.

"No, Ann, I don't. What the hell is going on?"

"I can't find him! It's my fault. He ran away. He took his school backpack with some of his favorite stuff and his savings, about a hundred dollars. I'm so scared!"

Ran away? He must have heard us. "How long has it been?"

"An hour, forty-five minutes, I don't know."

"Did you call Jeff and Gordie's parents?"

"But they're in San Francisco."

"That's likely where he's headed."

"I'll call them!"

"Call all the Berkeley cab companies. Call BART security. He may try to cross the Bay that way."

"All right. I already called the police. They said they put out a description and will send a car over."

"I'm on my way."

Now, as Reed guided his Comet along the interstate off-ramp for Berkeley, he could not stop blaming himself for dragging Ann and Zach into the cesspool of the self-obsession which blinded him to the toll it was taking on Zach. He would talk to Ann, tell her everything. Make one last intelligent effort to work things out before it was too late. If anything, anything happened to Zach, he'd never forgive himself. He glanced at the water below.

When Reed turned on Fulton, the hairs on the back of his neck stood up at the sight of a Berkeley patrol car parked in front of Ann's mother's house.

Ann was sitting at the kitchen table, talking through a crumpled tissue to a uniformed officer who was taking notes.

"Oh Tom!" she sobbed, hugging him tight. Letting him know that she needed him. Truly needed him. Reed's eyes stung. When was the last time he held Ann in his arms?

"Mr. Reed?" the officer asked.

"Yes."

"Officer Pender, Jim Pender, Berkeley PD. We've already got a description of your son out to radio cars. I'd like to talk to you."

"Certainly."

"Alone, please, sir."

Pender was a tall, black officer, at least six-four. He had a cropped goatee and exuded calm capability. His utility belt and holster gave leathery squeaks when he stood, his polished badge over his heart gleamed. The shoulder mike of his radio crackled, and Pender turned it down as the two men talked in the living room.

"Tell me what you think happened, sir." Pender said softly.

Reed told him everything. The officer's eyebrows shot up when he told him he was the reporter behind the Tanita Marie Donner controversy and had been fired that morning. When Reed finished, Pender said, "Okay, there's stress in your household. Zach overhears his parents arguing and decides to head out on his own. To his friends in San Francisco, you figure?"

Reed nodded. "Or my place in San Francisco."

"Okay, we'll add this new info to the alert we've already got out on your son. We'll notify SFPD and campus police." Pender checked his notes as they returned to the kitchen where Ann sat, face buried in her hands.

"Mrs. Reed, we'll do everything we can to find Zach," Pender said. "I'll ask you both again to try and put yourself in his shoes. Is there any material thing he wanted, a type of toy or something? Or any place he wanted to go, an arcade, a certain movie? Or any individual he would turn to? Give it some thought that way."

The Reeds agreed.

"Most kids who run away mad at Mom and Dad turn up within a few hours, especially the young ones," Pender said.

Ann tried a smile, but swallowed it. "At least the police shot the kidnapper yesterday in San Francisco," she said.

Pender nodded, but Reed caught something in his face.

"If the family is going to look for Zach, please keep someone here in case he returns or more information surfaces. I'm going to call this in. Then I'd like to search the house. Sometimes kids will crawl into a hiding spot to cool off for a while."

"Thank you, officer."

"Ann." Reed took his wife's hand. "I'm going to search

the area between here and the BART station. I'll call you every few minutes.''

"Yes." Her voice was barely audible.

"We'll find him, Ann, I swear." Reed hugged her, then caught up with Pender outside. He was in his cruiser entering his notes into his mobile computer terminal.

"What's up, officer?"

"How do you mean?"

"Your face registered something a moment ago when my wife mentioned SFPD shooting the kidnapper."

Pender contemplated whether to tell Reed whatever it was he knew.

"You're a police reporter, right?"

"That's right."

Pender scratched his goatee. The police radio blurted coded dispatches. "You reported on the big abduction cases of Danny Becker and Gabrielle Nunn across the Bay, right?"

"That's what got my ass fired, officer. Please."

Pender tapped his pen on his notebook, thinking. "Okay, I'm going to show you something. Get in."

Reed slipped into the passenger side, watching Pender's big hands dwarf the computer's tiny keyboard as he typed in commands. "SFPD and the FBI put out a new alert on the case. It's hot. I got it just before I got this complaint. Here you go. Says the task force now has a number one suspect in the Nunn-Becker cases and they're hunting him. Ever heard of a guy named Keller? Edward Keller?"

Reed was stunned. "Edward Keller—yes, I, Christ—"

"Nobody knows I showed you this." Pender pivoted the terminal to Reed, who devoured the short bulletin.

Edward Keller of no fixed address was wanted on a warrant for the kidnappings of Daniel Raphael Becker and Gabrielle Nunn.

"I was fucking right all along!"

"You know this guy?"

"I met him recently and thought he was weird, so I did some digging into his past." Reed shook his head in disbelief.

"Mr. Reed, do you think there's any link to your son's running away and Mr. Keller?"

Reed's heart stopped. No. There couldn't be. "No. I think it is a coincidence. Zach ran off because he heard us arguing about our problems. We had reconciled and we were on the brink of getting back together. Zach wanted that with all of his heart. But it fell apart this morning."

"I see. You said you started digging into Mr. Keller's past. Is there anything about him that you know that may be useful to the task force across the Bay? Anything we should pass on?"

"No. He's a lunatic, a Bible thumper. I met him on a story about university research on parents of dead children. He lost three a long time ago and babbled about resurrecting them with God's help. He was nuts. I tried to find him again, but I couldn't."

"Why did you want to find him again?"

"I had a gut feeling. But I wanted to find out what I could about him on my own before going to the task force, having been stung badly the last time I followed a hunch."

"Did you go to the task force?"

Reed shook his head. "And I was fired because my paper thought, given my track record, I was dangerous with my theories. It's complicated. Look, officer, I'm going to find my son. I have some ideas where he might have gone. Any other day, I'd be calling my paper, tipping them with that alert." Reed nodded to the computer terminal. "But fuck them. I was right. They were wrong and I don't work for them anymore. I've got more important things on my mind."

Reed moved to leave.

"Hold on there." Pender was friendly.

Reed waited. Pender stared at him. A streetwise cop with impeccable instincts, he was not going to let Reed leave him.

"Where's the first place you're going to look?"

Reed sighed. "Next to us getting back together, Zach wanted to buy a model of a ship."

"A hobby store then?"

"Thought I'd start with the nearest one."

"Buckle up."

"What?"

"There's one on University, I'll take you."

"Officer, I can take myself."

Pender started the engine and slipped the transmission into drive. "I think we should go together, Tom."

Pender double-parked his cruiser on University at a sliver of a store front called Dempsey's Hobby & Crafts. His head came within inches of the transom when he and Reed entered. The bald, potbellied, old man who ran the place was on the telephone.

"Yeah, Saturday's good. Sure—" he noticed Pender and Reed. "I told you, it's fine with me. . . . Yes . . . listen, Burt, I gotta go. . . . Yes, it's good. Burt, I gotta go now. I'll call ya later."

He hung up and spread his hands over the glass countertop in a bartender's what'll-it-be? fashion. He peered over his bifocals with the unpracticed seriousness of a shopkeeper unaccustomed to adult visitors, nodding to Pender because the shop was on his beat.

"Hello, Jim. How, are things in local law enforcement?"

"George," Pender said, "I need your help."

George Dempsey's eyes shot to Reed, then to Pender.

"This about that gang shooting in Oakland?"

" 'Fraid not." Pender leaned on the counter and into Dempsey's personal space. "This is Mr. Tom Reed. He's looking for his son, Zachary." Pender studied Dempsey's face. "He may have come in here within the last ninety minutes. Nine years old and how tall, Tom?''

Reed held a hand to his chest.

Pender continued. ''That tall, blond hair, new sneakers, school backpack, and interested in model ships.''

Dempsey tugged thoughtfully at his fluffy sideburns. ''Ships? Sure, was a kid like that in here a while ago.''

''How long!'' Reed stepped to the counter. Pender raised his big hand to warmly caution him.

''How long, George?'' Pender repeated, softer.

Dempsey twisted his sideburns before guessing: ''Hour?''

''An hour?''

''Yes, then he left with that other cop.''

''What!'' Reed said. ''They found him!''

''What other cop, George?'' Pender took out his notebook, glancing at his watch. ''Think.''

''He was plainclothes, uh, special state investigator, white guy six foot.''

''He definitely said special state investigator? You sure?''

''Absolutely.'' Dempsey scratched his chin. ''Flashed his badge, name was Lamer? Lampson? No—Lamont, Randall Lamont.''

''He left with the boy?''

Dempsey nodded.

''Which way?''

''Well, I didn't see. Say what's this about?''

''Tell me exactly how it happened.''

''Not much to tell. Kid walks in, goes to the shelf there all doe-eyed over the *Kitty Hawk,* then this Lamont comes in a few minutes later asking—yeah just like you—asking if I'd seen a kid. Then he goes to him, they have a little chat, then leave together.''

''What was the boy's demeanor?''

Dempsey blinked and looked at the ceiling. ''Scared, like he just got some bad news.''

Reed felt the first stirrings in his gut. His worry about Zach's running off was about to be swallowed by a greater terror.

Pender scanned the shop. "George, you ever do anything about your shoplifting problem, like I told you?"

"I did. I got security video installed couple months ago. It works just fine and— I see what you're askin'."

"Let's run that tape, George."

Dempsey hoisted a small black-and-white video monitor to the counter, angling it so Pender and Reed could see.

"I was plagued by little thieves until I got this." Dempsey grunted, squatting to operate the video controls from a low shelf behind the counter. A montage of ball-capped boys coming, going, and buying things, swam in super-fast motion on the monitor. "Glue, paints, scale model racing cars, electric motors. One kid stuffed the *Titanic* under his shirt. It all adds up. There he is!"

Dempsey slowed the tape. Reed watched Zach enter the store and sit on the floor before a shelf of models. Dempsey advanced the tape to the entrance of a man in a suit, wearing dark glasses, showing identification.

"You know this guy?" Reed said to Pender.

He shook his head without removing his gaze from the monitor. "You?"

"No," Reed said as the man approached Zach. They talked, then left together. Reed's face flushed. His heartbeat quickened. He couldn't believe what he was seeing.

"George, take it back to when the cop walks in," Pender said.

Dempsey reversed the tape.

"You have any audio?" Pender said.

Dempsey nodded. The tinny sound of homemade videos, with hard noise amplified and monotone voices, hissed from a tiny speaker on the monitor: "I'm looking for a boy, about ten years old, blond hair, backpack, sneakers. He was seen in this area within the last half hour."

"Could be the fella you want, drooling over the *Kitty Hawk* there. He just came in. Anything to do with that gang shooting in Oakland?"

"I'm not at liberty to discuss the matter."

Pender was staring at Reed. A fist covered Reed's mouth, the veins of his neck were pulsing

"You recognize that voice, don't you, Tom?"

"It's Edward Keller."

Where was Keller's beard and long hair? Reality stabbed Reed with switchblade suddenness. Keller had Zach. Had his son!

Have you ever lost a child? No. You have children? A son, Zach. He's nine. My eldest boy was nine when he died.

Pender seized his portable police radio.

67

Sirens.

Wailing. Yelping. Screaming.

It wasn't real. Couldn't be real. It was a terrifying drug-fueled dream. Reed was numb. Detached. Alone in the shop, watching everything unfold. Detectives talking to him as models of World War II fighters strafed them from above.

"Mr. Reed, anything you can remember about Keller that might . . ."

His mouth wouldn't work. What were his lines? What was he supposed to say? My little boy. My son. My only child has been taken. What was he supposed to do? Faces in his face. Dead serious. Faces at the shop window. Police cars. Flashing lights. A crowd gathering. A TV news camera, no, two—three. Coffee-breathed detectives who wore strong cologne clasping his shoulder.

"Mr. Reed, Tom, we need your help. . . ."

Zach needs me. My boy. I did this. Zach. Keller, his hand on Zach's shoulder.

Sirens. Wailing. Yelping. Screaming.

Sirens—the score of his profession. The chorus cueing his entrance upon a stranger's tragedy. And it was always a stranger, it always happened to other people. It never touched him. Oh, it grazed him in the early days. But he grew skilled in his craft. He knew the bridges into their pain, knew his way over the crevasses that would consume you if you failed in your mission, knew how to cradle their suffering long enough to serve himself.

The city shares your grief. Now is the time to say the things that need to be said, by way of tribute.

And in virtually every case, they would struggle to help. Stunned by their loss, they would recite an inarticulate requiem for their son, daughter, father, mother, husband, wife, sister, brother, or friend. Some would scrawl tearstained notes, or show him the rooms of the dead, their accomplishments, their dreams, their disappointments, the last things they touched.

And would you be able to provide the paper with a picture?

Dutifully, they would flip through family albums, rummage through shoe boxes, yearbooks, wallets, purses, reach to the mantel for photos. Drinking in each image before placing it tenderly in his trusted hands. But there were times a relative would see him for what he truly believed he was. They knew.

Oh, the years-off-the-street, J-school profs and burned-out hacks could pound their breasts about the unassailable duty of a democratic free press, safeguarding the people's right to know, ensuring no one dies anonymously and secretly on American streets. But that constitutional crap turned to dust when you met bereavement face-to-face, took it by the hand, and persuaded it to expose itself. You steeled your soul with the armor of a champion. The sympathetic, respectful reporter. Democracy's champion. But at the bottom of your frightened heart, you realized what you were: a driver ant, leading the column to the carrion, overcoming and devouring the mourners who open their door to you, those too pained to flee.

And before he left, they would usually thank him.

That was the joke of it. They would thank him. For caring.

He was shoved, prodded, and paid to succeed at this, and they thanked him. For caring.

Don't thank me. I can't care. I can't.

But he would smile, professionally understanding, all the while fearing he might never find the bridge back, for his ears rang with tormented voices chanting:

Wait until it happens to you. Wait until this happens to you. Now it had.

He was paying the price for the sum of all his actions. This was his day of reckoning. The toll was his son.

Zachary, forgive me.

"—Where is he? You let me go!"

It was Ann. Pender struggling to hold her, failing. She ran to Reed. He opened his arms to take her. A horsewhip crack of her hand across his face.

"Bastard!"

Reed saw stars and Franklin Wallace's widow, her accusations resurrected with Ann's voice. It was his fault.

"You bastard!"

Pender must have told her everything. "Ann, please." His face burned. "You don't understand."

"I understand and I blame you! You had to get close, had to keep digging for the sake of a story! Well, you've got a good one now, don't you? You used my son for it!"

"Mrs. Reed." Pender and another uniformed officer subdued her.

Sirens. Screaming. Ann screaming.

"Come with us, Mrs. Reed." Pender took her to a back room.

Reed turned away, meeting the rheumy eyes of George Dempsey, who was pretending he hadn't seen what he had seen, along with the police people in the shop. Dempsey was showing a detective the U.S.S. *Kitty Hawk,* the one Zach had held less than an hour ago.

The last thing he touched.

Suddenly the model fighters suspended from the ceiling began trembling, the shop windows vibrating. Quake? No. A chopper was circling. Reed overheard someone say they had a partial description of the suspect's van from a clerk at the bakery nearby. The pounding intensified when the door opened. Merle Rust and a posse of FBI agents arrived, flashing ID's, assuming command, from Berkeley PD, going to Dempsey's video. Sydowski, Turgeon, and a few other dicks from the task force were with them. Sydowski put his large, warm hand on Reed's shoulder, just like Reed's old man used to do whenever Reed lost a little league game.

"Hang in there, Tom. We're going to need your help."

Reed swallowed, then told them, "It's Edward Keller. It's been him all along. I met him for a story"—Sydowski and Turgeon tried to interrupt him, but he continued—"his three children drowned. He's a religious psychotic—thinks he can resurrect them. I was secretly researching him. My paper found out before I was finished and fired me. Keller asked if I had a son. I never suspected. I-I-I think he's going to drown . . . the Farallons where he lost his kids!"

"Tom, Tom, Tom!" Linda Turgeon's compassionate eyes offered comfort. "We know it's Keller."

"We found out this morning. I called you," Sydowski said. "We need you to help us get him."

"Martin! Dr. Kate Martin, did you try—"

Sydowski nodded. "She told us everything she knew. Tom, what did you find out? Addresses? Relatives? Anything?"

"Okay," Rust said from the counter where the FBI and SFPD people huddled around the video monitor. "It's ready."

Reed watched the videotape again. Then FBI Special Agent

Rust turned to him. "You're certain that man is Edward Keller?"

"Yes," Reed said. "All the information I have on him is at the paper. Keller lost his kids near the Farallons and made pilgrimages there from Half Moon Bay with a guy named Reimer."

"The Coast Guard's been alerted. They're watching the islands. We've got a team going to Half Moon Bay now and local people there have been alerted," Sydowski said. "Let's go, Tom. Merle, we're going to the *Star* news department."

"Okay, first, Tom, give us all the addresses Zach knows, so we can put people there in case he escapes or tries to call."

Their home in the Sunset, his room in Sea Park, Jeff and Gordie's houses, Ann's mother's on Fulton. Rust wrote it down.

"Let's get going, Tom." Sydowski took his arm.

"I have to talk to Ann."

Dempsey's back room was a moldy storage closet. Boxes of ancient model cars, planes, and ships teetered near the ceiling. There was a coffee-stained sink, a hot plate, a small table, and a door to a toilet. The air reeked of cardboard, cigarettes, and loneliness. Ann sat at the table across from Pender staring at pictures of Zach.

"Ann," Reed said.

She did not acknowledge him. The floor creaked when he squatted down and took her unresponsive hand.

"Ann, I have to go with the police. I have information that could help us find Zach. It's at the paper. Ann?"

She was not there.

Watching her and Reed, Pender said, "Crisis people are coming."

"Ann, I'll bring him home, I swear. I swear to you."

Reed tried to hug her, but it was awkward. She did not react until he started to leave. She lunged from her chair at him, crushing his neck in her arms, filling him with pain, love, and courage.

* * *

Sydowski and Turgeon shielded Reed from the tangle of reporters and photographers waiting outside the hobby shop. He recognized some of them and instinctively stopped. Sydowski pushed him into the backseat of an unmarked Caprice. Familiar voices hurled questions.

"C'mon, Reed, just give us something!"

"Tom, please just make a statement!"

"Is it really your son? Give us a break!"

One guy smacked the car in frustration. Reed imagined him returning to his newsroom, telling editors, as he himself had done many times, "I couldn't get anything good—the father wouldn't talk to us." Cameras pressed against the glass, their eyes probing, invading.

Wait until it happens to you.

Turgeon drove. The dash-mounted cherry blazed, and she gave a few blasts of the siren, inching through the crowd. The Chevy parted traffic, gliding, speeding through Berkeley, Oakland. All the while, Sydowski and Turgeon said nothing, allowing Reed his privacy, never once capitalizing on the chance to ask him how it felt to be in the spotlight. They were above that.

Sydowski broke the silence as they sailed through the tolls of the Bay Bridge to San Francisco.

"Tom, I don't think we have much time to find Keller. Tomorrow's the anniversary of his children's drownings. If he's going to do anything, I think he'll do it then."

Reed looked at the Bay, remembering the time Zach was a year and a half old and toddled into his study where he was working. His tiny, determined hands grabbed and tugged at him as he scaled his way to his father's lap, where he went to sleep, sucking his bottle. How Reed leaned back in his chair, savoring his warmth, his sweet smell, and vowed to keep him safe from all the bad things in this world.

68

Zach Reed's heart hammered in his chest as he ascended from sleep to consciousness, racing through a mental systems check. It was all coming back to him, bubbling to the surface.

He was not dreaming. He was waking to the nightmare.

He was kidnapped.

His mouth tasted salty. Kidnapped by some religious creep who talked about God. And this dungeon place stunk big time. Oh boy, he was in deep trouble. Mom and Dad were going to kill him because he ran away, because he got sucked in by a weirdo. He had to get himself out of this mess because Dad was going to kick his butt.

Squeak-creak.

What was that? Sounds of a TV somewhere. Where was he? He was lying on a bed. He opened his eyes. Two faces swam into focus, jolting him alert. Kids.

These kids were familiar for some very bad reason. Zach heard the rocking noise above them.

Squeak-creak. Squeak-creak.

"Who are you?" he said.

"Who are you?" the girl asked.

Zach went numb, like the time he was five and saw little Luke Petric get run over by an eighteen-wheeler, mowed down like a rag doll, and all Zach could do was stand there screaming, his scalp tingling as if he'd been electrocuted.

The kidnapped kids, the ones everybody was looking for: Danny and Gabrielle.

Squeak-creak. Squeak-creak.

That was him! Above them. The man who took them was upstairs. What was going to happen? It was getting hard to breathe. Something inside was overwhelming him, on the verge of breaking. Hang on. Calm down. Take slow breaths. Just be cool. He wanted to cry for his parents.

He was only nine.

But he was the biggest kid in this place.

The boy and girl looked different from their happy, smiling pictures. Zach wanted to cry, but Danny and Gabrielle were looking at him. Like he was supposed to save them or something.

"Who are you?" Gabrielle repeated coldly.

"Zach Reed. How do we get out of here?"

Squeak-creak. Squeak-creak.

"We can't. Mr. Jenkins has got everything locked up."

"Who?"

"Mr. Jenkins." Gabrielle pointed at the ceiling.

"Well don't worry, that doof is not going to hurt us!"

Danny started to whimper. "Can you take me home, now? I want to go home."

Zach put his arm around him. "Don't worry, Danny. It's going to be okay. I'm gonna fix it so somebody comes for us."

Garbage covered the floor—fast food bags, wrappers, and containers. The basement's only window was barred and covered with newspapers. Zach noticed the door was wide open.

"Where are we, Gabrielle? San Francisco? You know what street?"

Gabrielle shrugged.

"Are there any other people here?"

"Just Mr. Jenkins. My dog Jackson was here, but Mr. Jenkins said he ran away. Did you see him? He's a blond cocker spaniel."

"No."

Squeak-creak. Squeak-creak..

Gabrielle burst into tears, triggering Danny's sobs.

Zach didn't know what to do, so he hugged both of them, fighting his own tears. "It's gonna be fine. Shhh-shhhh. It's okay."

"He's a crazy man!" Gabrielle sobbed. "He killed a rat and he's always praying to us on his knees! He calls us by other kids' names, shows us old movies of them and makes us wear their old clothes! I'm so afraid! We tried to run away, but he's got us locked up, and he keeps making us sleepy!"

"Does he hurt you?"

Gabrielle shook her head. "He just baptizes you."

"What?"

"You're going to get it soon."

"What are you talking about?"

"He puts you in the tub and dunks your head. After that, he starts calling you by another kid's name. He told us you're the last one he was looking for."

"The last what?"

"Angel."

Squeak-creak. Squeak-creak..

Zach saw the door and thought. "Does he always leave the door open?"

"Uh-huh. So we can go upstairs to the bathroom."

Zach looked around for something, anything that might help him try to escape. He was surprised to see a corner of his backpack protruding from the stinking garbage. He fished it out.

The creep had never even touched it. Zach dumped the contents, grabbed his father's business card, his cash, his portable video game, then his tiny Swiss army knife. He opened it and ran his finger over the three-inch, razor-sharp blade. He folded it and stuffed it in the crotch of his underwear. Bad guys always frisked you, but a guy never checked another guy there. He was not supposed to. It was like a world rule, or something.

"Does this house have a phone, Gabrielle?" Zach said.

"In the kitchen, on the wall."

Squeak-creak. Squeak-creak.

"All right." Zach glanced at the ceiling and sniffed. "I've got a plan to get us outta here."

69

Reed pushed his way through the throng of reporters, photographers, and TV crews waiting in the lobby of the ancient fourteen-story *Star* Building in downtown San Francisco.

"Reed, is it true you know the kidnapper from a story?"

This was real. It was happening.

"Has there been a ransom demand?"

Something was roaring in his ears.

"Did this guy take your son because you were suspicious he abducted Danny Becker and Gabrielle Nunn?"

He couldn't concentrate clearly.

"Any connection to the Donner case and Virgil Shook?"

His only thought was of his son.

"Can we have a picture of Zach?"

"I can't talk now," Reed managed.

Cameras flashed and TV lights burned as he shouldered his way in. Sydowski, Turgeon, Rust, and half a dozen other police, shields hanging from pockets and neck chains, surrounded him, ensuring no one else got on the elevator with them. It was closing when a security officer wedged his arm between the doors.

"What the hell you doing, Butch?" Reed demanded.

The plump, gray-haired guard felt the hard glare of the detectives and he cleared his throat. "Uhm, sorry, Tom. But orders are that you've been terminated. Barred from the building. Mr. Benson's orders."

"Back off," Sydowski growled.

"Just doing my job. Good luck, Tom." Butch saluted.

As Reed and the police swept through the newsroom, heads snapped around, conversations stopped and people gaped. By now, the entire department knew Zach had been abducted. And everyone knew Reed had been fired.

He hurried to his desk, whispers following his wake.

His only crystalline thought was for Zach. Finding his son. Ann was right. It was his fault, and if it was the last thing he did, he would find Zach. Alive. Nobody would stand in his way. Every molecule of his being was focused on his son.

Everything remained on Reed's desk exactly the way he left it yesterday when he was still employed. He rifled his paperwork: his yellow file on Keller was gone. Sydowski and the others encircled his cubicle as he searched in vain.

"It was right here, a yellow legal-size folder!"

"Tom?" Molly Wilson materialized, her teary voice thickening. "I know everything. What Benson did. Zach. I'm so sorry, Tom."

"I need help, not sympathy, Molly. Where's my Keller file?"

"I'll help you, Tom." She sniffled, eyes going to Benson's office. He was on the phone, reading from a yellow file folder. "I'll help you right now!" Wilson ran off, bracelets chiming.

Reed burst into Benson's office, snatched the Keller file, and returned to his desk to show Sydowski and the others.

Benson leapt after him. "What do you think you're doing, Reed?" Benson grabbed the file back.

"Give me that file, Benson!" Reed spat.

"Tom, I'm terribly sorry about what's happened. Really. But you have to calm down and think rationally. This file is the property of this newspaper and you, as a former employee, are trespassing."

"What!" Reed was incredulous. "What did you say?"

"I'm afraid the only way to take this file is with a warrant."

Sydowski said, "We'll get one right away. Linda."

Turgeon picked up a phone. "What number to get out?"

"Nine," someone said.

FBI Special Agent Ditmire rolled his eyes. "I don't believe this. This is a hot pursuit. Can't we charge this man with obstruction, Merle?"

Reed thrust his face to within an inch of Benson's. "The clock is ticking on my son's life! If you don't give me that file now, it starts ticking on yours."

Benson blinked.

Reed continued. "Give me that file now or I hold a news conference outside and every parent in the Bay Area will know what Myron Benson at the *Star* is doing! Then I'll join the Beckers and Nunns to sue you for the wrongful deaths of our children."

"Myron, give Tom his file, now." It was Amos Tellwood, the publisher. Molly Wilson stood beside him. Newsroom activity ceased.

"I've just been fully enlightened. Tom, you have the paper's unbounded support." Tellwood turned to Sydowski. "I am the publisher and you have full access to anything we have that will expedite finding Tom's son. We shall not lose another second debating it. Tom, you remain a *Star* employee. Myron, in my office. Now."

Reed opened the folder. Sydowski and the others took notes, and went off to telephones. Tom told Sydowski and the others about Keller's pilgrimages to the drowning spot at the Farallons. Sydowski told him Keller had bought a boat.

The hunt for Zach Reed, Gabrielle Nunn, and Danny Becker intensified. The FBI doublechecked with the U.S. Coast Guard: Yes, the Farallons had been sealed. And the FBI and California Highway Patrol each put choppers up, searching for a new white van, possibly with rental plates, or anything trailing a boat like the one Keller had bought in Calaveras County. They had a team of police at Half Moon Bay, and alerts to all marinas.

Statewide bulletins with photos and more information were continually broadcast. Police stationed at every known point in Keller's past were watching for him and the children. Detectives went to the homes of Danny Becker, Gabrielle Nunn, and Reed's mother in law in Berkeley, where a phone trap was being set up. They were setting up a trap on Reed's newsroom line.

The SFPD tightened its surveillance of William Perry Kindhart, and undercover cops tuned their radar for any street talk on the kidnappings. Detectives questioned other members of Keller's bereavement group; others canvassed every car rental and leasing outlet in the Bay Area. The FBI's psych profiler pored over Reed's file on Keller and discussed it with Dr. Martin. The photo department kicked out three clear pictures of Keller taken secretly when Reed had sat in on Martin's research group and duplicated Reed's wallet snapshot of Zach. It was more recent than the framed one on his desk. Other newsrooms were calling the *Star* for Reed—for quotes, for photos.

Reed found a moment's sanctuary at an empty corner window desk, where he had a partial view of the Bay Bridge between the office towers. In his hand he held a picture Ann had snapped on a cable car a month before the breakup. He traced Zach's face with his finger.

He remembered Nathan Becker, sitting in that boutique in Balboa, drowning in fear, clutching Danny's picture, and Nancy

Nunn pleading before news cameras for Gabrielle's life, and how he thought it was sad for them, but a dynamite news story.

What had he become?

Wait until it happens to you.

Sydowski rolled up a chair beside him. They were alone. "How you doing, Tom?"

Reed shook his head, unable to answer.

"Hang in there. If we have anything going for us, it's that we know more about the bad guy than we ever did, thanks to you."

"Do you think Zach's dead?"

The two men searched each other's eyes.

"No." Sydowski gave him the truth. "Not yet."

Reed turned to the window.

"Tom, I think whatever he's going to do, he'll do it tomorrow on the anniversary."

Reed agreed.

"Look, Tom, you met the guy. What does your gut tell you?"

"He's a madman."

"You know we're doing everything conceivable to find him. Right now we've got nothing—no driver's license, no record with Pacific Bell, utilities, voter's registration, taxes, credit cards, nothing. On paper he doesn't exist. We've got people dealing with Fargo, following the bill he paid for the flowers on his family's grave. We may get a lead there. It's a question of time."

Reed nodded.

"Tom, this is the guy you wanted to tell me about after the Nunn case, after you met him at Martin's group and saw the rough home video we had from Nunn's party?"

"I held off because of the Donner fiasco."

Sydowski wanted to tell him everything about Franklin Wallace and Virgil Shook, but decided it wasn't the time. "Go home and be with your wife, Tom. She needs you. If something pops, I'll call you. We'll be moving everything to the Hall of Justice very soon.''

''Walt?''

''Yes?''

''He's our only child. He's all we have.''

''I know.'' Sydowski patted Reed's shoulder. ''Be strong, for him,'' he said, then left.

Reed rubbed his thumb over his son's picture, picked up a phone, and called his mother-in-law's house in Berkeley.

Ann's mother answered, her voice quavering.

''It's Tom, Doris. Is Ann there?''

''She's resting. A doctor from the university came over and gave her a sedative. There's lots of police here— Oh, they're signaling not to tie up the line.''

''I'll be there soon.''

''Tom, I'm praying for everybody.''

''I'll bring him home, Doris. I swear I'll bring him home.''

Reed covered his face with one hand. His life was slipping away, slipping through his fingers and there was nothing he could do. The eyes of the whole newsroom were on his back. He heard a familiar tinkle of jewelry and knew Molly was near. She touched his shoulder.

''Molly, I don't know what to do. Talk to me, about anything.''

''Go home to be with Ann, Tom.''

''I don't know if I can face her. She blames me.''

''Tom, no one on this earth can think clearly when something like this happens. No one.''

Reed turned to the window. ''Thanks for getting Tellwood.''

''Benson's a vampire. He sent me to Berkeley. I don't think you saw me in the pack.''

Reed looked at her.

''He went crazy when he heard Keller's name over the police scanners. He grabbed your file, pulled up the Keller feature you wrote yesterday, and said he was going to turn it into a

Pulitzer. Planned to keep you out by saying you were too distraught to be reached but your exclusive *Star* probe led to Keller, who retaliated by taking Zach before police could catch him.''

''What?''

''It's true.''

''He's diseased.''

''Tom . . .'' Wilson's voice broke. ''Tom, don't hate me, but what's happened is news. I've got to write a story, Tom.'' She glanced at the news desk and swallowed. ''They want me to interview you.''

Disgusted, he shook his head. But he knew the truth, better than anyone. From across the newsroom, a telephoto lens was aimed at him.

He had become the carrion and the ants were coming.

70

Zach Reed stared into his hand before closing his fingers around their ticket out of this rat hole.

Squeak-creak. Squeak-creak.

Zach crouched at the bottom of the basement stairs, primed to make his move. It was all planned. Gabrielle and Danny had gone upstairs to the bathroom. They were going to flush a whole roll of tissue paper, plugging the toilet, then call the man.

Squeak-creak.

A TV was blaring upstairs. Good, that would help. The toilet flushed, gurgled. It flushed again.

"Mr Jenkins!"

Good, Gabrielle. Good.

The *squeak-creak*ing stopped. Someone walked from the TV to the bathroom. A man's voice over loud, rushing water cued Zach. He padded up the stairs, breathing quickly, panting. Had to be brave. Only gonna get one shot at this. Adjusting to the light, his eyes widened at what he saw. Nothing had prepared him for this.

Enlarged pictures of Gabrielle and Danny covered the living room wall. A worktable was cluttered with a computer, books, and papers that had cascaded to the floor. The paint was peeling, blistering. Ignored. Windows were sealed with ragged sheets. The place was desolate. Something icy, something decomposing, reeking of death dwelled here. He spotted the three binders, the printed names of Joshua, Alisha, and Pierce, paired with Danny, Gabrielle . . . and Michael.

Michael? How did he know his middle name?

Pasted to one wall were news clippings about the baby girl they found last year in Golden Gate Park. Some of them were his dad's. Zach's stomach knotted.

He's going to kill us!

His eyes stung. The faces of his mother and father circled him. He was going to collapse. The ceiling was coming down on him. Stop it! Stop it! Stop it! Nobody's gonna get you outta here but you. Quit being a baby. Quit it! Hurry up!

Fists balled, he found the kitchen, scoured it until he found the phone. A wall phone with a long cord and the dial pad in the handset. He reached it easily, scanning the filthy counter for a magazine, a phone bill, anything with an address. Nothing. He swallowed.

The splash of water on linoleum echoed from the bathroom. Hurry!

He couldn't stop shaking. He sniffled, stretching the cord from the kitchen to the rear entrance. Wait! He tried the door. Nope. Locked solid. From the inside. Try the front door? No. No time. The cord was long, allowing him to hide in the rear closet. Leaving the folding door open slightly, he opened his fist and by a shaft of light read his father's business card.

TOM REED
STAFF WRITER
THE SAN FRANCISCO STAR
415-555-7571

It was his dad's direct line

Zach pressed the buttons for the number, shaking so badly he misdialed. Please, he sniffed and redialed. There. He put the phone to his ear, the line clicked, and began ringing.

Squeak-creak. Squeak-creak.

Keller sat before the TV news coverage of Zach Reed's abduction, his finger unconsciously caressing the body of Christ on the silver crucifix around his neck.

They have not died. I can bring them back.

"... it is unbelievable what has happened ..."

Skip Lopez, a green reporter for Channel 19's *Action News* team gripped his microphone

"Zach Reed, the nine-year-old son of Tom Reed, a reporter with *The San Francisco Star,* was abducted this afternoon from this hobby store in Berkeley. Reed had been covering the earlier kidnappings of two other San Francisco children, Danny Becker and Gabrielle Nunn, when this latest abduction occurred. ..."

Squeak-creak.

W-what was—Keller heard little voices. Water? The bathroom?

"Mr. Jenkins, sir." Gabriel was calling.

Keller left the living room and found Daniel and Gabriel in the bathroom, fearful. "What is it?" Water cascaded from the toilet, puddling on the floor. Obviously it was backed up. He found a plunger under the sink.

"Step away," he told them. A few solid churns cleared the blockage. "Use the towels," he pointed to the spilled water. Returning to the news, he stopped in his tracks.

Michael?

He hurried back to the bathroom.

No sign of Michael.

71

Sydowski shouted Reed's name again.

Why was he yelling his name, holding up his phone?

"Tom! Tom, it's Zach!"

Zach?

But Zach's kidnapped, how could he be calling? . . . Zach!

The impact of the call hit Reed like a bullet, nearly short-circuiting his brain. He flew across the newsroom, seizing the phone from Sydowski.

"Zach!"

"Dad?" He was crying.

Reed lost his breath. Had to think clearly.

"Zach, where are you?"

"I don't know, I think we crossed the Bay Bridge."

"Are you hurt?"

"No, but I think he wants to do something bad to us."

"Us?"

"GET A NUMBER, ADDRESS, AREA CODE," Sydowski scrawled on the note he thrust into Reed's face.

"Zach, is there a number—"

"The other kids are here too, Dad, Gabrielle and Danny."

"Zach, is there a number on the phone? Something with an address? Can you see any buildings you know? Run to a neighbor?"

Zach left the line and Reed heard him moving the handset.

"We're locked in and all it says on the phone is 4-1-5."

"4-1-5? That's all it says?" Zach was in the city.

"We don't have a tap up yet! He's in the city. Tell him to hang up now and dial 9-1-1. An address will flash for the dispatcher!"

"Daddy, I don't know what to do." Zach was whimpering.

"Zach, son, listen to me carefully—"

"Tom, do it now!"

"Dad? He tricked me, Dad, he tricked me so good. He said Mom was hurt and—"

Reed gulped. "He lied. Listen—"

"Now, Tom! Tell him to call 9-1-1 now!"

"Zach, listen to me. Hang up now and—"

"Hang up! Dad, no! You come and get me!"

"Son, listen, hang up and dial 9-1-1! We'll get the address!"

"Dad, you have to come and get me, please!"

"Zach, listen to me! Do as I say!"

"Dad, don't yell at me."

Reed covered his face with his free hand.

If only he could reach through the Pacific Bell cables and pull him to safety. If only he could touch him. He didn't want to lose him this time, this was his last chance. His only chance.

Sydowski was talking softly, forcefully, to someone on another line then turned to him. "Goddammit, Tom, do it now!"

"Zachary, you do as I tell you! Hang up and dial 9-1-1 now!"

"Daddy, I'm afraid."

"Do it, son, I'm going to hang up!" Reed sniffed.

"Dad, don't. Daddy! Don't, please!"

"I love you. Call 9-1-1 now!"

"Dad, he scares me, he's going to do something to us!"

Reed squeezed the phone, clinging to the fiber-optic thread connecting him to Zach. The plastic handset cracked under his grip.

"You call 9-1-1 now, or I'm going to kick your butt. Do it!"

Reed slammed the phone down, his heart breaking as he buried his face in his hands. The newsroom was silent, except for a camera's clicking, and Molly Wilson's tape recorder being switched off. People had gathered around Reed's desk; men muttering curses, women covering their mouths. The lifeline to Zach had slipped through Reed's fingers, paying out deeper into an abyss with each second.

Wait until it happens to you.

Sydowski remained on his open line to the 911 supervisor. A minute passed, two, five. The newsroom had caller ID, but Zach's call had come up blocked. Finally ten full minutes ticked by with no 911 call to the emergency line from Zach. It should have come within thirty seconds.

Something had happened. Something went wrong. It was in Sydowski's face.

"Tom." Sydowski squeezed his shoulder gently. "Tom, the fact that Zach called is a good sign for many reasons."

Reed waited to hear them.

"He's alive. He's thinking. And he got to a phone."

"Why didn't he call 9-1-1?"

Sydowski shook his head. "It might not have been safe for him to call again."

"He could make that call in two seconds. I'll tell you what happened—Keller caught him on the phone!"

"You don't know that and you're gonna eat yourself up playing the worst case scenarios, so shut it off."

"You tell me how."

"Go home to your wife."

"I can't."

"You can't?"

"She blames me for this and she's right."

"Tom, don't beat each other up over this. It won't help."

"I can't go home without Zach. I promised I'd bring him home."

Sydowski's eyes met Reed's, acknowledging the unspoken truth. Given what they both knew about Edward Keller, the children had less than twenty-four hours.

"I've got to stay, in case he calls me again. I'll stay here all night and the next night, if that's what it takes."

"Okay. Just remember, he hasn't defeated us. We're not out of this, not by a goddamned long shot." He patted Reed's knee, then left him at his desk.

Molly Wilson approached Reed to console him, but Reed waved her away. After that, no one dared go near him. He sat alone, waiting for his phone to ring.

72

"Where's Michael?" Keller demanded.

"I think he's still in the room." Gabrielle sniffled.

Keller rushed down the stairs and searched the basement in seconds. Michael was not there. Keller bounded up the stairs.

"Michael!"

He searched the main floor. Not a trace. His eyes locked on to the phone in the kitchen. It was off the hook! The cord stretching out of sight!

He was on the fucking phone!

Keller smashed it from the wall, then grabbed Zach, who was cowering in the closet.

"Please, mister. Don't hurt me. Please."

"Who did you call?"

"No one, I—"

"Who did you call!"

"I-I. Hospitals, my mom. I have to know if she is—"

"Liar!"

"I swear, I was asking the number for hospitals. I . . . I . . ."

"You are lying to me!"

Rage darkened Keller's face. "Satan is near. The Fallen Angel is among us, the Father of Lies! King of Whores!"

Keller hoisted Zach over his shoulder and hurried to the bathroom. Gabrielle and Danny screamed and scattered. Zach's struggling was futile. Keller laid him in the tub, and opened the faucets.

"Let me go, you sick freak!"

"I will not drink from the cup of devils! You cannot thwart that which is preordained!"

"Let me go!"

"The Lord is my sword and my shield!" Keller seethed. It was bad enough that the dog somehow got away last night. Now this. A phone call. Keller realized he was being challenged by powerful forces. But God was his shield.

"It is time," he said. "Time to come to Him and receive His light!"

Zach writhed, kicked, and pounded the tub, still clutching his father's card, aware of his knife hidden in his underwear as water gushed from the tap, dampening, soaking his clothes. Keller's crucifix raked across Zach's face as Keller's large, powerful hands seized Zach's head in a viselike grip.

"Reborn of water and the Holy Spirit in the sacred font. . . ."

He pulled Zach's head under the running water.

"By the mystery of your death and resurrection, cleanse this child in Your celestial light! Make his life anew!"

"D-dad, help me, Dad, he-help—"

Keller closed his eyes. Above the water's rush, the thunder, the storm, Pierce was calling from the darkness.

Daddy!

Holding Zach's head under the flowing water, Keller lifted his own face to heaven.

> *"This is life's eternal font,*
> *water made sacred by the death of Christ,*

cleansing all the earth.
You who are bathed in this water
are received in Heaven's kingdom.''

Suddenly it was over.

Zach sat up in the tub, coughing and gasping after Keller released him, shut off the water, and fetched him a large dry towel.

''Come with me.''

Zach followed Keller into Keller's bedroom, watching him pull out a big cardboard box marked ''Pierce,'' filled with boys' clothes that looked about his size.

''Find some dry clothes right away.''

Zach sniffed, but didn't move, dripping water with the towel cloaked around him.

''Do as I say! We're leaving!''

73

Reed spent the night in the *Star*'s newsroom, praying for Zach to call. Every half hour, he phoned Ann's mother's house in Berkeley, on the safe phone the FBI had installed, to see if Zach called there.

"Still nothing, sir," the agent assigned to the line told him.

"May I speak with my wife, or her mother?"

"I'm sorry, sir. They're still sleeping. The doctor says the sedative should wear off by mid-morning."

Reed said nothing.

"Mr. Reed, we fully understand your concerns and we will get you the instant we have something at this end."

"Yes, thank you."

"But sir, please check with us as often as you wish."

"I will."

Reed did not keep his vigil alone. Molly Wilson was among the newsroom staffers who waited with him, comforting him, assuring him Zach would be found safe with the other children, although she dozed off a few times. She was sleeping with her head on her folded arms on the desk next to Reed, when Myron Benson appeared, briefcase in one hand, jacket draped over his arm.

"Tom"—he nearly looked him in the eye—"I know you won't believe this coming from me, but I apologize and hope with all my heart it works out well for you."

Reed suspected Tellwood had put him up to this, but said nothing.

"I never liked you, Tom. I knew you resented me for lacking talent and I resented you for having an abundance of it. I was wrong. Anyway, you have more important things to deal with here. Good luck."

Benson extended his hand. Reed contemplated it for a moment before deciding to accept it.

"What did the old man have to say to you, Myron?"

"He fired me."

Reed was speechless.

Benson managed a weak smile before leaving.

An hour after sunrise, Reed was at the Hall of Justice, fear twisting his stomach.

Was Zach dead?

He had never made another call.

The task force had nothing, nothing at all at Half Moon Bay. The Coast Guard had nothing at the islands, nothing in the water. No boat, no trailer on the coast, no van. Nothing!

Reed was alone at an empty desk in Room 400, the SFPD Homicide Detail, watching Sydowski, Rust, Turgeon, Ditmire, and the others studying material on Keller. Rust and Bob Hill, the FBI's profiler from Quantico, were poring over Keller's psychiatric records, preparing for the eight A.M. news conference at the hall. Reed had not slept and, between adrenaline rushes, was nearly drunk with exhaustion. Sitting there as the ringing phones and voices faded, something triggered his memory, and the fragrance of baby powder, the feel of terry cloth, and the tenderness of Zach's skin when he was six months old washed over him. Reed was holding him, watching him as he sucked down a warm bottle of milk, gazing upon him during the commercial breaks of *Monday Night Football* with the sound off, knowing he possessed one of the earth's treasures.

And there was Zach, a lamb tied to the stake, staring at Reed now from the morning newspapers scattered around the Homicide room. Zach's picture, Keller's, those of Danny Becker, Gabrielle Nunn, and himself, all tormenting him with the truth.

Zach was gone. Gone.

And the headline haunting him.

THIRD CHILD ABDUCTED IS SON OF REPORTER
WHO INVESTIGATED KIDNAPPER

"Dammit! These press calls are supposed to be screened!" Ditmire hung up angrily. "That was the fourth fucking TV network asking if they can land their helicopter on the roof!"

Overnight the task force tip line lit up with calls as the story grew. Word leaked from the White House that the President and First Lady were following it. The national press were hitting it hard. So were the tabloid TV shows. More news outlets in London, Paris, Stockholm, Sydney, Tokyo, and Toronto were flying in reporters. Network breakfast shows insisted on an interview with Reed and Ann, promising exposure. Reed held off.

"Look outside," Turgeon said. A dozen news trucks were lined up along Bryant, deploying satellite dishes.

"This is nuts." Ditmire shook his head.

"The attention could help us, Lonnie," Rust said.

Sydowski finished a call to Ann's mother's house in Berkeley and somberly went to Reed.

"Ann's awake now, Tom. I just spoke with her."

"How is she?"

"Holding up." Sydowski's gold crowns glinted as he put his hand on Reed's shoulder. "I'm sorry, but she did not want to talk to you."

Reed understood.

"Tom, she insisted on being here for the news conference. We've got people driving her across the Bay."

Reed nodded. He was starting to get the shakes from too much caffeine, no food, no sleep. He craved the taste, the sensation of Jack Daniel's on his tongue, rolling down his throat, warming him.

"If either of you get second thoughts about making a public appeal, just say the word."

"No, no. We have to do it. We have to."

Sydowski ran his gaze over him, thinking. "We got a couple of rooms around here with sofas. Want to grab some rest? You've got nearly two hours until the press conference."

No. Reed could not be alone with his fear. Was Zach dead? He forced his thoughts away from children's corpses, caskets, and cemeteries. He could not be alone, he told Sydowski.

"Okay, well, I've got an electric razor, cologne, and stuff if you want to spruce up a bit."

"Thank you, but I'd just like to wait here for Ann."

"Sure, Tom." He stood to leave.

"Walt?" Reed's eyes were brimming. "Is my son dead?"

Sydowski looked at him for a long, hard moment, searching for the right words, deciding on the truth. "We just don't know, Tom. You must prepare for the worst, but never give up hope."

"But today's the anniversary of the drownings. And you said if Keller's going to do anything, he'll do it today."

"Yes and we are doing everything we can, we're chasing down every lead. You've got to hang on."

"What does your gut tell you, huh? He's beaten you guys three times now."

"I don't know. What do you think?"

"He's either very lucky, very smart, or both."

"In Danny Becker's case, he left us with nothing. In Gabrielle Nunn's case, we got his blood, got him on a piece of video, then a fingerprint and a name. In Zach's case, we have more video and, thanks to you, his motive."

"So, what does that mean?"

"We're gaining on him."

Ninety minutes later, a female FBI agent arrived at the Homicide Detail with Ann Reed, who was dressed in a white blouse, a dark blazer, and slacks. No makeup. Reddened eyes, taut jaw, betrayed a heart that had stopped beating. When Reed moved to embrace her, she was unresponsive. The doctor had given her two Valium before she left Berkeley. She looked as though she was going to a funeral.

No one moved until Rust said, "Let's get going." He and Sydowski escorted Reed, while the others took Ann to the elevator, all of them riding together to the press conference. In the elevator car, Ann apologized for being late.

"Not a problem," Rust said respectfully.

"I was trying to decide what to wear."

No one spoke as the elevator hummed.

"What do I wear to plead for my son's life?"

It seemed to take forever to arrive in the basement where the Hall of Justice cafeteria had again been transformed into a pressroom. Some two hundred newspeople were waiting there.

Reed and Ann were isolated, each alone with their pain. He was at the bottom of a well, blurry faces peering into it. Microphones and camera lights made the packed room hot, but he was shivering, his stomach seething. Copies of *The San Francisco Star* were everywhere. Faces staring at him. Reed was the man who had allowed his son to be kidnapped, and pushed an innocent man to suicide. Reed was on trial.

The FBI agent in charge of the San Francisco office, flanked by San Francisco's police chief, stood before a half-podium placed on a cafeteria table. He led off with a summary of the abductions, promising to take questions after Zach's parents spoke. He turned to the Reeds. Ann went first, her voice no more than a murmur.

"At the podium, please, Mrs. Reed!" Reporters urged her.

Reed helped her there, standing behind her as she clutched a folded note bearing her elegant handwriting on her store's stationery.

Ann began: "Edward Keller, I am Zachary Michael Reed's mother. He is my only child." Her monotone voice was alien to Reed. It was as if he was hearing a Jaycees address. "I want my son back and I am begging you to return him. I have spoken with the families of Danny Becker and Gabrielle Nunn. Please, let the children go safely."

Camera flashes rained on her.

"We've done nothing to hurt you and understand you must be suffering terribly, as we are suffering now. Our hearts are linked in our pain. Only you can end it safely. The children are innocents. Zach, Danny, and Gabrielle have done nothing to you. Please, please, I beg you to find it in your heart to let the children go."

Ann finished, declining to answer questions as she left the cafeteria with the help of two FBI agents. Cameras trailed her as Reed stood alone, unprepared, gripping the edges of the podium. The attention turned to him. He cleared his throat.

"Edward, if you are watching us, I'm sure you remember me, Tom Reed. Our understanding is that no one has harmed the children. I know you are a good man, Edward. Please release the children. The city, the entire country, now knows your tragedy, knows your pain. Do not extend it to others who have never harmed you. Release Zach, Danny, and Gabrielle, anywhere safely. By doing that, you will prove to everyone that you are the good man I know you are, Edward. You are a smart man, who means no harm to anyone. You have already proven so much, now is the time to let—'' Reed stopped, ran a hand over his face. "Please, let the children go. Please."

The reporters opened fire.

"Tom, do you think Keller took your son because you were getting close to learning he had kidnapped the other children?"

"I don't know, it's possible. I—"

"What kind of man is Edward Keller, Tom?"

"I— Well, I only met him briefly, so it's hard to describe—"

"Today being a tragic anniversary for Keller, do you think he is going to reenact some fantasy with the children?"

"I fear that might happen, but I hope not."

"What about Franklin Wallace and Virgil Shook, Tom?"

"What about them?"

"Both are dead. You reported last year that Wallace killed Tanita Donner. You still think so, or do you feel he died innocently?"

"I don't see what this has got to do with—"

"What I'm wondering is if there is a chance police shot the wrong guy in the Donner case. That maybe there's a connection to Edward Keller and the unsolved abductions?"

"The Donner case is still under investigation," San Francisco's police chief interjected. "We have nothing linking it with the kidnappings of Danny Becker, Gabrielle Nunn, and Zach Reed."

"Have you ruled out the possibility of a connection?"

"Our focus is on the children, who we believe are still alive and being confined somewhere by Edward Keller."

"That's right," the FBI agent in charge of the San Francisco office added. "I think we're getting off track. Now, we have something to show you. If you'll just watch the monitors."

He signaled to begin. Clear security video from the Berkeley hobby store rolled, showing Keller approaching Zach and leaving the store with him. It silenced the conference for half a minute.

"We've made copies to distribute and we've enhanced the suspect's face in still photos. We have a news release detailing the facts of the case. I want to reiterate the enormity of the investigation and that the reward for information leading to an arrest in this case now stands at $300,000."

Reed worked his way out of the room while the conference continued. But he wasn't free. With reporters in tow, he tried to find Ann. He caught up with her outside in the Hall of Justice parking lot as she was getting into a car with the FBI agent. Three camera crews were on her.

"Ann!" Reed called.

Reporters were shouting, jogging after Reed as he ran to Ann. He turned to them. "I just want a private word with my wife, so give us a break. Can you do that, please!"

"Come on," the agent said to the reporters, "back off!"

Reed slid into the backseat with Ann and rolled up the windows.

"Tom, I just want to go home to wait at my mother's house."

"Ann, I—please—"

"I have nothing to say to you right now and it's best we leave it that way. I have no time for you. Every fiber of my being is focused on my son.

"Our son, Ann. Our son."

"He's my son, he's your story."

Reed absorbed the blow.

"Ann, I swear, I'll bring him ba—"

"Get out of the car, I want to go."

"Ann."

"Get out, now!"

In the Hall of Justice, four floors up in the small waiting area of the Homicide Detail, San Francisco cabbie Willie Hampton was holding his cap, watching live coverage of the news conference on the little TV at the desk of Homicide Detail's secretary.

"Like I said, I don't know if that's the dude on the TV there," he repeated. "I just got back from Hawaii and seen this tragedy all over the news. Sorrowful thing."

Willie hung his head and shook it.

"I'm catchin' up on the news an' somethin' specific catches me 'bout that little Danny, the boy got stolen from BART at Balboa. Something's ticklin' my memory sayin' 'Willie, you got to check this here,' see. So I get my calendar, check my ride sheet for that day. Sure enough I was workin' around Balboa Park when that boy got taken."

Willie leaned forward, dropping his voice: "Between you an' me, my last fare was a curbside, off the books, right 'fore I left on my vacation." His tone rose back to normal conversation. "Picked up a dude carryin' a kid near Balboa same time they say Danny got taken. Somethin' strange 'bout the man. The kid was a girl, maybe five, but I recollect her hair looked kinda phony, like a wig maybe. I dropped them at Logan and Good, near Wintergreen. Somethin' funny 'bout it all. Somethin' not right. That's all I'm sayin', see."

Willie examined his cap for a moment.

"Miss, how much longer you figure 'fore someone talks to me?"

Turgeon took notes as Willie Hampton told her and Sydowski about his strange fare to Wintergreen. This was it, the real thing. Sydowski felt it in his gut as Willie recounted how he got lost on the dead-end street, turned around to find his way out, then saw his fare walking with the child over his shoulder before entering the broken-down house. When Willie finished his story, Sydowski had one question.

"Can you take us to this house now, Mr. Hampton?"

"Well, yes, sir. I think I can."

Half an hour later, Sydowski, Turgeon, and Willie Hampton sat in an unmarked police car, a few doors down the street from Edward Keller's house.

74

Dispatches about the break in the case sizzled on police scanners. Reporters who covered that morning's news conference scurried to Wintergreen. Local TV interrupted network shows with live reports from the curb. The house and entire yard were sealed. Identification experts from the FBI and SFPD, clad in white hairnets, surgeon's gloves, and coveralls—"moon-walking suits"—dissected the scene. The feds took the inside and the city team took the garage and yard. An FBI chopper equipped with Forward Looking Infrared able to trace body heat, even that of corpses, hovered overhead. The city guys covered every square foot of Keller's yard, using a probe and vapor detector, which picks up the presence of body gases from decomposition. Military camouflage canopies were erected over the area to hamper news helicopters from broadcasting the excavation of bodies, should the task force find any.

The scene inside the house was chilling. Nothing could have prepared Sydowski for it as he suited up with Rust to go in.

"Never seen anything like this," an FBI agent mumbled to

them as they entered. Huge surveillance photos of the children were plastered on the living room walls, which bled with quotations from the Scriptures. A claw of colored wires sprouted from the kitchen wall where the phone had been. It was a violent testament to the menace, thought Sydowski, deducing how Keller must have smashed it when Zach called for help. The solitary rocking chair before the TV underscored Keller's insanity. Rust went to the worktable and thumbed through Keller's journals, reading the criteria he used to select the children: angel names, ages matching his dead kids at the time of their drownings. How he sought them through birth notices, traced their families through public records, studied, and stalked them. Ident detectives were going through his computer.

Sydowski took the stairs to the basement room.

As he stepped off the last step to Keller's basement, Sydowski was assaulted by the stench of excrement, urine, and garbage, and pulled up his surgical mask. The children were gone, yet he braced himself for whatever awaited him in the room. Two FBI Ident experts were working there, breathing through gas masks. They nodded to Sydowski as he entered, watching him take in the scene, the knee-deep garbage of half-eaten fast food and wrappers, the soiled mattresses, the rats, the barred, papered window, and the bloodstained baseball bat.

"It's not human blood, Walt," one of the Ident guys said, his voice muffled from under his mask.

Sydowski nodded, blinking quickly. It was Golden Gate Park all over again—the rain, Tanita Marie Donner in the garbage bag, the stink, the maggots, flies, the gaping slash across her doll's neck, nearly decapitating her. Her snow-white skin, her tiny body on the slab, her beautiful eyes imploring him, beseeching him, reaching into him. All these fucking years on the job. All the fucking stiffs. It was supposed to get easier. Why wasn't it getting easier? Were three more child corpses waiting for him somewhere? Was that the way it was going to play out? His stomach was seething, his heartburn erupting. Give us a

break here. We're so close to this guy. Sydowski gritted his
teeth. So close.

He returned upstairs to confer with Rust in the living room.
A funereal atmosphere permeated the house. Everyone was
working quietly, cataloging evidence, bagging and hauling it
to a van which would deliver it to a plane waiting to fly it to
the state forensic lab in Sacramento. Few investigators spoke,
those who did, used low, respectful tones. Rust was still studying Keller's maps and binders, amidst the clutter. "Are we too
late, Walt?"

"I don't know, today is the anniversary. Seems he's geared
up to it. You going to look downstairs, where he kept them?"

"Right after we talk to Bill, here."

Bill Wright, the FBI's Ident team leader, sighed, removing
his gas mask, his reddened face damp with perspiration. "Well,
we can definitely put all three children in this house based on
the stuff we've found so far. Clothing. Hair. But the kids are
gone. We've got nothing outside, nothing inside. We've gone
through the attic, X-rayed the floorboards, walls. The last call
made from this address was the one Zach Reed made to *The
San Francisco Star* newsroom. The bills for the past three
months show little. No receipts in his trash. We're going to
take the plumbing apart in case he flushed anything. But our
guy's fled, likely with the kids. I'd say last night, judging from
the oil and coolant stains in the driveway. We'll keep the house
for as long as we need it to gather evidence for whatever comes
up."

"Thanks, Bill."

Sydowski pulled Rust aside. "Keller lost his kids, late in
the day, right?"

"Late afternoon, evening. The file put it between four and
nine."

Sydowski checked his watch. "Gives us a couple of hours,
maybe."

"Maybe."

* * *

Outside, the air was electric with rumors that the police had found bodies. Reed was with the parents of Danny Becker and Gabrielle Nunn, who also rushed to Wintergreen, jostled through the press gauntlet, and converged on the police command center as TV news helicopters circled overhead. Uniformed police had taken the parents aside to a secure area near the bus to await some official word. Their perspective allowed them to see the bagged evidence being removed from the house. Nancy Nunn sniffled, sharpening her focus on one clear bag. Gooseflesh rose on her trembling skin as she recognized the flowered print dress she had made for her daughter.

Paul Nunn caught his wife and struggled to quell her choking sobs, his own voice cracking, "Is somebody going to tell us what the hell is going on here!"

Reed saw Ann arrive and hurried to her, plucking her from reporters, pulling her to the sanctuary for the parents as the choppers pounded above. Ann wept. The agent who brought her left, to get some answers.

"Tom, is he dead?"

Reed tried to get his wife to focus on him. "Ann! We don't know anything. No one is telling us a word." He hugged her.

"Something is happening," Gabrielle's father said, "because this morning we found Jackson—Gabrielle's dog—scratching at our back door, looking pretty frightened."

"Why the hell is it taking them so long to tell us something?" Nathan Becker demanded. "Officer, please get us someone! We deserve to know what is going on. What have they found?"

The uniformed cop nodded, turned away, and spoke into his radio.

Reed held Ann. He was numb with helplessness. Fear. What was he going to do if they started carrying out bodies? His son. His only child. Only yesterday, Zach had locked his arms around him, enthralled with the hope his mom and dad were going to move back to their house.

Daddy you have to come and get me!

Sydowski emerged and ushered the parents away from the chaos and toward the relative tranquility of the bus.

"All we can determine is that Keller has fled with the children."

"Where?"

"We're trying to determine that right now."

"What about Half Moon Bay?"

"We've got people there."

"When did Keller leave?"

"We think sometime in the night." Sydowski then raised his hand. "We have nothing to show they've been harmed, outside of being held in a foul, scary environment."

"But the clothes?" Nancy asked.

"He's likely changed their appearances, to make it difficult to find them."

Phones were ringing inside the bus.

What were they doing to find Keller, Paul Nunn wanted to know.

"We suspect he is going to put to sea, somewhere along the California coast. The Coast Guard is on full alert. We've got every available search plane—"

"Inspector?" an officer with his hand covering a phone interrupted. "Sir, it's the Ranger Station at Point Reyes."

75

George Hay sat at the counter of Art's Diner in Inverness, eating a clubhouse sandwich. The front page of *The San Francisco Star* was folded precisely beside his plate and he read while he chewed.

He was engrossed in the multiple kidnapping case. It was fantastic. Had to be a ball-breaker for the people on it, he figured, reaching for a French fry. All that glory. Sure. And all that career-busting political bullshit, too. He took a hit of coffee. Admit it though, you miss the action, he told himself. Cases like that gave you a helluva rush. Yeah, he missed it, like he missed not being in pain.

Damn, he winced, putting his cup down to massage his leg.

Two years back, a carjacker's bullet had shattered his right thigh, leaving him with a partial pension, a bastard's attitude, and a permanent limp after fifteen years with the San Jose Police Department. A succession of rent-a-cop security jobs and lost weekends sunk his marriage. To hell with it. Allana was not the stand-by-your-man type; she was the kick-you-in-the-teeth type. George still had trouble believing that right before she walked out on him he was actually contemplating knocking off an armored car for her, thinking the money would keep them together. He shook his head. That was when a buddy got him work as a U.S. Park Ranger in Point Reyes, the national seashore park, just north of San Francisco.

He spent his first months swallowing what bits of pride he had left and going through the motions of his job. Gradually, he buried the things that made him an asshole and came to appreciate the therapeutic qualities of the park. He was even good natured about the ribbing he got from old police friends. "Collar any perps with pic-a-nic baskets, George?" He found a postcard-perfect cabin near Dillon Beach and was secretly trying his hand at writing a police mystery. Instead of a drunk, he had become a philosopher, a seaside poet. So fuck the world, old George was doing fine with the hand that was dealt him. There, his leg felt better. He gulped the last of his coffee and tucked a crumpled five and two ones under his plate. "See ya, Art."

A fat man, wrapped in the grease-stained white apron, peeked through the kitchen's serving window, waving as he left.

George clamped a toothpick between his teeth and inhaled the salt air, limping to his U.S. Park Service Jeep Cherokee. A Coast Guard spotter plane roared in the distance as he climbed into the Jeep, grabbed his Motorola mike, and checked in with park headquarters in Bear Valley, seven miles away.

"Forty-two here, Dell. Got anything? Over."

"Pretty quiet, George, except for— Just a sec . . ."

That was Dell, always misplacing something. George pried a piece of bacon from between his teeth. Three hours left in his shift, then four days off. While Dell searched, George flipped through the papers on his clipboard: faxes, alerts, and bulletins. Routine stuff about amendments to laws and regs dealing with the park, and the Gulf of the Farallons, overlooks from Sonora and Marin counties, Coast Guard notices. Usual crap. Ah, there

it was. The stuff from the FBI on the Keller kidnappings.
George read it again, awestruck by the magnitude. Details on
the boat, the trailer, the vehicles, background on Edward Keller,
the children, that reporter. Helluva case. Bet Keller took them
to Half Moon Bay, where he took his own kids twenty years
ago. He heard they had heavy surveillance going down there,
Coast Guard, FBI, the state boys.

"You still there, George?"

"Ten-four, Dell."

"Okay. Lou at the Valente place called. Saw some trespassing headlights late last night. Must've been kids partying
on the property again. Wants you to check it out when you
can."

"The spot down by the old cow path to the beach?"

"That's it."

"On my way. Ten-four."

Overnight and through the morning, the park was cloaked
in chilly fog. By midafternoon it had yielded to the sun and a
sparkling clear day. George hummed to himself driving from
Inverness, on Tomales Bay on the north side, to the Sir Francis
Drake Highway, meandering west across the sixty-five-thousand
acre park. He loved, no, he revered the Point, its majestic,
craggy terrain, its Bishop pine and Douglas fir forests, the
estuaries slicing into its sloping green valleys where dairy cattle
grazed; the mist-shrouded beaches and jagged shorelines, glistening today with sea spray as sea lions basked in the sun. And
the place had wild weather, simultaneously throwing up hot
California sunshine, cold fog, and damp, pounding winds all
within a few miles, manifesting the mood of the peninsula. It
sat on the San Andreas Fault, rendering the rocky shelves of
her coastal waters a ships' graveyard. But beyond the beautiful
treachery was the celestial Pacific and eternal hope. That's what
did it for him. The Point was a living, breathing deity. Damn.

He had become a tree-hugger! Admit it. He laughed out loud. Laughed until his goddamned leg hurt.

The Jeep curled past Schooner Bay, Drakes Estero, and the sea. George passed the overgrown ruins of the ancient mission church. He once read of plans to rebuild it years ago. Wonder what happened? About a mile before Creamery Bay, he left the highway for Valente's property. It stretched in a near perfect two-mile square between the road and the Point's north beach. He kicked the Jeep into four-wheel drive, bumping his way down a tractor trail that meandered to a small lagoon at a valley bottom. The path was long abandoned, but now and then local kids trespassed, usually in ATVs, to party. Looked like it happened again. George spotted fresh tire tracks at the valley bottom. Seemed strange. They were deep, mud-churning troughs, going to the shore, then disappearing into the tall, dense brush. But no tracks led out. No vehicles were in the area. Nothing. George stopped.

"What the hell is this?"

He cranked the emergency brake, killed his engine, and got out to investigate, pulling on his rubber rain pancho because much of the brush here thrived with poison oak and thorns. Slipping on work gloves, he followed the tire impressions into the thicket, using his baton to slap aside branches. Suddenly, he froze. Something chrome reflected the sun. He moved to it. Looked like the ball of a trailer hitch. It was! George chopped his way deeper, coming upon a tarp, barely concealing a late-model van. A rental by the looks of it. Who would take time to hide this stuff? he asked as the answer, rolling on a wave of knowing, crashed down on him.

The van was unlocked. Frantically, George scoured inside. Nothing. He jotted down the tag, struggled through the bush again, finding a manufacturer's plate for the trailer, jotting down its number. This was it. He knew it. Nettles snagged him as he fought his way back to his Jeep, snapped through the pages on his clipboard, and checked the trailer. This was it!

This was the goddamned trailer! George looked up and down the shore. "Where's the boat?"

No trace of a boat. He stared at the ocean. Keller put to sea here. He launched here. George pounded the wheel. That was right, everyone would be sitting on Half Moon Bay. From here, around the westernmost point at the lighthouse, it was only twenty miles to the Farallon Islands. Was he too late? Didn't Lou see the headlights last night? George snatched the radio mike.

"Dell, it's George! I've got something here! You're going to have to make some fast phone calls!"

The radio hissed with silence.

"Goddammit, Dell! Are you there? For Christ's sake!"

76

A great blue heron glided in the sunlight a few feet above, head extended forward, neck folded back on its shoulders, soft plumage drooping as it stalked prey along the beach.

Lady of the waters. Keller smiled, looking up from his worn Bible, eyes brimming with tears. He gazed at the afternoon sea: water made holy by the suffering of Christ, *you who are washed in this water, have hope of Heaven's kingdom.*

I am the resurrection, the way, and the light.

The light, the light . . . under cover of the night. The Lord was with him, guiding him, thwarting Lucifer's every attempt to interfere. Yes. After he had intercepted Michael's phone call, Keller gathered the Angels and took the back routes of the East Bay, driving here in a Taurus station wagon he had prepared weeks earlier. It had Nevada plates and each rear window was curtained in black with a small silver cross affixed to its center. Keller had magnetic signs custom made for the driver and front passenger doors, reading: A & B MORTUARY SERVICES, CARSON CITY, NEVADA. The children, who were sedated, slept in a large, oblong cardboard box in the wagon's rear. Along the way, Keller stopped to pick up the trailered boat and switched the station wagon to another rental van, which he hid in one of the double-size garages of a self-help storage facility in Novato. He drove to the park, launched the boat in darkness, concealing the van and trailer in thick brush.

Keller knew Point Reyes from his pilgrimages. Years ago, he had submitted a bid to rebuild the old mission church. "Upon this rock I will build my church; and the gates of Hell shall not prevail against it. And I will give unto thee the keys of the kingdom of Heaven." Three days after he put in his estimate, he lost his children. Out there, near the Farallons. "But Satan shall not prevail, for God had given him the keys to the kingdom." Divine Destiny.

Navigating by moonlight with the running lights off, Keller inched the boat safely around the Point Reyes Lighthouse, Overlook, Chimney Rock, and along some twelve miles of shore to this hidden cove near Drakes Estero, where he had taken sanctuary for the night, anchored and tethered to the nook's jagged rocks. Bitter, cold winds fingered into the cove, knocking the boat against the rocks. Keller did not risk a fire. Again, he sedated the children, leaving them to sleep aboard under blankets and tarps. He cloaked the entire craft with camouflage netting. Keller did not sleep. He huddled nearby under a blanket, as the wind rocked the boat, reading Scripture by penlight, keeping a vigil, counting down the hours, talking with God.

Now, afternoon had come. He could hear the children under the blankets, waking groggily. Keller could not stand it any longer. It was time. For twenty years he had waited, suffered, repented, and prepared for this day, this day of celestial glory and light.

Sanctus, sanctus, sanctus. Dominus Deus sabaoth.

Keller checked his watch. From their location, it would take over an hour to reach the islands at the right moment. He had memorized the charts. Everything he needed was in the boat. He was ready. Why was he waiting? It was time. But as he moved to the boat, his adrenaline-driven euphoria had given way to exhaustion, fear.

It should have been you, you bastard!

Accept that you cannot change reality. You must forgive yourself and move on.

The children are innocents.

The entire world knows your pain. Do not extend it to others who never harmed you.

Whoever committed this desecration shall be damned all the days of his life!

It is time, Edward. Your children are waiting.

Are you doubting Divine Will?

I am the resurrection and the life.

Your children are waiting.

Through his tears, Keller saw his son Pierce.

"Why are you doing this?"

Keller was in the boat, holding his hand, his small warm hand.

Pierce was alive! Here, talking to him.

The resurrection and the life.

"Please, don't hurt us."

Oh Pierce. Keller stretched out his hand, caressed the boy's shivering head, his young hair. Enraptured, Keller wept, his heart rising and falling with the boat . . . the black waves rolling. His children screaming: Joshua, Alisha, Pierce. Like lambs in the night. The cold darkness swallowing them, devouring them.

Joan's body twisting in the attic.

Keller squeezed the child's hand and scanned the cove.

Something humming, growling in the air. A search plane, far off, over the sea near the horizon.

Satan would challenge him to the end.

"You won't win this time! It is destined," Keller shouted at the sky. He glared at Zach. "Get back under the tarp! Now!"

Keller raced to the console, started the twin Mercury engines, pulled a machete from under the seat, and sliced the tether lines. The coastal waters were heavy with afternoon traffic, pleasure craft, charters, fishing boats, and commercial ships. He raked the back of his hand over his parched lips.

Sanctus, sanctus, sanctus. Dominus Deus sabaoth.

Easing the throttle forward, Keller set off for the islands.

77

The spires of the Bay Bridge, then the Golden Gate, passed below the FBI's Huey helicopter after it lifted off from Hamilton Navy Air Force base in Alameda near Oakland. It headed west over the Pacific.

Mid-afternoon. Visibility, excellent.

Langford Shaw, the San Francisco FBI's SWAT team leader, felt the tension aboard. He glanced from his notes to his men, while listening over his headset to the play-by-play of the bureau, the Coast Guard, the Navy, and the task force in Wintergreen. It was a massive rescue operation and he was in charge.

Four years to retirement and fate drops this ball-breaking fucker in your lap. A fuckup here and you were done. Well, he was a veteran agent of many wars and he'd be damned if he would allow that to happen. Shaw's face betrayed nothing, although his gut hardened when he got the call to activate: the kidnapping case again. The FBI's elite Hostage Rescue Team was en route on a Lear from Quantico, but they were hours away. Until then, it was all on Shaw's shoulders and those of his team.

Intelligence put Keller in a twenty-one-foot, twin-engine, open craft with three child hostages somewhere in the Gulf of the Farallons, between Point Reyes and the islands. Each SWAT member was handed photos of Keller, his boat, the children. The top theory said Keller would kill them at sea between four and six P.M., if he hadn't already done so. What they had here was a life-and-death hot pursuit and Shaw expected to execute the final option.

The Coast Guard's C-130 Hercules out of Sacramento and two Twin Otter auxiliaries were flying track crawl search patterns over the area. The guard also had its HH-65 chopper with the rescue hoist and divers scouring the islands. The *Point Brower,* a 110-foot cutter, armed with a three-millimeter cannon, had long since put out from Yerba Buena, making for the islands at twenty-five knots. Two high-speed, aluminum, diesel-powered "loaders" were searching the region. A second cutter, the *Point Olivo,* was coming down from Bodega Bay. The guard offered to scramble two Falcon jets from L.A. Shaw accepted. He then requested a U.S. Navy chopper pick up four additional SWAT team members at Hamilton, drop them at sea on the *Point Brower.* That would give him two sniper teams at sea level and another angle on the target, should they find him.

Shaw's bird was the command post where everything was being coordinated. Once more, he checked assignments, setting up the Huey's sniper points. "Mitch, you'll take starboard, and Ronnie, you set up on aft for a clear shot." Shaw indicated Fred Wheeler, his negotiator, on the satellite phone to Professor Kate Martin, learning about Keller's background and stress points. "Fred will try to talk him out of it, if he gets the chance. The rest of you are assault, depending on how we unwrap this one." Shaw switched from the chopper's intercom to his team radio. "Roy, Doc! Call when you put down on the cutter."

As they passed over San Francisco's shoreline, Shaw was called from the FBI's office on Golden Gate Avenue with word that another bureau Huey, just in from L.A. on a maintenance run, was empty and available. Good, he wanted two more sniper teams picked up for a third angle. And he had another idea. "After getting my guys at Hamilton, pick up some task force members on the house at Wintergreen. We could use them up here. Put a rush on it."

FBI Agent Merle Rust took the relay call from Shaw to the mobile command center at Keller's house in Wintergreen, then requested the SFPD clear the park a block west of the house for a helicopter landing.

"Walt," Rust told Sydowski, "they want us in the air as observers. A chopper will be here in fifteen minutes. You and me."

"They spot anything out there yet?" Sydowski followed Rust out of the bus after they informed the others.

"No." Rust shielded his eyes. "Chopper's landing in the park west of here."

Tom Reed appeared before Rust and Sydowski, looking like hell.

"Take me with you."

"What? How did you—?" Sydowski said.

"I was coming to the bus and overheard. I want to go."

"Impossible, Tom. I'm sorry," Rust said. "It's against policy."

"I have to know." He was determined.

"Tom"—Sydowski softened his voice—"stay here with Ann. She needs you. You can help the others. You should be together."

"Ann overheard you, too. She wants me to go. We have to know. Whatever happens. I have to know."

"We're sorry, Tom," Rust said, walking quickly with

Sydowski to his car. "You will be told the minute we know anything."

Reed walked with them. He was unrelenting. "I'm the only one here who has seen Keller, talked with him. Please. I know this man. You could regret not having me there."

The FBI's Huey was in sight.

At the car, Rust and Sydowski looked at each other, saying nothing. The helicopter approached, blades whipping, slicing, descending to the park as the news choppers reluctantly backed off. The press was going to be out there anyway, Rust figured.

The ground plummeted beneath them and in minutes, Reed was thundering over the Pacific, sitting knee to knee with FBI SWAT Team snipers. Seeing their weapons, their icy faces, and hearing their muted radio chatter, nearly smothered him. Someone passed him a radio with an earpiece so he could listen, hear clearly the voices of unseen forces. Saviors. Planning a rescue from the immaculate blue sky. If it wasn't too late.

From the chopper, the Pacific seemed a universe of changing hues and eternally deceptive whitecaps that were, or were not, boats. How could they ever find anyone down there? His stomach lurched. It was futile. He was peering into an abyss.

Forgive me, Zach. Please forgive me.

Reed's hands were clasped together as the chopper banked hard for an immediate northwest heading.

78

Zach's eyes adjusted to the dimness under the tarp.

The rumbling hum of the twin Mercuries pushing the boat, which leaped and skipped over the water's surface, was deafening, rattling him alert.

That rotten taste was in his mouth again. His head hurt, his leg was throbbing, and he was hungry. Danny and Gabrielle were lying on the deck with him, stirring, as the vibrations shook their bodies.

The boat was moving fast.

Ouch—something was sticking him in his groin—what? He reached into his underpants, remembering his pocketknife. He still had it. He tightened his fingers around it. Okay, he sniffed, don't sit up, just take a look around, see what's going on. What's that? He looked down at what was causing the painful pressure in his lower leg.

Heavy, yellow plastic rope was tied around his ankle and encased in a cast of silver duct tape. Zach followed the rope. It was coiled in a nearby bundle, knotted and heavily taped to four cement cinder blocks. Danny and Gabrielle? It was the same with them; rope and tape around their ankles, tied to the blocks. Another line ran from the bundle away from the tarp. Holding his breath, Zach lifted the tarp slightly, following the line along the deck to the front of the boat where it ended in a taped knot around the creep's ankle.

They were all connected. What was it for? Zach struggled to understand. Suddenly, it hit him, harder than anything in his life: The creep was going to kill them all!

Zach wanted his dad. Where was he? Don't scream! Where were the police. Didn't anyone care? Don't move! Aren't they looking for us? Think! Just think! Where are we going? Think! C'mon! He rubbed tears from his eyes and felt—the knife! Yes! He felt the knife in his hand. Okay. He could do something.

He shifted closer to the rope and opened the blade. It shrank next to the diameter of the heavy rope, like a steak knife against an oak tree. He sniffled and began sawing away. The tiny blade was sharp and cut into the rope, but it was going to take forever. Damn! He might not have time to cut Danny and Gabrielle free. He concentrated. He could stab the creep. No. The blade was too small. Panic washed over him. Think, Zach! Think!

Cut the rope and jump out? He could swim. For how long? What about sharks? What about Danny and Gabrielle? He didn't know. He didn't know anything, only that he had to do something quick. If he tried hard enough, he could cut through one piece of rope. Which one? He moved closer to the bundle, examining the coils. One line connected the cement blocks to the lines wrapped around the children's ankles. Which one? He double-checked the web of rope. Okay. Here goes.

He gestured to Danny and Gabrielle to keep still and quiet, then he gripped his knife and began slicing through the yellow rope.

79

From a thousand feet up, through the Coast Guard spotter's bubble, it looked like a meteor speeding across the heavens, cutting a southwest path across the sparkling sea, leaving a fading trail of white water. Another check through the binoculars to be certain. Twin outboards. Mercs. Northcraft. Affirmative.

"Air C-351, sighted the craft! Copy?"

"Roger, C-351. Coordinates? Over?"

"Got him running hard at . . . standby . . ."

The guard's C-130 Hercules had locked on to Keller's boat in the gulf about seven miles off Point Reyes, bearing southwest to the islands at forty-three knots.

Within six minutes, the guard's rescue chopper, at five hundred feet, moved in behind the boat, hanging back about a quarter mile while the cutter *Point Brower*, with two FBI sniper teams aboard, now within a mile, was coming from the south to intercept.

"We've got a visual," Langford Shaw acknowledged, as the bureau's Huey, pounding at maximum speed, came up fast taking the lead. It held at two hundred yards behind Keller's boat, stern portside. Altitude: three hundred feet.

Through binoculars, Shaw and his chief observer checked the suspect and the boat against enhanced photos from the hobby store security camera and the buy and trade magazine.

"Move up another hundred yards," Shaw told the pilot as he and the observer continued comparing pictures. "It's Keller," Shaw concluded. "And that's the boat. Pull back a hundred."

"No hostages," the observer said. "Wait, I see—"

"Sir," blurted one of the snipers looking through his scope, "edge of the tarp at eight o'clock!"

Part of a child's sneaker was sticking out from under it.

The second FBI helicopter arrived, taking a mirror point to Shaw's chopper at Keller's starboard stern. Listening to the radio dispatches, Reed requested and was given a pair of high-powered binoculars. Focusing on the tarp, he glimpsed Zach's shoe!

His shoe moved. Didn't it?

"That's my son's foot. That's Zach!"

The sniper team in Reed's chopper also locked on to Keller, his head bouncing in the scope's cross-hairs.

Why was a rope tied to Keller's ankle?

A Navy ship? No. Keller saw the markings. U.S. Coast Guard. The cutter appeared out of nowhere a few hundred yards ahead. Turning broadside. To block him!

"Edward Keller!" His name boomed out—a bullhorn?

He eased back on the throttle.

"FBI, Mr. Keller. Stop your craft now! I repeat, this is . . ."

                              * * *

"Movement under the tarp, sir," a sniper reported to Shaw.

"Drop him a line, Fred," Shaw ordered the negotiator.

The chopper tracked directly above Keller, matching his speed.

"Mr. Keller, we're dropping a phone to you now."

A line with a padded bag at the end of it was paid out from the chopper, landing safely on Keller's deck. The rope slackened, collapsing on him like netting. Keller shrugged it off, then tossed the bag into the ocean.

The noise was frightening, hurting his ears, but Zach realized police were trying to save them, and worked even harder at the rope. Gabrielle and Danny watched frozen in fear, hands over their ears.

Come on! Zach's fingers and wrist ached as he sawed.

Keller vanished from the snipers' scopes.

Slamming the throttle down, twin engines growling, the boat veered south, cutting a magnificent white-capped swath as crosswinds swept the tarp back revealing everything: the children, the ropes, the cinder blocks.

Shaw's throat tightened.

"Get on him now! We're going to take him out! Warn him, Fred!"

"Mr. Keller, surrender now or you will be fired upon!"

Shaw ordered the sniper teams in both choppers, and those on the Coast Guard cutter, to lock on Keller. He turned to his three-member assault team. They would be first in the water for a rescue in advance of the guard's chopper.

"Move in everybody! Now! Now! I want him now!"

Out of the corner of his eye, Shaw saw them. Four of them! And two more coming in the distance. News helicopters hovering over the scene. He'd be damned if they were going to see dead kids on the fucking news! He went on his intercom to Agent Fred Wheeler.

"Fred, get on the same frequency as the press pilots. Tell them to back off. This airspace is sealed for two miles!"

It was too late. The entire drama was unfolding live on every U.S. network. The parents of the children watched on TV monitors set up for them by news crews outside Keller's house in San Francisco. Cameras trained on them provided live reaction.

"Put a warning shot in his quarterdeck," Shaw ordered.

"I got it," answered Agent Lyle Bond, a sniper on the second chopper with Reed.

"Take it, Lyle, go!" Shaw said.

Bond's marksmanship scores were in the FBI's top one percent. Keller's boat swayed gently within Bond's scope as he stayed with him, partners in a tragic ballet, waiting for the precise moment—there it was—Bond squeezed his trigger.

The round ripped through the deck of Keller's boat like a sledgehammer, shattering the hull below, leaving a baseball-sized hole inches from his foot. He began taking on water.

"Mr. Keller stop your craft now!!"

Keller yanked on the throttle, killing the Mercs, stopping the boat, his own hissing wake washing around him, water rushing in through the gap in the hull.

The choppers were pounding.

Whoop-whoop-whoop-whoop.

In one smooth motion, Keller tossed Zach overboard, then

Gabrielle, then Danny. The long yellow ropes attached to their ankles slithered prettily on the surface.

The children thrashing.

Screaming.

Jaws dropped.

Eyes widened in horror.

Reed watched from the helicopter.

The other parents watched the TV monitors at the house.

Fast. It was unfolding too fast.

"My God! I can't believe this!" one network anchor's voice broke across the nation.

In a heartbeat, the two FBI helicopters swooped in—taking their points starboard and portside—locking on Keller as he muscled the cement blocks overboard.

"Green light! Green!" Shaw ordered. "Take him in the boat!"

Bullets rained on Keller, smashing into the boat, into him. A round passed through his right thigh, another exploded in his shoulder, a third grazed his skull as he dove into the water, disappearing beneath the surface.

Zach treaded water rapidly, witnessing the scene, unable to find Danny and Gabrielle. The noise, the surface spray was overwhelming. The choppers moved. So close, he can almost touch—

"Help!"

Instantly the blocks jerked violently at his ankle, dragging him under with Danny and Gabrielle . . . water bubbling, rushing past, filling his ears, mouth . . . until the tension overcame the point where he had cut at the rope, forcing it to snap, freeing all three children some twenty feet beneath the surface.

* * *

Keller remained tied to the blocks, plummeting feet first, crimson bubbles trailing his descent. Dazed from his wounds, he tilted his head, his lungs filling with water, losing time, lost in time as he gazed into the light. The children were silhouetted against the sun—floating, flying in the resplendent waters.

Sanctus, sanctus, sanctus.

Then it happened. As ordained by God.

The sky above, heaven above, blossoming . . .

Once. Twice. Three times.

Three beings, celestial entities summoned from eternity, each gliding, floating to each child, taking them to their breasts, severing their lines to him . . . the brilliant yellow rope floating away. He grew deeply tired, watching them ascend with the children, to the sun, to God.

He was forgiven.

He was at peace.

80

The shake was strawberry, Zach Reed's favorite. He sat up in the hospital bed to take it from his father.

"Thanks, Dad."

Zach's mother continued stroking his hair. She had never left his side once the doctors and the psychiatrist finished looking at him. Danny and Gabrielle were across the hall with their parents. Every now and then, they could be heard laughing, along with the sound of Gabrielle's cocker spaniel barking.

"The children are fine. They've suffered some shock, exhaustion, dehydration," one of the doctors told Ann and Tom. "We want them to eat. At this stage, pizzas, burgers, shakes, and fries are good medicine." He winked at Zach, adding, "We'll have them spend the night here resting. Let him sleep naturally when he gets drowsy. And Dr. Martin's available anytime, if anybody wants to talk some more."

The doctor left, closing the door softly.

"Everything's going to be okay, right?" Zach said.

"Sure, honey." His mother brushed his cheek.

Zach set his shake aside and bit his lip, worried about the fallout for breaking all the rules, for talking to that psycho doof, believing his lies. Still a little juiced from everything, he thought about how cool it was going to be telling Jeff and Gordie about the choppers. But the idea went away. He had almost drowned. He was still frightened. And there were a lot of other things. Things he couldn't understand. That nice lady doctor, the psychiatrist, Dr. Kate whom Dad knew, said she could help him with that when they talked some more. She actually knew the creep and promised to answer all the questions she could. She was smart. Even after their short talk, she seemed to know what was going on with Zach. She didn't get him wrong. He was happy, but he was still a little scared; scared about his mom, his dad. Everything. Well, Doc Kate wanted him to talk about it to his folks, so here goes: "I mean, I'm sorry about all this mess, for running away from Grandma's, getting in that creep's van. I made a mistake."

"Oh, sweetie." His mother crushed him in her arms.

"Zach, it's not your fault." His dad smiled. "You did good, calling me like you did, son. Very good."

"You're not mad at me?"

"No." Ann touched her eyes with a crumpled tissue.

He stared at his parents. They looked different, older, relieved, like something had been decided.

"So, are we going to talk about living together again?"

"I don't think so." Ann reached across the bed, taking Tom's hand, fingering his wedding band, looking into his eyes. "I don't think we need to talk anymore. I think it's settled."

"We're all moving back to our house? Together?" Zach said.

"Yes." Ann smiled.

Zach hugged them.

"Hey," Reed told him, "we'll let you in on a secret. The President is going to be calling from the White House later."

"The President? No way!"

"Come here." Reed took Zach to the hospital window. TV satellite trucks and news crews jammed the parking lot below.

"You're big news, Zach."

"Awe-Some! Wait 'til I tell Jeff and Gordie!"

A quick knock on the door. It was SFPD Inspector Linda Turgeon. "Sorry to interrupt. Could I see you, Tom, about your statement?" She smiled at Ann and Zach. "How you doin', sport?"

"Good. Great, actually." He sucked on his shake.

Outside in the hall, Reed and Turgeon talked in a quiet alcove. A news conference with the children, parents, and police was set for the hospital's lecture room in ninety minutes. And tomorrow, Reed was to go to the Hall of Justice, to give his statement on the case.

No problem. He took Turgeon's hand.

"Thank you, everybody, the FBI, the task force. I thank you."

"You and Zach helped break this."

"Where's Sydowski? I'd like to see him."

"He wants to see you, too. Downstairs in the coffee shop."

Heading downstairs, Reed passed Danny's and Gabrielle's rooms, smiling at the joy, the relief flooding the hallway. Professor Martin waved at him from Danny's room. The uniformed officers standing guard outside grinned at Reed, slapping his back.

Downstairs, he met Molly Wilson coming from the gift shop with balloons. She threw her arms around him, her bracelets chiming.

"Tom! Oh, Tom, I'm so glad it all worked out!"

"Yeah, yeah, me, too." He stepped back, gazing into her blue eyes. "Everything worked out the way it was supposed to."

She smiled her perfect-teeth smile. "That's good."

"You here working, Wilson?"

"Yes, but—" She remembered she had a bouquet of over-sized balloons. "These are for Zach."

Reed stared at them, then Wilson, saying nothing. Thinking. "Maybe I'll just have them sent up," she said.

"Wait for me here. You can give them to Zach yourself."

"Sure."

"And I suppose you would like an exclusive chat with him?"

"Yes, I would, if it's all right?"

"Let me talk with Ann. I think it would be fine."

"Thanks, Tom."

"Molly, I appreciate what you did back in the newsroom. Getting Tellwood's help when I needed it." Reed turned to leave.

"Tom, are you coming back to the paper? Tellwood's left the door open for you and Benson is gone."

"I don't know. I need time to think things through."

Reed found Sydowski alone, huddled over a coffee, peering through his bifocals at bird show brochures.

"Well, well: Tom Reed. My favorite *voychick.*"

"Why you hiding out?"

"Reporters are dangerous to my health."

Reed saw the gold in Sydowski's smile and it was like the shit a year ago never happened. He sat across from him, looking him in the eye. "Thank you, Walt. Thank you for everything."

"No need to thank me."

"And, I want to apologize for the fuckup with Franklin Wallace in the Tanita Marie Donner case. I was wrong."

Sydowski shook his head, sipping some coffee. "You were never wrong," he said.

"But, Virgil Shook was the guy, Wallace had nothing to do—?"

"You were half right at the time. But we could never tell you. I wanted to, but we couldn't tell anybody."

"Wallace was involved?"

"Yes. But Shook killed her. You scared the shit out of us digging up what you did. You didn't know that it was Shook who tipped you to Wallace, thinking we would put it all on Wallace. We knew Wallace was involved, but he wasn't alone. We needed him to bring us his partner, who turned out to be Shook."

"So you let me hang, the disgrace, the lawsuit?"

"It hurt me seeing you go through that shitstorm, but you hanged yourself, Tom. I told you to sit on your stuff."

"Wasn't Shook afraid Wallace would roll on him?"

"No. Shook dominated him psychologically. Fed him crap, faked his own suicide over the phone to Wallace. That's what did it, left him thinking we were coming for him. And when you got there first, well, that closed the lid on his casket. Shook was a clever bastard."

"What about Keller?"

"What can I tell you? You knew him as well as anyone. You practically solved the case, but I'll deny I ever said that." Reed chuckled.

Sydowski continued. "Edward died at the bottom of the Pacific, like he wanted. Now he's on a slab in the hospital basement, out of his fucking misery, like Shook. And you know what? The world feels a little lighter without the burden of their presence."

"Feel a song coming on there, Walt?"

Sydowski downed his coffee, tossing the paper cup in the trash.

"Maybe. I got to check on my old man, head home, feed my birds. Why not drop by some time, Reed? I'll get some fresh kielbasa, some egg bread, sweet butter. And you can buy the beer."

"I think you owe me, I'm solving your cases for you."

"Listen, you're still young. It's not too late for you to join the SFPD. I'd put in a word for you. You think you can cut it?''

"Naw, I like being a hack. I like living dangerously."

"You want danger? Let my old man give you a shave and haircut."

Sydowski clasped Reed's shoulder warmly.

"Love your family, Tom."

Before heading upstairs, Reed stepped into a washroom to cleanse his face. He was haggard; he needed a shower, a shave. Parts of him were still tingling. Christ, he had come so close to losing it all.

And he would have done anything . . .

Like Keller?

". . . eyes that haunt my dreams . . ."

Reed knew he would never be the same.

He had been given a second chance.

"Book 'em!"
Legal Thrillers from Kensington

Your Favorite Mystery Authors Are Now Just A Phone Call Away